W9-BEN-721

THE ZERO NIGHT

BRIAN FREEMAN

THE ZERO NIGHT

Published in 2022 by Blackstone Publishing
Cover and book design by Kathryn Galloway English

Printed in the United States of America

First edition: 2022
ISBN 978-1-0940-8234-9
Fiction / Mystery & Detective / Police Procedural

Version 1

CIP data for this book is available
from the Library of Congress

Blackstone Publishing
31 Mistletoe Rd.
Ashland, OR 97520

www.BlackstonePublishing.com

For Marcia

"Which came out of the opened door—the lady or the tiger?"

–Frank Stockton

1

The man with the briefcase sat on a bench in the drowning rain.

When the wind gusted, Lake Superior punished him for his choice of location, rolling waves up and over the pier and drenching him with spray that was even colder than the downpour. In the twin glow of the lighthouses on either side of the ship canal, and beneath the ghostly light of the lift bridge, the muddy, wriggling surface of the water looked angry and alive.

However, the man on the bench seemed unaffected by the October storm. He sat motionless, his back straight, his fingers spread atop the leather briefcase on his lap. Coils of his curly blond hair clumped like loose springs on his forehead. He wore a navy-blue button-down shirt, a neon-yellow tie, and black slacks, all soaked to the skin. His eyes appeared to be closed. His tall, skinny body, sitting alone on the bench, was a silhouette framed against the horizon of the lake.

Lieutenant Maggie Bei watched the man from the sodden green grass of Duluth's Canal Park. Rain lashed her, too, and the gales nearly lifted her off her feet. She didn't like being here at three in the morning, wet and cold. The truth was, she also didn't much like the man on the bench. His name was Gavin Webster, and he was a lawyer. She didn't trust lawyers as a rule, but Gavin was a defense lawyer, which meant he was by definition a liar, an ambulance chaser, a headline hound, and a sworn enemy of the police. On the phone, he'd told her he was in trouble, which was enough to get her out of bed in the middle of the night. Then again, Maggie rarely believed a word that came from a lawyer's mouth.

She squinted into the driving rain, and her lips tightened into a grimace. Then she walked across the grass, listening to the squish of her calf boots. She tugged the belt of her trench coat tighter, but cold water dripped from the bowl cut of her black hair like fingers down her back. She shoved her hands into the coat pockets. When she got to the bench, she sat down next to Gavin. Her legs weren't long enough to reach the ground, so her feet dangled. Her arrival elicited no reaction. He knew she was there, but he still didn't move.

Gavin was a good-looking man, Maggie acknowledged grudgingly to herself. He was in his midforties, like her, but his thick, curly hair and baby-smooth skin made him look younger than he was. He had a long narrow nose over a long narrow chin on a long narrow face. He hadn't shaved in a while, giving him blond stubble. His mouth was a thin, pale slash.

Among the community of Duluth lawyers, Gavin had long been considered a plugger. That wasn't a compliment. The judgment on Gavin was that he was hardworking and intelligent, but not someone who had lived up to expectations. His former partner had cheated him and driven him into bankruptcy, which meant that the more respectable commercial firms wouldn't hire him. He was a sole practitioner now. He wasn't part of the legal upper crust, not a member of the Kitchi Gammi Club, where the real deals were done among the city's movers and shakers. The big cases never came his way, so he took public defender work to make ends meet.

He was a man on a treadmill, running fast to stay in place.

"Hello, Gavin," Maggie said.

The lawyer's watery eyes opened. His head swiveled, and he stared at her through the curtain of rain. His pale-blue eyes were his most distinctive feature, intense and oddly luminous in a way that Maggie had always found creepy. His gaze latched on to people and refused to let go, as if it were a staring contest that he was determined to win.

"Thank you for coming," Gavin replied in a voice that sounded low and lost. "I'm sorry to call so late, but I didn't know what else to do."

"What's going on?"

"It's Chelsey," he said.

Maggie didn't know Gavin well enough to know who that was, but she made the obvious guess. "Is Chelsey your wife?"

"Yes."

"What about her?" Maggie asked.

"Someone took her."

Maggie's eyes narrowed with concern. "Took her? What does that mean? What are you saying?"

"I made a mistake. I should have called you sooner. I thought I could deal with this myself."

"Gavin, tell me what happened to your wife."

With his thumbs, the lawyer undid the two locks of his briefcase. He popped the lid. The case was empty inside, and rain began to soak the worn, stained interior. He ran his fingers along the wet calfskin.

"I brought the ransom with me in this. I gave them the money. I did everything they asked. After that, they were supposed to call and let me know where she was, but it's been three hours, and nothing. They're not going to call, are they? I was a fool to believe them."

"Are you saying that your wife has been *kidnapped*?"

There was a tremble in his lower lip as he snapped the briefcase shut. It was hard to tell because of the rain, but she thought he was crying. "They said if I called the police, they'd kill her. So I didn't call. I thought if I just gave them what they wanted, I'd get her back."

He focused on Maggie with those strange, inscrutable eyes again.

"Now she's dead," he went on helplessly. "I've lost her."

* * * * *

Serena Stride noticed the time on the clock glowing beside the bed. It was just past three in the morning. Sometime during the night, she always woke up long enough to check the time. When she did, she remembered her magic number, which increased by one with every toll of midnight. Her brain made the calculation automatically; she didn't even need to think about it.

6,607.

That was the count tonight.

For eighteen years, she'd kept track of the total, day by day, night by night. She couldn't turn it off. Even when she tried to forget it or put it out of her mind, she would wake up somewhere during the dark hours, and the number would click forward one more digit.

6,607.

That was the number of nights she'd survived without a drink.

Normally, Serena would acknowledge the number and then turn over and go back to sleep. But she was restless tonight. Out of sorts. With her eyes open, she stared at the bedroom ceiling and listened to the rain hammering outside. She glanced at Jonny, who slept soundly beside her. His chest was bare despite the chill of a cracked-open window—he liked fresh air even in the freezing weather—and there was enough light for her to see the wrinkled scar where the surgeons had sewn up his heart the previous year. He'd been shot. He'd almost died. But here he was, still beside her. Even so, the scar was always there, reminding her that even Stride was mortal.

His salt-and-pepper hair, which he'd been letting grow longer than usual for more than a year, fell messily across his handsome, weathered face. With the barest touch of her fingertips, she pushed back his fore-lock. She thought about waking him up. A part of her wanted to talk to him and tell him what she was feeling; a part of her wanted to make love to him. He wouldn't complain about that. But she wasn't in a mood for romance; she was too agitated, too consumed by her thoughts. Actually, it had been months since they'd been intimate. Life kept getting in the way and pushing them apart. She missed the closeness, and her body missed the sex. She felt the absence of him inside her, but they were too distant emotionally to be physically close. So she slipped out of bed alone and crossed the cold wooden floor to the living room. She pulled the bedroom door shut behind her as quietly as she could, but the knob always rattled.

There was no mystery in why she felt unsettled. It wasn't just the strained awkwardness between her and Stride. The answer was also the open door on the other side of the living room, leading to the empty bedroom where Cat Mateo had slept for almost four years. Cat was gone now. Well, not gone—but she was moving on with her new life. She was in a dorm at UMD, where she was a freshman. Serena hadn't anticipated the empty-nest feeling she had without the girl around every day.

She went and turned on the lights in Cat's room. Some of her posters and pictures, the ones she hadn't taken to college, still decorated the walls. The air still smelled like her, floral and fresh. Serena could have texted her to say, *hello, how are you, do you miss me?* Cat was new to dorm life, which meant she was probably still awake, hanging out with the other freshmen until all hours. But this was Serena's problem. She didn't need to burden Cat with her own loneliness.

Behind her, a pulse of music filled the living room. It came from her phone, which was charging on a table near the bedroom door. Maggie was calling. She'd given Maggie her own ringtone: Peter Gabriel's "Big Time," a tribute to ego run wild. The other detectives always gave her a wry smile when they heard it. Maggie had taken over the major crimes unit for the Duluth Police after Stride was shot, and her new role had proved to be an uncomfortable fit. The assignment was supposed to be temporary, but Stride's leave had gone on for more than a year now, and people were beginning to wonder if he'd ever return. That made the rest of the cops nervous. The snarkiness and impatience that made Maggie a good number two for Stride didn't always translate well when she was the one snapping out orders. Serena felt that more keenly than the others because she worked most closely with Maggie day to day.

"Hey, what's up?" she said, answering the phone.

"I'm soaking wet, that's what's up," Maggie replied in a sour voice.

Serena eyed the tall, rain-streaked windows that led to the cottage's front porch. "Why do I get the feeling I'm about to be soaking wet, too?"

"Yeah, I'm in Canal Park. Guppo's already on the way."

"What's up?" she repeated, because Maggie sometimes seemed to think that Serena could follow her thoughts telepathically.

"We've got a kidnapping."

"Who?"

"Do you know Gavin Webster, the defense lawyer? It's his wife. Chelsey. Chelsey Webster. The abduction happened two days ago. Two days! He tried to deal with the kidnappers directly, and they screwed him."

"Took the money and ran?" Serena asked.

"Right. No call, no sign of Chelsey, no evidence of where she is or whether she's still alive. Anyway, that's Gavin's story, so we need to check it out."

"You don't believe him?" Serena asked because she could hear doubt in her voice.

"He's a *lawyer*," Maggie repeated, using the word like it was a piece of fish that smelled past its prime. "So who knows? Gavin looks like he's in shock, but lawyers are good actors."

"Where are you?" Serena asked.

"I'm taking him to the lobby at the Comfort Suites so we can get out of the rain. I'll interview him there."

"Okay, I'll see you in a few minutes."

Serena put down the phone.

She headed for the house's third bedroom. That was where she kept her clothes now, rather than in the closet of the master bedroom. Getting called out in the middle of the night wasn't uncommon, so she'd decided to use the other closet to avoid waking Stride up every time it happened. Not that he'd ever complained. She stripped, put on a bra and a red turtleneck, and zipped up snug jeans. Her legs were long, and when she put on her heeled boots, she cleared six feet. Staring into the mirror over the dresser, she used a brush to get some of the tangles out of her long, lush black hair, and then she tied it in a ponytail behind her.

She grabbed her keys. Her wallet. Her badge. Her gun.

Before she left the bedroom, she hesitated, studying her face in the mirror the way she would examine a suspect who was hiding things from her. Emerald-green eyes stared back in the gray light. Her nose was sharp and straight. Her skin still had a mellow brown glow from the summer days outside. She was a harsh critic of her own looks, despite Jonny telling her that she hadn't lost the glamour she'd brought to Duluth from her old life in Las Vegas. With a critic's eye, she noticed laugh lines making parentheses around her mouth and a tiny web of wrinkles near her eyes. Her cheeks were fuller than she liked; no matter how much she worked out, time and the Duluth seasons managed to keep her weight a few pounds above her target.

That was Serena at forty-three years old.

Forty-three.

The middle of life. As much behind her as ahead of her. How had that happened? She hadn't really come to terms with the reality that she was no longer young, and she didn't like it. Being *mature* was supposed to mean you had less to prove to yourself, but if anything, she'd become increasingly dissatisfied with herself and her life. She felt a hole in her soul, an emptiness that followed her like a shadow and was always with her.

Serena turned off the light and headed out of the bedroom. The rest of the cottage was dark, and rain thumped on the roof. In the kitchen, she plucked her coat off a hook near the back door, then grabbed a bottle of water from the refrigerator. Before she could open it, her cell phone rang again. Quickly, she dug in the pocket of her jeans to retrieve it.

The caller ID showed a telephone number she didn't recognize. Except for the area code, which she knew well.

602. Phoenix.

Serena tensed. Nothing good ever came out of calls from Phoenix.

"Yes?" she answered cautiously. "Who is this?"

"Ma'am, my name is Deputy Lawrence Moray with the Maricopa County Sheriff's Office in Arizona. I'm trying to reach a woman named Serena Dial, and this is the number I have for her."

"My name's Serena Stride now, Deputy, but you've got the right person."

"Okay, well, good, thank you." His voice stumbled uncomfortably. "The thing is, Ms. Dial—Ms. Stride—I found your name and number in the possession of a woman we've identified as Samantha Dial."

Serena sighed and squeezed her eyes shut. "Yes, of course, you did.

That's the way it always works. Samantha Dial is my mother, Deputy. I assume you have her in jail again. What has she done now?"

Drugs.

Assault.

Theft.

Even prostitution. Being in her sixties wouldn't stop Samantha from ringing that bell.

What was it this time, Serena wondered.

Deputy Moray cleared his throat in a nervous way that Serena had heard police officers use many times before. She'd used it herself when she had to deliver bad news. That was when she realized that this was a very different kind of phone call.

"No, ma'am, it's nothing like that," the deputy went on. "I'm very sorry to have to tell you this, and I really apologize for doing it on the phone. But you see, we found your mother's body tonight. She's dead."

2

Even when Jonathan Stride was asleep, his mind was usually conscious of his wife leaving their bed, of the crunch of her footsteps on the gravel outside the open window, of the growl of her Mustang's engine as she drove off. He knew when she'd been called away and wasn't surprised to wake up alone. But this time, his eyes opened with a start. He'd been vaguely aware of her getting up, but he hadn't heard her leave the house, and at least half an hour had passed since then.

He threw back the blanket and dropped his feet on the cold bedroom floor. As he did, he felt a tug in his chest, as if someone had given him a sharp punch to the ribs. Most of the pain had gone away over the past fourteen months of rehabilitation, after the surgery that had saved his life. He was running again, lifting weights again, feeling maybe 80 to 90 percent of the man he'd been before he was shot. However, his bones gave him a bracing reminder every morning of what he'd gone through on the operating table.

Stride went to the bedroom window and checked the driveway. He'd been right. Serena's car was still there. Bare-chested and barefoot, he went into the living room, where the lights were off. When his eyes adjusted, he saw Serena sitting on the brick hearth of the fireplace. Her chin was balanced on her hands, her head down, her black hair mostly covering her face.

"What's going on?" he asked quietly. "Are you okay?"

She didn't answer. She didn't move at all.

"Serena?"

She finally looked up stiffly, like a statue coming to life. "Samantha's dead."

Stride took a long, slow breath in silence. He hadn't expected that news, but he realized what it meant. Samantha dying created a labyrinth of emotions for Serena, and a Minotaur was hiding in those dark corridors.

When he went and sat down beside her, he didn't tell her he was sorry. She wouldn't have wanted to hear that. He also didn't try to comfort her. Given the history between Serena and her mother, this loss was prickly and precarious, and she didn't need empty gestures from him.

"Was it an overdose?" he asked.

"You'd think, right?" Serena replied in a flat, calm voice. "But no. Heart attack, they said. Although I'm sure all those years of addiction played a part."

"I imagine so."

"She was homeless again," Serena added. "They found her in a park south of the airport."

"Do you need to go out there?"

"It's not my responsibility," she retorted sharply.

"I didn't say it was."

Serena shut her mouth, as if regretting her outburst. He watched her foot tapping sporadically on the floor, a nervous tic like Morse code.

"The body's in the county morgue," she went on in a softer tone. "I told them I'd find somebody to pick it up and arrange for cremation."

"Okay."

"I really don't care what they do with her ashes."

"Okay."

"I could hear it in the cop's voice," she added with a little jerk of her head, like electricity had shot through her neck. "He was thinking, what kind of daughter lets her mother end up homeless?"

"I doubt he was thinking that."

"Oh, he was."

"You didn't owe Samantha anything, not after what she did to you."

"You don't need to tell me that. Believe me, I know."

"How long has it been since the last time?" Stride asked.

"I don't remember. Seven or eight years now. I figured she was probably already dead. The last time, I told the cops to let her know I was done with her forever. No more bail money. No more anything, never again. She was on her own. And that's how it worked out. She ended up dying alone in a park."

Stride said nothing.

"The cops found my name and number folded up inside a cheap locket," Serena went on. "That's how they located me. She still had my number, but she never called. I guess she got the message, huh? I didn't want to hear from her anymore. The cop also said there was a photo of a little girl in the locket. Jet-black hair, green eyes. Guess who?"

Stride exhaled sharply. He couldn't stop himself from saying it. "I'm sorry."

"Samantha," Serena hissed, like the name was poison on her tongue. "Did she think keeping my picture would somehow change my mind? That I'd forget what she did? I swear, I will never forgive her. Not ever."

"No one's asking you to."

Serena wiped her face, as if she should have been crying, but there were no tears. Then she got up from the hearth with another electric twitch of her head. "Anyway, I have to go. Maggie needs me on a case."

"Take the day off," Stride suggested. "Mags can get by without you. She's got Guppo."

"I'd rather work."

"Come on, we'll go for an early breakfast somewhere. Just you and me. Then we can drive up the north shore to Split Rock."

"I said *no*." She breathed raggedly, her chest swelling. "Right now, I just want to forget all about this, okay? Samantha's dead. That sorry chapter of my life is finally over. I can move on."

He stood up beside her. "Are you going to call Alice?"

Alice Frye was a therapist. Serena hadn't had good luck with therapists for most of her life, but Alice was different—a seventy-something ex-hippie who told filthy jokes and didn't treat Serena like a busted toy. For months, Serena had kept her visits to Alice a secret, but eventually she'd admitted that she'd been seeing her. That was a big part of how Serena, who'd been a closed door when he first met her, had finally opened up and let out the things she'd gone through as a child. But she'd concluded more than a year ago that she didn't go to therapy anymore. She was done. Cured. That was what she'd told him. Stride thought she was making a mistake.

"Samantha has been out of my life for years," Serena insisted. "This doesn't change anything. I'm fine."

"Maybe so, but talking to Alice couldn't hurt."

"I appreciate the concern, Jonny, but I'm *fine*. Why don't you go back to bed? I'll text you later."

"Sure."

He watched her go. At the back of the house, he heard the slam of the door as usual, then the crunch of her footsteps as usual, and then the roar of her Mustang as usual. She sped away with a squeal of her tires the way she always did.

She wasn't fine.

* * * * *

Maggie sipped coffee in the deserted breakfast area of the Comfort Suites tourist hotel in Canal Park. Gavin sat across the table from her with a blanket wrapped around his shoulders. He stirred hot chocolate that he'd made from a powder packet. A gas fireplace beside them gave off a little heat, but she still felt the chill of her wet hair and the dampness that had made its way inside her clothes. Outside, rain continued to pound the boardwalk. All she could see in the lakeside windows were their own blurry reflections.

"We'll be mounting a search for your wife," she told him, "but I need to know what happened. Tell me everything, right from the beginning."

Gavin worked the stirring stick around the cup without drinking any of the hot chocolate. "What day is it?" he asked, with the vacant stare of someone overwhelmed by the smallest details. "Is it Friday?"

"Yes. Early Friday morning."

"I got home late on Tuesday. It was after ten o'clock. I'd been with my parents in Rice Lake for a couple of days, and I drove home after dinner. It took about two hours."

"Why didn't Chelsey go with you to Rice Lake?" Maggie asked.

Gavin shrugged. "Spending time with the in-laws? That wasn't her thing."

"When did you last talk to her?"

"I called her before I drove home, to tell her I was on my way. That was around eight fifteen or eight thirty."

"Did she sound okay?"

"Yes."

"She was home?"

"Yes, she said she was watching a movie."

"Where do you live?"

"We have a little house on 5th Street on Observation Hill. We used to have a place on Skyline, but we sold it and got this place instead. It's a lot cheaper, but it still has a view."

"Do you have neighbors close by?"

"A few. One next door, plus some houses on the north side of the hill. They look down on our place."

"Okay, go on," Maggie said.

"I got home and parked in the driveway. We have a one-car garage, and Chelsey usually parks her car there. I went inside the house through the downstairs door and called out to let her know I was home. She didn't answer, which surprised me. Usually, she's up late. I checked the garage, and I saw her car was there, so I called again, but she still didn't respond. So I went upstairs to the main level of the house. The front door was open and the window shattered. There was a lot of damage in the hallway, furniture overturned, pictures off the wall, like there'd been some kind of fight. When I turned on the light, I saw—I saw blood, too. Not much, but some on the wall and the floor. Chelsey was gone."

"Why not call the police?" Maggie asked.

"I was about to do that when my phone rang. I didn't recognize the number, but—I don't know—somehow I knew I had to answer it. When I did, I heard Chelsey on the other end. She was screaming, terrified. Then she got cut off with a cry, like somebody hit her. And there was this voice. It wasn't a real voice. It was electronic. This voice said, we have your wife. If you call the police, she'll be killed immediately. Follow instructions, and you can get her back."

"The caller said *we*?"

Gavin nodded.

"When you were driving home from Rice Lake, did you notice anyone following you? Did you see anyone parked on the street near your house?"

"No, but it was dark, so I'm not sure I would have noticed."

"What instructions did the kidnappers give you?" Maggie asked.

"They gave me two days to gather one hundred thousand dollars in cash. They said I'd find a small red backpack in the kitchen. I was supposed to put the money in there after I got it."

"And then?"

"And then wait. They said they'd call back on Thursday evening with further instructions on where to drop the backpack. Then they told me again that if I brought in the police, I'd never hear from them. Chelsey would be killed."

Maggie eased backward, the front legs of her chair lifting off the ground. She studied Gavin over the steaming top of her foam coffee cup. "Did they give you any clue about who they were? Or anything that indicated their motive or their connection to you?"

"No, there was nothing like that," Gavin replied. "It was a short call. They made their demands and hung up."

"Have you received any threats lately?"

"No."

"What about unhappy clients?"

Gavin shrugged. "If I lose a case, clients are always unhappy."

Maggie nodded thoughtfully as she took another sip of coffee. "One hundred thousand dollars? That was the ransom demand?"

"Yes."

"And that's what you gave them?"

"Yes."

"I have some questions about that."

"I'm sure you do."

She dropped the front legs of the chair back on the floor and leaned across the table. "No offense, Gavin, but you're not some corporate partner. I see your ads on bus-stop benches. I can't imagine you coming up with a thousand dollars to pay off a ransom, let alone a hundred grand. Where did you get that kind of money?"

Gavin glanced around at the empty tables in the breakfast room, as if invisible people were listening to them. "My circumstances have changed recently."

"How so?"

"A few months ago, my only sister died of cancer. She was a widow and had no kids. She and I were close. I was her sole beneficiary."

"How much money are we talking about?"

"Around three million dollars."

Maggie whistled softly. "Who knew about this windfall?"

"I don't know. Probably a lot of people. Chelsey and I told a few friends, and I suppose my parents did, too. I have no idea how far it went from there, but gossip travels fast."

"So people knew you could afford a sizable ransom."

"I guess so."

"Bank accounts are one thing, but getting your hands on cash is another. You go to a bank and ask for that kind of money, they're going to ask questions. There are required disclosures. How'd you get it?"

"I can't tell you that," Gavin replied.

"Why not?"

He shrugged and still didn't answer.

"Attorney-client privilege?" Maggie guessed. "You went to one of your clients."

"No comment."

"Who was it?" she went on. "Someone in the drug trade who traffics in illegal cash? I imagine you paid a hell of a premium. What was the vig? A hundred and fifty will get you a hundred?"

"No comment," he repeated.

"Come on, I need a name, Gavin."

"I can't give you one."

"Hasn't it occurred to you that the kidnappers might be connected to your client?" Maggie persisted. "There aren't many ways to get your hands on that kind of cash, and yet these people knew you could do it quickly."

He shook his head firmly, refusing to tell her more. "The bottom line is, I got the money I needed. I had one hundred thousand dollars in cash stuffed in the red backpack."

Maggie frowned. "Go on. What happened next? When did they call?"

"Nine o'clock last night."

"Same phone number?"

"No, it was a different number this time, but the same electronic voice."

"Did you talk to Chelsey?"

"Yes. I said no money unless I talked to her. They put her on the phone for a few seconds and then cut her off again."

"So as of six hours ago, she was alive."

"Yes."

"What did they tell you to do?" Maggie asked.

"At exactly midnight, I was supposed to park on Harbor Drive where the road curves between the aquarium and the DECC. They said they'd be watching me. When they were sure I was alone—no cops—a car would come up beside me with its passenger window open. I was supposed to toss the backpack inside. When they verified the cash, they said they would call back and let me know where to find Chelsey. So I locked the backpack inside my briefcase and did what they said. I drove down here in the rain and waited."

"Why the briefcase?"

He shrugged. "It was a Hello Kitty backpack. If anyone saw me, I figured that would raise questions."

"Did the car show up?"

Gavin shook his head. "No. There was no car. They switched the drop. I got a second call at twelve fifteen, and they told me to take the backpack and get out of the car. I did. There was a motorboat in the bay right near where I was parked. The caller said to take the backpack to the water's edge and toss it to the person in the boat. So that's what I did. Once he had the backpack, he gunned the boat's engine and left."

"Toward the lake? Through the lift bridge?"

"No, the other way. Back into the harbor."

"How many people were in the boat?"

"Just the one."

"Did you see what this person looked like?"

"No. He wore a hood."

"You're sure it was a he?"

"Well, the build was male. Otherwise, I couldn't see any distinguishing features. He had a hood, raincoat, gloves. I couldn't tell you how tall he was or whether he was fat or skinny."

"What about the boat?"

"It was dark-colored, probably blue or black, but in the rain, I couldn't be sure. Sleek, very powerful, lots of speed. I only saw it for a few seconds, and it was gone."

"And then?" Maggie asked.

"And then nothing. I waited in my car to get the phone call. When it didn't come, I tried calling back the phone numbers they'd used. Neither one was in service. I imagine the phones are somewhere on the bottom of the bay. That's it, Lieutenant. That's all I can tell you. When almost three hours had gone by, I realized they had no intention of giving Chelsey back to me. That's when I finally did what I should have done at the beginning. I called you."

3

Serena leaned against her Mustang and waited under the porte cochere of the hotel parking lot. It was almost four in the morning, and the heavy rain showed no sign of stopping. The street through Canal Park was deserted at that early hour, but the platform of the towering lift bridge was up, giving entrance to one of the giant ore boats arriving from Lake Superior. She saw a glint of its red superstructure as it glided silently through the narrow ship canal into the inner harbor.

The hotel doors slid open with a *whoosh*. Maggie clomped down the wooden steps to meet her. She eyed Serena's face with an expression that was as close to sympathy as Maggie was likely to offer. "You don't have to be here, you know. Go home. Guppo and I can deal with this."

Serena frowned. "Stride told you?"

"Yeah, he sent me a text."

"Well, I don't need the poor-poor-pitiful-me routine."

Maggie shrugged, as if Serena had said exactly what she expected. "Look, I know how things were between you and your mother, but we're still talking about losing a parent. No one's prepared for that, even if they think they are. Take some time for yourself."

"I want to work," Serena replied curtly. "This is my call, okay? Bring me up to speed, and let me do my job."

With a sigh of surrender, Maggie quickly summarized Gavin Webster's story of what had happened to his wife. Serena shoved aside everything else out of her mind and focused on the kidnapping.

"A boat to collect the ransom?" she said.

"That's right."

"Clever. Even if Gavin had brought us in, I'm not sure we would have been able to cover that."

"Yeah. Exactly."

"Well, it's easy enough to check if he's telling the truth. We should be able to get camera footage from the bridge."

"Guppo's up there now," Maggie said.

As if the other detective could overhear their conversation, both of their phones chimed simultaneously with incoming texts. Max Guppo had sent them a video file copied from the bridge operator's computer. Silently, Serena and Maggie both watched it on their phones. The time stamp was at 12:13 a.m., and the video captured a wide-screen view of the inner harbor. Serena enlarged the images on the feed, which helped her make out the activity taking place near the DECC. Distantly, she saw a boat cutting a swath through the choppy water and then idling close to the pier. On land, a man got out of a car and walked toward the edge of the water, where he tossed something toward the boat. The craft was in darkness. She could see nothing of the person operating it, but seconds later, the boat sped away at high speed, throwing up a wake behind it.

"So it went down like Gavin said," Serena observed.

"It did," Maggie agreed. She sounded almost disappointed. "We need to find that boat ASAP."

"That won't be easy. It could have landed anywhere on the Wisconsin or Minnesota side of the bay."

Maggie nodded. "I'll call Lance Beaton and have him get the Superior cops to start searching on their side."

"Do you think the wife is alive?" Serena asked.

"I don't like her odds. Gavin says he talked to her at nine o'clock, but now that they have the money, they don't have much incentive to keep her alive. If the plan really was to give her back, they would have called before now."

"What do you want me to do?"

Maggie fished in the pocket of her trench coat and came out with a house key pinched between her fingers. "Gavin gave me the key to his place. Get over there and see what it looks like inside. I'll send Guppo to join you, and we'll get a forensics team to start gathering evidence. Wake up the neighbors, too. Maybe someone saw something on Tuesday evening or in the days before Chelsey was taken. If we're really lucky, maybe one of them has an outdoor security cam that looks out on the street."

Serena nodded. "Okay."

"See what the neighbors have to say about Gavin and Chelsey, too," Maggie added.

"Meaning?"

"Meaning how was their marriage."

Serena pursed her lips. "Understood."

She climbed into her car, but Maggie signaled her, and Serena rolled down the window. "Is there something else?"

"No, not about the case," Maggie replied. "But if you want to talk about Samantha at any point, we can do that. I know I'm not the first person you'd usually talk to, but sometimes a frenemy is better than a friend."

"I appreciate the thought, but I have it under control," Serena informed her in a starchy tone. "Got it?"

"Got it."

Serena rolled up the window. She shivered a little from the cold, then started the car and sped down Canal Park Drive toward the city. She left the radio off and drove in silence. After crossing over the freeway, she turned left on 1st Street past the quiet downtown buildings. At Mesaba, she headed sharply uphill and then took another left at a short road that led to 5th. The narrow street was terraced along the steep slope of the Observation Hill neighborhood. Its asphalt had been beaten into cracks and potholes by the freeze-and-thaw of winter weather. Rainwater poured down the shoulders.

A few blocks later, she parked outside Gavin Webster's house. The property was on the south side of the street and overlooked the lake, which was invisible through clouds of fog and rain. It was an older house, with chocolate-colored wooden siding and a tuck-under one-car garage. Duluth was one of those rare cities where buyers could still find middle-class homes with lake views, but the neighborhood had begun to gentrify. Immediately across the street, up steep steps from the sidewalk, were several homes that had been expensively remodeled and expanded. Their picture windows looked right down on Gavin's house.

In the rain, Serena hiked up the driveway past messy, overgrown shrubbery. The yard was small, just a little patch of lawn in the back and a picnic table and a Weber grill near the garage. Over her head was the house's second story, where a balcony and large windows took advantage of the view.

She drew out her pistol, then used the key to unlock the lower-level door. Once she was inside, she called out loudly, "Is anyone here? This is the police."

No one answered.

The house was quiet and cold, and the lights were off. The only sound was rainwater dripping from her clothes to the floor. She checked the garage and found a boxy yellow Volvo parked inside. Chelsey's car. When she climbed the stairs to the upper level, she found a drafty hallway near the front door. She switched on the hall light and could see broken glass where the window by the door had been smashed inward. Gavin had obviously nailed plywood across the opening, but he'd otherwise left the scene untouched. She spotted a smear of blood on the wall, and then more blood spattered on the living room carpet. A fragment of fabric that looked like it came from the sleeve of a blouse lay there, too.

In her head, she re-created the scene. The kidnappers—one or more—had broken the window and let themselves in through the front door. Chelsey, alarmed by the noise, had come running to see what was happening. There was a fight in the foyer, Chelsey screaming and trying to escape, the kidnapper throwing her against the wall and then chasing her down as she ran.

Was she unconscious as they carried her outside?

Or did they gag her to keep her quiet?

One way or another, they'd taken her from the house. The whole abduction probably only lasted a couple of minutes.

Serena went into the living room, adjacent to the entryway. It was compact and paneled in dark wood. The room itself showed nothing unusual: old furniture with fabric worn through to the foam, black-and-white family photos hanging crookedly on the walls, and leather-bound law books crowded on a set of built-in bookshelves. And yet she felt a vibe in this room that made her uneasy. She'd had a cop mentor in Las Vegas who told her to listen to the feel of a place, not just the people in it. Where suspects and victims lived, how they lived, the things they kept, the art they put up, always left echoes of who they were. You could learn a lot from them.

The echo of this place was dark. Unhappy.

She turned her mind back to the circumstances of the crime. She thought about Gavin getting home, finding the damage, and realizing that his wife was missing. He was about to call 911 to report it—but then the kidnappers interrupted him with their ransom demands. Their timing was oddly perfect, reaching out to him before he'd had a chance to bring in the police. That didn't feel like a coincidence.

Somehow they *knew* when he'd arrived home.

Maybe they were watching from the street. Or—

She eyed the stairwell that led from the lower level of the house. When she traced the line of sight from the hallway to the far side of the living room, she spotted a bushy split-leaf philodendron potted near the front window. She went to examine it. Carefully separating the leaves, she located a wireless spy camera hidden inside the plant, with a vantage on anyone climbing the stairs.

They'd been waiting for Gavin to get home. Watching. Listening. By installing the camera, the kidnappers had been able to reach Gavin while he was not thinking clearly and still in a state of shock. *We have your wife.* And the camera would also let them know if he disobeyed their instructions and contacted the police.

This crime had been carefully planned and executed.

Standing in the living room, Serena found her attention drawn to the black-and-white pictures hung on the wall. She examined the photographs and recognized Gavin from the times she'd faced off against him in court. The curly blond hair. The intense, Jude Law eyes and enigmatic little smile. In most of the photographs, Gavin was with a woman, and she assumed this was Chelsey. They looked happy together. Big smiles, his arm around her shoulder, her arm around his waist. But Serena had learned not to trust what she saw in pictures. Photographs were two-dimensional, and you couldn't see inside them, which made it easy for people to show a different face to the world.

She took a close look at Chelsey Webster. The largest of the pictures had obviously been taken at a wedding. Gavin was in a tux. His wife wore auburn-colored silk, glistening like liquid on her curves. She was as tall as he was, with a statuesque figure. She had full brown hair tumbling past her shoulders, as if the 1980s had never gone out of style. Her dark eyes were cool and intelligent, and her eyebrows arched sharply. Her blush was a little too pink, her lipstick a little too red, and her teeth a little too white. But the whole effect was of someone self-assured and attractive. She was certainly past forty, but the look she gave the camera celebrated her age, rather than hid from it. She looked tough, the kind of woman who had probably put up quite a fight when they came to take her.

"Serena?"

The voice came out of nowhere, like a whisper.

She whirled around, breathing hard, but she was alone and the room was empty. She felt sweat on her palms. What she'd heard was inside her head. She knew that voice; she could call it up just by closing her eyes and listening. Smoky, deep, always slurred by whatever she'd had to drink or whatever drug she was on.

Samantha.

She wondered why the photograph of Chelsey had triggered thoughts of her mother. The two women didn't look at all alike. And then she remembered: the wedding. Serena had gone to her first wedding when she was thirteen years old. The older brother of one of her school friends had been getting married, and Samantha had taken her. It was so exciting, wearing a long turquoise dress, putting on makeup, doing up her long black hair, wobbling on high heels.

Her father had stayed home; he knew when he was the odd man out. Instead, mother and daughter had gone together, looking like sisters. Serena remembered how much she'd liked hearing Samantha tell people the story of her name, with sparkling laughter in her voice. *"Serena? Well, do you remember that television show* Bewitched*? Here I am, natural blond, and that girl came out of me with that jet-black hair of hers, and I just knew she'd be my evil twin. I was Samantha, so naturally she was Serena."*

Her mother.

The prettiest woman in the world. Gorgeous, with that long sunflower hair and jewellike green eyes she'd given to Serena. Graceful where a teenaged Serena had still been clumsy. They'd danced together at the wedding, at least when Samantha wasn't dancing with other men and giving Serena winks from the floor. They'd people-watched, with Samantha whispering mean little jokes about the other women in Serena's ear, making her giggle. They'd smoked cigarettes outside the church like bad girls. They'd swiped a bottle of white wine after Samantha flirted with the bartender, and her mother had let her drink with her until past midnight as they lay in deck chairs by the Scottsdale pool. And when that bottle was gone, she'd brought them another, and Serena had gotten drunk for the very first time.

It had been the best night of her life. The best night ever. She'd gone home sick but high as a cloud, and she remembered how much she'd loved her mother for giving her that night, and how she would do anything in the world for Samantha. She wanted nothing else from the future but to grow up exactly like her.

And in the worst way, she had.

"Serena?"

This was a real voice.

She spun toward the noise from the shadows. Automatically, she lifted her gun and pointed it at a man standing at the top of the stairs.

Without even a second thought, she curled her finger around the trigger. All she could see was a threat, and all her brain could think to do was fire.

Max Guppo thrust his hands in the air at the sight of the gun. "Serena! It's me! It's Max!"

Serena didn't react immediately. It took time for Max's words to break through the fog in which she found herself. She stared through the dark room, and her mind finally came back to reality. She wasn't in Phoenix. She wasn't with Samantha. This was Gavin Webster's house in Duluth, and his wife was missing.

She lowered her gun and holstered it. Her skin flushed hot with shame and fear. "Christ, Max, I'm so sorry."

"I called to you from downstairs. Didn't you hear me?"

"No, I didn't hear anything. I was distracted."

Max waddled into the living room. He was short, mostly bald, and as overinflated as a child in Willy Wonka's chocolate factory. He was also a sweet, cheerful father of five daughters who'd had an innocent crush on Serena ever since she arrived in Duluth from Las Vegas. They were the best of friends.

"Are you okay?" Max asked.

"Yeah. Sure. Don't tell Maggie, okay?"

He cocked his round head with surprise. "I'd never do that."

"Thank you, Max."

"The forensics team is right behind me," he said.

Serena felt her hands trembling, and she curled her fingers into fists to steady them. "Just have them dust everything, okay? But I don't think we'll find any prints. Whoever did this was smart. I'm going to go wake up the neighbors and see if they can tell us anything."

Guppo nodded, but his face showed the same worry she'd felt from Jonny and Maggie. "Are you sure you're okay?"

"Yes. I'm fine." She looked around at the living room and saw the photos of Gavin and Chelsey staring back at her from the wall. "Right now, I just need to get out of this house."

4

Despite the early hour, the lights were on in the house across the street. It was one of the homes that had gone through an expensive renovation, with a large two-story addition and floor-to-ceiling windows. Serena could see the silhouette of a man downstairs, his hands on his hips as he watched the police activity at Gavin's house. Neighbors didn't like that sort of thing.

She climbed steep steps from the street. The heavy rain continued to fall, an October downpour that went on and on. Before she got to the door, she stopped, hearing a strange whimpering noise not far away. It was impossible to see the origin of the sound in the rain and darkness, but she picked her way across a narrow stone walkway, built above the sharp slope of the retaining wall. Near the corner of the house, she found a black-and-white Border collie tied to a post in the ground. The dog was curled up into a tight ball with no protection from the rain, but even so, he lifted his head as Serena came closer, and his bushy tail flopped up and down in a puddle. Serena squatted, stroking the dog's sodden fur. He didn't look fully grown; she would have been surprised if he was even a year old.

"They left you out here?" she asked.

The dog licked Serena's hand, then laid his head over her foot. His personality was sweet, and his sad eyes looked up at her like he'd found a savior. She stayed with him for a few more minutes, talking softly to him and hearing his whimper become a happy rumble at getting attention. Then she kissed the dog's wet head and returned to the house's front door. Her badge was in her hand.

A man and a woman answered as soon as she rang the bell. They were both in their thirties, annoyingly fit and genetically blessed. The man wore a tank top and shorts, and he'd obviously been exercising because the shirt was soaked with sweat. The woman looked pretty but mussed in a T-shirt and baggy pajama bottoms.

"I'm sorry to bother you so early," she told them. "My name's Serena Stride. I'm an investigator with the Duluth Police. I'd like to ask you a few questions."

The man didn't seem inclined to invite her into the house. "What's this about? What's going on at Gavin's place?"

Serena didn't answer. "May I come in? It's a little wet outside."

The couple exchanged glances, and the man reluctantly stood aside to let Serena into the foyer. The house had a smell of new construction about it, and the modern look of the furniture and art told Serena that the owners had money. A lot of Twin Cities professionals had been moving to the north shore to work remotely in recent years, and they'd been snapping up lake-view houses and driving up prices. Locals weren't happy about it.

"By the way, your dog is outside," Serena said.

The man eyed his wife, as if it were her fault. "Goddamn it, the kids left the dog out all night again."

"I'll talk to them," the woman replied in a weary voice.

"The whole goddamn deal was that they would take care of the thing. That's the only reason I said yes."

"I know."

"I didn't want the dog in the first place, and I told you it wasn't going to be me feeding it and walking it and picking up its shit."

"As soon as the kids are up, I'll talk to them," she repeated.

Meanwhile, neither one made a move to go out and rescue the dog from the rain. Serena bit her tongue hard between her teeth to suppress her anger.

The man led her into the expanded section of the house, which had a cold, elegant feel, sleek but not welcoming. When it wasn't raining, the room obviously offered a stunning panorama toward the lake and the downtown skyline, but for now, there was nothing to see outside. The man grabbed a couple of copies of *People* magazine from a rack and spread them on a cushioned chair. He gestured for Serena to sit on the magazines.

"This furniture costs a fortune," the man explained.

Serena sat down, hearing the glossy pages crinkle beneath her.

"I'm Dale Sacks, this is my wife, Krystal," he went on in a curt voice. The two of them took seats on a blue sectional sofa near the windows. "Now can you tell us what the hell's going on? We don't like waking up to see police cars swarming the neighborhood."

"I understand."

"We've got two boys, seven and nine," his wife added. "Are they safe? Do we need to keep them home from school?"

"We don't know of any danger to anyone else at this time," Serena replied.

"Well, that's not much of an answer," Dale replied sourly. He went and poured himself a cup of coffee from a wet bar on the other side of the room. He didn't offer any to Serena or his wife.

"Did something happen to Gavin and Chelsey?" Krystal asked.

"Mrs. Webster is missing," Serena told them.

Krystal sucked in a breath. "Missing! What happened?"

"We're still looking into that, but in a case like this, every minute counts while we're trying to find her. I'd appreciate it if you could answer some questions for me."

"Sure, yes."

"How long have you lived in this house?" Serena asked.

Dale Sacks was looking out the window toward the Webster house. "About eighteen months. I like the north shore, and now that the whole world's working remotely, we figured, what the hell."

"If you work remotely, does that mean the two of you are home a lot?"

"Most of the time, yes. My office is right above this room, so that's where I am all day. Krystal runs an eBay business, so she's back and forth to the post office a lot, but otherwise, she's around, too."

"Have you noticed any unusual activity on your street recently?" Serena asked. "Cars you didn't recognize or strangers in the neighborhood?"

"No," Krystal replied with a frown. "I don't think so. With small children at home, I keep a pretty close eye on things. I haven't seen anyone that concerned me. If I had, I would have called the police."

"What about your neighbors around here? Have any of them mentioned seeing anyone suspicious?"

She shook her head. "No, but we don't know any of them particularly well. We're newcomers, and we're from Minneapolis, so that's sort of two strikes against us. Honestly, Gavin and Chelsey were the only ones around here who made us feel welcome."

"Were you home on Tuesday evening?" Serena asked. "Between eight and ten p.m.?"

"Tuesday?" Dale replied. "Yeah, we were both home. I had a Zoom call with clients in Australia. I do global medical device sales. Krystal was watching a movie with the kids."

"Did you see or hear anything going on at the Webster house?"

"Not that I recall. I was staring at the screen, not looking out the window. My desk faces the other way."

"Nothing at all? Glass breaking, shouting, screaming?"

"No. Something like that would have gotten my attention."

"Mrs. Sacks, what about you?" Serena asked.

"I was on the other side of the house with the kids all evening."

"And your dog?"

"What?"

"Where was your dog? Inside or outside?"

"Outside. Dale doesn't like the dog tracking mud inside."

Serena frowned and said, "Did you hear him barking?"

"Actually, yeah, now that I think about it, he was barking like crazy for a while," Dale replied. "I had to text Krystal to get the kids to shut him up. The thing was interrupting my Zoom call."

"What time was that?"

Dale pulled out his phone and scrolled through his texts. "Right around nine o'clock."

"Did you hear anything else?"

"Just the goddamn dog barking his head off."

"Did you look outside?"

"No. Like I said, I was in a meeting."

"Mrs. Sacks, did you or your children check on the dog?"

She got a little flush on her face. "Actually, no. I told the kids to check on him, but we were almost at the end of the movie, so they wanted to wait. By the time we were done, he was quiet again. I mean, it couldn't have been more than a couple of minutes that he was barking."

"Have you seen or talked to Mr. Webster since Tuesday night?"

Dale shook his head. "No. He's a lawyer, and his clients aren't exactly the cream of the crop, you know? So he keeps odd hours."

"When did you last see either Gavin or Chelsey?"

"It's been two or three weeks, I guess," Dale replied.

"Do you know the Websters well?" Serena asked.

"I wouldn't say *well*, but we've had meals together maybe three or four times since we moved in," Krystal told her. "Like I said, they were more welcoming than the others around here. I know Chelsey better than Gavin. We occasionally have wine together in the evening."

"What were your impressions of the two of them?"

Dale shrugged. "Gavin's an odd duck."

"How so?"

"I don't know, he never talks about anything other than work. He seems to enjoy bailing lowlifes out of jail at two in the morning. It's weird. Otherwise, I don't know anything about him. He never says a word about politics, family, whatever. He doesn't even seem to like talking about the Twins or the Vikings."

"But he's very good-looking," Krystal added. "Those eyes of his . . . wow, they're so mesmerizing."

Dale shrugged. "I guess women go for that sort of thing. Me, I don't really like it. When he looks at you, you have no idea what he's thinking. Usually with men, you know where they stand, but not Gavin. He's a closed book."

"And Chelsey?" Serena asked. "What can you tell me about her?"

"Well, I imagine she was a Minnesota hot dish once upon a time," Dale commented. "But that was—Krys, do you remember how long Gavin said they'd been together?—fourteen, fifteen years?"

"Meaning what?" Serena asked.

"Meaning a man who found himself with three million dollars might start thinking about a trade-in to a younger model."

Serena struggled to keep her reaction off her face. Krystal rolled her eyes and shot her a look that said: *Yeah, I know he's a pig.*

"So you'd heard about the inheritance," Serena said.

Krystal nodded. "Chelsey told us."

"Fucking amazing luck," Dale added.

"Don't say things like that," Krystal interjected sharply, running out of patience with her husband this time. "His sister died of cancer. That's not luck, that's awful. I'm sure if he had the choice, he'd give up all of the money in order to get her back."

"And if you believe *that*, honeybun, you're naïve," Dale retorted.

Serena swallowed down her dislike for this man. "Mr. Sacks, did Gavin say anything to you that would make you think he wasn't happy with his marriage? Or was considering divorce?"

Dale shrugged. "Nothing specific. It's just a guess. But based on what Chelsey told Krystal, we wouldn't have been surprised to see them split up."

"Mrs. Sacks?" Serena asked. "What did Chelsey tell you?"

Krystal looked uncomfortable with the direction of the conversation. "This was just girl talk. It wasn't serious. We were gossiping over wine a couple of weeks ago, that's all. I'm not sure it's appropriate to be sharing it with the police."

"Chelsey is missing," Serena reminded her.

"I know, but I can't believe Gavin had anything to do with that."

"What did she tell you?" Serena asked again.

Krystal sighed. "Chelsey wasn't particularly happy with things. I mean, even before the inheritance, she'd talked to me about how Gavin worked all the time. She wondered if he was cheating on her. You know, he represents a lot of—well, a lot of interesting clients. Prostitutes, people like that. Chelsey didn't like it. And after they got the money, I don't know. You'd think she would have been happy about it, but Chelsey said Gavin was acting different."

"Different how?"

"She was vague," Krystal replied. "Chelsey said his behavior was making her a little uncomfortable. Like she'd catch him watching her when she wasn't paying attention, just staring at her with those eyes of his. She even made—I mean, it sounds bad now—but she made a joke about it."

Serena's face darkened. "What kind of joke?"

Krystal hesitated. "Chelsey said she wondered if she should have somebody tasting her food."

* * * * *

Outside, when she was back in the rain, Serena struggled to understand what she did next.

Before she left the house, she reminded Dale and Krystal Sacks about their dog. She told them that they couldn't leave the dog outside like that and that they needed to take better care of him. She said they had to bring him inside the house right now, and if they didn't, she'd refer them to animal control.

After they'd closed the door, she went over to the Border collie again. He was still whimpering, still soaking wet, but he greeted her arrival as if she were his greatest friend on earth. She sat with him on the wet concrete, and the dog flopped over in her lap so she could rub his white belly. Fifteen minutes passed that way. No one from inside the house came to take the dog out of the rain.

She waited another fifteen minutes after that. The Sacks kids were up now. She could hear them shouting and running around inside the house. But the dog had been forgotten.

Serena didn't ring the bell. She didn't call animal control.

She was done with these people.

She unhooked the dog's leash from the post, and she took the Border collie to her Mustang and put him inside.

5

For almost a year after he was shot, Stride didn't miss his job.

The shooting had happened in late July, when a bullet tore open one chamber of his heart. The surgeons had performed an emergency thoracotomy to save him, which meant cutting open his entire chest cavity. The odds of his surviving the surgery at all had been no better than one in four. He'd actually died on the operating table during the procedure, and they'd had to shock his heart back to life.

The doctors had warned him that it wouldn't be an easy or fast recovery, and it wasn't. It was well into the fall months before he felt strong enough to take daily walks on the beach again. Even then, a few minutes of effort would wipe him out for hours. The slow pace of his rehabilitation left him depressed, and the doctors had warned him about that, too.

The scars of trauma are emotional, not just physical.

You'll need to accept the reality that your life will never be exactly the same as it was before.

They were right.

Sometimes he would sit by the lake and question how the events of his life had led him to that moment. He dwelled on the mistakes he'd made, the people he'd lost. He felt like a stranger to himself, as if he were inhabiting someone else's body. He hadn't died, but he hadn't started living again, either.

So as fall bled into the frigid winter, he finally embraced his new normal. He went to physical therapy twice a week, and he bought a treadmill, and when the temperatures climbed above zero outside, he went and jogged up and down the Point, which was the narrow spit of land between the lake and the harbor, where he and Serena lived. By the time spring arrived in Duluth (late, as usual), he was feeling physically more like the man he'd been before the shooting. Older, still in pain, but in some ways stronger than he'd been in years.

But he still found himself reluctant to go back to the police.

There was a darkness in his job, and he didn't want to confront darkness, not after what he'd been through. He didn't want to deal with death, evil, lies, and betrayal anymore. Facing his own mortality had changed him forever, just as the doctors had predicted. And yet the only thing Stride had ever known, the only thing he'd ever wanted to do with his life, was be a cop. If he didn't want that anymore, he didn't know who he was.

He'd already put in more than thirty years on the force and was eligible for his pension. So he'd spent the summer thinking about retiring and wondering if there was a second act for men like him. Meanwhile, the other people around him were getting on with their lives. Maggie was dealing with his old job, Serena was working as Maggie's partner, Cat was getting ready for college. Each of them knew where they were going. Each of them had a direction, a place to be, a reason for living.

Then there was Stride, feeling restless, doing nothing more than treading water on a dark sea.

He knew it hadn't made him a good husband. His relationship with Serena had been difficult for months, including their sex life, which was nonexistent. He was so frustrated by his own lack of direction that he'd drifted into old habits, shutting her out of his life and ignoring everything *she* was dealing with. It had never even occurred to him how hard it would be for her to have Cat leave for college. He'd only realized it when she spent four nights in a row sleeping in Cat's empty bed. When she'd come back to their room in the mornings, he could see loneliness written on her face.

And now, on the heels of that loss, Samantha was gone, too. An old deep wound had been ripped open.

He could feel a crisis building for her, like an ocean wave pulling back before the tsunami comes in, but he felt utterly unprepared to deal with Serena when he'd lost touch with himself. He knew that his time had come. He couldn't put off his decision any longer. He had to make a choice, and then he could move on. There was no middle ground, no in-between, just yes or no.

Was he still a cop?

Or was he done with that life?

Maggie had left him a voice mail a week ago. He'd played it a hundred times since he received it. It was as if she knew that he'd reached a crossroads. Stride sat at the breakfast table in the cottage and played the message again.

"Hey. It's me. Big news. Abel Teitscher finally retired. He's on his way to New Mexico, can you believe it? Abel Teitscher sipping margaritas by some desert pool. No way. I think he'd had enough of reporting to me, even though we both know I'm a total frickin' delight *to work for. Anyway, it's crazy here, because now we're shorthanded, and the chief's getting the budget blues from the city council, so it's not like we're going to hire anyone soon. I need to go through Abel's desk and sort through the open cases, but I don't know who I'd give them to."*

He heard a long, long pause on the message. Maggie, who could dish it out better than anyone he knew, was having trouble getting out what she wanted to say.

"So, no pressure or anything. You want to say no, say no, and we'll forget all about it. But I mean, with Abel gone, it occurred to me that maybe . . . I don't know . . . maybe you're finally in a place where . . ."

Her voice drifted off again. Then she just said it. She shot out the words.

"Oh for fuck's sake, boss. It's been over a year. Are you ready to come back here and do your job?"

* * * * *

With the rain still coming down, Stride sat near the windows of Kirby Student Center at UMD and waited for Cat. When he saw her approaching with a group of students, coffee in hand, backpack over her shoulder, he almost didn't recognize her. It wasn't that she looked different; she was still exactly the same, with a waterfall of chestnut hair, golden skin, a little upturned nose, and bright, teasing brown eyes. But there was a new grace about her, a confidence that hadn't been there before. He could see it in her walk, her expressions, her gestures. When he'd met her four years earlier, she'd been a broken, homeless teenager in need of rescue. Now she was a young woman, at ease in her surroundings. Seeing her that way, he felt a warmth in his chest that had to be what all fathers felt when they saw their daughters succeed.

When she saw him, she broke from her group and ran to hug him, nearly spilling her coffee with excitement. Her girlish voice reminded him that she was still young. "Stride! Hey, this is a surprise. What are you doing here?"

"I can't just come for a visit?" he said.

"You can, but you don't. It's been a month. I assumed you'd be over here every other day making sure I didn't burn the place down."

"I figured I'd embarrass you if I showed up," Stride told her.

She gave him a sly little smile. "Oh, you'd definitely embarrass me, but I still want to see you."

"Well, Serena and I wanted to give you time to settle in. How's that going?"

Cat got a crinkle in her forehead. She had the surprised look of someone who'd parachuted out of a plane and wasn't really sure where she'd landed. "I don't know. Scary? Weird? Great? I mean, I kind of fit in around here. That's a strange feeling for me. Most people know about my past, and they treat me like I'm some sort of badass. I like it."

"You are sort of a badass," he told her. "How are classes going?"

She bumped her head in mock confusion. "Oh, shit, classes? Am I supposed to be going to classes, too?"

"Ha."

Cat giggled and sat down across from him. She put her phone on the table. She looked every bit the college student, with a UMD sweatshirt, black jeans, fluorescent sneakers, and her backpack stuffed fatter than a Thanksgiving turkey. She was hiding her right wrist and obviously hoping he hadn't noticed the black cat tattoo she'd put there, like a rite of passage. "Seriously. I love it. Thank you."

"Good."

"But your timing is bad. I only have a couple of minutes before calculus. Can you hang out a while and we can have lunch later?"

"I can't, but how about you come over for dinner tonight?"

Cat's eyes narrowed as she read his face. "What's going on? What's wrong?"

"It's just an invitation."

"Yeah, sure. Come on, something's up. What is it?"

Stride hesitated before answering. "Serena's mother died last night."

Cat made a quiet, unhappy little hiss. "Samantha? The Wicked Witch of the West? Ouch. How's Serena taking it?"

"Not well."

"In other words, she's pretending it's no big deal and she's tough and everybody should quit trying to baby her."

"You're too smart for your own good, you know that?" Stride said. "And yes, exactly. Plus, she misses you more than she lets on. Having you leave the house has been hard on her. I think she needs some Cat time."

"Whereas I suppose you don't miss me at all."

"Not true," he replied with a grin. "I cry myself to sleep every night."

"Well, I *am* pretty missable. Anyway, sure, dinner tonight sounds great."

"Good."

Her phone rang, and Cat's eyes flicked to the screen before she pushed a button to ignore the call. He thought he detected a guilty shadow cross her face, and he waited to see if she would tell him who it was. He was pretty sure he wouldn't like the answer, and he was right.

"That was Curt," she explained, rolling her eyes.

Stride frowned. Curt Dickes was part of Cat's bad old days on the street, a con artist addicted to get-rich-quick schemes. Even Stride, who'd arrested him a dozen times over a dozen years, had to admit that Curt's exuberant personality was difficult to dislike. But that didn't mean he wanted him in Cat's life.

"He still calls you?"

"Yeah, every day. I guess he misses me, too."

"Curt will get over it."

"Oh, he's not so bad," Cat replied breezily. "He's funny. He makes me laugh."

"If you want to laugh, watch Jimmy Kimmel."

Cat stuck out her tongue at him in mock exasperation. They'd had this argument many times before, and they both knew they would never see eye to eye about Curt. Then she leaned forward, changing the subject. "Anyway, how are *you*? You going back to work yet?"

Stride didn't have an answer for her. Instead, he took out his phone and played Maggie's voice mail. Cat arched her dark eyebrows at him as she listened.

"Looks like she wants you in your old chair."

"Looks that way."

"What are you going to do?"

"I haven't decided."

"Yeah, right," Cat snorted.

"What does that mean?"

"I see that glint in your eyes," she told him.

"The glint?"

"You miss it. You miss that life. You miss the police, and you're lying if you say you don't."

"I really don't," Stride said.

Cat gave an exaggerated sigh. "Fine. Be stubborn."

"I don't miss it," he insisted.

"Uh-huh. Okay. Well, one of us is right, and the other one of us is you."

He smiled. "All right, maybe I miss it a little. But only a little."

"Yeah, keep telling yourself that," Cat said. "You're going back. I know you. But keep fooling yourself if you want. I have to get to class."

"Go."

She got up from the table, then leaned down and kissed his cheek. "I'll see you guys for dinner tonight. Late, as usual? Nine o'clock?"

"Sounds good."

"We'll order Sammy's?"

"What else?"

"Thanks for letting me know about Samantha," she added.

"Sure."

Before she walked away, Cat whispered in his ear. "Hey, Stride? I'm glad to hear Serena misses me. I miss her, too. If she needs me, I'll always be there for her. You know I will. But you know what? She needs you more."

6

"We've located the boat," Maggie announced to the detectives in the police conference room. "Lance Beaton says his cops found it abandoned at a launch in Billings Park in Superior. Based on the registration papers, we think it was stolen from a marina on our side of the water. We're sending a forensics team to check it out, but Lance says it looks clean as a whistle. Looks like our man stole the boat, collected the ransom, and then ditched it."

"Was he alone?" Guppo asked. "Or did he have a partner?"

Maggie shook her head. "Not sure. We don't know whether he left a car in the park or whether someone met him there. Either way, once he was back on shore, he could have gone pretty much anywhere."

She went to the whiteboard on the far end of the room and used magnetic clips to post several photographs of Chelsey Webster. One was from driver's license records, and others had been printed from JPEGs that Gavin had sent her.

"Here's our missing woman," she said. "Chelsey Webster, forty-six years old, married to Gavin Webster for the last fourteen years. First marriage for both of them. She's self-employed as a marketing consultant, whatever the hell that means. Gavin is supposed to be getting us a list of her clients and friends. She has no local relatives. Parents are dead, one sibling in Oregon. She went to UMD, worked at a couple of local ad agencies, then opened her own business shortly before marrying Gavin. Right now, that's all we know about her background."

She paced on her short legs, not saying anything for a couple of minutes. In front of her on the table was a jumbo-sized Coke from McDonald's, and she sucked soda through the straw, making dimples in her cheeks. By now, the cops in the room were used to the way she did things. She thought on her feet, sifting through the facts, debating with herself in her head, before she was ready to talk. While the others waited for her, they checked their phones, and although it annoyed her, she'd given up complaining about it.

"Okay, we've got three tasks," she went on finally. "First, find Chelsey Webster, alive or dead. For the time being, we operate on the assumption that she's alive. We don't know whether she's still being held by the kidnappers or whether they've left her somewhere and moved on, now that they have the ransom money in hand. We've forwarded her picture to police around Minnesota and Wisconsin, plus the state patrol, park rangers, everybody. The chief has a press conference scheduled in an hour, and we'll blast information to the media, too. That will generate tips from the public, but it also means we'll be chasing a lot of dead ends."

She eyed Guppo and Serena, who were sitting in the chairs closest to her. Guppo was eating Fritos and crunching them loudly and licking salt and corn dust off his chubby fingertips. She couldn't recall a meeting where he wasn't snacking on something. She also noticed Serena looking out the window toward the trees, as if she were somewhere else altogether.

"What did you two find at Gavin's house?" she asked.

When Serena didn't answer, Guppo took over, quickly swallowing a large mouthful of chips. "The damage and blood inside the house confirm that Chelsey was taken from there. None of the neighbors have security cameras that face the street, and no one saw or heard anything on Tuesday evening, so we don't have descriptions of the kidnappers or their vehicle. One of the neighbors told Serena that their dog began barking right around nine o'clock. That's probably the best bet for when the abduction actually occurred. Knowing the time helps narrow down the search, but there are so many ways out of that area that we're not likely to pick anything up from cameras on the roads. Even so, we'll review all the video we can find along 194, 53, Central Entrance, and 35. Maybe we'll get lucky."

"Were there any reports of suspicious activity in the neighborhood in the last couple of weeks?" Maggie asked.

He shook his enormous head. "Nothing."

"Did you ask about maintenance vans in the area? Contractors, plumbers, whatever? Something that wouldn't necessarily attract attention if it was parked outside for a while."

Guppo nodded. "We did, but still no luck."

"Well, they had to know the layout of the house and the area to pull this off," Maggie went on. "So either they had personal knowledge"—she put a little emphasis on the words *personal knowledge*—"or they conducted surveillance as they planned the crime."

"Well, the camera that Serena found was hooked to the in-house Wi-Fi," Guppo told the group. "I checked the device activity on their Wi-Fi log, and the camera started operating five days ago. The kidnappers have been watching them ever since."

"So they were inside the house five days *before* the abduction?" Maggie asked.

"Right."

"Why take the risk of planting the camera early?" Maggie asked. "Gavin or Chelsey might have discovered it."

"Well, with the camera in place, they could see that Chelsey was home alone that night, so they knew when to make their move," Guppo speculated.

"Was there any local storage? Can we download video that was recorded inside the house?"

Guppo shook his head. "No. The cam wasn't configured to store data on the device itself. The feed went straight to an app."

"Well, at least we can talk to Gavin and see what was going on at the house on the day the camera was installed. Maybe they had workers or contractors on-site for some reason." Maggie looked at Serena. "Do you have anything to add?"

Serena started, as if coming out of a trance. "No, that's all we have for now."

"Okay, so these people basically grabbed Chelsey and vanished into thin air," Maggie concluded with a scowl. "That brings us to task number two. Let's find out *who* did this. Ultimately, identifying the kidnappers may also be our best bet at locating Chelsey, unless we get lucky with a call to the tip line. I checked in with police in the larger cities around the state to see if they had reports of similar abductions, just in case we have a kidnapping ring operating here that hasn't come to light yet. Nothing was on their radar. To me, that suggests that this was most likely a one-off crime specifically targeted at Chelsey Webster."

She paused.

"That also leads me to task number three. We need to decide whether Gavin Webster is a victim or a suspect. A few months ago, he was a struggling low-end lawyer. Now, thanks to his dead sister, he's got millions in the bank. One way or another, money is the obvious motive here. Either someone saw an opportunity to extort a big payday from Gavin, or Gavin decided he'd rather spend his windfall as a single person, not a married person. Regardless, I think there's likely to be some kind of connection between Gavin and Chelsey and whoever did this. Someone knew about the inheritance, and someone knew the two of them well enough to come up with this plan."

Guppo had finished his Fritos and was examining the inside of the bag for crumbs. "Does your gut lean one way or another on Gavin?"

"I . . . don't . . . know," she said slowly, because that was the same question Maggie had been asking herself since three in the morning. Normally, her instincts didn't waffle about suspects. She knew almost immediately whether she trusted what someone was telling her. But Gavin was different. Maybe it was all the time he'd spent confusing juries and lying to defend guilty clients, but she found herself struggling to get inside his head.

"If he was involved, he's covering it well," she went on. "For the time being, it doesn't matter, because our plan's the same regardless. I want to know everything there is to know about both of them. Gavin. Chelsey. Their marriage. Their work. Their clients. Their friends. I want phone records, credit card records, bank statements. And I want to know *who* gave Gavin one hundred thousand dollars in cash. He won't say, and that means the money is probably dirty."

She clapped her hands like a football coach.

"Okay, everybody, let's get busy. We'll meet back here in six hours for another update. If Chelsey Webster is still alive, she's at risk with every minute that goes by. I want to find her, and I want to find her *now*."

* * * * *

After everyone else filed out of the room, Serena watched Maggie slump into one of the chairs and put her feet up on the conference table. Maggie drank her Coke until there was nothing left in the paper cup, and then she worked her straw around the bottom, making an annoying slurping noise. Serena waited.

"I want you to go to Rice Lake," Maggie said finally.

"What's there?"

"Gavin's parents. They're his alibi. He says he was there for a couple of days, and he didn't head home until eight o'clock in the evening. I want to know exactly when he left, but don't let them know we suspect anything. And get everything you can out of them. The marriage. The inheritance. If they heard stories about any of Gavin's clients. Whatever you can find out."

Serena nodded. "The neighbors across the street said Chelsey was concerned about Gavin. She was wondering whether he was cheating. She told them he was acting odd about the money, too. Odd enough that she joked about her safety. It may be nothing. Then again—"

"Interesting," Maggie replied. "Well, see if the parents think the inheritance changed Gavin. That amount of money can turn people weird."

"I will."

Serena stood up, but Maggie used her index finger to direct her back to her seat. "Hang on. I'm not done."

"Okay."

Maggie took a long time to say anything more. "I can't believe I have to ask you this, but did you steal somebody's dog, Serena?"

Serena shrugged. She'd known what the question was going to be, and she knew that Maggie already knew the answer. "Yeah. I did. Well, I rescued a dog, actually."

"Are you out of your goddamn mind?"

The more upset she was, the more Maggie swore.

"These people were abusing their dog," Serena replied by way of excuse. "They left him out in the pouring rain, and they didn't bring him in even after I told them to."

"Then you call animal control. You don't just take it."

"I call animal control, and months later, maybe they do something, but more likely, they do nothing."

"You're a police detective, not the Humane Society."

"Yes, I'm aware of that."

"Well, you say you're aware, but then you went and stole a dog," Maggie snapped.

"What do you want me to do?"

Maggie rolled her eyes and opened her mouth to deliver what Serena assumed would be another expletive. Then she took a deep breath and stopped herself. She went on with a veneer of calm. "Serena, I know you're going through shit. I'm sorry about that. I feel for you, I really do. I already told you that you *don't* need to be here. I have no problem with you taking time to get your head together."

"I'm fine," Serena reiterated.

Maggie exploded again. "You are not fine! You fucking stole a dog!"

"Look—" Serena began, but Maggie interrupted her sharply.

"Stop. Listen to me. If you're going to be here, I need your head in the game. Is that clear? This is a big investigation, and we're dealing with a *defense lawyer*. Everything has to be done by the book. If Gavin is guilty, our case has to be bulletproof. If he's not guilty, he will crucify us in the media over any slipup. I can't cut you any slack because you're Stride's wife or because we're friends."

Serena opted not to point out that they weren't really friends. Instead, she simply said, "Understood."

"If you make a mistake, you're off this case. Got it?"

"Got it."

Maggie nodded. "Fine. Go to Rice Lake. Talk to Gavin's parents. And Serena?"

"What?"

"Give those people back their dog."

7

But Serena didn't.

While she drove south out of Superior on Highway 53 toward Rice Lake, the Border collie sat upright in the passenger seat and curiously watched the forested landscape passing by on both sides of the car. Dry now, the dog had a lush coat, black on his lower body with a white tuxedo vest, and a black head with just a ribbon of white fur running down the middle of his face to his nose. His head didn't seem to have fully grown into his big ears, which drooped a little of their own weight. His eyes were dark, and one seemed to open more than the other, which gave him a permanently mournful expression.

"So do you have a name?" Serena asked.

The dog, hearing her voice, seemed to know she was talking to him—she'd checked; it was a him—and his head swung to look at her. She spotted a collar nestled tightly in the fur of his neck, and as she drove, she worked with her fingers to find his red ID tag. She squinted at what was etched on it.

"Sad?" she said, shaking her head. "Seriously? They named you Sad Sacks?"

Hearing his name, the dog barked.

"Well, sorry, buddy, but I'm not calling you Sad. At least while we're together, we need an alternative. Any suggestions?"

The dog kept looking at her, his floppy ears pricking up a bit.

"How about Elton?" Serena said.

The dog didn't react.

"I knew another dog named Elton once. We're probably not going to be together for very long, so you're going to have to put up with it for a while. You good with that, Elton? I'm Serena, by the way."

With a little snort, Elton draped himself across the red-and-black leather of the Mustang's seats and positioned his nose across Serena's leg. Even dry, he still had a wet-dog smell, so she turned on the vents a little higher. The fan ruffled Elton's fur.

The rain had finally stopped, but the sun was still missing in action. Bubbly clouds hung low in the sky. The north–south Wisconsin highway wasn't crowded, so she put the Mustang on cruise control. A few minutes later, she passed the town of Solon Springs, which meant she still had an hour to go before reaching Rice Lake. It was almost noon, but she didn't bother stopping to eat. She'd filled up at a gas station before crossing the high bridge out of Duluth, and she'd bought a few microwave hot dogs for Elton, which he happily devoured.

Her fingers stroked the dog's head in her lap. Elton closed his eyes and enjoyed the massage.

"So tell me something," she said, not caring that this was a one-sided conversation. "Do you miss being with the Sackses? I mean, dogs are funny that way. They even love people who kick the shit out of them."

The dog exhaled with a noise that was part whistle, part snore.

Serena's mouth curled into a frown. "Then again, it's not like I can talk. I stuck around for a long time with someone who kicked the shit out of me, too."

She wasn't aware of driving faster, but her foot pushed heavily on the accelerator, overriding the cruise control, and the Mustang responded like a thoroughbred unleashed.

"Can I tell you a secret?" she murmured, although she knew it was still a secret. When she looked down, she saw that Elton was sound asleep. Plus, he was a dog, and dogs were good secret-keepers.

"When my dad left us, I didn't even miss him," Serena continued. "That's pretty pathetic, huh? I was fifteen years old. Samantha had already started doing drugs. She shared them with me sometimes, when I wasn't sneaking drinks from her vodka bottles. She was so much cooler than the other moms. They didn't want anything to do with her. Or me. They started keeping my friends away from me, but I didn't care. I didn't need them. I had Samantha."

The Wisconsin landscape whipped past them, lightning fast.

"My dad didn't even try to take me with him. He just left. I went out with Samantha to a club one night—she had a fake ID for me, and I looked a lot older than I really was—and when we got back, he was gone. Packed up, no note, no idea where he went. For years, I told people that he abandoned me, but that's not really true. I wouldn't have gone with him even if he'd asked me. I was a momma's girl. I wanted to stay with Samantha. Being with her, living the way she lived—totally free—that was magic."

She touched her face, wondering if she'd find tears on her cheeks this time. There were still none.

"I remember when we got home to the empty house at four in the morning and found the note. Samantha just shrugged when she read it and said, 'Fuck him.' Like it was no big deal that her husband had walked out."

In her lap, the dog stirred and gave a low *woof*, as if offended by the profanity.

"Sorry, but that's what she said. I said the same thing, just parroted it right back. Fuck him. I was *glad* my father was gone. He was a downer. Without him, we could do whatever we wanted. Stay out all night. Sleep all day. Samantha bought me all sorts of shit. Music. Video games. I had no idea that she'd lost her job, that she was maxing out one credit card after another, that she hadn't paid the mortgage in a year. I didn't think about the fact that she wasn't working. When you're drunk at a party, you never think about the party ending."

There was no emotion in Serena's voice, because she felt no emotion at all. Everything that had happened may as well have been scenes from a movie on a screen, something unreal that an actor had gone through, not herself.

"Eventually, the bank foreclosed on the house, and we got kicked out. We were homeless. We lived in the parks, under bridges, in shelters when we could find a bed. Samantha just dug the hole deeper. She and I sort of switched places at that point. I began taking care of her. I didn't mind. I would have done anything in the world for her. That was when I met my friend Deidre. She was homeless, too. She taught me the ropes: how to scam things, who would help you, who would rape you if you gave them half a chance. I burned through jobs, mostly because I stole all the time, and as soon they figured that out, I was gone. But Samantha would always tell me what a good girl I was, how proud she was of me. Then she'd take the money I gave her and buy more drugs. It was never enough, though. Not for her habit. She needed a more permanent arrangement to keep the coke flowing."

Serena finally glanced at the dashboard and saw that she was driving one hundred and ten miles an hour. Her foot eased off the gas.

"His name was Blue Dog," she said.

* * * * *

The parents of Gavin Webster lived in an old section of Rice Lake, only a couple of blocks from Main Street. Their tiny house faced a neighborhood playground across the street. The lawn was mostly made of weeds, and it was brown where a couple of huge oak trees blocked out the sun. Serena suspected that Gavin had used some of his inheritance to help his parents, because she noted that the paint on the house was fresh, the roof looked recently replaced, and there was a brand-new Subaru Outback parked outside the detached garage.

She'd called ahead, so Mary and Tim Webster were waiting for her. They invited her inside the house when she knocked. Elton stayed in the Mustang. The three of them sat in the living room that faced the street, and Mary switched off the local radio station, which was playing a Travis Tritt song. Serena took a seat in a leather armchair, and the Websters sat holding hands on the sofa by the window. Mary was short, and Tim was very tall, with skinny legs that seemed to jut out into the middle of the room. The air had the syrupy, floral smell of hot oil plugged into an outlet.

When Mary fixed her stare on Serena, she saw that Gavin had gotten his distinctive eyes from his mother. They were the same intense blue.

"Who could have done this?" she asked with a frantic tone of disbelief. "Do you have any idea who kidnapped Chelsey?"

"We don't know that yet, but we have a large team investigating the case and we're doing everything we can to find her."

The father, Tim, shook his head. He was mostly bald, with a neat triangular gray mustache and black glasses. "You won't find her."

Serena looked at him in surprise. "Why do you say that, Mr. Webster?"

"My cousin's a cop in Des Moines. He says if the kidnappers don't get back to you once they get the ransom, that's it. She's dead."

"*Timothy*," his wife interrupted. "Don't talk like that."

"Yes, I know you're both concerned," Serena said, trying to reassure them, "but it's way too early to assume the worst. In order to find Chelsey, we need to gather all the information we can. That's why I'm here."

The father snorted. "Don't play games, Detective. You're here to check up on Gavin. Right? My cousin said as far as the cops are concerned, nine times out of ten, it's the spouse that did it. Well, you're wrong about Gavin."

"Gavin *loved* Chelsey," Mary added. "He's devastated. A wreck."

"I'm sure he is," Serena said mildly. "I really just want to confirm what happened and get the facts straight. When did Gavin arrive at your house?"

"Early evening on Sunday."

"Did he stay here with you? Not at a motel or anything like that?"

"He stayed with us," his father said.

"And you spent time with him on Monday and Tuesday?"

"We were with him all day both days."

"We think the abduction occurred around nine o'clock Tuesday evening at your son's house," Serena said.

"Then you can rule Gavin out," his father replied firmly. "He left our house at eight thirty. Unless you think he beamed himself to Duluth, he didn't make it there until after ten."

"You're sure about the time he left?"

"Yes. He checked his watch and said he wanted to get home before Chelsey was in bed."

"When did you next talk to him?"

"In the morning," Mary said.

"Did he tell you what had happened?"

"No. He didn't say a word. It was obvious that something was wrong; we could hear it in his voice. He seemed to be under some kind of tremendous stress, but he told us it was one of his cases. We didn't find out what was really going on until today when he called us again. Gavin apologized for not telling us the truth. He said he couldn't risk word getting out and Chelsey ending up in any more danger. I'm sure he thought we'd call the police if he told us, and I suppose we probably would have. He knows he made a mistake by trying to deal with this himself, but he was in a panic. I'm sure the kidnappers were counting on that."

"Can you think of anyone who might have done this?" Serena asked.

"It must be one of his scumbag clients," Tim harrumphed. "You lie down with dogs, you get up with fleas."

"You don't sound too happy about your son's law practice," Serena said.

Mother and father exchanged glances. Tim's face looked sour.

"Our children's lives didn't go the way we hoped," Mary told her. She sounded like someone in a bathrobe on the street watching her house burn down. "It's been one tragedy after another for both of them, and none of it was their fault. Honestly, there are days when Tim and I wonder if we're cursed. That God is punishing our kids."

"I know you also lost your daughter—Gavin's sister—to cancer recently," Serena said quietly. "Is that right?"

"Yes. Susan. We'd known it was coming for a few years. She'd been battling it bravely, but I'm afraid the outcome was never really in doubt.

She lasted longer than the doctors thought she would, but in the end, well, death always wins, doesn't it?"

"I'm very sorry for your loss."

Serena found it hard to look away from Mary's ocean-blue eyes.

"As for Gavin, things started out so well for him," the woman went on with a sad smile. "After law school, he worked at a corporate firm in Minneapolis for several years. Then he moved to Duluth to start a firm with a friend of his. They worked with start-up technology companies. It was a very successful practice. For a while, he had everything. Big house on Skyline Drive. Smart, beautiful wife in Chelsey. That was a happy time. We were very proud of him."

Tim scowled. "He was naïve. He didn't watch his back with that fucking partner of his."

Mary looked pained by her husband's harshness. "I suppose that's true, but I can't really blame him for that. Gavin is too trusting. His so-called friend—his partner in the law firm—had a gambling problem that wiped him out. He began to embezzle money from the firm's clients. Gavin didn't pay enough attention to the books. When it all came out, his partner went to prison. Gavin nearly did, too. As it was, he and Chelsey lost everything. Money. House. They were wiped out. Gavin started over doing criminal law for—well, for not the best sort of people."

"Scumbags," Tim said again.

"Gavin always says his clients are just down on their luck," Mary corrected her husband. "He said he could relate to that, given what he went through. Actually, he told us he was happier doing criminal defense work than he had been when he was working with stock offerings and venture capital. He said he could see the impact of what he did on people's lives, and he liked that."

The look on Tim's face told Serena that Gavin's father didn't agree.

"Could we talk about the inheritance?" Serena asked.

Mary looked down at her lap, and Tim—for all his rough edges—also looked stricken, thinking about his daughter.

"About three years ago, we finally got a bit of bright news in the family," Mary went on with a sigh. "Susan got married. She was forty years old, so we'd sort of given up hope about that. But then she met a wonderful man—athletic, very successful, a senior health-care executive in Duluth. We had visions of grandchildren, which we'd assumed was never going to happen."

"Gavin and Chelsey didn't want kids?" Serena asked.

"Oh, they talked about it for a while in the early years. I'm not sure Chelsey was too crazy about the idea of putting her body through pregnancy. I can't really blame her for that. Anyway, after the setbacks Gavin went through, they didn't feel ready. Financially, emotionally, whatever."

"And Susan?"

Mary sniffled. "Like we told you, it's been one crisis after another. First, we went through all of Gavin's troubles. And then, Susan got the diagnosis. Aggressive uterine cancer. She hadn't even been married a year! At the time, the doctors told us she might only have months to live. We couldn't believe it. You'd think that would be tragedy enough, wouldn't you? But God piled on. Susan lost her husband the same year. A car accident a few months later. I was so angry. Angry at the world. There Susan was, battling to stay alive, and she loses the love of her life. Honestly, I thought the stress of it would kill her right then and there. She hung on for two more years, but you could tell her heart wasn't in the fight. This whole stretch of time has been like a nightmare."

"I'm so sorry," Serena said again.

Mary nodded. Tim stared out the windows.

"I understand that Gavin was the principal beneficiary of Susan's estate after she died," Serena went on with a little hesitation. "Obviously, we're wondering whether money was a motive in Chelsey's kidnapping. I'm wondering how widely known it was that Gavin received a substantial inheritance."

"Well, this is a small town," Mary replied. "People talk. We didn't hide it. I'm not aware that Gavin or Chelsey did, either. I mean, who would dream that something like this could ever happen?"

"How did Gavin feel about his newfound wealth?" Serena asked.

"Well, he had mixed feelings, of course. He was on stable footing again financially, but only because he lost his sister. That's not something he would have chosen in a million years."

"Did he talk to you about any of his future plans?"

Tim leaned forward, his hands on his knees. His voice was gruff. "What do you mean?"

"Was he thinking about any changes because of his new economic circumstances? Giving up his job? Moving? Anything like that?"

"Or giving up his wife?" Tim asked sharply. "That's what you're really thinking, isn't it? Gavin got a boatload of money and was looking for a cheap way to get rid of Chelsey."

Mary's blue eyes widened in shock as she stared at Serena. "You can't honestly believe that Gavin did this—"

"Of course, they can!" her husband interjected. "You heard what my cousin said. That's the first place the police go. Blame the spouse."

"I'm just trying to get the whole picture," Serena replied calmly. "I talked to one of their neighbors, and she indicated that Chelsey was a little concerned about Gavin. She said he'd changed after the inheritance. It sounds like things were strained between them."

"If Gavin was different, it's only because Susan died," Mary retorted. "That's all it was. Grief. He lost his sister."

"How were things between him and Chelsey?" Serena asked.

"Fine. He's crazy about her. You've seen her picture. She's beautiful. Why would he look anywhere else?"

"He hasn't mentioned any problems?"

"All marriages have problems, but I don't believe there was anything serious. We would have known if there was. When Gavin told us what happened, we could hear how devastated he was. That wasn't an act. We know our son."

Serena smiled. "I'm sure you do."

Tim's eyes narrowed. "Except you still think he was involved, don't you?"

"I'm just trying to piece it all together. That's what will help us find Chelsey."

"Well, you can take this to the bank, Detective," Tim went on. "Gavin had nothing to do with his wife's abduction. He didn't do it. Believe me, I know my boy. He would never hurt anyone."

8

The man stood among the graves of a rural cemetery a few miles south of Superior, Wisconsin. Thick trees grew around him, giving him shelter and making him mostly invisible. The wet grass under his feet was strewn with red-and-yellow autumn leaves that had been swept down by days of wind and rain. His car was parked on a cemetery road half a mile behind him, well off the highway so it couldn't be seen. In the quiet early afternoon, he was alone.

With his binoculars, he focused on the small house on the other side of the dirt road. It was a two-story house that hadn't seen repairs in a long time. The red paint was faded and flecked away. Dirt and leaves matted the shingled roof. The rest of the lot had the same boneyard feel as the house, the lawn unmowed, farm equipment rusting in the weeds. A white 1990s-era Ford Taurus sat in front of a detached garage, and an old Winnebago camper was perched on blocks beside it.

He checked both directions. There was no traffic. A few trucks had passed on the intersecting highway while he was studying the house, but their loud engines gave him enough warning that he could take cover before they saw him. The nearest neighbor was several hundred yards away, far enough that they were unlikely to hear the noise of gunshots.

Or if they did, they'd assume someone was taking care of a rabbit trespassing in a vegetable garden.

He reached into his jacket, removed the 9 mm Glock, and racked a cartridge into the chamber. His hands were covered in tight-fitting black nylon gloves.

His boots crunched through the brush as he broke from the cover of the trees that bordered the cemetery. He stopped at the edge of the dirt road and listened again for highway traffic. He heard nothing, but he wasted no time crossing the road and crouching out of sight by the side of the old Taurus. He checked the car doors, which were unlocked. Rising up just high enough to see over the hood, he examined the house again. One of the front windows was open, and he heard scratchy music playing loudly from inside.

Dean Martin sang "Money Burns a Hole in My Pocket."

Ain't that the truth, Dino.

He assessed the way in. The steps leading to the front porch looked warped and unsteady; they'd probably creak with the weight of his feet and broadcast his arrival. Best to use the back door instead. He circled behind the garage, where he was twenty or thirty feet from the house's rear steps. One of the upstairs windows faced this way, so if someone was looking, they'd see him. It couldn't be helped. He tucked the gun in his pocket and walked casually, a man with nothing to hide. When he got to the back door, he stopped to see if his arrival had prompted anyone to check the rear of the house. Nothing moved inside; no one had spotted him. He turned the knob, and the door opened. He slipped inside and found himself in a kitchen that smelled of burnt bacon. Dean Martin got even louder, that famous slur warbling from the other end of the house.

The hallway ahead was thick with dust and shadows. Near the doorway, he noticed a landline phone, and he removed the receiver, then put it on the floor. The phone hummed softly. He slid out the gun again and held it in front of him as he took a step toward the living room. The yellowed linoleum gave under his feet, making a noticeable creak as the floorboards shifted.

Over his head, he heard a rush of footsteps. He froze. Then a man's voice shouted from upstairs. "Mom, turn the music down, will you? Jesus!"

The footsteps retreated from the stairs. In the living room at the end of the hallway, the music kept on, as loudly as before. The man with the gun approached the doorway and peered around the corner, and he spotted an old woman, asleep in a rocking chair by the window. She sat beside an old record player, from which Dino crooned at the top of his lungs. He waited to make sure the old woman's eyes stayed closed, and then he crossed the room in a few quick steps. She didn't hear him through her snoring. He took up position behind her.

He didn't need the gun for her. It was better that way. He replaced the Glock in his pocket, then reached around to his backpack and slid out a coil of nylon rope from the lowest pouch. He extended a short length of the rope between his gloved hands and reached forward over the top of the chair. The woman's head bobbed slightly as she slept, but her neck was exposed, wrinkled, and frail.

Dean started singing "Standing on the Corner." The backup band played noisy brass.

The man lowered the rope.

When he crossed his hands and yanked the ends together, the woman awoke in a frenzy, unable to breathe or scream. The rocking chair jerked and twisted, scraping on the floor and lurching up and down. He held on tight through the struggle. Dean kept singing, cool as a well-shaken martini.

Then it was done.

He kept the rope in place long after the body stopped moving. When he finally let go, he didn't bother removing the rope, which was bloody now where it had bitten through the skin of her throat. He reached over to the record player and turned up the volume until Dean began to make the house shake.

Next song: "Hey Brother, Pour the Wine."

He edged away from the chair to a place in the living room where he couldn't be seen from the hallway. He raised the gun and steadied his wrist with his other hand. He didn't have to wait long. Seconds later, the same male voice bellowed again from upstairs.

"Did you hear me, Mom? For fuck's sake, turn it down!"

The music blared on. Heavy, agitated footsteps thundered down the steps.

The man with the gun tensed, his finger curled around the trigger. Like a charging bull, a huge man flew through the doorway into the living room, his face red with anger, his muscles rippling. The man was shirtless and wore cargo shorts and no shoes. The momentum of his charge took him six feet past the doorway before he skidded to a stop. His eyes took in the sight of the dead woman in the chair and widened in shock. Then, sensing movement, he shifted his gaze and saw the man pointing the black barrel of the Glock at his chest.

Bullets erupted one after another.

The first bullet hit the big man but didn't stop him. He stormed across the room, blood on his skin, his huge hands outstretched at the ends of his arms. The next bullet hit his chest again and slowed him. The third stopped him where he was, making him sway like a tree in the wind.

The man with the gun fired again, into the other man's forehead this time, a perfectly centered shot below his crew cut and above his dark eyes. The big man's knees crumpled, and he fell facedown, not moving.

He was definitely dead.

Still, the man with the gun didn't take any chances. He put the hot, smoking barrel to the back of the man's head and fired one last time.

* * * * *

Serena drove north in silence as she headed back toward Duluth. She normally played music in the car to keep her company, but this time, she preferred the quiet. The only noise came from Elton. With every car that passed in the opposite direction on Highway 53, the dog put his paws on the half-open window and barked hello at the other driver. He got multiple waves in return.

It was almost two o'clock in the afternoon. She still had half the drive back to Duluth, and she realized she was hungry. She hadn't eaten since the night before. As she got to the town of Minong, she remembered a greasy spoon she'd visited with Jonny once before. It was a couple of blocks east of the highway. She made a quick right turn, trying to remember exactly where it was, and she drove up and down a few blocks before she located the saloon with its weathered wooden front, looking like something out of an old Western.

"What about you?" she asked Elton. "You hungry?"

The dog didn't answer, but he put his nose to the window and inhaled the smell of barbecued pork wafting from the restaurant. Serena took the hint.

"Okay, pork sandwiches for all."

She got out of the Mustang and made her way to the bar entrance. Inside, the aroma of meat was even stronger, and she could hear her stomach growling. The interior was decorated in the same Gary Cooper kitsch as the outside, with old farm tools hung on hooks and black-and-white photographs mounted in cheap frames. She expected to find sawdust on the floor. There were only a handful of tables filled by people eating a late lunch, but it was midafternoon in Wisconsin, and the bar counter was crowded with plenty of drinkers.

The bartender was a busty blond in her early twenties. She greeted Serena with a big white smile. Alcohol bottles glistened in glass rows on the mirrored shelves behind her. "What can I get you?"

"Can I get an order to go?"

"Sure, check out the menu, and see what you like. Be back in a sec."

She handed Serena a menu, then retreated down the bar to pour a tap Michelob for a man at the far end. Serena decided on one pork sandwich for her, one for Elton, and a basket of onion rings for them to share. When the bartender got back, she rattled off her order. The girl wrote it down, then nodded at a large group toward the back of the restaurant.

"Just so you know, it'll take a few minutes to get it ready. Those folks just put in their order, so the kitchen's slammed."

Serena shrugged. "I'm in no hurry."

"You want a drink while you wait? Beer or something? I make a mean Bloody Mary, too."

Serena stared back at her, and her mouth went dry.

She took in the bartender's cheerful, pleasant smile. She was a small-town waitress asking a simple question. Serena had been asked that same question hundreds of times over the years by hundreds of different bartenders. After a while, the answers came without even thinking about it. Without any hesitation. Without longing or yearning or regret.

No, thanks, I'm good.

No. Really. Nothing for me.

Or maybe: *Just a Diet Coke.*

6,607 nights. Not a drop of alcohol.

And yet this time, sitting in the bar, Serena felt the old longing come back, like a dragon rising over the mountain, spreading its wings and exhaling fire. She could smell it in the bar around her. She could imagine it on her lips, cool and smooth. She could anticipate the sensation it would bring, the warmth in her chest that spread through her body, the numbness easing her mind and dulling away fear, anger, grief, frustration, longing, and pain.

Her tongue slipped across her lips, wetting them. She wanted it *so much.*

Sweat made a clammy film on her skin. It was the sweat of shame, of desire, of guilt, of indecision. *Yes,* she wanted to say.

Yes, Absolut Citron, two ice cubes.

Yes, yes, yes, yes, yes, yes, yes.

"I—sure, I—" she began. The word actually started coming out of her mouth with a wolflike hunger. *Yes.*

Then, coming to her senses, she slapped both hands on the bar and jerked up from the stool. "Skip it," she said, barely finding breath for the words.

"What?"

"Skip the food. I have to be somewhere. I can't wait."

The bartender looked at her with a puzzled expression. "I thought you weren't in a hurry."

"I was wrong."

Serena turned away with a flush of shame. Her voice was overly loud, and everyone turned to watch her. She could feel their eyes on her back as she ran from the saloon. When she got to the Mustang, she practically threw herself inside. Her chest heaved, and her lungs struggled for air. With a soft whimper of concern, Elton nudged his nose against her from the other side of the car, and she put her arms around the dog and buried her face in his fur.

"Oh my God," she murmured.

This time, she'd survived.

This time, she'd walked away and saved herself.

But Serena was under no illusions. The devil was awake again, and he was leering at her with cunning eyes and very sharp teeth.

9

Stride walked into the Public Safety Building for the first time since he'd been shot, and warning bells didn't go off, and the world didn't end. Passing through the maze of cubicles, he tried to act normal, as if he'd been doing this every day without the interruption of the past fourteen months. But that was impossible. Everyone saw him. Everyone stopped talking. Somehow, they could read his face and recognize that he didn't want special attention for this moment, and they gave him space. No one came up to him, or hugged him, or cried, or called out, *Welcome back.*

Their reaction was much quieter and, to him, more profound. One by one, as he made his way from one end of the building to the other, they all simply nodded at him. And they smiled.

He bypassed his own office, because for now, it wasn't his office anymore. The lieutenant's chair belonged to Maggie. The one empty office on the floor had been occupied until recently by Abel Teitscher, who'd spent decades on the force as a smart detective but a mostly unlikable man. They'd clashed throughout Stride's tenure, especially after Stride had returned from a short stint in Las Vegas with Serena. Abel had taken over the detective bureau during Stride's absence, but his personality had left the staff in near revolt, and Deputy Chief Kyle Kinnick—who went by the nickname K-2—had been more than happy to demote Abel upon Stride's return. Abel had never forgiven the insult.

Now he was gone—finally retired after all these years.

Stride wandered into the office, which had already been stripped of anything personal. Abel's photos and commendations had all gone with him. However, the man's dense musk cologne had seeped into the walls and would take a long time to dissipate. There were files on the desk and case summaries scrawled in Abel's handwriting on two whiteboards near the window. Most cops did that kind of thing by computer now, but Abel had always preferred writing out his notes on every case by hand. Stride actually liked that about him.

He sat behind the desk and looked out the window. The police had moved out of downtown a few years earlier, and now they were located high on a hill in a remote part of the city, close to the forest. Stride liked it here, liked not being among the politicians of city hall. Instinctively, like a muscle memory, he reached for a cup of coffee or a can of Coke on the desk, but of course, nothing was there. Caffeine was off the list for his postsurgery regimen.

Sitting there by himself, he thought: *Now what?*

He got out of the chair and went to the whiteboards and tried to decipher Abel's handwritten scrawl. There were at least a dozen cases summarized on the two boards. Some were cold cases that Stride remembered; others were new since he'd gone on leave. Abel, efficient as ever, had written them down in chronological order, from oldest to most recent.

Stan and Arlene Foster. Double homicide, Chester Park area. No obvious motive. Business partner remains a suspect.

Letitia Cray. Overdose in suspicious circumstances, Central Hillside. Was scheduled as witness against Fred Dirkson in murder trial (Dirkson case now dropped).

Jonah Fallon. Hit-and-run, Bayview Heights neighborhood, suspect vehicle red Toyota Highlander. No leads.

Ray Palen. Missing since April. Car found near Fish Lake. No evidence of foul play, no indication of suicide.

Ginny Ellis. Homicide (stabbing), body found in Blackmer Park. Husband is principal suspect, insufficient evidence for charges.

Stride checked Abel's mostly empty desk and matched the tabs on the man's investigative files to the whiteboards. Abel had left them in identical order from oldest to newest, and he'd written out a summary that he'd paper-clipped to each folder. Whatever else you could say about Abel's prickly personality, he'd been serious about his work, and he was thorough in passing the baton to the next investigator.

He snatched the file off the top—Stan and Arlene Foster—and put his feet up as he eased back in the chair. As he read the file, he idly squeezed the leather-bound right arm of the chair like a stress ball, a habit he'd had for years. It felt comfortable; it felt natural. It took him a few seconds to realize why, and a smile broke across his face. This was *his* chair, more than fifteen years old, a chair that had followed him through multiple offices and in the move from downtown. Everything about it was familiar. The worn cushioning on the arms that he'd rubbed away. The scorched hole from years earlier where he'd burned the chair with an illicit late-night cigarette.

Maggie had been pretty confident he'd be coming back.

For the next hour and a half, he read Abel's files. Cold cases had a way of staying cold, so little had changed about the open investigations he remembered. Most cases got solved in a few days or a few weeks, with nothing left to tie up before trial except some loose ends and evidence reports from the BCA in Saint Paul. But if they didn't get answers fast, they usually didn't get them. Sometimes they knew who did it—Stride was sure Byron Ellis had stabbed his wife and left her body in a park to make it look like a stranger homicide—but they simply had no way to prove it. Other times they had no leads, and without leads, there wasn't much else to do. Jonah Fallon had been struck and killed while jogging on a Saturday evening in May two years earlier on a country road near

Proctor. The damage left at the scene had helped them identify the type of vehicle involved in the hit-and-run, but they'd never located the car or the driver. Ray Palen was a thirty-three-year-old single accountant working for one of the region's indie breweries. He had no history of depression, wasn't involved in a serious relationship, and had purchased theatre tickets two hours before driving to Fish Lake. Then he vanished. No body, no blood, no evidence in the woods, nothing that indicated what had happened to him. And nothing new had been found in the fifteen months since Abel had last given him an update on the case.

"Well, well, well."

Stride looked up as he heard the familiar voice. Maggie leaned against the office doorway, eating McDonald's fries one by one, a sly grin on her face.

"I heard it was true, but I didn't believe it," she said. "Jonathan Stride in the flesh."

"Word is, you need some help around here," he replied.

"Who told you that?"

"I got a message from the new lieutenant."

She came and sat down in the chair in front of the desk. Still eating fries, she put her feet up, and the two of them made a matched set. "Between you and me, I hear the new lieutenant is a real bitch."

Stride smiled. "Yeah, that's what everyone tells me."

Maggie threw back her head and laughed. When she was done, she looked at him with that old warmth in her eyes. It was sort of like returning to a familiar beach you'd visited as a child and feeling as if nothing had changed. Except a lot had changed for both of them. They had a complicated history together—a history that included a brief sexual relationship that had crashed and burned—but their friendship had endured through all of the years in between. He was closer to her than almost anyone, maybe even closer than he was to Serena.

"It's good to see you, Mags." He added, "I'm catching up on Abel's files, as requested."

She waved a french fry in the air dismissively. "Oh, don't worry about those. They're stone-cold. They're not going anywhere."

"Then why did you call me back?"

She shrugged. "Because I need you here."

"Seems like you've got things under control."

"Okay, maybe I like having you around."

"Yeah?"

"Just for eye candy," she added.

"Mags."

"Well, I also got a call from somebody who said that you needed to get back to work ASAP because you were driving everybody crazy."

Stride wondered if it was Serena, but then he knew. "Cat."

"Yeah. I'm pretty sure she only went to college to get away from you."

"So that's why you called?" Stride asked.

"That's why I called."

Stride put his feet back on the floor. He leaned across the desk and stole one of Maggie's fries, which weren't on his postsurgery diet. "Well, I'm here. What do you want me to do?"

"I could use your help on the Gavin Webster case. It's all hands on deck."

"All right. Whatever you need."

Maggie couldn't restrain the little smirk that broke across her face. "Good. Then come on. I need to talk to a hooker."

* * * * *

Her name was Shanice. They found her leaning against an abandoned building just off Superior Street in the Lincoln Park area. She was negotiating with an overweight man in a dirty white T-shirt who had a cairn terrier on a leash. When the man saw Stride and Maggie coming, he spotted them as cops immediately and beat a hasty retreat in the opposite direction.

Shanice rolled her eyes as they approached. "Well, that's another forty bucks gone. Thanks a lot, guys."

"Hey, Shanice," Stride said, because all the cops knew her, and she knew all the cops.

"Hey yourself, Stride. You back in action?"

"A little relief pitching. We'll see how it goes."

"Hey to you, too, Lieutenant," Shanice added with a mock salute at Maggie. "You guys getting bored up on the hill or something? How do I rate having the city's two top cops hassling me?"

"No hassles," Stride said. "Just a couple of questions."

Shanice shrugged. She was as short as Maggie and chicken-bone skinny. She was only twenty years old but had been a fixture on the Duluth streets since she was fourteen. Her oval face was pretty but overly made-up, with dark pencil liner drawn around her full lips, rainbow shadow above and below her eyes, and narrow black eyebrows studded with several piercings. Thick dreadlocks hung to her waist. She wore a necklace made from purple-and-green stones, dragon earrings, and a tight T-shirt cut off just below her breasts. Below the bare expanse of her tattooed stomach, she wore frayed jeans and four-inch heels.

"Knee pads?" Maggie commented, pointing at red neoprene padding on Shanice's legs. "Are you kidding me?"

"Girl's gotta be practical," Shanice replied, grinning. "I blow a knee, that's what you call a career-ending injury. I got a wrist brace, too. Not taking any risks with that corporal tunnel shit."

"Well, we won't keep you away from your workouts for long," Stride told her slyly. "This isn't about you. It's about Gavin Webster. Based on court records, you seem to know him pretty well."

Shanice stuck her thumbs in the loops of her jeans. "Oh, yeah. I got Gavin on speed dial. A lot of my friends do, too."

"Have you heard what happened?" Maggie asked.

"You mean his wife? Sure. It's all over the city that somebody grabbed her. Feel bad for the guy. Some lawyers, they look at me like I'm something they gotta scrape off the bottom of their shoe. Not Gavin. He's okay."

"When did you last . . . need his services?" Maggie went on.

"About two weeks ago, middle of the night. When it's that late, a lot of lawyers will just let you cool your heels in a cell until morning. Gavin came over right away, dressed in a suit like it was noon and he was going into court. Got me out, made sure I was okay, took me home. Class act, you know?"

"What are his rates like?"

Shanice gave Maggie a sideways look and ran her tongue over her teeth. "You mean, do my knee pads count as cash with him?"

"Yeah, that's what I mean."

"No, not Gavin. Believe me, if I can pay somebody with jizz, I'm happy to do it. He's cute, too, so what the hell. If he asked, I'd throw it in as a little bonus. But that's not his thing."

"Any of your friends tell a different story?"

"Nah. They all say Gavin's a straight shooter."

"We heard his wife wasn't so sure."

Shanice snorted. "Wives always wonder about that, and most of the time, they got good reason. But if Gavin was sampling the goods, he wasn't doing it with me or my girlfriends. And our goods are pretty sweet."

Stride knew Shanice well enough to believe that if she said there was no hanky-panky, there wasn't. "What's the word about the kidnapping? You hear any rumors about who did it?"

"Plenty of people are talking, but you ask me, they're just pumping gas. I haven't heard any names, and something like this, you can't keep it quiet. If it was a brother on the streets, I'd know. This smells like a pro job. Upscale."

"But no names?"

"If I knew, I'd tell you," Shanice said. "Like I say, I like Gavin."

"Could this have been personal? Did he have any enemies?"

"Nobody that I heard about. If he did, it wasn't anybody who talked about going after him or his wife. That's serious shit."

"Did you ever meet Chelsey?"

"Nope, never had the pleasure."

"Did Gavin talk about her?"

Shanice's jaw worked up and down on a piece of gum. "Come on, Stride. Guys don't see me and start bragging about the wife. But I saw a pic of her once. Nice. She looked like the right kind of cool and the right kind of hot."

"Have you heard anything that might help us find her?" Stride asked. "Whoever abducted Chelsey had to take her somewhere and keep her quiet and locked up. Plus, they had to come and go for two days. Somebody must have seen something."

"Not around here. Like I told you, you're wasting your time in this neighborhood."

Maggie shuffled on her feet impatiently. "What about money?"

"What about it?"

"Aren't you surprised that Gavin was the target? Why go after a low-end lawyer like him?"

"Don't play me for a fool, Lieutenant," Shanice complained, focusing an icy stare on Maggie. "You want to ask if I knew about Gavin's pot of gold? Just ask straight up, all right? Yeah, I knew. We all knew. Gavin is loaded now. His sister croaked and left him a shitload of bucks."

"How did you hear about it? Did Gavin tell you?"

Shanice shrugged. "Somebody comes into money, word like that gets around pretty fast. Gavin had some debts and suddenly he paid them off. People notice that kind of shit. They talk."

"Debts?" Stride asked sharply. "What kind of debts?"

"Gavin likes poker. Poker doesn't always like him."

"He plays?"

"Yeah. Pretty hard-core."

"Like how much?"

"I heard he owed twenty thousand at one point. Interest on that kind of cash runs steep. I mean, broken legs kind of steep. But he wiped the slate clean a few months ago. That's when word started going around about his sister."

"Where does he gamble? Fond-du-Luth?"

"Oh, hell no, the Indians don't want that kind of heat. This is off-the-books stuff. A private game, invitation only, high limit. Some real hush-hush shit."

"We need a name and a location," Stride said to Shanice.

"Yeah, and I need a boob job and a pair of Chucks. Guess we're both out of luck."

Stride dug in his pocket and extracted two twenties from his wallet. "At least we can pay you for the client you lost. Whatever you tell us, we forget where we heard it. Deal?"

Shanice licked her lips and studied the cash. Then she plucked the bills out of Stride's hand. "I hear the game runs out of some unmarked warehouse down by the water."

"That's a pretty downscale location for an upscale game," Stride said.

"Easier to keep it quiet that way."

"Who runs it?" Maggie asked.

Shanice shook her head. "You want a lot for forty bucks, Lieutenant."

Maggie pulled out her own wallet and produced two more twenties. "Does this help?"

The girl smiled as she pocketed the extra money. "I hear the guy behind it goes by the nickname Broadway. That's it. I don't know who he really is. I hear he's from the Cities, not local. He sets up the whole thing every Friday. Sounds like it's quite the party, too. By Saturday morning, they shut the whole thing down and the place is empty again."

"Friday?" Stride said. "So there's a game tonight?"

"Probably."

"And Broadway's the banker?"

"Yeah, that's what I hear. I don't know where he gets his money, and I don't want to know. But if you need cash, Broadway is the one who will get it for you."

Stride looked at Maggie, and he knew they were both thinking about one hundred thousand dollars in ransom money.

Cash.

10

As daylight bled into the dreary evening, Stride and Maggie bumped over railroad tracks and drove beside graffiti-covered train cars as they hunted through the streets of the Duluth Port for Broadway's secret poker game. Near the bay, they crossed dirt and gravel lots flooded with rainwater. Heavy equipment, huge storage tanks, and pyramids of taconite loomed on both sides of the road. There were dozens of rusting, windowless buildings within spitting distance of the harbor that gave no clue what was inside. If the gathering place for the weekly game were anywhere near them, it was well hidden.

After two hours of fruitless searching near the docks, they were almost ready to give up. Then, as Stride headed north to merge back onto the freeway, he saw a dark Mercedes turn left on a frontage road a quarter mile ahead of them. Acting on instinct, he followed, hanging back and giving the Mercedes plenty of space. When it continued around a tight curve, Stride turned off his headlights and slowed down, but when he emerged on the other side of the curve, the Mercedes had disappeared. On the left side of the road was a dirt lot where several empty semitrailers were parked. Elevated train tracks loomed on the other side of a line of trees. On his right was a green warehouse with several loading-dock doors but no exterior windows.

"Where the hell did it go?" Maggie asked.

Stride followed the road to an intersection at a stop sign, then did a U-turn because the Mercedes was nowhere in sight. He kept his lights off as he retraced their route to where they'd lost the other vehicle, and then he pulled his Expedition onto a grassy slope and parked.

"Shall we?" he said.

They both got out of the truck. The area around them had a strange, dead calm. Pools of water in the potholes reflected the gray sky. They were close enough to the I-35 freeway to read the billboards.

Side by side, they walked around the curve in the road. There had once been a railway bridge here, but it had been torn down, and netting had been laid on the hills to prevent erosion. Trees grew from the slopes where the train tracks had once run. They stayed in the shadows as they examined the empty lot and the green warehouse in front of them. Stride caught the faintest breath of cigarette smoke hanging in the air. Someone was here.

A dirt entrance road ran beside the warehouse, leading to a fence that blocked off access to the rear of the building. The fence looked new and had electronic controls for the double-wide gates. It was topped with concertina wire. The muddy road continued on the far side of the gates, but they couldn't see around the building walls. However, Stride could see fresh tire tracks.

He switched on the flashlight on his phone and aimed it at the warehouse wall. Near the roof, he could make out the white housing and pinpoint red light of a security camera focused on the gates.

"They know we're here," he commented.

Confirming that thought, the lone door on the side of the warehouse opened behind them, and the smell of cigarette smoke got stronger. A blond man wearing construction gear and a reflective yellow jacket approached them with a wary smile on his face. The man was heavily built and at least six foot five, and his hands were buried in his pockets, which likely meant he was clutching the barrel of a pistol. A walkie-talkie was clipped to his jacket.

He called to them firmly but pleasantly. "Folks, this is private property. I'm going to have to ask you to leave."

Stride held up his badge. So did Maggie. The presence of the police didn't soften the man's attitude.

"Do you have a warrant to be here?" he inquired.

"No," Maggie replied casually. "No warrant."

"Well, then once again, I'll have to ask you to leave. Cops or not, this is still private property."

"The sign says you manufacture and store children's playground equipment," Stride noted, with a glance at the sign on the warehouse wall. "This is quite the security operation for a business like that."

"We've had break-ins," the man replied.

"I guess you can't be too careful with those suburban mommies."

The man didn't laugh. He extended one arm toward the road. "Anyway, if you wouldn't mind, Detectives . . . ?"

"It's strange that you haven't asked why we're here," Stride went on. "Generally, when cops show up, that's the first question we get. You don't seem very curious about why we're standing at your fence."

"Okay. Go ahead and tell me. Why are you here?"

Maggie glanced up at the roof of the building and spoke toward the camera instead of the man in the construction jacket. "We want to talk to Broadway."

"Who?"

"You heard me," Maggie said.

"I don't have any idea who that is."

Maggie shrugged and pulled out her cell phone. "No problem. We must have made a mistake. And listen, I'm sorry to hear that you've had break-ins around here. That's not acceptable. Tell you what, I'm going to bring in a squad car and have a couple of uniformed officers park right here on the road all night. That should scare away anybody who's thinking about ripping you off."

She gave him a sweet smile, and the man's pale Scandinavian face darkened with anger. He backed away, whispered into his walkie-talkie, and then told them, "Wait here."

The man disappeared inside the warehouse door.

Not even five minutes later, they heard a noise from the other side of the fence. An overhead spotlight illuminated the rough ground. Another man emerged from behind the rear wall of the warehouse and walked into the light. This man was small, no more than five foot six, and probably in his midthirties. He had wavy, dark hair brushed back, giving him a high forehead, and wore sunglasses though it was well into the evening. He was dressed impeccably in a deep-purple suit, white shirt, tie, and pocket square. As he walked, he nimbly avoided the puddles that would have splashed his black leather shoes.

He came up to the fence and gave them a tight smile, which made dimples in his cheeks. "Lieutenant Bei, Lieutenant Stride," he said in a polite, youthful voice. "I understand you wish to talk to me."

"You're Broadway?" Maggie asked.

"I am."

"Want to tell us your real name?"

Another smile flickered on his lips. "I imagine once Cher became Cher, she didn't refer to herself as Cherilyn Sarkisian very often."

"Okay. Well—*Broadway*—how about we talk about the illegal gambling operation you're running inside this warehouse?"

He tugged on the cuffs of his shirt, making sure that the exact proper distance extended from the sleeves of his suit coat. When he answered her, it was with friendly condescension. "Maggie. Jonathan. Do you mind if we dispense with the formality of titles? I make it a point to know the police in the areas where my businesses operate, so I've been looking forward to having the pleasure of meeting you for some time. I'll also pay you the respect of not referring you to my lawyer or wasting your time making you apply for warrants that no judge is likely to grant. I'm sure the day may come when you'll think it's worth your energy to try, but for tonight, let's focus on why you're really here. Fair enough?"

"Why do you think we're here?" Stride asked.

"Gavin Webster."

"I take it you're aware that his wife has been kidnapped," Stride said.

"I am. What a terrible thing."

"Someone gave Gavin one hundred thousand dollars in cash to pay the ransom. Was that you?"

Broadway shrugged. "I'm not sure how it helps you for me to say yes or no. Neither answer gives Gavin his wife back. So why don't you pick a question that will actually assist you in your investigation, and I'll do my best to answer."

"Who else knew Gavin was part of your game?"

Broadway squinted one eye in what looked like genuine puzzlement. "Why is that a concern for you?"

"Because one hundred thousand dollars is a lot of money," Maggie snapped. "Most people—even rich people—can't put their hands on that kind of money *in cash* in a couple of days. But the kidnappers seemed to know that Gavin would have access to someone who could make that happen. Namely you. That suggests that the kidnappers knew about Gavin attending your private parties."

A frown creased Broadway's smooth face. "Interesting. That's a theory I hadn't considered, and I admit, it has some merit. Would you mind if we spoke hypothetically for a moment?"

Stride chuckled. "Go ahead. Who knew Gavin plays poker here? Hypothetically."

"Well, assuming one were to stage private gatherings in which people sought entertainment, any number of individuals might be aware of the participants. Other players, security guards, drivers, waitresses, bartenders, singers, strippers, magicians, what have you."

"What the hell do you have going on in there, Broadway?" Maggie asked. "Caesars Palace?"

He gave them another faint smile. "I'm merely saying it would be a long list."

"We're accustomed to long lists. Can you give us names?"

"Regrettably, no. As I indicated, I'm speaking purely hypothetically. And if you *were* to go after the records of my hypothetical business . . . well, you can imagine I'd need to decline in order to protect the privacy of my workers and guests. That would mean you'd have to have probable cause for a warrant, and I just don't think you'll get too far with that, even with a friendly judge. On the other hand, I will offer you this. I'll conduct an internal audit of my personnel, and if I find any information that I think might reasonably be of interest to you, I'll make you aware of it. In return, I'd ask that you not hassle me or my friends simply for the sake of harassment. Yes, I'm aware that you can inconvenience me and force me to relocate, but you're not going to shut me down anymore than you can shut down the drug trade or the sex trade. Supply follows demand, not vice versa."

Stride shook his head. Broadway was a cool customer. He had the quiet arrogance of someone who was sure he held all the cards. And he was right. They had nothing on him, no leverage to make him talk.

"Off the top of your head, can you think of anyone you'd consider a suspect in this abduction?" Stride asked. "Someone we should look at right now? You must know that time is critical. If Chelsey Webster is still alive, she won't be for long. We need to find her."

Broadway smoothed his lapels. "I'm not insensitive to your problem, Jonathan. I really do want to help, and if I believed I knew someone who could have perpetrated this terrible crime, I'd tell you. However, in all seriousness, I can't think of a name to give you. A person in my line of work tends to screen employees carefully. Guests, too. Any type of criminal record would get you crossed off my list."

Stride glanced at Maggie. There wasn't anything else to do here.

"All right . . . Broadway," she said. "We're done for now. Trust me when I tell you we'll meet again."

"I have no doubt. But I'm glad to have met both of you."

They headed through the gravel lot, but Broadway called to them before they'd gone too far, and they both returned to the fence. As they waited there, Broadway removed a remote control from his pocket and pointed it at the camera mounted near the roof of the warehouse. The small red light went dark.

"One more thing," he said. "This is a little bonus for you. Off the record, not from me, not for attribution or inclusion in any court filings. Consider it an investment in our relationship."

"What is it?" Stride asked.

"Hundreds. Look for hundreds."

"I don't understand. What does that mean?"

Broadway rubbed his fingers together, the unmistakable signal for money. "The ransom was paid in hundred-dollar bills. Exclusively hundreds. You might find that helpful in locating the kidnappers. If I were you, I'd keep an eye out in town for someone passing them around."

11

As Serena drove home that night, she passed through the Canal Park area and noticed an unusual number of people gathered on the green grass near the ship canal. October was still the tourist season, and the passage of an ore boat under the lift bridge always brought gawkers running to the piers. But this seemed to be something different. From her car, she spotted an odd display of multicolored lights flashing through the darkness in the middle of the park.

Rather than head across the bridge toward their cottage on the Point, she pulled off the street and parked her Mustang. Putting Elton on a leash, she took the dog and walked into the grassy park near the city's marine museum. A stiff, cold breeze blew off the lake and swirled her black hair as she approached the crowd. There were at least fifty people arranged in a circle around a man perched atop a coffin that glowed with green luminescent paint. The man was on stilts that lifted him high into the air, and he wobbled unsteadily in the gusty wind. He wore a tight-fitting black bodysuit that had some kind of plastic overlay studded with lights.

As Serena watched, the lights changed colors and transformed into various designs. First, the bodysuit became a skeleton, its white bones dancing. Then, a dozen orange Halloween pumpkins illuminated all over the performer's body. Then, a Christmas tree filled his chest, twinkling with red-and-green lights. Finally, the word *DULUTH* appeared on one leg, and *MINNESOTA* appeared on the other leg, and *#1* flashed on his torso.

That won a big cheer from the crowd.

The next message had a more mercenary tone:

XMAS LIGHTSUITS, $200!

From atop the stilts, the man spotted Serena standing in the crowd. She heard him calling to her. "Hey! Detective! It's me!"

She knew that voice. It was Curt Dickes.

Of course, it was. If a strange moneymaking scam were underway in Duluth, the odds were good that Curt was behind it. Over the years, she'd caught him peddling everything from homemade craft-beer growlers (which she suspected were poured from cans of Coors) to knockoff concert tickets and bags of marijuana. The jail had a revolving door with his name on it. He was mostly a low-level fraudster, but he was clued in to nearly every scheme on the Duluth streets, which often made him a useful source of information when she and Stride needed help.

Serena also suspected that Curt was in love with Cat. She didn't like that at all. The two of them had hung out for years, dating back to when Cat was living on the streets and Curt was in the business of recruiting pretty teenagers to dress up Duluth parties. Cat had left that world far behind, but Curt was still in the middle of it. So if there was one person that Serena wanted *out* of Cat's life forever, it was Curt Dickes.

"Come on down here, Curt," she called, drawing a disappointed groan from the crowd.

Curt nimbly hopped down from his stilts and landed with a thump on the coffin. He began passing out business cards to people around him, and when Serena grabbed one, she saw an advertisement for curtslightsuits.com. With a sigh, she pried the rest of the cards from Curt's hand, then beckoned him toward the water. Elton followed on the leash, his nose to the ground.

They stood by the rocks, where the whitecaps of Lake Superior erupted in spray. A few wet fall leaves blew across the grass. Whenever

Curt moved, the plastic on his light suit crinkled, and the lights flashed. Tourists kept coming up to ask where they could buy one, and Serena shooed them away.

"Curtslightsuits?" she asked. "Really?"

"You bet, I'm taking orders now!" Curt replied with his usual enthusiasm. "If you want one, you should do it fast and beat the Christmas rush. I figure these things are going to sell like crazy over at Bentleyville."

"And you'll be delivering these orders when?" Serena asked.

He lowered his voice to a conspiratorial whisper. "To be honest, my delivery time is a little uncertain. I'm still negotiating with a supplier in China."

"Uh-huh."

He flashed a cheerful grin that didn't really try to hide the scam he was running. That was part of his charm and part of why Cat found him attractive. Yes, he was usually on the wrong side of the law, but he had so much fun doing it that it was actually hard to dislike him.

Curt was tall, but without much meat on his bones. He had greasy black hair that he usually wore down to his shoulders, but which was now tied into two pigtails jutting out of his head like antennae. His bodysuit didn't show much skin, but Serena could see a tapestry of tattoos stretching from beneath the fabric onto his hands and face. He was almost thirty, but still had the boyish looks of a teenager. She thought of him like a misdemeanor version of Peter Pan.

"Shut the site down," she told him. "Got it? I'll be clicking over there in the morning, and I better not find it online."

"Yeah, yeah, okay."

Serena didn't ask how many people he'd already conned into placing advance orders at two hundred bucks a pop. She figured they'd get complaints about that at the station soon enough.

Meanwhile, Curt squatted in front of Elton, and the black-and-white dog responded to his charm, too. The dog licked his face and then tumbled over on the park sidewalk for a tummy rub.

"Who's the pooch?" Curt asked. "When did you guys get a dog? I can't believe Cat didn't tell me."

"He's sort of a loaner," Serena replied without going into details.

"Well, he's cute. You guys need a dog. I mean, now that you don't have a Cat anymore, why not get a dog?"

"Ha."

"Speaking of Kitty Cat," Curt went on.

"Let's not."

"Aw, come on, Serena. We're just friends. She and I text every day. It's no big thing. I'd never cause her any trouble, I swear."

"You've already caused her plenty of trouble," Serena reminded him.

"Well, don't worry, I'd never lay a finger on her. Absolutely no funny stuff. I value my life too much. You and Stride know too many places to hide bodies."

Serena couldn't help but chuckle at that. "Cat's doing well at UMD, so I want you to leave her alone, okay?"

"Tell you what, how about I leave Cat alone and you leave my website alone?" Curt asked with a wink. He pushed a button on a small plastic box to make the lights on his body chase each other from head to toe. The display gave Serena a headache.

"How about you tell me what you know about Gavin Webster?" Serena replied. "And turn off those damn lights."

Curt switched off the controller with a loud sigh, and his light suit went dark. "Gavin? Sure, I know Gavin. He's helped me out a few times. What's the deal with the kidnapping? Did he do it? I bet he did it."

"Why do you say that?"

"Hubby inherits a fortune. Wife disappears. Connect the dots."

"Do you have any evidence to back that up?"

Curt put a finger on the side of his nose. "No, that's just how it smells to me."

"Well, forget how it smells. Right now we're trying to figure out who grabbed Chelsey and where they're hiding her. You got any names of people I should talk to?"

Curt looked around to make sure no one was within earshot. "You know about Broadway?"

"Yeah, Stride and Maggie just talked to him. Stride filled me in about Gavin and the poker games."

An eyebrow shot up on Curt's forehead. "Stride? The big guy's back in the lineup? I knew he couldn't stay away forever."

"I'm sure he'll be thrilled to have your support, Curt. Now, do you know anyone who could be involved in the abduction? Any people connected to Broadway?"

"Well, I've been known to put Broadway in touch with local assets from time to time," Curt admitted. "He's a Minneapolis guy, so he doesn't have the connections around here that I do."

"What kind of connections are you talking about? Players?"

"No, that's all him, but he likes a class operation. Entertainers. Musicians. Studs behind the bar to pour drinks, pretty girls to take their minds off the cards. All of that is sort of my specialty."

"And Gavin?"

"He's been hip-deep in the whole thing from the beginning."

"He's not just a player?" Serena asked.

"Oh, no, he helped Broadway set it up. There have been a few legal hiccups along the way, and Gavin made them go away. A security guy had a DUI. One of the players got carjacked with a lot of cash in the car. Gavin smoothed it all over. In return, Broadway staked him in the games."

"We heard Gavin was in some heavy debt for a while."

"Yeah. He loves poker, but he's no good at it. Between you and me, I think Broadway liked having Gavin in hock to him. A lawyer makes for a nice house pet. But then Gavin got a windfall from his sister and paid it all off."

"Is it possible Broadway got nervous about Gavin inheriting all that money? Like maybe Gavin would walk away and expose the games?"

"Hard to say. Broadway's a slick dude, but you don't want to cross him."

"What about Gavin's wife? What do you know about Chelsey?"

Curt made a little growl. "The cougar? Nice body, I'm told. She stays in shape. Better shape than the marriage."

"Who told you that?" Serena asked.

"One of my favorite party girls also works as a masseuse. She met Gavin at one of the gigs. She's not always strict about adhering to the no-happy-endings rule, so she calls Gavin for help sometimes when you guys haul her in. Gavin said his wife was looking for a massage and asked Toni to give her a rubdown. No funny business, Chelsey wasn't into that, at least not with girls. But Chelsey must like her because Toni's been giving her massages for a while now."

"What did Chelsey tell Toni?"

"You'd have to ask her for the details. Toni just said Chelsey was worried about getting dumped now that Gavin had money." Curt snickered. "But I don't suppose she figured that meant getting dumped in a landfill."

"This masseuse, Toni. Where do I find her?"

"I'll text you her number," Curt replied. "Might as well get a massage while you're there. She has magic fingers, if you're into that sort of thing."

"Please stop talking, Curt."

"Yeah, sure. We done here?"

"One more question," Serena said. "Stride got a tip from Broadway. Have you heard about anyone passing around hundred-dollar bills today?"

"C-notes? What, like from the ransom payoff? No, but like I said, I'll put out the word. Something like that's easy to spot. If I hear anything, I'll give you a call."

"You do that."

Serena tapped her thigh, and Elton scrambled up next to her as if they'd been training together for months. She also crooked a finger at Curt, and when he leaned in, she took hold of Curt's collar and whispered. Something about the gesture and the sound of her voice made Elton realize that Curt wasn't a friend, and a mean rumble emerged from the dog's throat.

"By the way, I don't like hearing that you're still recruiting girls for parties," Serena murmured. "My advice is that you get *out* of that business if you know what's good for you. And if I ever—*ever*—hear that you've invited Cat to one of your parties, then you'll be the one getting dumped in a landfill."

Curt held up his hands in surrender and laughed nervously at the threat.

Serena didn't laugh at all.

* * * * *

Late in the evening, Stride sat in Maggie's office with his feet up on her desk. This had been his office and his desk before he was shot. She sat on the other side, with her own feet propped on the window ledge. Beyond the glass, the woods were lost in the darkness of the night. The overhead office lights were off, so the only light came from the glow of her computer monitor. They were both quiet.

When Stride inhaled, he realized that the smell of the office had changed. It didn't smell like him anymore. It didn't look like his office anymore, either. Serena's picture and Cat's picture weren't smiling at him from frames on the wall. The souvenirs he kept from old cases were gone. Nothing was the same.

Maggie opened the bottom drawer of the desk and removed a bottle of Dublin whiskey, something he never would have kept there. "Teeling?"

He shrugged. "Why not?"

She took out two shot glasses and filled them high. He drank his in a single swallow and enjoyed the mellow warmth that spread in his chest. Like so many other things, alcohol wasn't on his postsurgery diet, but he didn't care. He'd decided that the key to not dying wasn't to quit all the things that made life worth living.

"Today was good," Maggie said.

"I'm not sure we're any closer to finding Chelsey," Stride pointed out.

"I mean good as in having you back."

"I'm not back," he clarified.

"Well, even if it's just a trial balloon, I'll take it. You, me—I miss that."

He didn't answer. She was right about him and about the day. Part of him *was* hungry to be back. Part of him wanted to sit behind that desk again and call the shots and feel the surge of adrenaline in his veins. Another part of him wanted to leave it all behind.

"I don't know what to think about Gavin Webster," Maggie admitted.

She poured another shot for herself, but Stride waved his hand over his glass.

"I don't either," Stride said.

"When I hear about gambling debts and inheritance windfalls and secret poker games, I think he has to be guilty. He wanted to get rid of his wife, so he got somebody to abduct and kill her, and he used the ransom money to pay the person off."

"Could be."

Maggie shoved a stack of papers across her desk. "We got a copy of Gavin's cell phone records."

"And?"

She pointed at an incoming call highlighted in yellow. "See that call? It was made the day that Guppo says the surveillance camera was placed in Gavin's house. The number is the same burner phone that was used to demand the ransom on Tuesday night."

"So the kidnapper contacted Gavin *before* Chelsey was abducted?"

"Yep."

Stride shook his head. "If Gavin's guilty, that's a pretty careless mistake."

"I agree. And yet most criminals—even smart criminals—make mistakes. Good thing, or our job would be a lot tougher."

"We need to talk to Gavin about it."

Maggie tipped her glass toward him. "You want to take the interrogation?"

"This isn't my case," Stride said. "It's yours."

"Yeah, but you're better at this than me. I tend to scare people, and they shut up."

Stride looked at her. "I'm not back, Mags."

"Well, you're here now, and hopefully, you'll be here tomorrow. Talk to Gavin in the morning. See what he says."

He shrugged. "Okay. If that's what you want."

"Thank you."

She drained her shot of Teeling, and then she held up the bottle.

Stride didn't bother turning down the whiskey this time. She filled both crystal glasses, and they clinked them together in a toast.

"To old times," she said.

"Old times."

Maggie drank the shot, put the glass down on the desk, and then said, "So. What are we going to do about Serena?"

12

Cat climbed the dunes behind the cottage. When she got to the top of the weedy slope, she could see Lake Superior spread out in front of her. The beach ran along the peninsula toward the Duluth skyline that was framed against the hillside, and waves thundered against the sand. She saw Serena near the edge of the surf, with the high wind making a mess of her long hair. Not far away, a dog ran back and forth through the water, returning to Serena like the fixed point of a compass.

Being here felt like home. She'd spent a lot of time at the lake with Serena, talking about life, men, sex, parents, and guilt. It was a kind of mother-daughter closeness that neither one of them had seen coming. Cat's own mother had been killed by her father when she was six years old, and after that, she'd bounced between foster homes and life on the streets. When she'd moved into the cottage, her relationship with Serena had built in a slow, difficult way. With Stride, it had been easy. Stride was Stride. Cat loved him. But she and Serena had struggled. They'd started out jealous of each other, Cat for the fact that Stride loved Serena, Serena for the fact that Stride sometimes opened up to Cat more than to her. Cat was also naturally rebellious, not just like a normal teenager, but as a girl who'd lived through trauma and spent years making her own rules. Stride took some of that defiance, but Serena got the brunt of it.

However, as time passed, Serena began letting Cat make her own mistakes. In return, Cat found herself leaning on Serena more and more. She began to realize that she and Serena had a lot in common in their pasts, and she started to ask Serena for advice, even if she didn't always take it. And although Serena had never pretended to be a surrogate mother to her, Cat began to look at her that way. She liked it now when Serena referred to her as her daughter.

She took the wooden steps to the thin strip of beach. It was a cold, crisp night, radiant with moon and stars. The dog galloped her way, as if recognizing a friend without being introduced. He rolled over on the sand, and Cat squatted and gave him plenty of attention. When she was finished, the dog jumped up and shook a cloud of sand off his fur, which made Cat laugh and cough. She came up beside Serena, where the waves slipped in almost to her feet.

For a long time, she felt no need to say anything. They both stood next to each other, arms crossed on their chests, the water dark and blue in front of them. Far out on the horizon were the stationary lights of an ore boat, awaiting a berth in the harbor.

Finally, Cat said, "So what's the deal? Did you replace me with a dog?"

"That's a long story," Serena said.

"Is he a permanent addition?"

Serena sighed, and Cat heard sadness in her voice. "No. Just a visitor."

"Well, he's sweet."

"Yes, he is."

They both fell silent again. The waves kept coming and going.

"Curt says you threatened to kill him," Cat said a couple of minutes later, with her usual girlish giggle.

Serena gave a little shrug. "I probably wouldn't do it."

"Probably?"

"It's better that he's not completely sure," Serena said.

"You do know that you don't need to worry about me and Curt, right? That's ancient history."

"I'm glad to hear it."

Serena turned toward her in the moonlight. Cat saw a glassy shine in her eyes, but no actual tears. As she stood there, Serena reached out with one hand and stroked Cat's chestnut hair. She looked her up and down with a kind of wonder.

"You've only been away a month, and you already look different," Serena said.

"Different how?"

"Older. Wiser. In control of your life."

"Thank you."

"Sorry for not texting more," Serena said. "I wasn't ignoring you."

"I knew where you were," Cat replied. She closed the gap between them and folded Serena up in a hug. Serena was much taller and stronger, but Cat held her tight. When she let go, she tilted up her head and whispered, "Stride told me about Samantha."

"I figured."

"You okay?"

"No. Not really."

"Wanna talk?"

"Yeah."

Serena walked down the wet beach into the water, as if she needed the jolt of the chill to open up. The waves rushed in, soaking her shoes and ankles. The dog ran through the surf and barked at them happily. Cat joined her and put an arm around Serena's waist and leaned her head against her shoulder.

"So what are you thinking about?" she asked.

"The bad old days in Phoenix," Serena murmured, her voice barely louder than the lake.

"Sure."

"I kick myself for letting it happen. I should have gotten out right away. I should have run as soon as I met Blue Dog. But I didn't."

"Yeah, but you were what, sixteen?"

"It didn't matter how old I was. I knew what was going to happen. I knew what he was going to do to me, but I couldn't leave Samantha. Back then, I couldn't imagine life without her. It was my job to take care of her."

Cat had heard the story before. "I was sixteen when you found me, too. Remember? I blamed myself that my life was such a mess. You were the one who kept telling me that it wasn't my fault."

"It wasn't."

"Well, what Samantha did to you wasn't your fault, either."

There was enough moonlight for her to see Serena slowly shaking her head, as if she still didn't believe it.

"I stayed," Serena said, sweeping the hair impatiently from her face as the wind gusted. "That was my choice. She needed me, so I stayed."

"What she needed was more drugs. Samantha *sold* you. Blue Dog was her dealer, and she let him rape you over and over to keep herself in cocaine. How the hell does a mother do that to her daughter?"

Serena stared into the distance. "It was what Samantha wanted. That was the only thing that mattered to me. I was desperate to make her happy. She would sit in the corner of the bedroom and watch us, high as a mountain with those glazed eyes, and I would smile at her, because I wanted her to know everything was okay."

Cat failed to keep the anger out of her voice. "Stop it, will you? I don't want to hear shit like that. Blue Dog was a fucking animal. And I'm sorry, but so was Samantha. In fact, she was worse. You were a teenage girl getting *abused* over and over by the woman who was supposed to keep you safe. You don't owe her a thing. Let her go. Let that bitch rest in hell."

The dog heard their voices. It stopped, frozen, and then splashed through the surf and reared up to put its front paws on Serena's stomach. Serena cupped the dog's head between her hands. Cat realized, watching them, that there was something more intense in Serena's affection for this dog than she was letting on. It was as if Serena were clinging to the Border collie for sanity, and if she let go of him, she would let go of herself, too.

"Do you want me to stay here with you tonight?" Cat asked.

"No."

"Why not? It's no trouble."

"You don't live here. You live in the dorm."

"It's only one night."

Serena gave her a tired smile, as if someone had told a joke with a punch line that was more sad than funny.

"What is it?" Cat asked.

"You. You're trying to take care of me."

"So?"

"I guess that's a tradition in my family," Serena said. "Sooner or later, mother and daughter always trade places. Now it's our turn."

* * * * *

Stride arrived home late.

He found half a Sammy's pizza on the dining-room table. Cat had already come and gone. He called Serena's name, but she didn't answer him. When he went to look for her, he found her in bed, lying atop the blanket in a T-shirt and shorts. She had the fresh, damp smell of the shower. A beautiful black-and-white Border collie lay asleep in the curve of her torso. When Stride came in, the dog opened one eye, wagged its tail briefly, and then fell asleep again.

Serena's eyes were open, but she didn't acknowledge him. Fully dressed, he climbed onto the bed beside her. The backs of their hands brushed together. They both stared at the ceiling.

"How was your first day?" she asked quietly.

"Disorienting. Energizing. Exhausting."

"I've gotten a lot of calls. Everyone wants to know if you're back for good. If you're ready to be a cop again."

"I don't know the answer to that."

Serena didn't reply immediately, as if she were looking for the right words. "I think you made your decision when you walked through the door. Now it's just a question of realizing that your mind is made up."

"Maggie said the same thing. We'll see."

"And that's all you've got to say?"

"What more is there?" Stride asked.

Serena exhaled with something like a hiss. "You've been struggling with this for months, but we haven't talked about it. You talk to Cat. You talk to Maggie. Not me. I'm your wife."

His hand nudged away from hers. "I know."

"You love me, Jonny, but even after all this time, I'm not sure you trust me."

"I could say the same about you."

"Yes, I guess you could."

He propped himself on one elbow. "What's really going on with you?"

"I wish I knew."

"Now look who's keeping secrets," he said.

"I'm not. I swear I'm not. I'm being honest. Losing Samantha is—it's bringing up things I've never dealt with before. Things I didn't even know I felt before. I was wrong to say I'm fine. I admit that. But I don't know what I am."

"How can I help?"

"I'm not sure you can. You have your struggle, I have mine. I have to deal with this on my own."

He wanted to fight that idea. He wanted to tell her: *No, you're not alone. Your fight is my fight.* But he didn't. That wasn't how they dealt with things. They avoided the hard stuff because it was easier to stay locked in their own worlds.

"I'll give you space if that's what you need," he said.

She didn't look surprised by his surrender. Her head turned; her green eyes stared at him. "I'm only going to ask you for one thing."

"What's that?"

He could see a strange battle going on behind her eyes. "Maggie told you about the dog, right? I'm sure she told you I stole him. I'm sure they keep calling about him."

Stride nodded. "Yes. You're right."

"Don't make me give him back," she said fiercely.

"Serena—"

"I need more time with him. Don't make me give him back. Not yet. Do whatever you have to do."

"Why is this so important to you?" Stride asked.

"I shouldn't have to tell you that. If I ask for something, that's all you should need."

"Okay. You're right. I don't need an explanation."

Serena shook her head. "Liar."

Stride felt as if she'd slapped him, but she wasn't wrong. She wasn't acting like the woman he knew. He didn't understand what was happening to her, and he needed more than a leap of faith.

"Tell me," he said. "What is it about this dog?"

"Blue Dog had a pit bull," she murmured in reply.

"What?"

"A pit bull puppy. Elton. The dog was in the apartment when Samantha and I moved in. It hardly ever moved from the corner of the bedroom. If it barked, Blue Dog would kick it. If it whimpered, he'd burn it with cigarettes. Elton learned to stay in the corner and not move."

Stride closed his eyes with a stab of grief. This was brand new. This was a story she'd locked away from him. He shook his head in dismay, feeling as if he and his wife were still strangers after all these years. All the things she'd told him about her past, and she'd left out the dog. She'd left out something that obviously still convulsed her with guilt.

"When it was just Elton and me in the apartment, I would talk to him," she went on. "I would tell him that someday, we'd both run away. I'd leave, and I'd take him with me, and we'd be free. I swore to him that I would give him a better life and he'd never have to be afraid again."

Serena rarely cried, but he watched tears begin to slip down her face like a river slowly escaping from the winter ice.

"But I left," Serena said. "When I finally ran away to Las Vegas with Deidre, I didn't take Elton with me. I left him there. I was supposed to save him, Jonny, and instead, I abandoned him. I left Elton to die with that son of a bitch."

"Serena, you couldn't go back to that apartment. It wasn't safe. You had to get out of there."

"I should have taken him with me," she insisted.

She reached out with her hand, and the dog beside her woke up and nudged forward to put his nose against her cheek. Serena just closed her eyes and continued to cry softly and silently.

Serena, who was normally a pillar of strength. It scared him.

Stride let a few minutes go by, and then he said, "I'll do what I can. I promise."

* * * * *

Sometime later it was dark. Serena awoke from sleep, felt the warm lump of Elton still beside her, and heard Jonny sleeping on the other side of the bed.

Her head turned. She noticed the clock, as she always did. Midnight had passed again.

"6,608," she murmured to herself.

But that night it didn't feel like a victory.

13

On Saturday morning, Serena texted the masseuse named Toni, using the phone number that Curt Dickes had given her. She asked for a meeting at a budget motel across from a car dealership on the north side of the city. Guppo's brother owned the motel, and he was always happy to help the police by letting them borrow an empty room. Toni responded to her text immediately with a time, a price, and a string of kiss emojis.

From the motel's first-floor window, Serena watched the parking lot. Elton kept his paws on the window ledge, alert to every car passing on the highway. He'd slept beside her all night, and when she'd gotten up early to go for coffee, he'd run to the Mustang ahead of her and waited for her to open the door. She felt a kinship with the dog. He seemed to be attuned to her moods, although she didn't know if that was true or if she simply wanted it to be true.

She'd stayed awake most of the night, picking her way through the minefield of her memories. She found herself wondering why she'd kept the story of the dog in Phoenix from Jonny for all these years. But she knew. It was because her life in Phoenix had always been more complicated than she'd let on. To Stride, to Cat, to Maggie, to Guppo, to everyone who knew about her past, she'd been a victim, a prisoner who finally escaped. Except nothing was that simple. Everything Samantha had asked her to do, she'd done, and she'd never once said no. If her mother wanted it, then she wanted it, too.

Elton barked.

Serena looked through the sheer curtain and saw a red Kia pulling into the motel parking lot. It parked, by chance, right next to Serena's Mustang, but there was nothing on her own car to identify her as police. The door of the Kia opened, and a petite woman in her twenties got out. She had shoulder-length blond hair and wore boots, leggings, and a long cowl-neck sweater dress. The woman opened the rear door of the car and removed a square carrying case, which Serena assumed was for a portable massage table.

Shortly after Toni headed for the motel lobby, Serena got a text from Guppo's brother. *She's on her way.* A few seconds later, knuckles drummed on the door of Serena's room.

She opened the door. The young woman gave her a bright smile from the hallway. "I'm Toni."

"I'm Serena. Come on in."

Close up, Toni was pretty and even younger than Serena had suspected. She was probably barely twenty. Her eyes were a kind of pale flecked gray, and her makeup was skillfully applied, including peach-colored lipstick and just the right amount of blush. Her nose was round and small. Her fingernails were short but painted glossy red. She wore a charm bracelet loosely on one wrist, and Serena noticed a silver UMD bulldog among the charms. Toni was probably a college student.

"Hey, beautiful dog," Toni commented, noticing Elton, who'd jumped up on the motel bed.

"Thank you."

She came into the room, and Serena closed the motel door. Toni propped the black carrying case against the bed. "So who gave you my number?"

"Curt Dickes," Serena replied.

Toni hesitated, her smart eyes reassessing Serena with surprise as if to say: *Oh, so it's going to be that kind of massage?*

"How do you know Curt?"

Serena stood in front of the door, blocking it. "I've arrested him a few times."

Toni stiffened, and her smile vanished. "Hey, come on. Are you kidding? What the hell? You texted about a massage, I gave you a price for a massage. Period. I didn't promise anything else."

"I'm not trying to set you up, Toni. I just want information."

"You could have told me that in your text," she snapped.

"Somehow I didn't think you'd be as likely to show up that way," Serena replied.

Toni shrugged and didn't disagree. She sat down on the bed, crossed her legs, and began petting Elton. "Are you going to tell me what this is about?"

Serena took a chair from the small motel desk, and she sat down, too, keeping herself between Toni and the door. "Chelsey Webster."

"Sure. Guess I should have seen that coming."

"Do you know anything about her disappearance?"

"Only what I see on TV."

"Do you have any idea who might have abducted her?"

"Well, my bet would be Gavin," Toni replied, "but I can't prove it. It's always the husband, isn't it? But I have no idea who he got to do the dirty work for him. So is that it? Can I go?"

"Relax, Toni. I booked you for an hour. I'll pay you for an hour."

Her eyebrow arched with surprise. "Seriously? Well then, it's your dime. You want a massage while we talk?"

"No, thanks."

Toni's shoulders bobbed, and she went back to petting the dog. "Your loss. I'm really good."

"Tell me how you met Chelsey."

"Through Gavin," Toni replied. "He said his wife liked to play tennis and she'd screwed up her shoulder and wanted a massage. I owed Gavin for some legal work, so it was on the house. Chelsey liked my style, and she's been bringing me back ever since. She pays cash. Nice tipper, too."

"How long have you been giving her massages?"

"About a year, I guess."

"How did you first meet Gavin?" Serena asked.

"I told you. He's a lawyer."

"I heard differently," Serena said.

"Oh?"

"Curt says you're part of the decorations at Broadway's poker games."

"Curt has a big mouth," Toni retorted sharply.

"Is it true?"

"I have nothing to say about Broadway."

"You sound scared."

Toni's jaw jutted with defiance, but one of her boots bounced nervously on the carpet. "If you want to talk about Broadway, you can keep your money, and I'm out of here."

"Okay, no Broadway," Serena went on. "Tell me more about Chelsey."

"What do you want to know?"

"Start with what she's like. I've never met her."

"Chelsey's one of those fortysomething women who was hot in her twenties and thinks she still is." A wicked smirk bent across Toni's face. "No offense."

Serena shrugged. "Your time will come, kid."

"Yeah, well, Chelsey thinks she can turn back time if she works out hard enough. Tennis, kickboxing, weight lifting, running—she keeps in pretty good shape."

"You mean for her age?"

Another smirk. "Yeah, for her age. But you can't hide from your masseuse. I see her naked, so I notice what's sagging and what's not."

"Does she ever talk to you about Gavin?" Serena asked. "About her marriage?"

"All the time."

"And? What does she say?"

Toni twisted the charms on her bracelet. "Chelsey thought she was buying a Birkin bag and wound up with a knockoff. At least until recently, that is."

"What does that mean?"

"She told me that when she married Gavin, he was on the way up.

Big-shot corporate lawyer, nice house on the hill. Fundraisers at the Kitch. Nice life, right? Then they lost everything. That was quite the comedown. She said Gavin turned into a different person after that. Angry, bitter, always pissed off about not having any money. She said he hated the work he was doing."

Serena frowned. "His parents told me Gavin preferred the criminal work to his old corporate law practice."

"All I can tell you is what Chelsey said," Toni replied. "But we all tell our parents what they want to hear, right? Trust me, I don't exactly brag to my folks about how I pay the tuition."

"And their marriage?"

"Strained," Toni said.

"Did Chelsey know about the gambling? About Gavin losing money at Broadway's poker games?"

Toni swept some of her blond hair away from her eyes. "I told you, I don't talk about Broadway."

"For now, I don't care about him. This is about Gavin and Chelsey."

The girl took a long time to answer. "Yeah. Chelsey knew."

"How did she find out?"

"Someone saw Gavin at the games and told her about it."

"Who?"

Toni shook her head. "I don't know. She didn't say. But she found out how deep in the hole he was, and she was furious. That was money they didn't have. They had a hell of an argument over it."

"Why not divorce him?"

"Who knows? Love's a weird thing."

"She still loved him?"

"That's what she told me."

"What about Gavin? Did he love her?"

"I guess that's the million-dollar question."

"Did Gavin ever talk to you about his wife?" Serena asked.

"No. He wouldn't do that. He knew I saw Chelsey for massages all the time. I'm sure he figured anything he said would go straight back to her."

"Did Chelsey talk about the inheritance?"

"Yeah, for a while, she was pretty upbeat about it. She thought it would finally change things for them. And it did. But not the way she was expecting."

"How so?"

"Well, she noticed that Gavin was very careful about keeping the money he got from his sister in a separate bank account. His name only. That way, Chelsey couldn't see how he was spending it. She worried that he'd gamble a lot of it away. Plus, she was afraid he was thinking about dumping her and taking all the money. If you inherit stuff, apparently it's yours, and your spouse can't do shit about it. So Chelsey thought he might be looking to get rid of her."

"She said that? Those words?"

"Yup."

"When did she tell you all this?" Serena asked.

"Not long ago. A few weeks. There was definitely trouble in paradise."

"What else did she say?"

"Sex was a problem, too," Toni said. "I mean, she even asked me if *I'd* ever fucked Gavin."

"Had you?"

"No, but the fact that she asked told me she thought he was cheating on her. She said he was getting weird in bed, too. He'd gotten a daily Cialis prescription, and she said it was definitely not like he needed boner pills every day for their love life. She also said he'd been pressuring her to try stuff."

"Stuff?"

"Like X. He said he'd heard it would heighten her arousal, and he knew where to get some."

"Where?" Serena asked.

Toni rolled her eyes. "I'm not talking about that."

"Broadway?"

"I'm not talking about that," the girl repeated.

"And this happened recently?"

"Very."

Serena frowned. She tapped the side of her thigh, and Elton immediately scrambled off the bed and ran to her. She stroked the dog's fur as she contemplated what Toni had told her.

"Did Chelsey ever tell you that she feared for her safety?" Serena asked.

Toni hesitated. "Not in so many words."

"In what words?"

The girl played with the cowl on her dress. "Well, it's just that—I don't know whether Gavin was cheating on Chelsey, but I'm pretty sure that Chelsey was cheating on him."

"She told you that?"

"Kind of. I was giving her a massage, and I noticed—well, I noticed what looked like a bite mark on her ass. I made a joke about Gavin being a vampire, and she went white as a sheet. She swore and asked me how noticeable it was. I said it was pretty obvious."

"So you got the idea that it wasn't Gavin who gave it to her?"

"Bingo."

"Do you have any idea who it could have been? Did Chelsey ever say something to give you a clue?"

"No."

"When was this?"

"A while ago. Maybe a year? It may have been the first time I gave her a massage. So it was long before they had any of the money from his sister."

"Did Gavin know?" Serena asked.

"I don't think so. Chelsey looked panicked about the bite mark. She said Gavin had a temper. If he thought she was cheating on him, she wasn't sure what he would do to her."

14

Reporters were gathered outside Gavin Webster's house when Stride arrived. It was almost noon, and the TV journalists were getting ready to go on the air for the midday news. He squeezed through them without answering questions or making a statement. But he noticed that the tenor of the questions had changed from the previous day, when the kidnapping was first announced to the press. Yesterday they were asking whether the police had any hope of finding Chelsey Webster alive.

Today they were asking whether her husband was a suspect in her disappearance.

Stride walked up the driveway and knocked on the lower-level door. The lawyer answered a few seconds later with a mug of coffee in one hand. As he invited Stride inside, he looked at the reporters clustered at the end of the driveway.

"I see the vultures are out in force," Gavin said.

"Yes, they are."

"Do you think I should talk to them? Make a personal plea to the kidnappers?"

"That's up to you," Stride replied, "but I don't think kidnappers tend to be swayed by sentiment."

Gavin stroked his unshaved chin and shook his head. "Unfortunately,

I agree with you. Plus, whenever I see a victim make a public plea, I usually say to myself, 'Yeah, he did it.'"

Stride made no comment.

"Apparently you think so, too," Gavin added.

He led him upstairs to the main level of the house. Stride noted the front door, which still showed the aftereffects of the break-in. He followed Gavin to the rear of the house, where an open-air deck looked down the hillside toward the lake. The clouds and rain of the previous day had given way to cool sunshine. The view was magnificent, the city buildings sharp and clear, the blue lake water glinting. They both sat in wicker chairs, and Gavin shifted his chair so he was facing Stride directly. His curly hair was messy, and he wore a dirty sweatshirt and sweatpants. His blue eyes were tired and red, his face pale.

"I honestly didn't expect you to be the one grilling me, Stride. I thought you were done with this."

"We're shorthanded. I'm helping out."

"Well, I'm glad to have you involved in finding Chelsey. You're the A team, as far as I'm concerned. Plus, you and I go back a long way."

That was true.

Stride had worked with Gavin Webster since the man's early days in criminal defense law, and they'd been on opposite sides of interview tables and courtroom witness boxes several times. Maggie disliked all defense lawyers, but Stride viewed them as one of the cogs in the machine that made the system work. He expected them to exploit any loophole that would advantage their clients, and to Stride, that just made him work harder. He'd actually had more ethical troubles with prosecutors over the years than he'd ever had with defense lawyers.

On the other hand, he didn't know Gavin outside of the man's work. Some lawyers made a point of building personal relationships with the police, figuring that would help their clients when they needed a rule bent or a misdemeanor overlooked. Not Gavin. He was smart, committed, and hardworking, but he was also an enigma, hiding his personality behind those strange blue eyes. Over the years, he'd shared almost nothing about his private life or his family. Stride hadn't even known that he was married until he heard about the abduction. It was difficult to trust someone who was a stranger.

"So what can you tell me about the search for Chelsey?" Gavin asked.

"The tip line has been up and running for more than twenty-four hours, and we're getting dozens of calls. So far, nothing has panned out, but everyone's on overtime pursuing leads."

"I hear you're talking to my clients. I can't say I like that."

"Crimes like this typically don't involve random victims. You were targeted. That means the likeliest suspect pool is people who know you."

"I understand that," Gavin replied, "but just because I'm the victim, don't think I won't come down hard on the police if you harass my clients. I'm still their lawyer. So tread lightly."

"No one's being harassed. We're just asking questions."

Gavin gave a cynical grunt, then reached for his coffee. He glanced up at the blue sky, noting a helicopter flying low along the lakeshore. "I've been seeing a lot of helicopters yesterday and today."

"Yes, they're part of the search," Stride replied.

"Search," Gavin said, curling his lip at the word. "You mean they're searching for a body. Follow the lakeshore and the banks of the river. See if a corpse washes up. I know the protocol, Stride. You don't have to pretend with me."

Stride wasn't going to lie to him, because Gavin was right. "Have you had any further contact from the kidnappers?"

"No. Do you have any suspects?"

"Not yet."

"Except me," Gavin said.

Stride shrugged. "You're not a suspect, Gavin, but we do have questions. That's one of the reasons I'm here."

"Naturally." He got up and went to the railing with his coffee. His sweatshirt fit loosely, which made him look even skinnier than he was. "One of my clients called and said she'd heard people were asking on the street about hundred-dollar bills. I assume that means you know about the ransom. I also assume that means you found out about Broadway."

"Yes."

"Well, I'm not talking about him. Attorney-client privilege."

"Privilege doesn't cover the other people at the games. And someone at the games could easily have been involved in the kidnapping. Anyone seeing you there would have known you'd come into money and that you had access to large amounts of cash."

"Sorry, it's all off-limits."

"You'd rather protect Broadway than help us find your wife?"

"I'm a lawyer. That means I have professional responsibilities. Those don't change based on my own circumstances."

"Well, I'm not asking about your work as a lawyer. I'm asking about you as a player. You found yourself in a lot of debt, didn't you? And Chelsey knew about it?"

"Yes."

"Who told her?"

"I don't know."

"You two argued about it?"

"Yes, but I paid it all off."

"Except you were still playing, weren't you? She was afraid you'd blow through the inheritance. Gamble it away."

"I have a problem. I admit that. I'm getting help for it."

"When did you last play?"

He hesitated. "No comment."

"How was your marriage, Gavin?"

Gavin turned around, and his luminous blue eyes seemed to levitate. "Well, we're down to it now, aren't we? You must love this part."

Stride said nothing, but in fact, he didn't love this part. He took no joy in exposing the things people liked to keep hidden about their lives. Their secrets. Their lies. He hated ripping off the masks they wore, showing all their vulnerabilities for the rest of the world to see. Being forced to do it made him not like himself very much. But that was the job.

"Your marriage," he said again, like a dog with a bone.

Gavin looked up at the sky, as if in prayer, and then back at Stride. "Chelsey and I weren't always happy. I'm sure you've already guessed that. She married a corporate lawyer, a man who was supposed to do patents and IP deals and sip martinis at Black Water and hobnob with the city council. Instead, she wound up with a man who bails out drunks and hookers at three in the morning. If there was one tiny bright spot in the horror of losing my sister, it was that I wouldn't have to make Chelsey struggle anymore."

"She was afraid you were going to divorce her," Stride told him. "Take all the money and leave."

His eyebrows knitted together. "Don't be ridiculous."

"It's not true?"

"No."

"You never talked to a lawyer about divorce?"

"Never."

"Then why would she think you wanted to split up? Because that's what she told a friend."

"I don't believe that."

"She told one of your neighbors that the inheritance had changed you. She was concerned for her safety."

"That's a lie, Stride. I can't believe you would make up a story like that."

"I'm not lying. Chelsey said it, Gavin. We also heard that she may have been having an affair."

His mouth was a thin flat line. "I wondered."

"Do you know who it was?"

"No."

"Did you confront her about it?"

"No. Honestly, I didn't want to know whether it was true. And it's not like I've been the best husband."

"So you've had affairs, too?"

Gavin ran his hands through his curly hair in exasperation. "Yes. A few times, with clients. It was years ago, when I was depressed and angry about my life. But not since then. Have I been neglectful? Maybe. Working too hard, not paying enough attention to her? I guess. But that's married life. The fact is, I was trying to change."

"By taking Cialis? By trying to get Chelsey to try Ecstasy?"

Shock registered on his face. "Jesus. How did you hear about that?"

"That's not important. Do you see why we're concerned, Gavin? You inherited millions. You've got a gambling problem, and you're involved with a criminal enterprise you won't talk about. Your marriage is rocky; your wife is telling people she's afraid of you. And in the midst of this, she gets kidnapped, and you don't call the police until the kidnappers have vanished with one hundred thousand dollars and no sign of your wife. What part of that do I have wrong?"

Gavin slammed the mug down on the railing of the deck. Coffee spilled over his hand and onto the grass below.

"Watch your temper, Gavin," Stride said quietly. "People might get the wrong idea."

"It doesn't matter what I say. You already have your mind made up, don't you?"

"No, I don't. That's the truth. But I do want a direct answer. Yes or no. Did you arrange to have your wife kidnapped and killed?"

Gavin sat back down and started to laugh. "Amazing. I see it with clients all the time. I know the shit that the police pull, but wow, you still don't see it coming when it happens to you. How you people twist and manipulate the ordinary ups and downs of someone's life to make them look guilty."

"Inheriting millions of dollars and having your wife disappear a few months later is not ordinary, Gavin. Not ordinary at all. And you didn't answer my question."

"The answer is *no*. I didn't do it."

"Do you have any idea who did?"

"No!"

Stride waited, letting the angry flush fade from the man's pale face. Then he continued. "You were under surveillance for several days before the abduction. We found a hidden camera in your living room."

"A camera? They were watching us?"

"Yes. That way, the kidnappers knew when Chelsey was alone. They knew when you got back from Rice Lake. They were probably also making sure you didn't call the police after they made the ransom demand."

Gavin shook his head. "Bastards."

"The camera was planted last Thursday. Did you have anyone inside your house that day? Clients? Workers?"

The lawyer took his phone and checked his calendar. "No."

"Were you home?"

"During the day, yes, but not in the evening. We had a dinner with one of Chelsey's marketing clients."

Stride reached into the pocket of his sport coat and drew out a piece of paper. It was an excerpt from Gavin's cell-phone records. "That same evening, you got a two-minute call on your cell phone. What was that call about?"

"I have no idea. I receive dozens of calls every day."

"The phone that called you is the same phone that was used to let you know that Chelsey had been kidnapped."

Gavin's surprise looked genuine. "Seriously? Is that true?"

He examined the page that Stride had put on the table and noted the yellow highlight on the two calls.

"I swear, I had no idea."

"What was that call about?"

Gavin rubbed his hands over his face and made a show of trying to think. "I don't remember. It was probably just a wrong number."

"For two minutes?"

"I don't know. Or maybe it was a cold call from a potential client. I get those all the time. People ask for information, I tell them to make an appointment."

"Are you the only one who answers your phone?"

"Yes."

"So you talked to the person who called?"

"I suppose I did."

"Was the person male? Female?"

"I'm telling you, I don't remember the call!"

"It's interesting that this call was made on the same day that the kidnappers planted the surveillance camera in your house."

"So what? Maybe they wanted to make sure I wasn't home before they broke in."

"Or you were telling them the coast was clear," Stride said.

Gavin inhaled sharply, as if ready to explode again. Then he closed his eyes and calmed himself. When he reopened his eyes, he slid back the chair and stood up. He spoke in a low, firm voice. "That's it. We're done. I'm not answering any more questions."

"Okay."

"You can show yourself out."

Gavin slid open the sliding glass door and went inside, leaving Stride alone on the deck. The lawyer left his mug of coffee behind.

For a show of outraged innocence, it was convincing. Stride was almost ready to believe him. Then again, he had learned long ago that all lawyers were actors at heart. Storytellers. And whoever told the best story usually won.

* * * * *

Rex Samuels pulled his tow truck into the crowded Saturday parking lot at the Pike Lake Golf Course. Pontoons and paddleboats dotted the nearby lake, and golfers lined up putts on the greens of the flat nine-hole course. It didn't take him long to spot the car he was looking for. The blue Subaru WRX was parked not far from the lakeshore and close to a lineup of golf carts. The owner leaned against it, scrolling through his phone. The man glanced up and shot him a wave when he saw Rex's truck arriving. The Subaru had a slight lean to it, thanks to the driver's front side tire, which was dead flat.

"You're a lifesaver," the man said when Rex pulled up next to him and hopped down from the truck.

Rex shrugged. "No problem. You got no spare, huh?"

"Guess not. I bought the car used a few months ago, didn't even check whether the spare was in there."

"Well, I'll get you sorted out," Rex told him. "I brought two tires with me. Lotta people, they replace the tire on the other side, too, so they both wear the same. But it's up to you."

The man shrugged. "You're here. Might as well do them both. Cash okay?"

Rex grunted his approval.

He wasn't surprised that the man didn't ask about the price. And he wasn't surprised that he hadn't checked his car for a spare, either. The Subaru driver was tall, in his thirties, with a cool car, cool haircut, cool clothes, and a cool phone. He probably didn't know how to change a tire. People didn't know how to do the stuff that mattered anymore. If you could pay cash for new tires without asking the price, well, you had too much money.

Having too much money had never been a problem for Rex, but he didn't complain. He'd worked behind the wheel of a tow truck since he was nineteen, pulling cars from accident scenes, yanking repos, jump-starting batteries when it was twenty below zero, and changing tires for people who didn't know how to change tires. Now he was almost fifty. He had what his wife called a Budweiser belly and a Bigfoot beard. All the matted brown hair on his chin compensated for having almost no hair left up top.

"This'll take a few minutes," Rex said.

The man whipped a hand through his slicked-back brown hair. "Take your time, man. I'm in no hurry."

Rex got started. The afternoon sun was warm on his shoulders as he jacked up the Subaru and attacked the lug nuts on the first tire. They were tight, and he had to lean his weight into the wrench to make them turn. The driver stood so close that he practically cast a shadow over Rex, but he was focused on his phone and not on the work being done to the tire.

"How about this kidnapping thing?" the man said. "That's crazy, right?"

Rex gave a grunt, and his muscles rippled. "Huh?"

"You know, the lawyer whose wife got abducted? What do you think, did he do it? That's what everybody's saying."

"Don't know what you're talking about," Rex replied.

"Seriously? It's all over the news."

"I don't watch the news."

"Oh. Well, I can't blame you for that. It's mostly shit lately."

"Shit all the time," Rex said.

He got the first tire off, and he rolled the new one over and had it attached in a few minutes. He lowered the car, then got ready to do the second tire. He went around to the opposite side, and the owner followed, as if Rex couldn't be trusted to do the job alone.

"Guy looks guilty to me," the man went on.

"Who?"

"This lawyer."

"Yeah?"

"Yeah, look at those eyes. Creepy, huh?"

The man held his phone in front of Rex's face. Rex had no choice but to stare at the screen, where he saw a photograph of a man with curly blond hair, a narrow pale face, and blue eyes that looked like something out of a zombie movie.

"Creepy," Rex had to agree.

He focused on the lug nuts again, which were just as tight on this side of the Subaru. He sweated as he worked and found that he had to use his boot on the wrench to get extra leverage. Finally, he got the first nut off. The others usually came faster. He repositioned the wrench, but he found that he was distracted, and he wasn't really sure why.

Then he realized that the photograph of the lawyer kept hanging in his mind. The hair. The blank expression. And yeah, especially those eyes.

"Can I see that guy again?" Rex asked.

The driver glanced down at him. "Who, the lawyer? Sure."

He put the phone back in front of Rex's face, and Rex let go of the wrench and squinted at the picture. He got so close to it that his nose practically brushed the screen.

"Yeah, that's him," Rex said.

"What do you mean? That's who?"

"I did a job for that guy last weekend."

The Subaru owner did a double take. "This guy? Gavin Webster?"

"Yup. Flat tire, just like you. Small world, huh?"

"I guess." The driver squatted in front of Rex and gave him a curious look. "Where was this? Where did you see him?"

Rex rocked back and wiped his brow. "Some dirt road near Island Lake. Took me forever to find him, because there's nothing but trees up there."

"What was he doing out there?" the man asked.

"Don't know. He didn't tell me, I didn't ask. I mind my own business. But I live in an area like that. Lotta strangers come down our road. Most of the time, it's because they're dumping something they don't want anybody to find."

15

"Who's next?" Maggie asked Guppo impatiently.

Max checked the roster of Gavin Webster's clients he'd downloaded from court records. They'd already made the rounds to a dozen men throughout the afternoon, looking for connections to Broadway and for faces that twitched when they asked about a stolen boat abandoned on the Wisconsin side of the Saint Louis River. So far, they hadn't found anyone Maggie considered a suspect.

"His name's Hink Miller," Guppo said.

"Hink? You mean Hank?"

Guppo shook his head. "Nope. The charges list him as Hink."

"What kind of a name is Hink?" Maggie asked irritably.

"What kind of a name is Guppo?" Max replied with a chuckle.

"Yeah, all right. What's the deal on this guy?"

"We arrested him for assault in a downtown parking ramp last year. Some guy backed out of a spot and dinged his old Ford Taurus, and Hink took it badly. Put the guy in the hospital. Gavin was the lawyer, and Hink walked, charges dropped. The victim developed memory problems, and the county attorney didn't think she could make the case. Thing is, Hink's employment history includes a lot of work as a bouncer, arena security, tough-guy stuff."

"Sounds like someone Broadway might have on the payroll," Maggie said.

"Exactly. The last known address we have is a third-floor apartment on 2nd Street on the hill over the courthouse."

"Okay. Let's go."

Maggie gunned her Avalanche along Highway 2, heading back to the city. As she drove, a loud crunch of gravel rumbled from under her tires as she veered accidentally onto the highway shoulder. Guppo cleared his throat to alert her, and she steered back into the lane, overcorrecting across the yellow line and prompting a horn blast from an oncoming truck. Maggie didn't hide the fact that she was a terrible driver. She'd totaled more than one Avalanche already, and her current model looked like she'd been driving in Beirut rather than Duluth. Stride and Serena refused to drive with her, but Guppo never seemed concerned.

"How's Troy?" he asked her.

Troy Grange was the health-and-safety manager for the Duluth Port and also Maggie's on-again, off-again boyfriend. The off part was primarily her fault, not his. He'd asked her to marry him two years earlier, and she'd said no. Then she'd had a brief affair with a Florida detective named Cab Bolton, who was as tall and suave as Troy was lumpy and short. That definitely hadn't helped their relationship. But to his credit, Troy kept coming back into her life, and she was running out of excuses to push him away. She couldn't say she loved him, but she'd never really loved anyone other than Stride, and that affair had crashed and burned as quickly as they both had known it would.

"Troy's fine now," Maggie said.

"Now?"

"Well, he had a little problem last month. I'm not sure he'd like the word to get around."

"Come on," Guppo prompted her, obviously smelling dirt.

Maggie glanced away from the road, and Guppo reached over and grabbed the wheel to straighten it as the truck swerved. "You know how they say to contact a doctor if you're still ready for action after four hours?"

"Uh-oh," Guppo said.

"Yeah. So he and I had a good morning. A really good morning. Three times worth of good morning, and he was still ready for action. When he hit five hours, we went to the ER. Trust me, you haven't lived until you've seen a cute little twentysomething nurse use a big-ass needle to drain the blood out of your boyfriend's dick. It's kind of like watching one of those Macy's parade balloons deflate."

She pantomimed with her index finger slowly toppling, and Guppo gave a little shiver. "That's an image I'll never get out of my mind," he said.

"You asked."

"At least it sounds like you guys are still together," Guppo added.

"Yeah, we're still together. Despite my best efforts."

Maggie kept driving. They reached the city a couple of minutes later, and she screeched to a stop at the red light across from Miller Hill Mall, nearly rear-ending a city bus. A uniformed police officer in a squad car pulled up in the lane next to them, glanced over with a grin, and made the sign of the cross at Guppo. Maggie responded by lifting her middle finger.

As they started up again on the green light, Maggie said, "You mind if I ask your advice about something, Max?"

"Go ahead, but isn't Stride your Ann Landers?"

"Not this time. It's about Serena."

Guppo glanced at her with surprise, and words burbled out of his mouth. "She told you about that? Aw, jeez. Look, it was a reflex. The house was dark, and she didn't realize it was me."

"What the hell are you talking about?"

"Um, what are you talking about?" Guppo asked.

"About her walking off with the damn dog."

Guppo frowned. "Oh. Yeah. The dog."

"What am I missing, Max? What did Serena do?"

"It's nothing. Don't worry about it. I told her I'd keep it to myself."

"Max, spill it," Maggie snapped.

"Okay, okay. Look, it wasn't a huge deal. She didn't hear me call out to her when I got to the Webster house. I went upstairs, and she—well, she drew her gun on me."

Maggie pounded the steering wheel. "Fuck, fuck, fuck!"

"She wasn't going to fire," Guppo insisted. "Come on, we've all made worse mistakes at one time or another."

Maggie bit her lip hard and didn't say anything more. Sergeant Maggie would have unloaded on Guppo for not telling her, but Lieutenant Maggie tried to keep a stranglehold on her tongue, rather than blame the messenger. Serena was the problem, not Guppo. She also knew Guppo was sweet on Serena and would do just about anything to protect her. But this was a disaster.

She kept a rein on her temper for another ten minutes, until they got to the small apartment building on 2nd Street. With a squeal of her brakes, she bumped over the curb and parked three feet onto the sidewalk. After she jumped down to the street, she slammed the door hard behind her and didn't wait for Guppo. She went and jabbed her finger repeatedly into the buzzer for the third-floor apartment.

A woman's whiny voice blared back over the intercom. "Who is it? Lay off the goddamn buzzer, will ya?"

"Police. We're looking for *Hink*."

"Who?"

"HINK!" Maggie shouted. "How many Hinks do you know?"

"There's nobody here with a name like that."

"His name's right on the damn label on the damn buzzer," Maggie insisted. "Hink Miller."

"Well, he must have had the place before me. I only moved in last month."

"Do you know where he went?"

"Not a clue. Never met him."

Maggie heaved a sigh. Next to her, Guppo was already running searches to locate a new address for Hink Miller. Before he could find anything, however, a window slid open on one of the first-floor apartments, and a skinny man in a white T-shirt leaned outside. He had a can of Bent Paddle in his hand. His face was freckled, and he had wiry hair the color of sand.

"You looking for Hink?"

Maggie nodded. "Yeah. You know where he is?"

"Moved out," the man said. The expression on his face didn't look sorry that Hink was gone.

"How about where he works?"

"He does security gigs mostly. Nothing permanent. Any place where they need muscle."

"Well, do you have any idea where we can find him? Where did he move to?"

The man shrugged. "I don't know the address, but I think he's over in Wisconsin now. His mother had a stroke, so he lives with her. She's got a little house just off the highway south of Superior."

* * * * *

For most of her life, Serena had never believed in premonitions, or intuition, or a sixth sense. She was too practical for things like that. She'd never believed in God, either, not after the things God had let happen to her in Phoenix. But over the past few years, she'd begun to wonder if it was arrogant to think that there was nothing else to the world but what you could see with your eyes.

A couple of years earlier, she'd met an actress named Aimee Bowe who claimed to be psychic. Serena had dismissed the idea as foolish. And yet when Serena had been hunting for Aimee after she'd gone missing, there had been a mental connection between them that Serena couldn't rationally explain. She'd felt Aimee reaching out to her. Guiding her. The only word that fit was *telepathy*.

Then there had been Stride's surgery. Serena, who never prayed, had prayed that day as if God were real. When Stride lived, she told herself it was the skill of the doctors that had saved him and nothing more. And yet, deep down, she couldn't help but wonder.

As Serena drove down the Point, exhausted and confused, she had another premonition, but this time it was of dark things coming. A bad moon rising. She didn't doubt her instincts for a second. She looked over at the dog in the passenger seat and knew their time together had come to an end. And she knew that, without him, she would be heading over a precipice.

"I'm sorry, Elton," Serena told him. "They're going to take you away from me."

He seemed to understand her because he bumped his face against her arm repeatedly until she took one hand off the wheel to pet him.

When she got to their cottage on the lake side of the Point, she saw a slick, expensive SUV parked outside, and she had no doubt that the truck belonged to Dale Sacks. She pulled into the driveway and put her arms around Elton, and she held him silently and kissed his head. Then she attached the leash to the dog's collar and brought him into the house through the back door.

In the living room, Jonny stood by the stairs that led to the unfinished attic. He was in hushed, intense conversation with Dale Sacks, who sat on the red leather sofa. She knew perfectly well that Jonny was trying to convince Dale to give Serena more time with the dog, and she knew equally well that Dale was having none of it.

When the man spotted Serena and Elton, he bolted to his feet, his face red with rage. He swore at her, and that made Jonny take a step toward him, his attitude calm but menacing.

"I know you're upset, Mr. Sacks, but do *not* talk that way to my wife."

"It's okay," Serena murmured to Stride. "He's right."

She squatted next to Elton and held the dog's face. "You have to go home now, sweetie."

"*Sad*," Dale Sacks commanded, snapping his fingers. "Over here. With me, right now."

Sad Sacks. Serena still couldn't believe this son of a bitch would name their dog Sad. She patted Elton's backside and whispered, "Go on. It's okay. You need to go with him."

Elton whimpered and refused to move.

"*Sad!*" the man shouted, but his command had no effect.

Serena stood up and used Elton's collar to pull the dog to his feet. With the leash, she dragged him across the room against his will, and then she handed the end of the leash to Dale Sacks.

"I apologize for my behavior," Serena said calmly.

Dale swore at her again, and Elton growled, and Stride looked ready to throw a punch.

"Elton, you need to go with him," Serena told the dog.

Dale yanked on the leash, but Elton dropped back on his hindquarters and refused to stand up. The man grew exasperated. "Do I have to carry you? I'll fucking carry you if I have to."

Serena caressed the dog's head and pointed at the front door. "You can go, Elton. It's okay. You need to go."

And then to Dale Sacks: "I expect you to treat him better. Is that clear? Animal control will be following up with you."

"Fuck off, you crazy bitch."

Serena had to stand in front of Jonny and hold him back.

Elton whimpered again, but now he let Dale pull him across the room. The front door was partially ajar, and Dale and the dog disappeared through it, and the man slammed the door behind them. His footsteps thumped down the porch, along with the scratch of Elton's paws. Serena didn't move at all, but she grimaced when she heard the dog howl in grief from the front yard. It made no difference. She stared at the windows, saw the headlights of the SUV shine to life, and saw the U-turn as it drove away toward the lift bridge. Elton was gone.

"I'm sorry," Jonny apologized. "I did everything I could. I offered him any amount of money to let you take him."

"I know."

"We can get you another dog. We'll go to the Humane Society; we'll find you a rescue dog."

Serena shook her head. "No."

"What can I do? Tell me what to do. Tell me what you need."

"There's nothing you can do, Jonny."

She turned around and headed to the rear door of the cottage.

"Where are you going?" he asked.

"Out. I need to be somewhere else."

"Let me come with you."

"I want to be alone," Serena said.

"I'm sorry about Elton," he repeated.

"There's nothing for you to be sorry about. I knew it would end this way."

"Serena, stay here with me. You shouldn't be alone feeling like this."

She couldn't keep the edge out of her voice. "How do you think I feel, Jonny? Tell me."

That was cruel.

Cruel to put him on the spot. Cruel to show him how little he really knew her.

He spread his arms wide, looking more helpless than she'd ever seen him. "Lonely. Abandoned. Heartbroken. I don't know if you won't open up to me. How do you feel?"

"I don't feel anything, Jonny," Serena answered in a robotic voice, which she knew was like turning a knife into him. "Nothing. I don't care about anything. I don't care about anyone. Not me. Not you. I really don't know what the hell I'm doing in this world. I might as well be dead."

16

"Are you laughing, Samantha?" Serena said aloud. She found herself waiting for an answer, but her mother didn't give one.

"I bet you think this is pretty funny. All these years later, and you can still totally mess up my life. I never took that power away. I never figured out how to protect myself. I'm sure you like that. Everything was all about you when I was a girl, and somehow it still is."

Serena sat on a bench in Enger Park, with the nighttime lights of Duluth spread out below her. The evening breeze had turned cool. No one else was around, but the wind rustled loudly through the brush. She felt numb, not conscious of time passing. She'd lost track of the hours she'd been here.

A bench. That was appropriate.

They'd found Samantha stretched out on a bench, her heart stopped. The police had sent her a picture because they needed someone to identify the body. It had taken Serena hours to gin up the courage to open the image and look at it. The years hadn't been kind to Samantha, but it was definitely her. The lush blond hair had turned gray. Her pretty skin had grown blotchy and wrinkled and sunken against the bones of her face. Her eyes were closed, hiding the electric emerald green. Her mouth held no smile, and that was strange because Serena couldn't remember a time when Samantha hadn't been smiling. No matter the situation, Samantha smiled, no teeth showing, just a little bend of the lips. She smiled at the good. She smiled at the bad. She smiled when Blue Dog was stripping her teenage daughter naked and taking her to bed. She smiled when Serena told her she was pregnant and needed an abortion.

Seeing her dead body, Serena had still expected a smile, but apparently, even Samantha couldn't bluff her way out of that one.

"I walked out on Jonny tonight," Serena went on. "Somehow I chose you over him. Amazing. What the hell is wrong with me? That's why I cut you out of my life, you know. I have no willpower when it comes to you. If you snapped your fingers, I'd go running back to your side. I hate the control you have over me. I hate it. I've spent decades trying to break the chain, and I still can't do it. Is this your last joke, Samantha? You want to bring me with you wherever you are? I can see you looking back and crooking your finger. *Come on, sweetheart. It'll be fun, just us girls, just like the old days. No boys allowed.*"

Serena swore out loud and tried to sort through the chaos in her head.

Her first instinct was to run away. That was what she'd done years ago. Her friend Deidre had been with her during that horrible, horrible abortion and in the days she'd spent bleeding at the hospital afterward. As soon as they released her, she and Deidre had run away to Las Vegas. No call to Samantha, no way for her or Blue Dog to follow them. Cut the cord, leave everything behind.

Run.

That was how she'd survived the first time. If she hadn't run, she would have died in Phoenix. She'd already started drinking, already started doing cocaine. She was becoming a miniature version of Samantha, the black-haired yang to her mother's blond-haired yin. If Serena had stayed, she'd be the one who was dead. Stretched out on a bench. Samantha, standing over her. Smiling.

Yes, she could run again. Leave Jonny. Leave Duluth. Leave everything behind. She could steal Elton from the Sackses and put the dog in the Mustang, and then she could drive away and never come back.

But it didn't matter how far she ran, or where she tried to hide. Samantha would always find her.

Her chest swelled as she inhaled slowly. She held it, then exhaled, counting to ten at each stage. Her therapist, Alice, had told her to soothe herself with breathing exercises when the stress came.

She did it several more times, and then she said out loud, "I will not run."

Okay.

But she felt as if her soul had broken in two. She stood on one bank of a river, nothing but a cold, empty shell. An orphan. On the other side of the river was her whole life, her marriage, her friends, the people she loved, her happiness, her sanity. While she'd had Elton with her, she'd felt as if there were a tiny little bridge across the river, just wide enough for her to walk with the dog. But now the bridge was gone. Now she had no way to get back to the person she wanted to be. No way to get back home.

Her phone rang, disturbing the quiet and shattering her edgy nerves. The phone was sitting on the bench beside her, and the screen lit up. The caller wasn't Jonny, or Cat, or Maggie, or Guppo. They'd all tried, and she'd ignored their calls. Of all people, Curt Dickes was calling her. She thought about ignoring it, but she closed her eyes and then grabbed the phone.

"What do you want, Curt?"

"Ouch," Curt replied. "In full bitch mode tonight, I see."

"Believe me, you do not want to see me in full bitch mode."

"Fair enough, fair enough. I'm actually calling to cheer you up."

"How?"

"Information!" Curt replied happily. "I have dirt. A break in the case."

"What is it?"

"No, no, no, first you have to say please. Pretty please, with sugar on top."

"Curt, I am not in the mood for this shit."

"Wow, you are definitely crabby. Little tiff with the Stridemeister?"

"*Curt.*"

"Okay, fine, but you owe me big. Seriously big. Remember you asked me to keep an ear to the ground for people passing hundred-dollar bills?"

Serena was immediately alert. "What did you find?"

"See, now you're interested. 'Please, Curt.' That's all I want to hear. Come on now, let me hear you say it. 'Puh-leez, Curt.'"

"Please," Serena hissed in annoyed surrender.

Curt chuckled. "There now, that wasn't so hard. Anyway, yes, I did exactly what you asked and put the word out about C-notes. Made sure everyone in the Big Dickes network was clued in. I got a text a few minutes ago from a buddy of mine who works behind the bar at a joint on Grand. He said he pulled a breakfast shift at one of his other jobs, and a guy there paid him with a crisp hundred-dollar bill. My buddy didn't want to make change and asked if he had anything smaller. So the guy opened up his wallet, and that was all he had inside. Hundreds. Lots of them."

* * * * *

It was almost midnight when Serena got to the bar, which was located in a downscale stretch of the Denfeld neighborhood in West Duluth, not far from the high school. The place was small and nothing to look at, with cutouts of sports players hung on the aluminum siding like decals and neon beer signs glowing in the handful of tiny windows. The door was open, letting out noise from inside, and a few smokers lingered on the sidewalk. The bar was still crowded. It was Saturday night, and motorcycles and cars were parked on the street and in the asphalt lot in the back. The neighborhood around the bar was an odd mix of worn-down houses and commercial businesses. A funeral home. A shoe store. An insurance agency. An old garage. Down the street was a thick dark line of trees.

Serena parked on Grand and got out of the Mustang, but she didn't cross the street immediately. She tried to remember why this place felt familiar to her. She'd never been inside, but she knew the name. Then she realized that the location had come up on a previous case. She had a memory of seeing the bar listed on a victim's credit card receipts and of noting in her police file that this was a hangout she should investigate. But she never had. Now she couldn't even recall what the case was.

She crossed to the bar and entered through the open street door. It was a small place, with walls paneled in light oak and a stubby counter that accommodated half a dozen stools. All of the stools were taken, and almost forty people filled the rest of the space and occupied the high-top tables. They held fruity cocktails, mugs of beer, and glasses of wine. The bar featured the usual accoutrements: pool table, pull tabs, dartboards, televisions hung in the corners, big-ass swordfish on the wall. She'd been in bars like this many times when she was younger, and the atmosphere rushed back to her as if she were a teenager in Las Vegas again. The voices, the laughter, the music, the low light and shadows, the clinking of drinks, the anonymity mixed with the intimacy of strangers—it was like going back in time. When she and Deidre had run away, places like this had felt like home to them. They'd gone there to fake their age for drinks, pick up men, and find beds for the night.

Her mind flashed a warning, like one of the neon signs on the bar walls. This was a bad place for her to be right now. But she ignored it, because she didn't care. She felt the hunger for a drink on her lips, and she was tired of saying no, tired of shutting off who she was, tired of the battle.

Samantha was right there next to her. Smiling. *You know you want it.*

One of the men at the counter gave up his stool. Serena slid onto the warm seat and took his place. She was alone and attractive, and the men all noticed her. So did the women. Even the younger ones shot her unpleasant stares, as if new female competition wasn't welcome. It made her feel good. It made her feel not forty-three years old for a while.

The bartender noticed her, too. He was younger than she was, no more than his midthirties, and he had a tall, lean physique and a very handsome face. He wore his thick, wavy brown hair combed back on his head and short on the sides. His eyes were dark brown, his nose pointed and slim, and he had a long face with a smooth, dimpled chin. He wore a crew-neck T-shirt that fit him like a second skin, revealing muscled arms and a taut stomach. It was warm inside the bar, and his skin had a faint glow of sweat.

"What can I get you?" he asked.

He propped his elbows on the varnished counter and leaned closer, ostensibly to hear her over the noise, but she knew his real goal was to get his face nearer to hers. She didn't mind. She found herself liking the attention. His smile was wide and confident, and the arch of his thick eyebrows gave him a devilish sexiness. One diamond stud glittered in the lobe of his left ear.

"Are you Jagger?" Serena asked.

The bartender rocked back and studied her with surprise. "I am. Who are you?"

Serena flipped the lapel of her leather jacket to reveal her badge pinned to the pocket. She saw a faint shadow of worry cross his face. Every innocent person saw the badge and wondered what they'd done, but the bartender recovered quickly. His cocky smile returned.

"You're a cop, huh? I like the look. You've got that Mariska Hargitay vibe going on."

Serena refrained from pointing out that Mariska Hargitay was fifteen years older than she was. "Serena Stride," she told him. "Curt Dickes gave me your name. He says you may have some information that can help us."

Jagger chuckled. "You know Curt, huh? Lucky you."

"I don't think I'd go that far."

"Yeah, he's one of a kind, that's for sure."

"Do you have a few minutes to talk?" Serena asked.

He looked around the bar with a frown. "Somebody called in sick, so I'm the only one back here, and it's still pretty crazy. Tell you what, we close in about an hour. Can you wait until then? At that point, I'm all yours."

"Sure, I can wait," Serena said, because she had nowhere else to go.

"Let me get you a drink of something. On the house. Even cops can drink on Saturday night, right? You look like a cosmo girl, and believe me, I make a hell of a good one."

Serena closed her eyes for a moment, absorbing the atmosphere of the bar. The memories of Las Vegas, of hot nights off the Strip, blew through her like sand on the breeze. Her breath caught in her chest. And just like that, she was gone. Done. No hesitation, no regret, no self-doubt. She'd already known when the day began how it would end. What scared her was how easy it was to throw away years of sobriety, to accede to years of want and temptation. It felt natural, normal, right, as if the last time she'd been drunk was yesterday, and it was no big deal. She could feel how the glass would fit in her hand. She could hear the clink of the ice and smell the scent of lemon like a breath from a California grove. And then the vodka would be cold and smooth sliding into her chest, and all her pain would be banished.

Jagger watched her, as if he could hear some unspoken dialogue going on in her head. "You okay?"

"I'm fine. Give me an Absolut Citron. Two ice cubes."

"Lady knows what she wants."

"Yes, she does."

She watched him walk away like some kind of man-god in his tight shirt and jeans. He grabbed a lowball glass, dropped in exactly two ice cubes. He was a man who knew drinking, knew what customers wanted. His hand reached for the thick Absolut bottle, gave it a little Tom Cruise twirl, and drew it back high over the glass as alcohol spurted from the stainless steel pourer. Serena almost moaned at the sight of it. And then he brought it to her, and his fingers grazed hers as he put it in her hand. The whole experience had a sexual power that felt like electricity exploding in a shower of sparks.

The glass, the liquid, the ice, caught the light. She swirled it. She let it waft into her senses.

6,608.

That was the number. She glanced at the clock on the bar wall and saw that it would be midnight in ten more minutes. One more day. One more number. One more night without a drink. But this time she wasn't going to make it. There would be no upward click to 6,609. This was the night she'd known was coming sooner or later, the night when nothingness won, but it felt so good to have the drink in her hand that she wondered why she'd denied herself this pleasure for so long.

She brought the glass to her lips and took her first cold, strong, blissful sip. Time melted away, and just like that the new number of the night was in her head.

Zero.

17

Serena had forgotten how high the high was. How amazing it felt. After one drink, which took her no more than a minute or two to finish, she felt as if a lake wave had washed away all of her cares. Relaxation spread through her body, made her skin tingle, made her happy. She felt strong. Confident. She pointed a finger at the man named Jagger, and he read the desire in her face and brought her another drink, which disappeared just as quickly.

The third drink made the second seem distant and far away. The fourth brought a smile that was as wide as the bartender's. That was the insidious thing. She'd always been a cheerful drunk. There were those who got angry, or morose, or foolish, or numb, but alcohol unlocked Serena. She saw the world more clearly, with a kind of twenty-twenty vision into the recesses of her soul. She'd never felt better or more in control than when she was drunk to the point of oblivion. It was only when the alcohol wore off that she crumbled into nothingness, and cried, and shrank, and screamed. Her head would split open; her stomach would turn over, and she'd wake up covered in her own vomit. But that prospect seemed so far off, so unlikely, so impossible, that she couldn't worry about it. What mattered was right now, and Serena felt incredible.

"What kind of a name is Jagger?" she asked the bartender in a flirty voice, when it was one fifteen in the morning, and the bar was closed, and they were the only ones left inside. He was cleaning up, wiping down the counter with a towel, and she was watching her seventh drink float in front of her eyes.

"I'm a rolling stone," he replied.

"Yeah, right."

"Well, it's true, actually. I've lived in the same apartment in Duluth for about five years, but that's one of the longer times I've spent anywhere. Before that, I was in Boston. Before that, Amsterdam. Before that, Dubai. Before that, Auckland, Honolulu, Bali, a few other places. Before that, Wichita."

"Wichita?"

"Born and raised and quick to leave at eighteen."

"Why Duluth? Why not Helsinki or Barcelona or some new exotic place?"

"Why do you think?" Jagger asked, showing her his white teeth again.

"A girl."

He tapped a finger on his sharp nose. "Ding ding ding. Her name was Dayan. I met her in Amsterdam when our bicycles collided. I moved back to Boston with her, mostly to make her college girlfriends jealous, I think. Then I followed her to Duluth when she had some pipeline to protest. But she got bored of that and bored of me and moved on. I think she's in Alaska now."

"Bored of you?" Serena asked.

"I know, hard to figure, right?" Jagger replied with another grin. "I'm still deciding where to go next. For now, I kinda like it here. Anyway, that's the fun story of my name, but the real story is that I'm called Mick Galloway. Mick became Jagger during one long night with some punk band while I was in Jakarta, and the nickname stuck."

"You look like a Jagger," Serena said.

"So people say," he replied. "Plus, I do a mean 'Under My Thumb' on karaoke nights."

"I'll bet you do."

She tapped her empty glass again. Without any hesitation, he added two fresh ice cubes and refilled it from a newly opened bottle of Absolut Citron. He hadn't charged her for any of the drinks, which made her wonder if he had other forms of payment in mind. She had no intention of sleeping with him, but every drink made him even more handsome, and it was hard not to picture him naked. And hard.

"So Curt says you told him about C-notes," Serena said. She had the advantage and curse of being a functional drunk, able to pretend she was perfectly sober right up until the moment she passed out.

He noted the same skill and seemed impressed. "Back to business, huh? Yeah, that's right. Curt sent out a group text, me and like fifty other people. Said he was looking for somebody passing hundred-dollar bills."

"How do you know Curt?"

Jagger rolled his eyes. "Oh, he's a flake, but he's clued in, so I help him when I can. Welcome to the new economy, right? I have part-time hours at four, five places, plus the usual bartending gigs when I can get them."

"And the C-notes?" Serena asked.

Jagger eyed her curiously. "You want to tell me what this is about?"

"Sorry. Police business."

"Not even a hint?" he asked. "You have a lot of self-control for someone who's downed almost a whole bottle of vodka by herself."

"It's a gift. The C-notes?"

"Well, one of my part-time gigs is waiting tables at The Kitchen in Superior. I was in there first thing this morning, and one of the regulars was there. He ordered his coffee and chicken-fried steak like he normally does, and when I gave him the check, he passed me a hundred-dollar bill. Well, I hate breaking shit like that, so I asked him if he had anything smaller. He had this big grin and opened his wallet to show me, and I swear, he must have had ten C-notes in there, all crisp, perfect bills."

"Who is this guy?"

"No idea. All I know is his name. Hink Miller."

"Hink?"

"Swear to God. He moved into his mother's place south of Superior a few weeks ago. I guess he takes care of her. Since then, he's been in for breakfast most weekend days when I'm there. For all I know, he comes in the rest of the week, too."

"Is it usual for Hink to have a lot of cash?"

Jagger shrugged. "Well, he's not a big tipper, and most of the time, he pays with crumpled fives and tens. Hundred-dollar bills? No way."

"Did you ask him about it?"

"Sure. I said, 'That's some cool dough, Hink, where'd you get it?'"

"What did he say?"

"He said he did a job for a friend."

"What kind of job?"

"No idea," Jagger replied. "And no, I don't know who the friend would be. Like I said, it's not like I know Hink. He's just a big bruiser of a guy who likes chicken-fried steak, gravy on the side, hash browns with extra onions, and three eggs over hard."

"Hink Miller," Serena said.

"That's him."

"Do you know his address?"

"No, but I think the house actually belongs to his mother. Seems to me Hink said her name is Florence, but I'm not sure."

"Did Hink ever mention a man named Gavin Webster?"

Jagger's brown eyes narrowed. "I don't think so, but the name's familiar. Why do I know that name?"

"It doesn't matter. Does Hink ever come in with anybody else?"

"Not while I've been there."

"Okay. You've been a big help. I appreciate it."

"My pleasure," Jagger replied. "Do you need anything else?"

"No. Thanks. I need to go."

Serena began to slide off the barstool, but Jagger took her wrist with a gentle touch. His fingers were warm and firm. He lowered his voice and stared right at her. "Hang on, how are you planning to get home? Cop or not, I can't let you drive. You've had way too much."

"I'm fine," Serena protested, although he was right and she was in no condition to get behind the wheel.

"Hey, come on. You're too smart to do something stupid like that. If you get into an accident, your cop buddies will arrest me for letting you get on the road. You either need to call someone, or you need to sleep it off somewhere."

"I suppose you have a suggestion about where I should do that?" Serena remarked, meeting his eyes.

He laughed, a charming laugh. He swept a hand through his dark hair, and she noticed the muscles of his arms again. "Well, my apartment's just a couple of blocks away, but I don't think my girlfriend would appreciate you showing up. You don't have to go home, but you're not driving. You want me to call your husband? Or an Uber?"

"What if I promise I won't drive?" Serena asked.

"Alas, I don't listen to promises like that. Easily made, easily broken."

Serena stood up, not wobbling. She grinned at Jagger and spread both of her arms wide, then swung a finger toward her face with the intention of tapping the tip of her nose. Instead, she nearly poked out her right eye with a long, perfectly painted fingernail.

"Shit," she said.

Jagger was kind enough not to laugh. "What's your husband's name and number?"

She surrendered and gave it to him, and he wrote it down and grabbed his phone. Watching him, she flushed and felt hot with a wave of shame. She didn't want to face Jonny, didn't want him to see her like this, didn't want him to realize she'd fallen hard. She didn't even want him to meet Jagger and realize she'd been in a bar alone with a man who looked as good as this one.

"I'm going to wait outside," she said. "I need some fresh air."

Jagger made a beckoning motion with his fingers. "First, your car keys."

"You really don't trust me, do you?"

"You I trust. But not the Absolut."

Serena fumbled in her pocket and found her key ring. It took her several tries to separate the Mustang fob from the other keys she had, but eventually she slapped the fob on the bar. "I wasn't going to drive, you know."

"I know."

She stalked away from Jagger toward the front door of the bar. Fumbling with the doorknob, she let herself out onto the sidewalk. There was no traffic on Grand Avenue. The cool night air hit her face but did nothing to revive her. Her buzz gathered speed like a skier at Spirit Mountain, and she could feel her body and brain breaking into pieces. Her Mustang was parked across the street, and she thought about waiting for Stride inside the car, but then she realized it was locked and she didn't have her key anymore.

With her head hung low, she wandered down the sidewalk toward the corner. A potholed asphalt road dipped sharply as it led toward the thick line of trees. She bent over and steadied herself with her hands on her knees and her hair spilling forward. The pavement at her feet was overgrown with weeds pushing up through the cracks. A foul odor wafted from a nearby sewer grate, and she was afraid it would make her sick. She straightened up too quickly, feeling a wave of dizziness, and she turned her face to the sky, where the stars seemed to streak like comets.

She closed her eyes.

Opened them.

And that was when she saw the woman in the street.

The woman wasn't far away, maybe twenty yards. She looked to be about Serena's age, and she had messy, highlighted brown hair tucked behind her ear on one side and falling over her face on the other. She was short, with a bony figure emphasized by her skinny red jeans. Her dark eyes were wide and scared. Her skin was a ghostly shade of white, which made the river of blood that was going down her forehead stark and shocking.

The blood spread into a crimson pool at her feet.

Serena did a double take. It was as if the woman had come from nowhere. She saw the blood and shouted, "Hey, are you okay? What happened?"

The woman ran away toward the trees.

"Stop! Wait!"

Serena took a couple of steps, then swayed, lost her balance, and nearly fell. She squeezed her head with both hands as if she could squeeze the vodka out of her skull like juice from an overripe lemon. Ahead of her, the woman's hair flew, and her arms pumped as she disappeared down the short street. Serena shouted again—"Stop! I want to help!"—but the woman kept running without looking back. When she reached the trees, she plunged inside and disappeared.

Fighting her nausea, Serena followed in the darkness. She managed a stumbling half-run down the middle of the street. At the trees, she hesitated, seeing no sign of where the woman had entered the brush. She made her way forward through the weeds. The tree branches were still wet from the rain, and they soaked her clothes and covered her in damp leaves and scratched her face with sharp edges. She followed a rough trail. There was litter all over the ground: cans, bottles, cups, old tires, chunks of asphalt. On the other side of the trees, she came to a chain-link fence that surrounded the sprawling lot of the city's street maintenance facility. There was no sign of the woman.

"Hello! Are you there? Where did you go?"

Getting no answer, Serena climbed the fence. The metal was slippery, and she struggled to keep a grip. At the top, she fell hard on the other side and landed in mud. She got up and wiped herself off and studied the deserted lot. Puddles made lakes across the gravel. Piles of crushed rock, black dirt, and road salt rose like mountains, some with weeds growing out of them. There were plows and yellow maintenance trucks parked everywhere and a giant tent like an aircraft hangar. If the woman was here, she had many places to hide.

Serena listened but heard nothing. She called, "I'm with the police. It's okay. Where are you?"

Silence.

She walked out into the middle of the dark lot, but she was completely alone. There was no sign of the woman anywhere. Then it all caught up with her. Grief. Guilt. Alcohol. Loneliness. Unconsciousness came rippling toward her. She took two more steps, kicking up a cloud of silver dust, and made it as far as the slope of one of the heaps of crushed rock. Slowly, like a proud tree falling, her body slumped sideways to the ground.

* * * * *

Stride stared down at Serena. He felt his heart break. Her eyes were closed, her wet, dirty hair across her face, her clothes torn and muddy. While unconscious, she'd obviously vomited, and it was a good thing she wasn't on her back because she could easily have choked to death. He squatted next to her and stroked her face with the back of his hand. She didn't respond.

"Serena," he said softly.

When she was quiet, he shook her shoulder gently. "Serena."

Slowly, unhappily, she stirred. Her eyes fluttered. He watched her try to focus, and for a while, she didn't seem to recognize him in the darkness. He helped her sit up, and she wrapped her arms around her knees and buried her face between them and said nothing for a while. He sat down next to her.

When awareness finally dawned on her, she looked up and took note of where they were, but she refused to meet his eyes.

"I'm sorry," she said.

Stride didn't need an apology. "How are you?"

"Okay except for the axe someone buried in my head."

He gave a short, humorless laugh. "You scared the hell out of me."

"I know."

"What are you doing here?"

Serena seemed to remember something, and she tried to leap to her feet, but she fell back down against the rocks. He caught her and steadied her. "Take it easy. There's no rush. You're not ready to move yet."

"There was a woman," Serena said.

"A woman?"

"I saw her in the street. She was injured. Bloody. I followed her this way, but then I lost her."

"Do you know who she was?" Stride asked.

"No, I have no idea—" Serena began, but then she stopped. Confusion crossed her face, and her brow furrowed. She shut her eyes, wincing at what seemed to be a stab of pain. "Actually, that's not true. Now that I think about it, I recognized her face. I'd seen her before."

"Do you know where?"

She shook her head. "No, I don't remember. I can't place her. But I definitely knew her face."

"Was she hurt badly?"

"It looked that way. Blood was everywhere. I mean, it was pooling in the street at her feet. I think she'd been shot in the head."

Stride frowned as he stared at her. "Shot in the head? But she was walking around?"

"I know it makes no sense."

He let the silence stretch out. Then he said, "I didn't see any evidence of someone else around here. Definitely not anyone who was injured. I didn't see any blood on the street."

"I didn't imagine her, Jonny," Serena said.

Stride didn't challenge her, even though he was certain that she *had* imagined it. But for the moment, it didn't matter.

"How did you find me?" she asked.

"I dialed your number. I heard the phone ringing beyond the trees."

"You got my car keys from Jagger?"

He nodded. "I'll have someone pick up the Mustang."

"I suppose he told you—I drank. I drank a lot."

"I think I would have figured that out," Stride said.

She finally turned her head to look at him. She met his eyes, blinked, and looked away, but he took her chin and moved it back. Her face, her hair, was a mess. He leaned in and kissed her, tasting alcohol, sweat, mud, and vomit. She looked far away, lost, on a road that led nowhere. He had never seen Serena like this, and it worried him, because he didn't know how to deal with it. He was used to her being fierce and fearless, not broken, not exposed. Even knowing that Samantha had always been her weak point, he hadn't expected her mother's death to knock her off her feet like this. All those years after Phoenix, after all the abuse, and Samantha could still manipulate her daughter from the grave.

He wanted to ask Serena how to help, but he didn't think she knew, and he didn't think she would ask him for help even if she did.

Her face was inches away. Her green eyes looked solemn and self-aware.

"I'm falling apart, Jonny."

He pulled her head into his chest and put his arms around her. For now, that was all he could do. "I know."

18

In the morning, at police headquarters, Serena found herself taken off the Gavin Webster case for good. She didn't blame Maggie for benching her. A shower, fresh clothes, and mouthwash weren't enough to cover the aftereffects of the night. When she studied herself in the bathroom mirror, she saw what she looked like. There were dark sleepless circles under her bloodshot eyes. Her face looked pale, almost cadaverous. The fluorescent lights made her squint, her head throbbing. She wasn't drunk anymore, but she still felt drunk, as if the poison hadn't left her blood.

Stride wanted her to go home, but Serena knew if she left the station, she would go straight back to the bar in West Duluth and ask Jagger to keep pouring drinks for her, until she'd recaptured the bliss of letting go. That was how it always went. There was never just one zero night. Somehow she had to find a ledge to grab onto, something that would stop her from falling any further.

Maggie seemed to understand that, so she didn't force Serena off the job entirely. Instead, while Maggie and Stride left to find Hink Miller in Superior, Serena stayed behind at police headquarters, closeted in her cubicle. She took four Advil, but it didn't help the throbbing behind her eyes. She unwrapped and ate some dry crackers, but they tasted like dust.

Most of all, she thought about the woman she'd seen on the street. That woman had become an obsession for her.

Who was she?

It was true. Serena *knew* her. The face hadn't clicked in her mind right away; she'd only noticed the blood. But she'd seen that face before. Not in person and not recently. The woman wasn't someone she'd met, and that was what made it disorienting to see her on the street. Serena knew her only from photographs, from witness statements, from being in the woman's house, from seeing her bank statements and credit card records.

She'd seen that woman's face in a police file somewhere. Serena was sure of it. She had a mental block about the woman's name and what had happened to her, but she also had the sense that there was unfinished business between them.

Who was she?

She started by reviewing cold cases. She dug out the handful of files from her desk that were unsolved and stalled, lacking new evidence. Drug cases. Missing persons. One homicide involving a homeless person on the Lakewalk. She reviewed everything she'd gathered on the open investigations, looking for a photograph that matched the woman she'd seen, but she came up empty. And it felt like she was searching in the wrong place, because she didn't believe she would have forgotten someone who was part of her active caseload.

Next, she pulled up computer records of the other cold cases spread around the department. There were dozens of them, and even though she wasn't the lead detective, she would have gotten updates and seen pictures of victims and suspects at Maggie's team meetings. So maybe her mystery woman was hidden in one of those files. She went through them one by one. The Cray overdose, the Mathers home invasion, the Karpeles Museum theft, the Fallon hit-and-run, the threats sent to half a dozen local judges, the break-in at the DECC, the Palen disappearance, and more, until the brightness of the screen made her headache unbearable.

While she was in the midst of her research, Guppo stopped by her desk. He made no comment on how bad she looked—she knew Guppo always saw her through rose-colored glasses—and instead, he apologized profusely for letting the truth slip about the incident with the gun at Gavin Webster's house. Serena kissed his cheek and told him to forget about it. Gun or no gun, she would have been kicked off the case anyway.

Then she asked for his help.

Serena described the woman she'd seen on the street and asked if the details rang a bell with Guppo from any of their old cases. Max had a good memory for faces. He huffed a little, his breath smelling like cheese popcorn, and his eyes narrowed into a squint. Then he made her repeat the details.

"You actually *saw* this woman?" Guppo asked.

Serena hesitated. "Yes, I did."

She didn't want to believe what Stride suspected. She couldn't accept that she'd imagined the whole thing, that the image of the woman was nothing more than a drunken hallucination. But in the cold light of day, she really didn't know anymore.

"Then no," Guppo replied, shaking his head. "I can't place her."

Serena frowned. "It sounds like the description reminded you of somebody. Who?"

"Nobody you could have seen on the street," he said with a smile.

"Please, Max. Who?"

"Nikki Candis," Guppo replied. "Remember? Two years ago? This woman sounds exactly like her. Skinny red jeans and all. But obviously, it couldn't be her."

Nikki Candis.

Yes. Everything came rushing back as soon as Serena heard the name. The face. The photograph.

The body on the bed.

"Thank you, Max," she said.

"Sorry I couldn't be more help."

"No, you were. I appreciate it."

Guppo heaved his sizable girth out of the chair, gave Serena a strange look as if she were an angel with a broken wing, and disappeared toward his own cubicle. As soon as he was gone, Serena opened her desk drawer.

Not the open cases. The closed cases.

Nikki Candis.

She yanked out the thin file—there hadn't been much to investigate—and she opened the manila folder. Nikki's photograph was right on top. The photograph they'd taken when they found her. There was no doubt about it. The hair, the face, even the clothes down to those red jeans, were all the same. They matched the picture in her head precisely.

This was definitely the woman that Serena had chased into the trees last night.

But there was also no denying the fact that Stride was right. It hadn't been real. The image on the street, the pursuit into the woods, had been nothing but a dark fantasy dredged up by a bottle of Absolut Citron.

Nikki Candis was dead. She'd shot herself in the head.

* * * * *

Stride parked on the dirt road across from the house belonging to Hink Miller's mother. The house was quiet, and there were no signs of life inside. He kept an eye on the curtains, but they didn't move. There was a Ford Taurus parked outside the detached garage, and based on the tire tracks left in the mud, it had been driven sometime during the most recent rainstorm.

Next to him, Maggie checked her watch. Her knee twitched impatiently as they waited for the Superior Police to arrive. "Where the hell is Lance?"

"The judge needed to sign off on the warrant," Stride reminded her. "Let's face it, our probable cause is pretty thin."

Maggie shook her head. "Hink's a Gavin Webster client, and he was flashing a wallet full of hundred-dollar bills a few hours after the ransom payout. Plus he's got a history of assault. That should be enough."

"Depends on the judge."

"Lance is just making us wait," Maggie complained.

"Well, that's possible, too," Stride agreed with a smile. "You know Lance."

He lowered the window of the SUV. Cool October air blew through the truck, and a few dead leaves rolled toward them down the dirt road. Through the trees on his right, he saw the monuments of a quiet cemetery. As they waited, he glanced at Maggie. They hadn't talked about Serena or the events of the previous night or Maggie's decision to kick her off the Webster case. And Stride hadn't mentioned the woman on the street. He knew Serena was lucky not to be suspended entirely, but if Maggie suspected that Serena was having hallucinations, she'd demand a psych evaluation before letting her back in the building.

Maybe that was what Serena needed. Time and a couch.

Stride had gone through it himself. Over the summer, as he debated whether to return to the police, he'd visited with the department psychologist several times. She'd had to clear him to go back if that was his choice. Stride had never been a fan of sharing secrets with people closest to him, let alone with strangers, but he'd tried to overcome that. The shrink had asked about death and loss; and his late wife, Cindy; and Serena and Cat. She'd asked about being the lieutenant and about not being the lieutenant. Eventually, she'd told him that the only way he'd know if he was ready was by going back and seeing if he was ready. He'd asked her wryly how much she was billing the city for that insight.

She'd cleared him anyway.

He glanced in the rearview mirror of the SUV. Behind them, two squad cars from the Superior Police turned off Highway 35. Both vehicles pulled ahead of him and parked on the dirt road. Four cops got out: three men, one woman. Stride and Maggie got out, too, and one of the men waved a piece of paper in his hand like he'd just been awarded an Oscar.

"Got your warrant," Lance Beaton said. "You're welcome. It wasn't easy. The judge didn't like your hearsay report on the C-notes, and without that, let's face it, you don't have shit. But I pushed hard on the idea that we've got a kidnap victim who might still be alive."

Stride watched Maggie's face tighten with annoyance. She refrained from sarcastic retorts, which he considered an example of personal growth. They both knew the Superior detective well. Whenever they crossed the bridge from Minnesota to Wisconsin, Lance was their primary interdepartmental contact. He had a habit of taking credit on every break in every investigation. If they had to make arrests on the Superior side of the bay, news reports invariably played up the role of the Wisconsin detectives and downplayed the work done in Duluth. Stride had learned to ignore it, but Lance still managed to bring smoke curling out of Maggie's ears.

He was not yet forty years old, with thinning brown hair and a tall, slightly underfed physique that made his uniform look baggy. He had dark, straight eyebrows and a dark, straight mustache, as if his face had been highlighted by a whiteboard marker. His gray eyes had a fixed look that Stride described as *sleepy* and Maggie described as *vacant*. He never smiled, and Stride suspected that was because he wanted the world to see him as a Very Serious Cop.

"Was Hink on your radar before today?" Stride asked Lance.

"No. He's kept his nose clean over here, but that's only been a few months."

"Is there anything to tie him to the boat you found in Billings Park?"

"Negative, the boat was wiped clean," Lance replied. "No prints, no DNA. That was all in my report."

"Can we get on with this?" Maggie asked. She headed toward the front of the house but stopped when she saw that Lance's feet were still rooted to the ground. The other Wisconsin cops deferred to him and didn't move.

"What do you want us looking for in there?" Lance asked, his hands on his hips.

"First and foremost, Chelsey Webster," Maggie replied. "And send someone around back in case Hink does a rabbit."

Maggie didn't give Lance a chance to overrule her. She marched for the house again, and the Wisconsin detective took long strides to keep up with her. One of the other cops headed for the rear of the house, and Stride and the remaining two cops followed Maggie and Lance. They crossed the dirt road to the weedy lawn and approached the front porch, and as they did, wind gusted across the roof. Stride saw sheer curtains blowing from inside an open window.

When the breeze reached him, he caught an odor on the air and barked, "Stop."

Maggie looked back, her eyebrows arched. Then her nose wrinkled as she caught the smell, too. "Shit."

They both drew their guns.

Lance's brow furrowed. He hadn't figured it out yet. "What the hell?"

"Body," Maggie said.

She ran to the front door and pounded with her fist, and Stride made his way to the house's open window. As he got closer, the smell from inside intensified. He stayed to the side of the frame and watched the thin fabric of the curtain whip in and out like a ghost. He listened for movement, but heard nothing. With his gun in his right hand, he glanced into the living room, and at first, his eyes struggled to distinguish anything but shadows. Then he saw a shape on the floor, and a moment later, he noticed a figure slumped in a chair.

"We've got two bodies," he called. "A woman and a man."

"*Police!*" Lance announced immediately in a loud voice. "We're coming in!"

He signaled to one of his burly cops, and like a bull in a china shop, the cop threw his body against the door and crashed it inward in a shower of splinters. Lance went in first, gun level, and Maggie followed. Stride did the same, and a few seconds later, they were all standing with their hands covering their noses and mouths in the house's small living room. Two other cops began a room-by-room search.

The bodies had been dead for a while. An elderly woman sat in a rocking chair, her head down on her chest. She looked as if she could be sleeping, except for the ruby-red line of dried blood that stretched around the visible portion of her neck. On the floor, Stride squatted beside a heavyset man in a large pool of blood, multiple gunshot wounds to his chest and head. Shell casings were sprinkled around the hardwood floor. The killer hadn't bothered retrieving them.

Maggie looked down at the corpse. "Hink Miller."

"Somebody's been cleaning up loose ends," Stride said. "Making sure nobody's around to talk."

"How long do you think they've been here?"

"At least twenty-four hours."

The cop who'd broken in the door returned to the living room from upstairs. The lone woman on the Wisconsin team rejoined them at the same moment from the basement. They both shook their heads.

"There's nobody else in the house," the woman reported. "Also no sign that your vic was ever being held here."

Lance waved his hand toward the front door. "I want everybody out. I need to call the medical examiner and get a forensics team over here. Until then, I don't want anyone spoiling the scene."

Stride saw Maggie open her mouth to protest delaying a full search, but she closed it again without complaining. They both returned outside. On the front lawn, Stride studied the house, then walked around it, looking for anything out of place. Nothing caught his attention. The killer hadn't left obvious clues behind. When he returned to the front yard, he noticed that the side door of the detached garage was open. Maggie stood in the doorway, shining her flashlight inside. He joined her, and they examined the interior. There was winter plowing equipment and fertilizer stored there, but little else.

"Let's check the Taurus," Stride said.

They headed for the car that was parked outside the garage, its white paint and tires splattered with dried mud. Glancing through the windows, he saw empty food wrappers on the passenger seat and a sweatshirt crumpled on the rear floor. He opened the driver's door, and using the cuff of his sleeve, he popped the lever that opened the trunk. When they went to the back, Stride leaned forward, taking a whiff of the interior.

"Smell that?" he said.

Maggie leaned over the trunk and frowned. "Perfume."

"Yeah." He took out a pen and used it to drag a small plastic bag from the back of the trunk. It was torn open at the top and filled with plastic zip ties. Then he pointed at a few reddish drops on the trunk's shell. "That looks like blood to me."

"Chelsey was in here," Maggie concluded.

"That's my bet."

"But she's not in the house or the garage, so where the hell is she?"

Stride nodded. "And is she still alive?"

19

In May two years earlier, Serena had been called to a house in Proctor by uniformed officers responding to a 911 emergency. Outside, she'd found a fifteen-year-old girl named Delaney Candis sitting on the front porch in a state of shock. Inside, Serena had found Delaney's mother, Nikki, in bed, dead of a gunshot wound to her temple, a long-barreled Smith & Wesson revolver clutched in her hand. As death investigations went, it appeared open-and-shut. Suicide.

The question for Serena was why her drunken mind had conjured Nikki Candis outside the bar. Why *her*? She might have expected to see a vision of Samantha. Or Deidre. Or someone else from her teenage years, taunting her as she slipped back into her alcoholic past. Instead, her mind had resurrected a suicide victim, one of dozens she'd investigated in her career, from a case that had no real mystery.

At her desk, she reviewed Nikki's file, but there wasn't much to it. According to her daughter, Nikki had battled severe depression off and on for years. She was also a heavy drinker. She'd been divorced from Delaney's father since the girl was five; he was out of the picture and not part of their lives. Nikki had run a catering business, and although their house had a sizable mortgage, they didn't seem to be in serious financial jeopardy.

Delaney didn't know where Nikki had gotten the gun. Serena's research revealed that the gun had been stolen in Cincinnati years earlier, so it was likely that Nikki had bought it illegally. But there was no indication of when she'd bought it, or who she'd bought it from.

"Suicide," Serena murmured again.

There was nothing suspicious about the scene. She had no reason to think that Nikki's death was anything other than what it appeared to be.

Except Serena saw in the file that she'd written a note to herself two years ago: *Delaney isn't telling us everything.*

Had she missed something?

She'd wrapped up the investigation in three days. Three days. That was fast. She noticed a comment from Nikki's father that she'd circled in the file: *Something was bothering Nikki, but she wouldn't say what it was.* Normally, that was the kind of question Serena would want resolved before putting a case to bed. If something had been bothering Nikki, maybe that was what had forced her over the edge to kill herself. Or maybe it was something else entirely. Regardless, it was an open issue in the midst of a death investigation.

And yet Serena had let it go.

She closed the file, but she removed two photographs as she did and put them on the desk in front of her. One was the violent picture of Nikki, dead of the gunshot wound. The other was a picture that Delaney had provided of the two of them together. In that photograph, Nikki looked untroubled by depression. Mother and daughter had arms around each other's waists, both of them smiling. Nikki had golden-brown hair that matched Delaney's, and Serena could see the family resemblance in their faces. They were pointing at T-shirts they wore with the logo of Nikki's business: Catering by Candis.

Every suicide masked a complex family tragedy. This one wasn't any different.

Serena hadn't gotten pushback when she closed the case. Guppo had agreed with her. If she went back to him right now, he'd say what he'd said back then: *Suicide, case closed.* Stride had reviewed her findings, as he did on every case, and he'd asked no questions. It had been a busy time in the department, so she'd moved quickly. She and Guppo had been helping Abel Teitscher on the Fallon case, and a wrongful death investigation took priority over a suicide. She'd done what the circumstances required, and she'd made the right call.

But that wasn't the whole story. Not for her.

She stared at the pictures of Nikki Candis and tried to sort through what she felt about this woman. Her job was to shut down any emotional reactions to a case, but she'd failed to do that with Nikki. She remembered exactly how she'd felt, because the same emotion erupted as she picked up the file again. Anger. She felt angry at this woman. That was why she'd closed the case quickly, not because she was busy, not because it was open-and-shut, not because she'd answered all the questions. She'd wanted the case done, put away, over.

Because the life and death of Nikki Candis pushed too many of her own buttons.

Alcohol abuse. That was the first hot button. She remembered now why the West Duluth bar on Grand had felt familiar to her. It was all over Nikki's credit card records. She'd been a regular. There was also a note from a pastry chef who'd worked on catering jobs for Nikki: *She was a blackout drunk.* And another comment from a waiter: *When the party was over, she'd celebrate hard. Really hard.*

By itself, that didn't bother her. Serena was an alcoholic, too, so she didn't judge others who struggled with the same disease. No, what upset her was the toll it had taken on Delaney. Nikki had abandoned her daughter, not just by committing suicide, but by letting her demons overshadow her duties as a mother. Talking to Delaney, Serena saw everything she remembered from her own teenage years. Defensiveness. Denial. It was obvious to Serena that Nikki and Delaney had switched places in that household long ago. Mother became child. Child became mother.

Just like she and her own mother had done. Nikki and Delaney may as well have been reflections of Samantha and Serena. That was why she'd bailed on the investigation as soon as she could.

But reviewing the file reminded her that she'd felt *off* about the whole case from the beginning. Something was wrong about it. Something didn't add up.

Delaney isn't telling us everything.

Serena opened the file again and retrieved the phone number for Nikki's parents. They lived ninety minutes south of Duluth in the small town of Mora. She dialed the number, which rang for a long time before an elderly man answered.

"Hello?"

"Is this Paul Vavra?" she asked, using Nikki's birth name.

"Yes, it is." His voice had a raspy, solitary quality to it, as if talking to anyone was a bother to his day.

"Mr. Vavra, this is Serena Stride with the Duluth Police. I interviewed you and your wife two years ago after the loss of your daughter."

He was quiet for a while. Then he cleared his throat. "I remember."

"I'd like to ask you and your wife a couple of additional questions."

Again there was a long silence.

"My wife passed away last year," he said.

"I'm so sorry."

"Losing Nikki took the wind out of her."

"Yes, I understand."

"I'm not really anxious to revisit what happened, Detective. I'm trying to remember my daughter's life, not her death. It's taken me a long time to get to this point. Is there a reason you're bringing this up again now?"

Serena chose her words carefully. She certainly wasn't going to tell this man that she'd had a vision of Nikki outside a bar while she was dead drunk. "I'm going through some of my old case files. In reviewing the file on Nikki's death, it seemed to me that there were questions that I didn't fully answer."

"That's not how you felt two years ago," Paul said.

"Yes, I know."

"Two years ago, you couldn't shut down your investigation fast enough."

"You're right about that, and I apologize. If you'd rather not talk to me, I understand. But if I made any kind of mistake two years ago, I'd like the opportunity to rectify it. Back then, you and your wife were convinced that Nikki did not commit suicide. You told me there had to be some other explanation for what happened. I don't know whether that's true, but I'd like to find out."

She could hear the old man breathing on the other end of the line. She thought he might be crying.

"Nikki did *not* kill herself," Paul reiterated. "Nothing about that has changed in two years. I know what I know."

"If Nikki didn't kill herself, that means someone else killed her and made it look like suicide. When we talked, you didn't have any idea who could have done that, and you weren't aware of anyone who had a motive to harm your daughter. Is that still true? Or is there something more you can tell me that might help with the investigation?"

The man made a little sigh on the phone. "I can't imagine anyone who could have done this to Nikki. The whole thing makes no sense."

"I made a note during our original interview that you and your wife thought something was bothering Nikki in those last few days."

"Yes, that's true."

"Do you have any idea what that could have been?"

"I don't. We asked her about it. She shrugged us off, which was typical. She didn't open up about things to us. Nikki had a lot of problems, Detective, I won't deny that. We didn't always have the best relationship with her, because we thought some of her behavior put Delaney at risk."

"You mean the drinking?" Serena asked.

"Yes."

"How bad was it?"

"Very bad. She had a serious problem and didn't seem capable of dealing with it. There were times I'd have to go pick her up on a street somewhere. Or strangers would take her home and spend the night. A couple of times Delaney even had to go get Nikki by herself, even though Delaney was only fifteen and had no license. So no, we weren't happy about any of that."

The description gave Serena flashbacks of her own teenage life. Her own blackouts. And Samantha's, too. She remembered all the times she'd brought Samantha home herself, just like Delaney had done with Nikki.

Fifteen years old. No license.

A reflection in the mirror.

"However, Nikki being an alcoholic doesn't mean she killed herself," Paul Vavra went on firmly. "She would never have left Delaney alone. And even if that was what she chose to do, believe me, she would have found some other way to kill herself before she used a gun."

"Oh? Why is that?"

"Nikki *hated* guns. She was adamant about it. She didn't want a gun in the house because of Delaney."

"I don't recall your mentioning that when we talked two years ago," Serena said.

"Maybe I didn't, but you were halfway out the door the whole time, weren't you?"

"Yes. Again, I'm sorry. So you don't have any idea what was troubling Nikki before her death? She didn't say anything?"

"No."

"Did you talk to Delaney about it?"

"We asked once, but Delaney shut us down. She's a little like her mother that way."

"Do you think she knows?"

"I have no idea."

"According to my notes, Delaney was staying with you that weekend in May. Nikki was home alone in Proctor. Is that right?"

"Yes."

"Was there a reason Delaney was staying with you?"

"No. She did it a lot. My wife liked fussing over her granddaughter. I also think Delaney sometimes needed a little break from her mother. In some ways, Delaney was the adult in that house, and there were times when she needed an opportunity to be a child again. I suppose that makes no sense to you."

"Actually, it makes a lot of sense," Serena said.

"I'm afraid Nikki liked time alone, too. It was easier to drink that way."

"Did you talk to your daughter that last weekend? Or do you know if Delaney called home?"

"Not that I recall."

"How is Delaney?" Serena asked. "Does she still live with you?"

"No. She's a freshman at UMD. She has an apartment near campus."

"Really? My adopted daughter, Cat, is a freshman there, too. Delaney must be pretty young to be in college, though, isn't she?"

She heard a note of pride in Paul Vavra's voice. "Delaney is incredibly bright, as well as being a beautiful girl. She skipped fourth grade, so she's always been a year younger than her classmates. Even with everything she went through losing her mother, she never lost a step academically. We told her she could take time off, but she didn't want that."

"I remember thinking she was a special girl," Serena said.

"Yes, she is."

"Do you mind if I talk to her? I'd like to ask her some questions."

"Talk to her if you want, but I don't think she'll be very responsive."

"Why is that?"

"Delaney spent a lot of time getting past the death of her mother," Paul explained. "And then the death of her grandmother, too. She's known a lot of loss for someone so young. Her focus is on the future, not the past, and that's as it should be. She almost never talks about what happened to Nikki. In fact, she hardly ever mentions Nikki. But I suppose she still thinks about her mother, even if she pretends it's all behind her."

"Yes," Serena replied. "Yes, believe me, she does."

* * * * *

Lance Beaton looked like a cat who'd snatched a bird right off a tree branch. Stride watched the detective from Superior march toward them from Hink Miller's house, where Lance, a dozen of his officers, and the team from the Douglas County Medical Examiner's office had spent the last two hours examining the crime scene. Even without a smile, Lance's face boasted a whiff of self-satisfaction. He carried a paper grocery bag from Super One Foods, and his hands were covered by tight plastic gloves. There was no indication of what was in the bag.

"Lance found something," Maggie said with a groan.

"Yup."

"We're never going to hear the end of this."

"Nope."

"Look at him. He's got a hard-on."

"Mags."

"I'm serious. He's flying the flag. Do you know what the Superior cops call him?" She made a vulgar motion with her right hand. "Beatin' Beaton."

"Mags."

"How many Lance Beatons does it take to change a light bulb?" Maggie continued.

"Mags."

"Oh, come on."

Stride gave in and said, "How many?"

"None. You don't change a dim bulb."

Stride finally chuckled, and Maggie grinned wickedly.

"See? You missed me."

"I never said I didn't."

Lance crossed the dirt road to join them. The grocery bag swung in his hand, but he held it in a way that they couldn't see what was inside. Maggie shot a quick but obvious look at the cop's loose trousers and gave Stride a wink.

"Beatin'," Maggie whispered.

Stride had to choke back another laugh.

"I figured I'd give you two an update," Lance said.

"An update an hour ago would have been even better," Maggie replied.

"We were busy."

"Did you find any sign of Chelsey Webster?" Stride asked.

Lance shook his head. "No. Even if you're right that she was transported in the trunk of the Taurus, there's no evidence to suggest she was kept on the property. We searched the house, the basement, and the garage, and we had people go through the woods to look for any signs of a burying place. Your vic isn't here."

"What about the bodies?"

"The ME thinks they were killed sometime yesterday afternoon. The gun used on Hink was a 9 mm. When we recover the bullets, we'll feed them into the system and let you know if we get a match."

"Is there anything else in the house?" Maggie asked.

"We're going through Hink's computer, but so far, there's nothing but porn. We'll make copies of any electronic and paper records we find, since I assume you'll want all of that."

"Yes, we will," Stride said.

"Plus you can throw in the porn," Maggie added.

Stride smothered a laugh and waited for Lance to do the same, but the detective remained stoically immune to Maggie's sense of humor.

"Did you see anything that would link Hink Miller to Gavin Webster?" Stride asked.

"No, nothing."

"What about a man who goes by the name Broadway?"

Lance looked puzzled. "Broadway?"

"It's a nickname. We think he runs an illegal poker game near the docks in Duluth. Gavin Webster's part of it, and we'd like to know if Hink was, too. The word we got is that Hink did a lot of freelance security."

"If we find anything, I'll let you know," Lance replied.

Maggie gestured at the grocery bag. "So what's in there? You run out to Super One to get some Pop-Tarts?"

Lance still didn't smile.

"We found something hidden in a plastic garbage bag inside the salt reservoir for the water softener."

He made a show of snapping his plastic gloves. Then he reached inside the grocery bag and emerged with a small red child's backpack that was designed to look like a strawberry. It had a Hello Kitty face on the outside.

"Shit!" Maggie exclaimed. "That's the ransom bag."

"Did you look inside?" Stride asked.

Lance nodded. He delicately opened the zipper of the backpack and separated the flaps so they could see the interior. Stride expected multiple wads of cash, but instead, he saw only a single sheaf of bills held together with a rubber band. The outermost bill was a crisp hundred-dollar note.

"Are those all hundreds?" Maggie asked.

"Yes. We found Hink's wallet upstairs, too. There were a handful of C-notes inside, just like your witness said."

Stride frowned. "Did you count the cash?"

"We did. It comes out to eighty-nine bills or eight thousand nine hundred dollars. There was another nine hundred dollars in Hink's wallet, which puts him two hundred short of an even ten thousand."

Maggie looked at Stride. "*Ten* thousand? Gavin said the ransom was *one hundred* thousand."

Stride put on his own gloves and removed the band of bills from inside the backpack. He flipped through the stack to confirm they were all hundreds, and his face darkened. "Where's the rest of the money?"

20

"Do you know a girl named Delaney Candis?" Serena asked Cat.

The two of them stood next to Serena's Mustang in a parking lot across from the main library at UMD. Cat was eating a PowerBar, and she had a laptop bag slung over her shoulder. She wore shorts that highlighted her sleek golden legs and a maroon UMD hoodie over her torso. It was a cool, bright afternoon, and the nearby sidewalks were crowded with students and faculty.

A little smile crossed Cat's lips at the mention of the girl's name. "Oh, I know *of* Delaney, that's for sure. I bet she knows me, too."

"Why is that?"

"Our calculus prof posts everybody's tests scores online with a class ranking. She says competition makes us work harder. The first test, Delaney ranked number one, and I ranked number two. That pissed me off, so the next test, I studied my ass off and made sure I beat her out for the top spot."

"I take it she's smart?"

"Oh, yeah, she's really smart. I just want to prove I'm smarter."

"Have you met her?"

"No, but I tutor one of the guys in class. He's Delaney's boyfriend. Or he used to be when they were in high school. Sounds like they don't hang out anymore."

"Why is that?"

Cat shrugged. "Don't know, probably just a college thing."

"What's the boyfriend's name? The one you tutor."

"Zach Larsen. I'm pretty sure he likes me. That's why he asked me to help him. And he needs the help. Math is definitely not his subject."

"What about you? Do you like him?"

"He's okay, but he's just a kid," Cat said, which made Serena smile. "What do you want with Delaney?"

"It's an old case. I want to make sure I didn't miss something."

"You? Not likely."

"Well, there were special circumstances," Serena replied. "Anyway, I called Delaney, and she's supposed to meet me here. I figured I'd see how you were doing first."

"I'm glad you did." Cat finished her power bar and crumpled the wrapper. "Hey, I heard about the dog."

"Elton? Yeah. He went home."

"Sorry. Is there any chance you'll get him back?"

"I don't think so. The whole thing was just—I don't know what it was. My circuits got fried with Samantha dying, and Elton helped me through it. But that's over."

Cat gave her a look that said nothing was over. "You think Stride didn't tell me? Come on."

"Fine, okay," Serena admitted, feeling annoyed that she had to say it out loud. "I had a bad night."

"Um, yeah. No kidding. Have you called Alice?"

"I don't need a shrink."

"It sounds like you need something. Just call her."

"I don't need *you* acting like a shrink, either."

"Well, fuck that, I don't care! Who do you think you're talking to? Get pissed off at me if you want, but I get to be worried about you, all right? You did a cartwheel off the wagon, and the next day you're over here crapping around with old cases like nothing happened to you. What's that about?"

"This is my therapy," Serena told her.

"Sounds more like a river in Egypt to me," the girl muttered.

"*Enough*. Knock it off, okay?"

Cat didn't look satisfied, but in fact, Serena wasn't in denial about how bad off she was. Or at least, that was what she was telling herself. Working on this case did feel like the therapy she needed. Dealing with the death of Nikki Candis was her mind's way of dealing with the death of Samantha.

Two mothers, both of whom had failed their daughters.

Two daughters, both determined to protect their mothers. Regardless of the cost.

"What did Stride say when he found you?" Cat asked.

"He was very sweet, which bugged me."

"What a shock." Cat shook her head in exasperation. "What the hell is it with the two of you? Was I the only thing holding you together?"

Then the girl shrunk back, as if her temper had carried her too far. "Sorry. That was a shitty thing to say."

"Yeah. It was."

"Except I'm not wrong, am I?"

Serena wanted to scream at the girl, but she pushed down her frustration. With Cat. With Stride. But mostly with herself. It had a bitter taste.

"No, you're not wrong," she acknowledged wearily. "Jonny and I love each other, but we still don't know how to rely on each other. I know I should be turning to him for support, and I'm not. But it's not like he's asking me for help, either."

"Are you going to drink again tonight?" Cat asked.

Serena could have lied, but what was the point? "Probably."

"Just like that?"

"You asked for the truth, Cat," Serena snapped. "If you don't want it, don't ask, okay? I'm not *planning* to drink, but I know myself. I already want another drink right now. I want a dozen drinks right now. It's taking every bit of self-restraint I have not to drive straight to a bar from here. So I'm not kidding myself. Yeah, odds are, I'm going to drink tonight. I'm a big girl. I can make my own decisions. Even bad ones."

"You want me to go with you?"

"I definitely do *not* want that."

"I'd do it. I'd hold your hair back when you throw up."

"I know you would, but I'm not dragging you into my disease. Got that?"

Cat bit her lip, as if struggling to find something to say. "At least don't drive."

"I won't."

"If you can't call Stride, call me."

Serena softened. "Yeah. Okay."

Cat was about to head to the library, but Serena took her shoulder. "Hang on. One more cop question."

Cat smiled. "Sure."

"Curt says he solicits UMD girls to go to parties for money. Particularly for somebody named Broadway who runs an illegal gambling racket. Have you heard anything about that?"

"Yes," the girl admitted.

"I hear it's good money."

"Very good."

"Did Curt ask you to go?"

Cat's brown eyes flashed. "Yes."

"I'm going to tear him limb from limb," Serena said calmly.

"You don't need to do that. I said no. I told him if he asked me again, I'd cut him off for good. And maybe cut off other things, too."

"I may still kill Curt."

"Don't. He's not worth it."

"Have you heard anything more on campus about Broadway? Any rumors about who he is?"

Cat shook her head. "Only that he's someone you don't want to mess with. The girls say he comes across as mellow and cool when you meet him, but if you let him down, he's like January ice."

* * * * *

When nearly half an hour passed after Cat went into the library, Serena began to think that Delaney Candis had decided to skip their meeting.

Then she spotted a girl getting out of a blue Highlander SUV in the library parking lot, and she recognized Delaney from the investigation two years earlier.

The teenager had grown up in the time since then. She was very attractive, with a willowy build and slightly messy brunette hair down to the middle of her back. She wore a white-and-yellow blouse and what looked like a Ragstock skirt in a sunny shade of orange. Her brown eyes reflected a keen intelligence, so Serena wasn't surprised to hear that Delaney was in a battle with Cat for the top spot in class. In pictures, Serena had also seen the girl wearing a warm, magnetic smile. But looking at her now, she saw no smile, just nervous apprehension.

"Delaney, I'm Serena Stride," she said as the girl approached her near the red brick walls of the library.

"Yes, I know."

"I appreciate your meeting me."

"What is this about?"

"I've been reviewing the case file about your mother's death, and I have a few more questions."

"My mother died two years ago," Delaney said in a strained voice. "What other questions do you have? Why are you bringing this up now?"

Serena hesitated. Other students kept passing in and out of the library doors near them. "Do you mind if we go somewhere else to talk? This might be a little easier with more privacy."

"Fine. Whatever."

They headed down the sidewalk away from the library. Serena made small talk, but otherwise, they didn't say anything to each other. At the Swenson engineering building, they turned right and headed toward the university stadium. There was a large stretch of green grass near the stadium parking lot, and Serena led them there. The sun was high in the blue sky overhead.

Serena had been debating exactly what to say, but she decided to be honest with the girl about everything. There was something about Delaney that made her think she would respond better to the truth than to anything else.

"I want you to know something right up front," Serena told her. "I'm an alcoholic, like your mother was."

The surprise on Delaney's face was obvious. She hadn't expected a confession like that. "Oh. Okay."

"My own mother was an alcoholic, too," Serena went on. "She was also a cocaine addict. There's a strong genetic component to addiction, and I got the family disease. I've struggled with it my whole life. I hear you're very smart, so I assume you're smart enough to know that you're probably at high risk, too."

"I don't drink," Delaney said. "And I don't intend to start. No drugs, either."

"Good for you." Serena looked away, squinting into the sun as she figured out what to say next. "When I was a teenager, I ended up taking care of my mother most of the time. I did a lot of things to make her happy. Sometimes it meant being in abusive situations. It hurt me in ways I'm still dealing with today. Something tells me you faced similar things with Nikki."

"I loved my mother. I didn't mind helping her."

"I loved my mother, too. All I'm saying is, I have an idea where you're coming from."

"If you say so."

But Serena could hear hostility in Delaney's tone.

"My mother died a couple of days ago," Serena went on.

"I see. I'm sorry."

"Thank you. It knocked me off my feet to an extent I wasn't ready for. I didn't see it coming. I've been sober for a lot of years, but last night, I slipped up. I got very, very drunk at a bar in West Duluth. And outside the bar—I saw something. I don't even know how to explain it."

Delaney's brown eyes narrowed with curiosity. "What did you see?"

"I saw your mother. I saw Nikki. I know how that sounds, and believe me, I'm not saying it was real. It was just a hallucination."

"This was the bar on Grand Avenue?" Delaney asked.

"Yes."

A cynical shadow crossed the girl's face. "Well, if my mother was going to haunt anywhere, it would probably be there. That was her place."

Serena nodded. "Look, I don't believe in ghosts. I don't think that's what this was. All I'm saying is, my mind was sending me a message. I think the message was that I missed something when I was investigating your mother's death. That's why I decided to take another look at the police file. I've been through it in detail now, and there are some questions that I failed to answer properly. That's why I wanted to talk to you."

"I don't know what else I can tell you," Delaney said.

"Well, your grandparents thought something was bothering Nikki in those last couple of weeks before her death. Do you have any idea what that was?"

"Um, yeah, like she was thinking of killing herself."

"I get that, but was there anything else? You told me she'd suffered from depression for a long time, but when people actually make a decision about suicide, there's often a triggering event. Some kind of stress or crisis that pushes them over the edge. Can you think of something like that?"

Delaney's face reddened. "I don't want to talk about this."

Serena put her hands up in a kind of surrender. "Okay, let's put that aside. I promise, the rest of this won't take long. What about the gun she used? Did you know she had one?"

"No."

"Your grandfather was surprised that Nikki would have a gun in the house. He said she'd always been adamant that it wasn't safe."

"Well, it wasn't safe, was it?" Delaney snapped.

"Do you know where or when Nikki got the gun?"

"No. If I'd known she had it, I would have told her to get rid of it."

"Okay. There's something else. I found a reference to it in my notes when I was going back through the file. When I got to your house that day, there was a UPS package on the porch. We opened it as a matter of procedure, and there were two things inside that struck me as curious."

Delaney shrugged, as if she didn't remember the package. "What were they?"

"One was an angel figurine. It had the message 'I'm sorry' written on it. Do you know why Nikki bought that?"

"No."

"Do you know who it was for?"

"I assume she wanted me to have it after she was gone. After . . . what she did."

"Did you keep it?"

"No, I threw it away."

"Okay," Serena replied, but she found that answer surprising. "The other item in the package was a set of deer whistles. You know, like you attach to your car. Apparently, they give off a high-frequency whistle, and it's supposed to deter deer from crossing in front of you."

"Yeah, so? Mom hit a deer years ago. She was paranoid about them after that."

"It just seems like an oddly practical item to be purchasing two days before you kill yourself."

"I don't know what to tell you," Delaney said. "I really don't know why you're asking me any of these questions."

"I guess I want to make one hundred percent sure that your mother's death was what it appeared to be."

"What else could it be?"

"Your grandparents were convinced that Nikki didn't kill herself," Serena said. "The fact is, from a forensic standpoint, the medical examiner couldn't rule out the possibility that someone put the gun in your mother's hand. My investigation declared her death a suicide, and I just want to be certain I didn't make a mistake."

"You didn't."

"Are you sure? Can you think of any reason someone might have wanted to harm your mother?"

"No." Delaney's voice was clipped. "No, and I hate the fact that you're dragging me through this again. Mom killed herself. That's what happened. You're not helping me or her by bringing it up after all this time."

"I respect how you feel," Serena said.

"Then drop it. We're done. I have to go."

"Just one more question."

"What is it?"

"My adopted daughter, Cat Mateo, is a freshman here, too. She tutors a boy named Zach Larsen. I understand Zach was your boyfriend at the time of your mother's death."

Delaney's whole body twitched at the mention of Zach's name. "So what?"

"Why did you and Zach break up?"

"What business is that of yours?"

"I was wondering whether it had something to do with your mother's death."

"It didn't," Delaney insisted. "Are we done? I have class now."

"Sure. Thank you, Delaney."

The girl hurried away in quick, nervous steps—practically running—as if she couldn't get away fast enough. Watching her, Serena thought that the note she'd made in the file two years ago was still true.

Delaney wasn't telling her everything.

21

Stride had sat in an interview room in police headquarters with Gavin Webster several times in the past, when Gavin was an attorney representing his clients. This time, Gavin was alone. He'd expected the man to arrive with his own attorney, but Gavin had the usual lawyer's arrogance of thinking that the advice he gave to his clients didn't apply to himself.

They sat on opposite sides of the table. Stride read the attorney his rights. He was taking no chances with procedure. Gavin didn't flinch at the recital or make any effort to halt the interview.

When he was done, Stride said, "Do you want some coffee? Water?"

"No, I'm fine."

"Are you hungry?"

Gavin chuckled without humor. "If you're trying to play the good cop, you must really think I'm guilty."

"To tell you the truth, I don't know what to think, Gavin."

"I already told you that I didn't do it," the lawyer said.

"Yes, I know that's what you said."

"Are you any closer to finding Chelsey? Do you have any leads?"

Stride nodded. "Actually, we do. We believe a client of yours, Hink Miller, played a role in Chelsey's kidnapping. He may have transported her in the trunk of his Ford Taurus. There's a scent of perfume in the back.

We also found zip ties and traces of blood. We'll be testing the blood to confirm whether the DNA matches your wife, but we think it's likely."

Gavin sat back in the chair as if he'd been struck. He covered his nose and mouth with his hands and breathed loudly. "Did you search Hink's house? Did you find any evidence of where he took her?"

"There's no sign of Chelsey on the property. So far, the only connection we've found is the car."

"Do you think Chelsey's dead?"

"We don't know any more than what I've told you. But let's talk about Hink. When's the last time you talked to him?"

"I represented him in a case sometime last year," Gavin said.

"Have you seen him since then?"

"I don't think so. Not after the case wrapped up."

"How did he happen to choose you as his attorney?"

Gavin hesitated. "A third party brought me in."

Stride made the obvious leap. "Broadway? Did Broadway hire Hink to do security at the poker games?"

"All I can tell you is that I only represented Hink the one time last year. We've had no substantive communications since then. Honestly, I can't believe he would have been involved in Chelsey's kidnapping. Have you talked to him? Did he admit it?"

"Hink's dead," Stride said.

"*What?*"

"He was shot to death yesterday afternoon. His mother was strangled at the same time. Their bodies were found at her home south of Superior."

"Jesus Christ!"

"Where were *you* yesterday afternoon, Gavin?" Stride asked. "The police were at your house, so we know you weren't there."

Gavin didn't answer at first. He looked in shock. "I drove around."

"All afternoon?"

"Yes."

"Where?"

"I don't know. I was in a daze."

"Did you go to Wisconsin?"

The lawyer blinked and took a few seconds to answer. "Yes, actually, I did. I thought about going down to Rice Lake to see my parents, but I decided not to drive that far, so I turned back."

"Did you go to the house where Hink Miller was staying?"

"Of course not. I had no idea Hink was even in Wisconsin. Last I knew, he was in Duluth. All I did was drive around by the water and then I crossed the bridge back to Minnesota. I went up the north shore for a while."

"Did you murder Hink Miller and his mother?" Stride asked.

"Don't be ridiculous. No, I didn't."

"Do you own a gun?"

Gavin's blue eyes took on a squirrelly look. "I do."

"What kind?"

"A 9 mm Glock."

Stride stared back at him. "Hink was shot with a 9 mm."

"It's a very common gun, as you know."

"We'd like to run ballistic tests on your Glock."

Gavin stared back across the table, and his upper lip glistened with sweat. "Actually, my gun is missing."

"Missing?"

"I went to look for it on Thursday night. I wanted to bring it along to the ransom drop. I didn't know what I was dealing with, and I thought it would be safer if I was armed. But I checked our bedroom closet, which is where I always keep it, and the gun wasn't there."

"It didn't occur to you to mention this before now?" Stride asked.

"In the panic of everything else, I forgot about it. All I can assume is that the kidnappers took my gun."

"Why would they do that?"

"I have no idea."

"How would they know you had a gun? Or where you kept it?"

"Again, I don't know."

Stride nodded. "Remind me how much you paid in the ransom drop."

"One hundred thousand dollars."

"In cash?"

"Yes."

"In hundred-dollar bills?"

"Yes."

"How did you transport the ransom?"

"In a red Hello Kitty backpack that the kidnappers left for me. I already told you this."

Stride slipped a glove onto his right hand, and he leaned down to the floor and reached inside a box. Keeping it far enough away that Gavin couldn't touch it, he held up the backpack that Lance Beaton had found in Hink Miller's basement. "Is this the backpack?"

Gavin's blue eyes widened. "Yes! Where did you find it?"

"Hink Miller had it."

He shook his head. "Hink. I can't believe this. So he really was involved. Why would he do this? It makes no sense."

"Did you recognize Hink in the boat on Thursday night?"

"No. I told you, the man was wearing a hood."

"But it could have been him?"

Gavin shrugged. "I suppose."

"And when you tossed the backpack to the man in the boat, it contained the full hundred thousand dollars?"

"Yes. Why?"

"We found less than ten thousand dollars in the backpack," Stride said.

"*Ten . . .*?"

"That's right. Not a hundred thousand dollars. Ten thousand. Where's the rest of the money?"

"I have no idea. Whoever killed him must have it. Obviously, Hink had a partner. They split up the ransom after the man brought in the boat."

"So you're saying that the kidnappers split up the cash between them overnight, but then one of them came back the following day and killed his partner? Why not just kill him right then and there and take *all* of the money? And why would Hink settle for ten thousand? If he knew there was more, why not demand half? Also, why would Hink have the backpack itself but only a small portion of the ransom money?"

Gavin laid his hands flat on the table. "Look, I can't explain any of this, but I know what you're thinking. *I* hired Hink to kidnap and kill Chelsey. I paid him ten thousand dollars, and that's what was in the backpack that I tossed to him in the boat. Then I went and killed him to make sure he wouldn't expose me."

"Is that what happened?" Stride asked.

"No! It's not. I wasn't involved in any of this. Not in kidnapping my wife. Not in killing Hink Miller and his mother. Someone else did this."

"Who?"

"I don't know!" the lawyer erupted.

Stride calmly tapped a pencil on the table. He watched Gavin Webster and tried to get inside the man's head. Typically, the easiest answer in any investigation was also the right answer. Husband inherits millions, decides not to share it with his wife, and arranges for his wife to disappear. And yet Stride still couldn't decide what he saw in the lawyer's eyes. If he was guilty, he was covering it well. If he was innocent, he was keeping secrets about something.

"Did you talk to Hink about your inheritance?" Stride asked.

"Of course not. Back then, I didn't have it! But I told you, word has gotten around. So maybe he knew. I have no idea."

"Did people at the poker games know about it?"

"No comment."

"Did you see Hink at the poker games? One of the people there could be his accomplice."

"I'm sorry, but I can't help you."

"Or *you* could be his accomplice," Stride added.

Gavin held out his wrists. "If you believe that, then you better arrest me."

Stride did nothing, and Gavin shrugged. "I guess that means I can go?"

"Yes, you can go," Stride told him.

Gavin stood up, and so did Stride, but when the lawyer went to open the interview-room door, Stride blocked his way by holding the door shut. "One more thing. I want you to make a phone call for me."

"To who?" Gavin asked.

"Broadway," Stride replied. "I need to talk to him again."

* * * * *

It was night. Late.

Serena drove around Duluth. She was trying desperately not to go where she wanted to go, and like a nomad, she cruised the city. She drove up London Road as far as the split at Highway 61, and then she turned around, retracing her steps. She took the turns of Seven Bridges Road into the rural areas north of the city, then crossed the desolate land to the airport, then made her way to Miller Hill Mall, which was closed for the night.

In the mall's empty parking lot, she sat with the engine running, the windows open, and the radio playing. John Anderson teased her with "Straight Tequila Night." She switched off the radio and closed her eyes and squeezed her fists together. The hunger of what she wanted left her mouth dry with desire. She could taste it, feel it, imagine the sensation in her chest. There was no hiding from it. The more she resisted, the more the need grew. She craved the peaceful, easy feeling of that liquid bliss coursing through her bloodstream.

Aimlessly, Serena drove again, still trying to stay ahead of the temptation. She went to Enger Park. To the docklands by the water. To the mean streets of the Central Hillside. Her phone kept blowing up. Stride texted her. Cat texted her. Guppo texted her. She ignored all of them. When the notifications kept coming, she turned off her phone.

From downtown, she made her way to 5th Street. Near Gavin Webster's house, she parked below the trees and got out. Down the hill, the lights of the city glowed like a ribbon next to the dark stain of the lake. Looking up, she saw the streak of a shooting star. The lights of Gavin's house were dark. It didn't matter, because she hadn't come here to see him.

Instead, Serena stared at the house of the Sacks family across the street. Standing at the base of the steps on the house's steep slope, she called out quietly.

"Elton?"

If the dog were outside, left on his own to the elements again, he would hear her. Smell her. Know she'd come back for him. If he were there, she would take him with her, and he'd protect her and keep her sober. But there was no bark this time, no whimper from a Border collie left alone. At least for tonight, the Sackses had brought him inside.

Serena got back in the Mustang in despair. Before she could drive off, she glanced up at Dale's brightly lit office window on the second floor. There, front paws against the glass, was Elton. Somehow he sensed her presence. The dog tilted its head, its snout pointed upward, and Serena opened the car window and heard a muffled, mournful howl.

Elton was calling to her. Missing her. It broke her heart. He needed her, and she needed him.

Dale Sacks came to the window. He yanked on the dog's collar to shut him up and take him away. The man looked down at the street but didn't see her car parked below the retaining wall. After a while, he turned around and disappeared, and a few seconds later, the lights in the office went out.

Serena turned on the engine and finally did what she'd known she would do all along.

She drove to the bar on Grand Avenue.

22

"This is a hell of a lot better than calculus," Zach Larsen told Cat as he passed her the joint.

She took a shallow hit and followed it with a deep breath of sweet, cool air. She thought about old men doing math, and something about that image made her giggle. "I don't know. I'm pretty sure Leibniz and Newton must have been stoned when they came up with differential equations."

"No kidding," Zach said. "You'd have to be."

Cat didn't feel stoned herself, just pleasantly mellow, as if the moon and stars were brighter and closer than they usually were. It was past midnight. The two of them lay on their backs on a blanket spread across the green grass of midfield in the UMD football stadium. Zach had a student maintenance job there, so he had the keys to get them in. Empty bleachers looked down on them from both sides of the field.

"It's a pretty night," Cat murmured.

"Yeah. Look at all the stars. See that really bright one there? I wonder what that one is."

"It's a planet," Cat replied. "That's Jupiter."

"Is it? You know that?"

"Yup."

"You know about stars?"

"Some."

She'd taken an astronomy course during her senior year in high school, and Stride had bought her a telescope. They'd spent hours on the beach behind the cottage mapping the sky. Most of what Cat read or saw, she typically remembered. She extended one arm and pointed out half a dozen constellations.

Zach shook his head in awe. "Wow. Calculus. Astronomy. Is there anything you can't do?"

Cat smiled. He was flattering her, but she didn't mind. His right hand grazed against her left hand, and she wondered when he would make his move. He'd looked embarrassed suggesting they go to the stadium instead of studying math, and the location, the stars, the blanket, the joint, all had make-out session written all over them. She knew that he had a little crush on her, but she wasn't interested. Maybe some kissing if the joint put her in the mood, but nothing more than that. They were both freshmen, but Zach was two years younger than she was, and Cat liked men, not boys.

Of course, Zach knew all about her past. Everybody did. The incident with the Hollywood actor who'd tried to rape her two years earlier had landed Cat on the covers of magazines and splashed her personal life across the internet. So far, reactions to her arrival on campus had run the gamut. Some people didn't care, some considered her a MeToo hero, some thought she was an attention-seeker, and some treated her like a kind of exotic zoo animal. That was Zach, who seemed tongue-tied whenever he was around her.

Zach was young, but she had to admit that he was also sweet and handsome. He had a shy smile and warm blue eyes. His blond hair sprouted up from his head like a weed, and his ruddy face was still a little broken out. He had the thick neck and limbs of a football player, but not the grace or speed to make the team. He'd actually apologized about that, as if Cat cared about such things. Apparently, Zach's lack of physical prowess had been a big disappointment to his father. Cat had known plenty of men like that, and she didn't like them.

"I beat your girlfriend on Wednesday's test," Cat said. "She didn't look too happy."

"Delaney's not used to anyone beating her," Zach replied. "In high school she was the valedictorian, you know."

"Oh, yeah?"

"Yeah, I never met anyone smarter than her. Not until you, I mean." He propped himself up on one elbow on the blanket. "And you know, Delaney's not my girlfriend anymore. We broke up."

"Too bad. She's really pretty."

"Yeah. She is. But I mean, so are you."

Cat took the joint from Zach's hand again and took another hit. "How long did you guys go out?"

She watched his mouth crease into something that was part smile, part frown. It was obvious he still had feelings for Delaney, even if they weren't together. Cat wondered if Zach's crush on her was mostly a substitute for his ex-girlfriend.

"We went out all through high school," he said, "but we've known each other since kindergarten. As kids, we were best friends. Then I guess our hormones kicked in around the same time, so we started dating. We were together all the time. My folks only live a couple of miles from where her house was."

"Was?"

Zach hesitated. "Yeah, she's not there anymore. Delaney's mom killed herself a couple of years ago."

"Oh, shit!" Cat exclaimed. She sat up on the blanket with her legs crossed. "I had no idea. I feel bad for her."

"Yeah, that sucked."

"I lost my mom, too. I mean, I was a lot younger than she was. I was only six. And my dad killed my mom, and I know suicide's different. But loss is loss. I should talk to her."

Zach shook his head. "It won't do any good. Delaney doesn't talk about it."

"Is that why the two of you broke up?" Cat asked. "Because of what happened to Delaney's mom?"

Zach lay back on the blanket. His face looked like a ball of confusion as he stared at the sky. He didn't ask for the joint back, so Cat smoked it herself.

"I have no idea why we broke up," he said quietly after a while.

"Well, losing somebody messes people up."

"I know, but it wasn't that. It happened before."

"She broke up with you before her mom's suicide?"

Zach nodded. "Yeah. One day everything was fine, and the next day—*boom*. She said she didn't want to see me anymore. We were done. Not boyfriend-girlfriend, not even friends. She didn't come to my house again, not once. At school, I kept pestering her to tell me what had happened, because I figured I must have done something to piss her off. She said that it wasn't me, but I didn't believe her. But I never figured out what went wrong between us."

"When did her mom kill herself?" Cat asked.

"Delaney broke up with me on a Friday. It was a week after that."

"Were there problems between them?"

"No, they were always really, really close. But it wasn't easy for Delaney, because Mrs. Candis had a big drinking problem. Half the time when I was at Delaney's house, her mom was drunk. Delaney would tell me stories that were just wild. Her mom would throw up, have blackouts, get the shakes. Strangers would take her home, and Delaney would find men in her mom's bed. Really bad stuff. But no matter what Mrs. Candis did, Delaney wouldn't hear a word against her."

Cat stretched out on her back and stared at the sky again. "I think Delaney was lucky to have you."

"That's what she used to tell me. She said I was her rock. I always figured we'd get married. I mean, we never talked about it, but it was just sort of understood between us, you know? But then she dumped me."

"Did you have an argument or something?"

"No. There was nothing like that. We'd just had a great weekend together. Everything was fine. Then the next day she started giving me the freeze-out. Ducking my calls. Ignoring my texts."

"Shit," Cat said.

"Yeah, it really hurt. But it was a couple of years ago. I've moved on."

Cat didn't think he'd moved on at all.

"What happened that last weekend?" she asked.

Zach shrugged. "Why do you care? You don't even know her."

"Well, it sounds like we have some things in common. Plus, come on, Zach, you're still in love with her, right? That's pretty obvious."

"I don't know," he replied wearily, as if he'd asked himself that same question many times. "My dad keeps telling me to forget her. He says she's a mental case like her mom. He says I should get laid. He says once I do that, I'll stop thinking about Delaney."

Zach's face flushed as he realized what he'd said. Cat shifted so that she was sitting up again. Her jaw hardened.

"Was that the plan for tonight?" she asked acidly.

"No! I didn't mean you."

"Did you bring condoms?"

"I—well—yeah—" he stuttered and then closed his eyes. "Shit."

"If you think I'm easy because of my past, you've really got it wrong," Cat told him.

"I don't think that. I swear. I only brought condoms because my dad, well, he always says, be prepared. But I didn't take you out here to have sex, Cat. I like you. You remind me of—well, you remind me of her."

Cat shook her head. "Wow, you're really bad at this."

"I know. I need to get past her. I just don't know how to do that. Not until I know what the hell happened."

Cat relaxed and settled back on the blanket again. "Well, there must have been something. Trust me, we girls can lose our shit over little things."

"I know, but there wasn't anything!" Zach insisted. "Delaney went camping with us that weekend. Me, her, my folks. We all had a great time."

"Delaney's mom didn't come with you?"

"No, she stayed home. Mrs. Candis never liked my dad. She thought he was crude. Which he is. Plus, Delaney said whenever she was away, that was when her mom used to really go nuts on the booze. So I guess Delaney knew what she'd come home to on Sunday."

"What happened on the camping trip?" Cat asked.

"Nothing. We fished. We hiked. Mom grilled the fish, and Dad drank too much beer. Typical trip. We stayed at the campsite Friday and Saturday, and then we went home on Sunday afternoon. I asked Delaney to stay for dinner, but she said she'd better check on her mom. So my dad drove her home, and that was that. No arguments, no nothing. When she was leaving, Delaney gave me a kiss. Everything was fine. Then the next day, she wasn't at school. Same thing on Tuesday. I kept texting and calling, and she didn't answer, and I was starting to freak out. By Wednesday, she was back, but she kept avoiding me. By Friday, I finally cornered her outside class and said I wouldn't leave her alone until she told me what was going on. That's when she broke up with me. Just like that. She said it was her fault, not mine, but she couldn't see me anymore."

"She didn't say why?"

"Nope."

"Did you talk to any of her friends?"

"Sure. They were blindsided by it, too."

"Have you talked with her at all since then?"

"I went by her place a couple of times the next week, but she asked me to leave. I pestered her with texts and shit, and she blocked me. My dad told me I should knock it off and leave her alone. But none of it made sense to me. I mean, you're a girl. What am I missing?"

Cat leaned across the blanket and gave him a little peck on the cheek.

"I don't know," she said, "but I can tell you one thing."

"What?"

"You should listen to what Delaney told you. Whatever happened, I don't think it had anything to do with you. This was about her. And maybe her mom, too. And it was big."

23

Serena savored the moment of surrender. The first swallow was always the sweetest. It was like spreading her legs for a lover. The vodka went down cold, and then it turned warm in her body, like hot sun blazing on her skin on a Las Vegas afternoon. All the swallows after that were nothing but pale imitations, but the first one made it worthwhile.

"I didn't expect to see you so soon," Jagger told her with a smile of surprise. He still looked as cool as the Absolut. Different T-shirt, just as tight. Black jeans. Closing time was coming soon, and only a few stragglers were nursing their last drinks in the bar. They may as well have been alone.

"And here I thought you'd miss me," Serena said, her voice slipping into a sultry pitch.

"Well, you were in pretty bad shape last night."

"I know. You were my hero. Thank you."

"I'm not so sure about *hero*," the bartender replied. "*Enabler* maybe. It's a fine line. Something tells me I shouldn't be serving you at all. I can spot problem drinkers, and you, lovely lady, have a problem."

"Do I look like I want a lecture?" Serena asked.

"No."

"Then let's assume I don't."

"Your husband asked me to call him if you came back," Jagger said. "I liked him. Something tells me I wouldn't want to wind up on his bad side."

"Yeah, Stride is tough as nails," Serena agreed. "Not like you."

"You don't think I'm tough?" Jagger asked, with a wide grin and a flex of his muscles.

"No, you're not tough. You're smooth. How old are you, anyway?"

"Thirty-five."

"A baby," Serena said.

"What about you? Want to confess your age?"

"I'm older than you, and let's leave it at that."

"No way you're over forty."

Serena smiled. "See? You're smooth."

She finished her drink and tapped a long fingernail on the bar. He went to get her a refill. Her eyes followed him from the back, where the view was as good as it was from the front. She told herself that her flirtation was innocent. The bar was a kind of closed universe where nothing was real. She could tease a man, and he could tease her back, and it didn't mean a thing. But she knew that the ice under her feet was thin. She was married, he had a girlfriend, but every drink made those things matter less and less. If she kept coming back, they'd be alone sometime after closing. She would kiss him, or he would kiss her, and then she'd be on her back on a table, and he'd be on top of her.

It would happen.

It had happened to her more than once in her long-ago past. Other men, other boyfriends, other disasters. She didn't want to cheat—she loved Jonny more than she loved her life—but she could see her future.

It. Would. Happen.

Serena took a deep breath. Her desires were scaring her, and she knew what she had to do. Get up and walk out of the bar. Skip the next drink and the one after that. Get from midnight to midnight sober, and move the number from zero back to one.

Instead, Jagger put a lowball glass in front of her, and she took another long, beautiful swallow.

"You're right," Serena said.

"About what?"

"I'm an alcoholic."

"I figured. First relapse in a while?"

"A very long while."

"Do you want me to kick you out?"

"No. If you kick me out, I'll just go somewhere else. When I'm ready to stop, I'll stop."

"Should I call your husband?"

"No, don't do that."

There. That was the first little crack in the ice. The secret conspiracy between them. *Don't call my husband.*

Addiction had such perfect aim. It was like a sharpshooter hitting targets. Marriage. Job. Home. Money. It had been that way with Samantha, too. Serena knew how it would go, a long fall down into darkness until she was lying at rock bottom with her life in ruins. She didn't want to go through that again, not the way she had more than 6,600 nights ago.

But there were two Serenas, and she was watching helplessly as the other Serena walked away from everything she loved.

She finished her drink.

Ordered another.

She finished that one.

And ordered another.

Down, down, down, she kept falling, looking for the ledge to take hold of, looking for anything that would break her descent.

Jagger put the next glass in front of her. "So why are you here?"

"What do you mean?"

"You can get drunk anywhere. Another bartender wouldn't give you a hard time about it. He'd just pour."

"Maybe I like your face," Serena said.

"Ah. Well, I like yours, too."

"I can tell."

His eyes weren't thinking about his girlfriend. His eyes said, *I want you, you want me.* And he was right. She did. She was so turned on she could feel an erotic tingling all the way down to her toes. She wanted the seduction;

she wanted the game. It was a game that ended with both of them naked and him buried inside her, her body writhing, their skin slippery with sweat.

She could hear the echo of Samantha laughing at the thought of it. Like mother, like daughter.

Stop, Serena told herself.

Don't do this, she screamed inside her head.

She frowned at the next drink on the bar. She pushed it away. Pulled it back. Pushed it away. She brushed back her hair and ignored the heat between her legs, and she tried to remember who she was.

A cop. A detective. That was her salvation.

She took a photograph from her purse and put it in front of Jagger.

"Do you recognize this woman?" she asked. "She used to come in here a lot."

He picked up the picture. "No, she doesn't look familiar."

"Her name's Nikki Candis."

"I can keep an eye out if you're trying to find her."

"You don't need to do that. She's dead. She died two years ago."

His eyebrows arched. "Two years? Well, I only started working here six months ago, but if you want, I can ask around. Other people have been here longer."

"Thanks, that would help."

She took the lowball glass in her hand. With a sigh of resigned acceptance, she downed the whole thing. Then she reached in and took one of the ice cubes and cupped it in her palm. She watched it melt on her hot skin.

"Another?" Jagger asked. His eyes said it all.

Yes, she wanted another. And another. She wanted what came after that, too. The man-woman dance. She felt herself possessed by an overwhelming urge to reach out and grab this man's face and get it over with. The first kiss. The kiss that would lead to everything else. She leaned across the bar. He was inches away, so close and so attractive. His eyes glittered, wondering what she would do. She imagined what his tongue would feel like. Not just on her mouth but elsewhere.

It. Would. Happen.

Unless she stopped right now. This second.

Unless she grabbed the ledge.

Touching him, not touching him, felt like a test of willpower. If she went the wrong way, there was no going back. She took a stuttering breath, utterly consumed by desire. Then she pinned her arousal down, which was like caging a feral cat that scratched and yowled. She leaned back and shivered to clear away the image of their bodies intertwined.

That was how recovery began, with one small victory.

She wasn't going to have sex with this man. She wasn't going to cheat.

There was no final exam. No declaration of mission accomplished. You won one little victory, and then another, and then another, and when you added them all together, you got to 6,608 nights without a drink.

"One more?" he asked again.

"No, I'm done," Serena replied. She repeated it for good measure. "I'm *done*."

Jagger looked at her with a faint shadow of disappointment. But he said, "I'm glad to hear it."

"That's all for me. I won't be back."

"Congratulations."

She didn't know whether he believed her. She didn't know whether she believed herself. Then Jagger held out his hand for her car keys. "You've still had too much to drive."

"I know. I'll text my daughter to come get me."

"Your daughter? She'd have to be, what, ten years old?"

"Smooth, smooth, smooth," Serena said to him. She lifted her phone and showed him Cat's photograph. "My adopted daughter. She's twenty. I'll wait for her in my car. And don't worry, I'm not going anywhere."

"Whatever you say."

Breathless, oddly exhilarated, she headed for the door. Jagger called after her.

"Hey, I'm curious."

Serena stopped. "About what?"

"This woman in the picture. If she died two years ago, why are you asking about her now? Does this have something to do with Hink? That guy with all the cash?"

"No, it's not part of that case," she replied, the vodka loosening her tongue. "It's something else. All the evidence from back then says that Nikki Candis killed herself, but there's something that bothers me."

"Yeah? What's that?"

"My gut," Serena replied. "My gut says that she was murdered."

* * * * *

Stride paced.

With the cottage lights off, he went back and forth from the front door to the back door in darkness. Every few minutes, he walked out into the crisp, clear night, listening to the thunder of the lake on the other side of the dunes. Then he went back inside. He'd already called Serena half a dozen times and gotten her voice mail. He'd texted, but his messages went undelivered.

She was off the grid. She didn't want him to find her.

Restlessly, he wandered into the spare bedroom where Serena kept her clothes. He knew it was a practical thing. She often got called in overnight. But he hated that she'd moved her clothes out, that when he opened his closet door, it no longer smelled like her perfume. She dressed and undressed here, where he didn't see her naked, and he missed the sight of her body. He longed to be close to her again, but this was all his fault. He'd been letting her creep away for months.

In her bedroom, Stride opened the top drawer of her dresser. Underneath her sweaters, he found the photograph she kept there. He picked up the picture and used the flashlight on his phone to illuminate it. The photograph was of Samantha and Serena when Serena was about fourteen years old, already stunning in her youth. The two of them wore matching pantsuits, holding hands, their heads leaning together, black hair against blond hair. Samantha was beautiful, too; he could see the amazing genes of mother and daughter. This picture had been taken before the worst of Samantha's problems, but if you knew what was coming, you could see the danger in her eyes. The selfish, self-centered, narcissistic need to be the center of the party. The willingness to sacrifice everyone else to get what she wanted.

There weren't many people in his life that Stride hated, but he hated Samantha. He'd never met her, and yet he *hated* her. He was furious over the things she'd done to her child, the physical and emotional scars that Serena carried to this day. Wherever Serena was, Samantha was with her. Her mother was dead, but she was never far away.

He swore out loud. He couldn't pretend or fool himself anymore. He and Serena were at a breaking point, and he needed to do something. He didn't care if she wanted space. He wasn't going to accept being without her. He marched to the back door of the cottage, grabbed his leather jacket, and went outside. There were places he could check around the city. The park at the end of the Point. Brighton Beach. Enger Tower. And the bar in West Duluth. That was the first place to look. He knew how Serena's mind worked, how it went in ever-decreasing circles as she homed in on the truth. If that bar was where she'd slipped, she'd go back there to slip again.

He was almost to the door of the Expedition when his phone rang. It was Cat.

"Hey," she said.

"Hey."

"Sorry to call so late," she told him, "but I figured you'd be up."

"I was."

"Are you out looking for Serena?"

"I was on my way."

"Well, don't bother. She texted me. My roommate's driving me down there to pick her up. I'll take her home."

"Where is she?"

"The bar on Grand."

He closed his eyes. "Damn it."

"She drank a lot, but she sounded okay."

"Good."

There was a long stretch of silence on the phone.

"You get that she doesn't want to look weak in front of you, right?" Cat asked. "That's why she called me, not you."

"Yes, I get that."

"Well, try not to be stupid when she comes home."

He laughed without any humor. "Yeah."

Cat hung up.

Stride felt a heaviness in his chest, but it didn't feel like stress on his heart. He walked to the end of the driveway and out to Minnesota Avenue, where he stood in the middle of the empty street. Around him, the houses on the lake and bay sides were dark. A streetlight cast his long shadow onto the pavement like a giant. Tendrils of mist made a kind of fog, obscuring his vision.

Then his phone rang again, surprising him. The number was one he didn't recognize.

"This is Stride," he said as he answered.

After a staticky pause, a muffled voice spoke. "You're a cop, right? I've seen you on TV."

"That's right. Who is this?"

More static. More silence.

"I don't want to give my name," the man replied finally. "Are you still looking for that missing woman?"

"Yes, we're still looking for Chelsey Webster," Stride said. "What do you know about her kidnapping?"

"I don't know anything. But I know where you should look for her."

"Where?"

"The woods near Island Lake," the man told him.

"That's a big area. Can you narrow it down?"

"No."

"Why do you think Chelsey is there?"

"Ask her husband," the voice said. "He was in those woods last weekend."

"How do you know that?"

"Some guy with a tow truck told me. He said he fixed a flat for Gavin Webster up in those woods. That's a big coincidence, don't you think? Him being up there in the middle of nowhere right before his wife goes missing? If you ask me, he was scouting where to hide her body."

24

"Do you really think someone *killed* Nikki Candis?" Cat asked Serena, as they drove through the deserted streets of downtown Duluth. "It wasn't suicide?"

Serena stared out the car window. In her head, she was going over Cat's description of her conversation with Zach Larsen. That was easier than thinking about the things she had to tell Stride.

"I don't know. I could be wrong, but there are a lot of things that don't add up."

"Like what?" Cat asked.

"Delaney keeping secrets. Nikki using a gun, when she hated guns. The breakup with Zach. And that package Nikki ordered. The angel figurine and the deer whistles. Something about those deer whistles bothers me. Put it all together, and I don't get the picture of a woman who killed herself."

"You don't think *Delaney* killed her mother, do you?"

Serena shook her head. "No, Nikki's parents told me they drove Delaney back from Mora that Sunday. The three of them were together when they found the body. And according to Paul Vavra, Nikki was alive on Friday when he picked up Delaney from the house. Of course, it's possible that the Vavras are covering for Delaney, but that's not how it feels. No, this is something else. I'm missing a piece of the puzzle, and when I find it, I think the whole thing will make sense."

"What are you going to do next?"

"I'll talk to Zach's parents in the morning," Serena said. "Usually, if the kids are close, the parents are, too. They may know something."

Cat was quiet for a while, and Serena didn't mind the silence. The girl crossed the lift bridge onto the Point and drove the Mustang toward the cottage, using the late hour as permission to blow past the speed limit. Serena rolled down the passenger window, and the cold air through the car helped clear her head of the aftereffects of the Absolut. She felt no need to throw up tonight, which was another small victory. First saying no to her hunger for Jagger. Then saying no to more vodka. She wanted to stack little successes on top of each other like blocks.

"You, me, and Delaney," Cat murmured as they got closer to home.

"What about us?"

"Well, we're like a little club, aren't we? We all had our mothers taken away from us in one way or another."

"True."

Cat grabbed Serena's hand and shot her a smile. "Except I was lucky. I got a second chance."

Serena felt her emotions bubble up like a fountain. Rather than let the girl see her start to cry, she turned her face away to the open window. They reached the cottage driveway a few seconds later, and Cat turned in and parked the Mustang next to Stride's Expedition.

"Do you want to go back to campus?" Serena asked. "I'm sure Jonny would drive you to the dorm."

"No, I'll just sleep here."

"I can drop you off at school in the morning," Serena said.

"Thanks."

"And I appreciate you coming to get me."

The girl kept a deadpan face. "I'm just glad you've never had to get *me* out of any trouble."

Serena laughed at the sarcasm. Cat laughed, too. They hugged and then got out of the car and went into the cottage through the rear door. The kitchen was dark, but in the shadows, she could make out a figure sitting at the dining-room table. It was Jonny, waiting for them. Cat saw him, too, and she went over and kissed his cheek and murmured something that Serena couldn't hear. Then the girl crossed the living room to her old bedroom and closed the door, leaving the two of them alone.

"Hi," Serena said, sitting down in the nearest chair. The heat of guilt and embarrassment burned on her face.

"I'm glad you're home," Stride said.

"Yeah. Here I am."

She had no idea what to say next. She had no idea where to start. The two of them simply stared at each other like wary boxers. The shadows deepened the furrows in his face, and his wavy hair covered most of his forehead. She could sense his frustration, his helplessness, because he didn't know how to reach her. She felt the same way about him.

"I have to leave before daylight," he said.

"Oh?"

"Yeah, we have a lead in the Webster case."

"What is it?"

He explained about the anonymous call.

"It may be a dead end," he went on, "but Maggie wants to find the tow-truck driver and get him out there early so we can search the area."

"Good idea."

"But if you want me to stay here, I'll stay," he added, nudging onto that thin ice between them.

"No, you should go," Serena said.

His stiff reaction told her that she'd said the wrong thing. He thought she wanted him to leave, but that wasn't true. She wanted him back on the case, back doing what he loved, because she was certain that was what he needed. The man who'd spent fourteen months wrestling with his future, going around in circles, wasn't the man she'd married. Jonathan Stride was a cop. He would never be anything else, and the sooner he realized that, the sooner he could start living his life again.

She could have said all of that, but instead, she let the silence linger between them the way it had for months. Until she couldn't take it anymore.

"You and me," Serena went on finally. "What do we do?"

"I don't know."

"Because I really want to find our way back. I need that."

"So do I. The truth is, I can't live like this anymore, Serena."

"Neither can I."

"You cut me out tonight. Why?"

"Because I'm a different person when I drink, and I don't like it when you see me that way."

"Why not?"

Serena shook her head. Was he really going to make her say it? "Because I'm *ashamed*, Jonny. Because this is not who I am."

"It is who you are, though. It's part of you."

"I hate being vulnerable."

"I understand that. Believe me. Do you know how hard it was for me to rely on you after I was shot? To let you take care of me when I was physically crippled? I could barely get out of bed or do anything for myself. I wanted to send you away until I was past all that."

"Why? I'm your wife. I love you. I loved caring for you."

"I love you, too, but that's not the point. I hated being vulnerable, just like you."

"You didn't ask to be shot. This is different."

"It's not different at all. You didn't ask to be an alcoholic. You didn't ask for a mother who abused you."

Serena fell back on what she always did. She tried to drive him away.

"I almost had sex with another man tonight," she interjected bluntly. She wanted to shock him. She wanted to make him realize how pathetic she was.

He didn't look surprised. "The bartender?"

"Yes."

"Well, did you?"

"No, but I thought about it. I wanted it. I *wanted* to do something stupid, something meaningless, something to make you hate me." Serena shook her head. "I wouldn't blame you if you walked away. My father left my mother. He was right to do it. He was smart."

"You're not Samantha."

"Are you sure? Because I'm acting like her. It's like she died, and this is what she left me."

The chair scraped on the floor as Stride drew closer to her. He stroked her cheek with the back of his hand. It was dark in the cottage, and his face was dark, too. His voice was a whisper.

"I was thinking earlier about how much I hated Samantha," he said. "And then it occurred to me that you still love her. That's what makes this so complicated."

She exhaled long and loud and tilted her chin to stare at the ceiling in the darkness. "How can I possibly love that woman?"

"She was your mother."

"I know. God help me, she was. And you're right. In some crazy, stupid way, I do still love her. I miss her. I miss what she should have been. I feel guilty that I abandoned her."

"You saved yourself. That's not the same thing."

"Do you think she hated me for leaving?"

"No. I don't think that at all. She kept your picture, remember?"

"I should have helped her. I should have done something more."

"Serena, some people are beyond help. You know that. Samantha wasn't the person she was because of you. She was just a lost soul. Her demons destroyed her."

"What about *my* demons?" she asked.

"You've beat them back for years. You're not your mother."

"I'm not so sure."

"Being weak during one terrible time in your life doesn't change how strong you are."

She pressed her fingers together, as if she were praying. She didn't feel strong at that moment, and she didn't even want to be strong. She needed other things. She needed not to be alone. She needed to let someone hold her and help her. Those were hard things to admit to herself.

"Let's go to bed," she said.

"Okay. You must be tired."

"Not sleep, Jonny. That's not what I want."

She stood up from the table. Quickly, firmly, she pulled him to his feet, too. She led him through the cottage until they got to their bedroom. Inside, she closed the door tightly, hearing the handle rattle. They stood close to each other in the darkness, nearly invisible, and she heard nothing but his breathing. She guided his hands to her shirt, and he peeled it up, and then he unhooked her bra, and her breasts came free. His fingers undid the buckle of her jeans and slid the zipper down. She stepped out of the rest of her clothes.

"Turn on the light," he said. "I want to see you."

She did. The glow was dimmed, barely more than the light of a candle. She stood naked in front of him, feeling strangely exposed. It had been too long, and she didn't feel like the woman she'd once been. But he didn't see any of her flaws. His eyes roved over her skin, getting to know her again; his fingers touched her everywhere, softly, intimately. Her body responded like fire; her lips parted in a soft moan. She reached out and began undoing his buttons, but then she stopped.

"I'm not out of the woods," she murmured.

"I know."

"I don't know how long it will take for me to be okay again."

"It doesn't matter."

"I'll call Alice. I will. I'll talk to her and get back in therapy."

"You do whatever you need."

"I need you, Jonny. That's what I need."

"I'm right here."

"Undress for me. I want to see you, too."

Serena watched him take off his clothes. Her eyes devoured him. His face, his skin, his body, his lean muscles. The pale scar dividing his chest that symbolized all of the divisions they'd been through in the past fourteen months. When he was completely naked, like her, she engulfed him in her embrace and molded her body against his, two halves making one whole.

Then she kissed him with all of her passion letting go, and she led him to bed.

25

The tow-truck driver named Rex Samuels guided Stride along the roads on the south side of Island Lake. Like a psychiatrist's inkblot, the reservoir sprawled across dozens of miles, creating strangely shaped inlets and a myriad of dead-end roads. Some of the roads were paved, but many weren't, and they all looked alike, densely lined with evergreens. It was still early, just before sunrise, but there would be no sun that day. Another storm front had rolled in from the west to block out the sky, and the first drizzle of rain began to spatter across Stride's windshield.

He was quiet as he drove. He should have been tired because he hadn't slept at all, but instead, he felt charged with adrenaline. His body ached, but it was a good ache. He could still feel Serena in his arms and remember the sensations of her body below his, of being inside her again.

Maggie sat in the truck's second row of seats. She nursed a cup of McDonald's coffee and an Egg McMuffin, and she wore sunglasses despite the gray light. Rex sat next to Stride. The tow-truck driver had a big thermos of coffee, and a few white sticky crumbs of what looked like oatmeal clung to his lumberjack beard. The man wore a white T-shirt that didn't stretch far enough to cover his stomach and loose-fitting jeans that were covered in grease stains.

"How'd you guys find me again?" Rex asked, sounding annoyed that they'd dragged him away from his business on a Monday morning.

"You fixed a tire for somebody on Saturday near Pike Lake Park," Stride said. "He called me. He said you were telling him about doing the same thing for Gavin Webster up in these woods last weekend."

Maggie slid a photograph of Gavin between the seats. "This is the guy, right? You're sure?"

Rex glanced at it. "That's him."

"Are we close to the spot where you met him?" Stride asked.

"Hmm." Rex leaned forward and squinted into the woods. "Not sure about that. Seems to me we took another wrong turn back there. Better turn around."

Stride sighed and maneuvered the SUV into a tight U-turn. His tires scraped on the dirt, and he had to back up into the brush and avoid the white trunk of a birch tree that bent over the road. They'd already made several wrong turns and gone all the way to the winding edge of the lakeshore before Rex confirmed that they weren't in the right area.

"Didn't you write down the location?" Maggie asked impatiently.

"I did when he called me. After that, I threw it away."

"Do you remember any identifying features?" Stride asked. "Were there houses nearby? Could you see the water?"

"Yeah, I remember some houses. Not where Webster was, but I passed some houses as I was going there."

"Well, that narrows it down," Maggie commented sourly.

"Did you go as far as Boondocks?" Stride asked.

"No, I'd remember that. The wife and I go there for beer and nachos sometimes. Webster was on the south side of the lake. I never went through town."

The rain got harder. Stride turned on his windshield wipers, and his headlights shined through the gloom. When he steered around a curve, they found themselves back at the paved highway of Rice Lake Road. Stride turned south. The land was more open here, with a few widely separated houses set back from the road and power lines following the highway. He accelerated through the spray. He hadn't gone far when they passed a small fire station. Rex suddenly came to life.

"Hang on, what's that?"

"The Gnesen Fire Station," Stride said.

"No, the road. What road is that?"

"It's County 295. Datka Road. But that heads toward Fredenberg Lake, not Island Lake."

Rex's big head bobbed up and down. "Yeah, I guess it could have been Fredenberg. I don't know. The roads all look the same up here. Anyway, I definitely remember turning at the fire station."

Stride could almost hear the sound of Maggie rolling her eyes in the back seat. He did another U-turn and headed left on Datka Road. The asphalt disappeared under his tires after about a hundred yards, and he drove through mud. Trees hugged the sides of the road, some pines, some birches that had cast yellow leaves into the ruts. They passed a few driveways and a handful of mobile homes built in the clearings. After a mile or so, they reached a fork, and Rex said confidently, "Yeah, go right. This is it."

Stride steered right at the fork. The farther he drove, the more the road narrowed, until it was barely wider than the SUV.

"Are you sure this is the place?"

"I'm sure. It was a bitch getting my truck down here."

They reached a junction where there was a wide trail leading into the trees. It was generous to call it a road, because it was overgrown with weeds and grass, and he spotted a couple of fallen tree trunks blocking the access. But there were tire tracks, so someone had been driving here.

"That's the spot," Rex said.

"Here?" Maggie said.

"Yeah. This Webster guy, his car was in that clearing."

All three of them climbed out of Stride's truck. The rain was heavy and loud in the trees, and the wind had begun to kick up, turning the air cold. This was a particularly deserted stretch of woodland. They hadn't passed a house in at least half a mile, and they were still another half a mile from the lakeshore. The area was dead quiet, missing the distant rumble of traffic that was usually in the background. Stride wandered down the grassy trail until it curved away into the trees.

Maggie came up beside him. "What was Gavin doing out here?"

"Good question."

They walked back to the dirt road and joined Rex by the truck.

"So what was wrong with Gavin's car?" Stride asked.

"I told you. Flat tire. Rear driver's side."

"When was this?"

"A week ago Sunday."

"Morning? Afternoon?"

"Morning. Pretty early. Normally I'd go to church, but a job's a job."

"Did you see anybody else out here?" Maggie asked. "Any other cars or people?"

"Nope. Nobody."

"Was Gavin alone? Or was anyone else in the car with him?"

"It was just him."

"How was he dressed?"

"Oh, hell, I don't remember."

"Was he clean or dirty?"

Rex thought about it. "Dirty. Looked like he'd been out in the woods."

"Did he say what he was doing out here?"

"No, and I didn't ask. I don't stick my nose into other people's business. They don't bother me, I don't bother them."

"Did he have any equipment with him?" Stride asked. "Did you see anything in the car?"

"Like what?"

"Rope. Zip ties. Any kind of weapon."

"Not that I saw. Shit, if he had a gun, I'd think twice about stopping. But it's not like this guy looked like some punk who was planning to jack me, you know? He looked legit."

"Did he give you his name?" Stride asked.

"No. No name. He called, told me where he was. That's all."

"Did you write down the license plate of the car? Or did you ask to see his driver's license?"

"Why would I do that? I changed the tire, and I was done."

"So you can't verify that it was him?" Maggie asked.

"Yeah, but I'm telling you, I recognize his face. It was this Webster guy."

"How did he pay?" Stride asked. "Did he use a credit card?"

Rex shook his head. "Cash. That was pretty nice, too."

"What do you mean?"

"Service plus the tire came to a little over four hundred bucks. Guy didn't have change and didn't want any. He peeled off five hundred-dollar bills from his wallet and handed them over and told me to keep the rest."

Stride exchanged a look with Maggie.

"He gave you *hundred-dollar* bills?" Maggie asked.

"Yeah."

"And this was last Sunday morning?"

"I already told you that," Rex complained.

Stride took Maggie's elbow, and the two of them retreated down the grassy trail again. He studied the road leading into the woods, and he felt the hammer of rain, not caring that he was getting soaked. Next to him, water dripped like a slow leak from Maggie's bangs. Over their heads, lightning split the dark clouds. A few seconds later, thunder beat loud enough that he could feel it inside his chest.

"Gavin had hundreds in his wallet before the kidnapping," Stride said. "Before the ransom demand."

"That doesn't prove anything," Maggie pointed out.

"No, but it's an interesting coincidence." He stared into the woods, which were thick and dark and stretched for miles. They were the perfect hiding place. A body left somewhere in those woods was unlikely ever to be found. It would just slowly disappear into the ground.

"Did anyone actually *see* Chelsey on Sunday or Monday?" Stride asked. "Or talk to her?"

"Not that I know of, but we weren't checking her whereabouts that early. Gavin says the abduction took place on Tuesday night."

"Right, but we only have his word for that. We also only have his word that he got proof of life from the kidnappers."

"You think he killed Chelsey and hid the body *before* he went to see his parents in Rice Lake?" Maggie asked.

"Maybe. Then he used Hink Miller to help him stage the ransom drop, and when he didn't need him anymore, he got rid of Hink."

Maggie frowned. "But there was evidence that Chelsey was transported in Hink's trunk."

"Gavin could have planted that evidence," Stride said. "It's part of the narrative. Make us think the kidnapping was real."

Maggie shook her head. "You see, this is why I hate lawyers."

Stride took a few steps into the woods. He inhaled the rain-tinged air. He looked for footsteps. Broken branches. Torn clothes. A path that would lead to a burying place. But there was nothing. Gavin wouldn't have made the truth that easy to find.

As he stood in the downpour, though, Stride felt something else, something that had been missing from his life for fourteen long months. A sense of belonging. A sense of purpose. The gears of his life were fitting together again. Serena. His marriage. And his job.

He finally had his answer. He was back.

"We better get the dogs out here," Stride said. "It's time to search."

26

In the morning, Serena took Cat back to UMD. They didn't say much, but Cat wore a sly smile on her face the whole time, which likely meant that Serena and Stride had been loud enough in their lovemaking for the girl to overhear. Serena didn't confirm what had happened, but she didn't feel any embarrassment, either. Instead, she felt exhilaration, as if she'd finally turned a page with Jonny. And with herself.

After she dropped Cat on campus, she headed south through the rain to the outlying town of Proctor. That was where Zach Larsen's parents lived. It was where Nikki and Delaney had lived, too. She visited Nikki's old house first. It had been sold since her death, but Serena felt no need to see the interior again. The house was located on the corner of a country road on the north side of town, in the shadow of a rusted white water tower. A swampy wetland festered near the street. The lot was large, but the house itself was a small rambler, dwarfed by tall birch trees surrounding it. An unpaved driveway led to a detached two-car garage. When she'd arrived at the house that Sunday in May two years earlier, she'd found Delaney sitting on the front porch, oblivious to the flashing lights and multiple police cars parked around her. Paul Vavra had been waiting inside with the body of his daughter.

His first words to her had been, "Nikki wouldn't have done this."

Serena sat in her Mustang on the quiet, rainy street and revisited the events of Nikki's last weekend. The medical examiner estimated that the body had been lying in the bed since sometime Friday night. According to Paul and Delaney, Nikki had been alive on Friday afternoon. The UPS package with the figurine and deer whistles had been delivered on Saturday and never claimed from the porch.

Nikki's credit card showed no activity on Friday. If she'd gone anywhere that evening, she'd paid cash. The doors and windows to the house had been unlocked, but Delaney had said that was how they usually left them. A burglar could have walked into the house and come upon Nikki in bed, but there had been no reports of break-ins in the area. The neighbors hadn't reported any unusual activity, no strange cars on the street. A couple of people had heard what they later assumed was the fatal gunshot sometime after midnight, but no one had been concerned enough to call the police.

That left Serena with the same questions.

If it really was murder, who did it?

And why?

Serena headed out of Nikki's neighborhood. The Larsens didn't live far away as the crow flies, but there was no direct route because of the railroad tracks separating the east side of Proctor from the west. She found their two-story home on a sprawling open lot on 4th Street. Through a marsh filled with cattails, she could see a lineup of brown CN railcars on the nearby tracks. An overlapping trill of birds filled the air. The Larsen house was larger than Nikki's rambler, and the property included a triple detached garage and a large workshop with high doors. Equipment and vehicles dotted the green grass, including a motor home, two motorcycles, a vintage Oldsmobile in the process of restoration, an F-150 pickup truck and large flatbed trailer, and a snowplow attachment for the winter season.

When Serena rang the bell, Zach's mother, Barbara, answered the door. She was an attractive brunette in her midforties. She had a trim figure and wore an untucked yellow blouse and tan slacks. Her smile was friendly, but she looked mildly curious to find a police detective on their doorstep. She led Serena into the living room and then went to get her husband, Ben, who was still having breakfast. As Serena waited for them, she noticed that the living room looked like a museum dedicated to Ben's college days at UMD. There were athletic trophies, framed newspaper articles, photographs of a teenaged Ben Larsen in his Bulldogs uniform, and even an old helmet prominently displayed on a shelf next to a Wilson football.

Barbara returned to the living room with her husband. Ben didn't look happy to have his morning interrupted. He was tall and still rather good-looking, as he'd been in his college pictures, but he'd put on weight over the years and had a protruding beer belly that looked hard enough to ricochet a quarter. He had black hair so thick and stiff it didn't look like it would move in a windstorm. His sweatshirt bore a logo advertising Larsen Auto Repair, and his jeans fit snugly below his stomach. He wore unlaced work boots. He sat down on the sofa near the front windows, and his eyes landed on Serena's breasts before he noticed her face.

"What's this all about?" he demanded.

Next to him, his wife added with concern, "Is Zach okay?"

Serena smiled reassuringly as she took out her notebook. "Yes, Zach is just fine. This isn't about him. I have some questions about something that happened a couple of years ago. The death of Nikki Candis. Delaney's mother."

Barbara Larsen's face bloomed with surprise. "Nikki?"

"What's there to ask questions about?" Ben interjected. "She popped herself."

Ben's wife shot him an exasperated look, and Serena got the feeling that looks like that passed between them regularly.

"I'm reviewing the file to make sure we didn't miss anything," Serena replied.

The man on the sofa checked his watch. "Well, is this going to take long? I've got to get to the garage. We're backed up with jobs."

"No, this shouldn't take long at all," Serena said.

"I don't see why you're talking to us," he added impatiently.

"Obviously, because of Zach and Delaney," Barbara hissed under her breath. Then she looked at Serena with another friendly smile. "We knew Delaney very well, of course. She and Zach were best friends from the time they were five years old. So naturally, I spent a fair amount of time with Nikki, too."

Ben fidgeted in silence, his face darkening. Serena remembered the comment that Cat had passed along from Zach Larsen. *Mrs. Candis never liked my dad. She thought he was crude.*

"Nikki's parents told me that something had been bothering her prior to her death," Serena went on. "They didn't know what it could have been, and Delaney won't talk about it. But I understand that Delaney and Zach also broke up unexpectedly a week before Nikki's death."

Barbara nodded. "Yes, that's true."

"It sounds like Zach didn't see it coming."

"Not at all," she replied. "He was completely blindsided. Zach really loved that girl."

"Do you have any idea why Delaney ended their relationship?"

"I don't. It's still a mystery to me. Zach tried to talk to her about it, but she wouldn't give him any reason at all. That was so unlike her. Delaney is such a sweet, smart girl. The whole thing makes no sense."

"Did you talk to Delaney's mother about it?"

"I tried to," Barbara said. "I called Nikki to find out what was going on, but she wouldn't talk to me either. I'm afraid I was pretty rude to her on the phone. I said Delaney had treated Zach badly and he deserved an explanation, and Nikki needed to talk to Delaney about it. At that point, Nikki basically hung up on me. But I could tell she was unhappy, too."

"So you think Nikki was upset about the breakup?"

"Oh, yes. Very. I think Nikki liked Zach a lot."

Serena flipped back through her notes. "I understand Delaney accompanied you on a camping trip a couple of weeks before Nikki's death."

"That's right. We took our motor home up to Cascade River and pitched tents. Zach and Ben stayed in one, and Delaney and I stayed in the other."

"Did the two of you talk?"

"Yes, of course. Delaney and I were a little like mother and daughter ourselves. She'd grown up around us. We chatted about everything. Sometimes it was a struggle for her, you know, because of her mother's drinking, and I wanted Delaney to know that our house was a safe space for her."

"You knew about Nikki's drinking?" Serena asked.

"Oh, yes, she had a terrible problem," Barbara replied. "Honestly, sometimes I was concerned about Delaney staying in that house. But Delaney was absolutely devoted to her mother. She wouldn't hear a word against her."

"Did Delaney talk about Nikki's problems during the camping trip?"

"No, not that I recall. Not that weekend."

"Were there any issues with Delaney and Zach? Arguments, disagreements, anything like that?"

"No, we all had a lovely time."

"When did the trouble start?"

"Well, almost immediately after we got back, I guess. We arrived home Sunday afternoon. Zach and Delaney were giggling, kissing, couldn't keep their hands off each other. I remember thinking that Ben and I needed to make sure that Zach knew the facts of life, if you know what I mean. Especially about protection. I was pretty sure that he and Delaney hadn't had sex yet, but you could tell it was on the horizon. At fifteen, they seemed all grown up, and Delaney was such a pretty girl. Anyway, that's why I couldn't believe what happened next. On Sunday they were two teenage lovebirds, and then it all fell apart."

"How so?"

Barbara frowned. "Ben drove her home on Sunday, and she was fine. After that, well, she just cut Zach out of her life. Us, too. I saw her at Nikki's funeral a few weeks later, but she wouldn't even talk to me. Then she moved to Mora to live with her grandparents. I don't think I've seen her since."

Serena turned to Ben Larsen, who had yet to say a word. "Mr. Larsen, when you drove Delaney home, did she say anything to indicate that something was wrong?"

"Nope. Not a thing."

"Did she say anything at all? Did she talk about Zach? Or about her mother?"

"No. She was playing with her phone, and I was listening to the radio."

"Were you surprised when she broke it off with Zach so soon after that?"

Ben shrugged. "I guess, but if you ask me, Zach's better off without her. She had that boy wrapped around her finger. Manipulative, you know? She was turning him into a pussy."

Serena watched annoyance flash across Barbara Larsen's face. That was a word she didn't like.

"When you took Delaney home that Sunday, did you see her mother?" Serena asked. "Was Nikki there?"

"I don't know. If she was there, I didn't see her. I dropped the girl off, and I left."

"How well did you know Nikki?"

"Not well at all. She always had her nose in the air, although I don't know what she had to be stuck-up about. Barb's right about her being a boozehound. When I saw her, she was usually drunk." He checked his watch again and tapped his foot on the carpet. "What's this all about anyway? Why are you asking questions after all this time?"

Serena chose her words deliberately. She kept her eyes locked on Ben's face and waited for his reaction. "I'm looking into the possibility that Nikki was murdered."

She heard a gasp from Barbara, but Ben looked at her with a kind of sour surprise, as if he'd found shit on the bottom of his boot. "Murdered? You're nuts."

"Why do you say that?"

"Who would bother murdering Nikki Candis? She was a nobody. A drunk. She took a gun and put herself out of her misery. End of story."

"You sound pretty sure about that," Serena said.

"Hey, it's not like it was such a big surprise. Delaney knows that better than anyone."

Serena frowned. "What do you mean by that?"

Zach's father hesitated, momentarily at a loss for words. "I just mean, she knew her mom was a loser. We all did."

"Ben," his wife chided him quietly. "The woman is dead."

"Exactly. She's dead. It's been two years. I don't know why you're dredging this up now. Did you talk to Delaney about it? Is this murder bullshit her idea?"

Serena stared at him. "No. Delaney's adamant that her mother committed suicide."

"Well, there you go. You should listen to what she says. She knew her mother better than anyone." He checked his watch yet again, although almost no time had passed in between. "Look, I'm busy. I run a business. Are we done?"

"Yes, we're done," Serena replied, measuring out her words.

Ben Larsen bolted to his feet. Without lacing up his boots or kissing his wife, he stomped across the living room and slammed the door on his way out of the house.

27

Rain poured from a dark sky as Stride returned to police headquarters. It was almost noon, and the search in the woods surrounding Datka Road and Fredenberg Lake had been underway for several hours. There were dozens of square miles to cover in wet, dense conditions that made it hard for dogs to pick up the scent of a body. He suspected they would be at it until nightfall.

As he got out of his Expedition, he noticed a black Mercedes on the far side of the lot. It was parked on a slant, taking up two spots. This was no ordinary Mercedes. Stride recognized the sleek AMG GT model, which was priced at well over a hundred thousand dollars and definitely wasn't a fixture on Duluth streets. The personalized Minnesota license plate read NIGHTS. His eyes narrowed with curiosity as he studied the car through the heavy rain, and as he started walking toward it, the vehicle flashed its headlights at him like a greeting.

The passenger door clicked open as he approached the car. He shook off as much rain as he could from his clothes, then climbed inside and pulled the door shut. On the other side of the front seat, Broadway sat behind the wheel. He was dressed in a similarly trendy suit to the first time they'd met, this time in royal blue instead of plum. His close-shaved chin came to a sharp point. He wore sunglasses, but he took them off as

Stride joined him, and Stride could see that the man's eyes were a honey shade of golden brown.

"Jonathan. Hello." His boyish voice, and the lightness of his eyes, made the man appear even younger than he was.

"Broadway," Stride said. "It's not game night, is it? What are you doing in town?"

"I have other business. I come and go a lot."

Stride ran his fingers along the car's leather seat, which had a rich, buttery feel. "Sorry to be getting your interior wet. It looks expensive."

"It is, but don't worry about that. Do you like the car? Some people don't think that a Mercedes can be cool, but they haven't driven the GT."

"It's impressive. Maybe I'll get one when I win the Powerball."

Broadway gave him the faintest smile.

"I noticed the license plate, too," Stride went on. "'Nights on Broadway'? Are you a Bee Gees fan?"

"It's Barry's world, and we're all just living in it," the man replied.

"You know I'll be looking up the registration as soon as I'm inside the building."

"Naturally. You won't find anything helpful, though. The car is registered to one of my companies. Actually, when you learn more about my identity, you'll be disappointed. I'm just a businessman."

"A thirtysomething businessman who runs an illegal gambling operation and drives around in a hundred-thousand-dollar car," Stride said.

Broadway's eyebrows flicked playfully. "The Stealth Edition is north of one hundred and twenty-five thousand, actually."

"But no chauffeur? No security guard? I'm surprised you're driving yourself."

"Gavin said you wanted to talk, and I assumed you wanted a private meeting," Broadway said.

"You're right."

"Well, here I am. Are you any closer to finding Chelsey?"

"She's still missing," Stride replied.

"That's very sad. And yet I understand you have a major search operation underway in the woods north of the city."

"How did you hear that?"

Broadway shrugged. "My police sources tend to be pretty reliable. I gather you're looking for a body?"

"No comment."

"Of course not. Well, on one hand, I want your search to be successful, so Gavin has some kind of closure. Then again, as long as you don't find Chelsey, there's still hope."

"Did you tell Gavin about the search?" Stride asked.

"No, I figured I would leave that to you. He's bound to take it as bad news. For what it's worth, he still appears to be genuinely shocked by his wife's disappearance. I like to think I have something of a knack for knowing when people aren't being sincere. Then again, I respect your judgment, too. If you consider him a suspect, I have to take that seriously."

"Who told you that he's a suspect?" Stride asked.

"Common sense would be enough, but actually, he told me that himself. He's a lawyer, so he knows how the game is played. You were bound to treat him as a suspect. It's an old story, isn't it? Husbands kill wives, and wives kill husbands."

"What about you? Are you married?"

"I'm not. Too busy to settle down."

"Have you ever met Chelsey Webster?"

Broadway played with the buttons on his cuff while he formulated an answer. "In fact, I have. She and Gavin were at the NorShor. I bumped into the two of them before a show. What an extraordinary restoration they did with that venue, don't you think? Chelsey and I had a lovely chat. Arts, city politics, climate change, whiskey. She has a very agile mind and a wicked sense of humor. Extremely attractive, too. I'd be hard-pressed to think Gavin would have much interest in trading her in for a younger model. In fact, I'd say he's the lucky one in that marriage. I was with a beautiful young woman myself that night, but I admit, Chelsey made me forget all about her while we were together."

"Did Chelsey know who you were?" Stride asked.

"You mean did she know about my . . . relationship . . . with Gavin?

No. Then again, I'm not exactly one of his typical clients, am I?" Broadway slipped a phone from inside his suit coat pocket, scrolled through a few text messages, and then replaced it. When he was done, he gave Stride another dimpled smile. "Anyway, you asked for this meeting, Jonathan. What would you like to talk about? I'll help if I can."

"Hink Miller," Stride said.

"Yes, Gavin told me that he may have had a hand in the abduction. That's very disturbing."

"Did he work for you at the poker games?"

"Hink was in my employ for a while as an independent contractor," Broadway replied carefully. "But I terminated him some time ago."

"Why?"

"I believe I mentioned that a criminal record is typically disqualifying for working with me. I run a clean ship. Hink was arrested for assault last year. I believe you know about that incident. Gavin helped put the legal issues to bed, but I grew uncomfortable with Hink remaining in my employ."

"Is it possible he held a grudge?" Stride asked. "Against you or against Gavin?"

"Anything's possible, but Hink walked away with a sizable separation bonus. I find that keeps ex-employees in line."

"Did Hink know about Gavin's inheritance?"

"I have no idea. However, Gavin's financial turnaround happened very recently, as you know. Hink was long gone by then."

"How did you happen to hire him? Who sent him to you?"

"He came via a mutual friend of ours," Broadway replied with a smile.

Stride rolled his eyes. "Curt Dickes?"

"Precisely."

"If you employ Curt, then you're not so religious about turning away people with criminal records."

"I don't employ Curt. He's more of a consultant. A headhunter, if you will."

"Supplying girls?" Stride asked. "If your games include prostitution, you're not going to like how this all turns out for you."

"I assure you, I'm not involved in prostitution in any way," Broadway replied, looking mildly offended at the idea. "That doesn't mean I don't dress up my parties with attractive people. I do. But those are two very different things."

Stride sighed. Broadway was like sand slipping through fingers. "Can you tell me anything more about Hink? Do you know whether he has ties to anyone else in your . . . enterprise? Obviously, someone murdered him and his mother, so we want to know if he had an accomplice."

"I understand. And no, I have no names for you right now, but I'll keep looking. I told you I would audit my people, and I'm serious about that. However, it takes time to find connections. Now, can I help in any other way?"

"The ransom," Stride said.

"What about it?"

"You were helpful in telling us about the hundred-dollar bills. I appreciate it."

"You're welcome," Broadway replied.

"But now I need to know, did you really give Gavin one hundred thousand dollars in cash? Because we only found a fraction of that amount at Hink's place. I need to know if Gavin lied to us."

Broadway tapped the steering wheel as if he were counting off the seconds on a clock. "May we speak off the record again?"

"For now," Stride agreed.

"All right. The truth. Gavin didn't lie to you. He came to me saying he needed ransom money, and I gave him one hundred thousand dollars in cash. All in hundred-dollar bills. In return for an appropriate fee, of course."

"When?" Stride asked.

"What?"

"When did he come to you for the money?"

"I believe it was close to midnight last Tuesday."

"And not before?"

"No." Broadway gave Stride a knowing look. "That doesn't sound like the answer you wanted."

"We've heard that Gavin had hundreds in his wallet a couple of days before the ransom demand," Stride said. "So we wondered . . ."

"Whether the kidnapping was staged? Well, I can't tell you anything about that, Jonathan. Gavin is a smart man, so if anyone could pull off something like this, he could. Although again, I really don't know why he would. Inherited assets aren't marital property, as you know. But the hundreds in his possession are no mystery. He had one of his rare winning streaks at the games on Friday." Broadway added again, "Off the record."

Stride frowned.

They were done; there was nothing more to ask. He got out of the car, shut the door, and heard the Mercedes's engine purr to life. As Broadway drove away, Stride stood in the parking lot and let the afternoon rain pour over his head. Now that he was back on the job, he couldn't escape that old frustration. Sometimes the more he dug into a case, the further he got from the truth.

He'd thought that he had finally found a flaw in the kidnapping scheme.

He'd thought that he finally had Gavin Webster on the ropes, but the man had managed to slip away again. Every question had an answer.

They still had no way of proving he'd killed his wife.

Unless he was what he said he was. Innocent.

28

Serena pulled off the highway near the railroad tracks in Proctor. Not far away, a freight train rattled northwest out of town, its cars piled high with taconite. Graffiti was scrawled on the metal walls. A stiff, cold breeze blew rain across her windshield, and the rust-colored ground near the tracks was thick with mud and pools of water. Power lines drooped overhead. Almost a hundred yards away, a group of three teenagers hiked between the tracks.

From where she was, Serena had a clear vantage on Ben Larsen's auto repair shop. It wasn't a large business, just a white garage with a set of three oversized doors, all of which were open. Cars, rusted trailers, and empty semitrucks were parked around the lot. With a pair of binoculars, Serena could see Ben and another mechanic working inside the garage underneath a dark-green sedan. She'd bought a sandwich in town, and she ate her lunch and waited.

Shortly after two o'clock, she saw Ben take a phone call. A couple of minutes later, he climbed behind the wheel of his F-150. He had a flatbed trailer hitched behind it. As he drove out to the highway, Serena ducked down in the Mustang so that he wouldn't see her. When the truck was out of sight, she jogged across the street, then hiked up the dirt lot toward the garage. She didn't know how much time she had before Ben returned.

When she'd first investigated Nikki's death, she'd been certain that Delaney was keeping things from her. Now she felt the same way about Ben Larsen.

She strolled into the open garage through a curtain of rain pouring from the roof. A handsome black man, probably in his midtwenties, worked below the green Dodge that was elevated by the car lift. He was dressed in blue coveralls and had earbuds in his ears. His head bobbed rhythmically as he worked, and he didn't hear Serena call out to him. She had to touch his shoulder to get his attention, and when she did, he jumped in surprise.

He popped the earbuds out of his ears and let them dangle down his shirt. "Sorry. Didn't see you there."

"That's okay."

"What can I do for you? You got a car that needs some work?"

"No, it's not that." Serena showed him her badge and introduced herself. "Do you mind if I ask you a couple of questions?"

"Well, you probably want the owner if you've got questions. That's Mr. Larsen. He just left. He's picking up a car in Cloquet, so I imagine he'll be back in an hour or so."

"Actually, I was hoping you could tell me more about Mr. Larsen," Serena said.

The young man frowned. He had short black hair and a trimmed beard, and he had the tall, lean build of a runner. She noticed that he was wearing a name tag on his coveralls that read: LEON.

"Not sure I'm too comfortable with that," Leon admitted. "I don't like talking behind anybody's back, you know?"

"I understand that. Anything you can tell me would help a lot. Have you worked for Ben long?"

"Five years. Since I got out of high school. That's the thing, I like the job. I don't want to mess that up."

"Sure. I'm really just gathering background information. I'm working on a cold case from a couple of years ago, and I'm talking to everybody who knew the victim."

"Victim?"

"A shooting death," Serena said.

Leon scratched his nose with a greasy hand. "Well, shit, okay. I don't want to mess around with that. I mean, if you think I can help, ask away."

Serena glanced around at the interior of the garage. The concrete floor was stained with oil, and even with the doors open, it smelled of gasoline. She saw stacks of old tires and a long worktable at the back lined with tools and parts. Three others cars were parked inside in various stages of repair.

"You must know Ben pretty well after five years," she said. "What's he like?"

Leon shrugged. "Ben's Ben. He has his opinions about things. I have mine."

"Do you know Ben's son, Zach?"

"Oh, sure. Before he went to college, Zach was in here all the time. I like the kid."

"How do Ben and Zach get along?" Serena asked.

Leon rolled his eyes. "Ben's pretty much the same as a boss or a daddy. He likes things done his way, and if you don't measure up, he'll let you hear about it. Ben was an athlete in school, so he figured Zach should be an athlete, too. But Zach isn't cut out for that. Big and strong, but kinda clumsy, you know? Ben always thought it was because Zach didn't try hard enough, and he'd ride the kid pretty hard."

"Zach used to have a girlfriend," Serena said.

Leon nodded. "You bet. Delaney."

"You know her?"

"Oh, yeah. She'd come to the garage with Zach a lot. Ben liked to put Zach to work on the cars, and Delaney would hang out in the back and do her homework. She's a brainiac. Really cute, too. Zach was crazy about her."

"They broke up. Did you hear about that?"

"Yeah. It was pretty sudden. I never heard why."

"Did Zach talk about it?"

"He said Delaney broke it off. That's all I heard. I was surprised.

I always thought Delaney liked Zach as much as Zach liked her. But teenagers are weird, huh?"

Serena eased smoothly into her next question. "What about Ben? What did he think about Zach dating Delaney?"

Leon glanced nervously through the open garage door, as if making sure Ben wasn't standing there watching him. Without answering, he went to the counter at the back of the garage and grabbed an open can of Dr Pepper. He took a drink, wiped his mouth, and came back.

"Leon?" Serena asked. "What did Ben think about Delaney?"

"I guess Ben liked her okay."

"Is that all?"

"I'm not sure what you want."

"It sounds like Delaney spent a lot of time with Zach's family. They went on trips together. She was over at their house. She was here at the garage. I'm wondering what Ben had to say about his son's girlfriend."

Leon scratched his nose. He checked his watch and studied the undercarriage of the car over his head. Anything to avoid answering her question.

"Come on, Leon," Serena murmured. "Talk to me."

"Hey, look. I like Ben. He pays me pretty well. He doesn't dump a lot of racist shit on me. That's why I stick around."

"I get that, but this is important."

Leon's face contorted unhappily. "Ben and Delaney . . . I don't know, he was just weird about her."

Serena frowned. "What do you mean?"

"Well, shit, you know how men are. I'm not going to pretend I don't notice when a girl's got it going on. But Delaney was Zach's girlfriend. Plus, she was what? Fourteen? Fifteen? Some of the things Ben said about her, I just couldn't believe it."

"Like what?"

"Oh, I don't know. Like talking about what kind of a hot body she had. Going on to me about whether I thought Zach was banging her. Talking about how she made him wish he was sixteen again. It was just creepy, creepy shit. Dads don't talk about their son's girlfriend that way, you know? And then one time—"

Leon stopped.

"Yes?" Serena prompted him.

"Well, one time, Zach and Delaney walked over to the garage from school. Delaney had been in gym class and hadn't had time to change or shower or anything. So Ben was like, use the shower in back, go for it, no problem. I could tell Delaney didn't want to, but Ben would *not* let it go. Kept pushing it and pushing it. So finally Delaney went in the office and took a shower just to shut him up. The thing is, after she changed her clothes, she forgot her backpack in there. So later—I mean, this is just too weird—later, Ben went into the office to get it for her, and when he did, he swiped her panties."

Serena did a double take. "He did *what*?"

"Yeah! He just took them. The next day he was showing them off to me like he was fucking proud of it."

Serena felt a sinking feeling deep in the pit of her stomach. "Did Delaney know about this?"

"About her underwear disappearing? How could she not?"

"What about Zach?"

"I don't know. Not unless Delaney told him. Ben didn't usually talk about Delaney in front of Zach. He saved that shit for me."

"The breakup between Zach and Delaney," Serena went on sharply. "Do you think it had something to do with Ben?"

Leon shook his head. "No idea. Zach said he didn't know why Delaney dumped him."

"What about Ben? Did he say anything?"

"Not a word. Zach would be crying about her, and Ben would tell him to shut up and grow a pair. He never talked about Delaney after that."

Serena frowned. "Did you ever meet Delaney's mother?"

"I don't think so."

"Did Delaney or Zach talk about her? Or did Ben?"

"Not that I recall."

Serena slid her phone out of her pocket. She opened up her photos and found a picture of Nikki from the police file. It was the photograph of Nikki and Delaney together, and she enlarged the pic so that the focus was on Nikki's face. She showed the phone screen to Leon.

"Do you recognize this woman?" she asked.

He squinted at the photo. At first, he looked ready to say no, but then he stopped and took a second look. "Oh, her. Yeah, that's her. That's the one."

"Who?"

"The woman who had the big argument with Ben," Leon said.

"When was this?"

"I don't know. A while ago. She came into the garage white-hot mad and went after Ben. I mean, she went *after* him. She hit his face so hard she drew blood. Ben pulled her into the office and shut the door, and the two of them started screaming at each other."

"Could you hear what it was about?"

"No, but it got so bad I called the cops."

"You called the police?" Serena asked.

"Yeah. I was afraid she was going to kill him. Anyway, they were in there for a while, and then it got real quiet, and the woman stormed out and left, didn't say anything else. Ben came out, and I told him the police were on their way, and he swore and said what did I do that for. He said she was just an unhappy customer, a drunk, it was no big deal."

"Did the police come?"

Leon nodded. "Yeah, and Ben told him it was nothing. He blamed me. Said I overreacted, and it was all a misunderstanding. He told them he didn't want to get the woman in any trouble and asked if they could forget about the whole thing. The cop was a bowling buddy of Ben's, so he let it slide. That was that."

Serena held up the photo of Nikki again. "And you're sure this is the woman?"

"I'm sure."

"All right. Thank you, Leon. I'd appreciate it if you didn't mention our conversation to Ben."

Leon looked relieved to be able to keep it to himself. "Whatever you say."

Her emotions churning, Serena left the garage and walked back into the heavy rain. She was thinking about Nikki, thinking about Delaney, and thinking about Samantha. She was thinking about daughters protecting mothers and mothers protecting daughters.

In the Mustang, it didn't take her long to retrieve the details of a 911 call in Proctor two years earlier at the location of Larsen Auto Repair. Ben was mentioned by name; the woman was unidentified. The resolution of the incident was written up simply as: *Customer assault. Owner declined to press charges.*

Serena was more concerned about the date of the altercation.

Nikki Candis had confronted Ben Larsen on a Wednesday afternoon. Two days later, she was dead.

29

The woods around Fredenberg Lake refused to give up their secrets. They'd been searching for hours through nearly impenetrable terrain and had still covered only a fraction of the land. It was slow work. Fallen trees blocked their way, making a tangle of moss and dead branches, their trunks sprawled like bodies. Birch trees grew tightly together like columns of snow soldiers, forcing them to step sideways to squeeze between them. There were sharp valleys everywhere, with treacherous footing and swollen creeks soaking their boots. Wind rumbled in the high treetops like ocean waves. The rain fell hard, as it had throughout the day, making everyone wet and miserable. Even the dogs looked unhappy.

What made it worse for Maggie was knowing they might never find what they were looking for. If the body had been buried deep, even the dogs might not smell it. If it hadn't been buried at all, then they would be lucky to find any random bones that had been left behind by wolves and scavengers. There were definitely wolves not far away. Every few minutes, Maggie would freeze as a bloodcurdling howl rose above the noise of the storm.

She checked her phone. Signal came and went with the wind, and for the moment, she had none. She folded her arms across her skinny chest and examined the forest, which got darker minute by minute.

"Do you think Chelsey is really out here?" Guppo asked. The round detective was flushed and breathing hard as he kept pace with her in the forest, but Maggie had never heard him complain.

"I don't know. Stride's going to talk to Gavin about what the hell he was doing up here two days before his wife was kidnapped. But I don't like it." She leaned her head back against the nearest birch tree. Briefly, she closed her eyes. "Did you talk to the neighbors around here?"

"I did, but there aren't many. Nobody recognized photos of Gavin or Chelsey or Hink. There's not much traffic on the road, but most of the houses are set back, so they can't see who's coming and going. Nobody mentioned suspicious vehicles."

"How about gunshots?"

"There are always gunshots up here," Guppo said. "People around here don't even notice. I asked about shouts or screaming, but nobody heard anything like that. Not a surprise. If somebody brought Chelsey up here, odds are she was already dead."

"Yeah," Maggie said again, with a sigh.

In the distance, a wolf howled again, mournful and ominous. Another chimed in, and soon they heard the chorus of an entire pack in the distance.

"They sound hungry," Guppo said.

Maggie shivered. "Man, I can think of a lot of ways to go, but being torn apart by wolves is really low on my list. One time I was up on the Gunflint, and I saw a deer by the lake. Half a dozen wolves came out of the woods and surrounded it. That was not a pretty sight."

"With me, they wouldn't need to eat again for days," Guppo said.

Maggie burst out laughing. Then she shook her head and wiped some of the rain from her eyes. In the gray forest around them, half a dozen police officers tramped through the wet leaves, leading dogs who kept their noses in the weeds. The searchers dodged around an uprooted pine and headed down into a steep gully, where they disappeared from view. With them gone, Maggie felt as if she and Max were alone in the woods.

"So is Stride back for good?" Guppo asked.

Maggie thought about what she'd seen in Stride's face that day. "I think he is. I figured once he got a taste, he couldn't stay away."

"What does that mean for you? If Stride's back, does he become the lieutenant again?"

"Hell if I know. That's up to K-2."

"You've been in charge for over a year. Could you go back to being number two?"

"With anybody else? No. With Stride? I guess that would feel normal." She was about to make a bad joke, but then she stopped herself. *I've been under him before.*

"Think it would work the other way?" Guppo asked. "With you as the boss?"

This time she couldn't resist. "Me on top? If history's any judge, I think he'd like that."

The joke flew over Guppo's head, and she was grateful.

"The thing is, his ego doesn't have to fill the room like mine," she went on. "But could I ever order him around? I don't know. Plus, I can't say I'd miss being at the front of the room. And you don't have to tell me that none of you would miss me."

"Not true."

"Serena's ringtone? 'Big Time'?"

Max chuckled. "Oh, you know about that, huh?"

"I know about it. You all think my ego's out of control. Which it is."

"It's not ego when you're good at what you do. And if we miss Stride, it's only because we miss Stride."

"Yeah. I miss him, too."

Maggie checked the time and squinted through the treetops at the charcoal sky. Where they were standing, darkness and shadow crept through the forest like a damp fog. The rain beat down on her head, as hard as ever, and showed no signs of letting up.

"We're going to have to knock off for the night soon," she said.

"Yeah."

"We'll start again in the morning."

She squeezed through the nest of sharp branches to the edge of the slope. Where the land fell off sharply, she could no longer see the bottom of the gully thirty feet down. The cops below her had switched on their flashlights, making a crisscross pattern of lights winking on and off through the trees. She cupped her hands around her mouth to call the team back to higher ground.

Then she heard a noise below her, and she froze.

One of the dogs barked. It was a frantic, excited bark, and it didn't stop. In the aftermath, she heard one of the police officers shout, then another, then another. The overlapping voices carried up the gully, and when she understood what they were saying, Maggie dove down the slope at a run.

"*We've found something.*"

* * * * *

Across the brightly lit UMD student center, Cat recognized Delaney Candis hurrying into the rain. The other girl was tall, and she walked fast. On an impulse, Cat gathered up her own books into her backpack and quickly followed. Outside, night had fallen, and the wind whipped her wet hair into her face. Delaney had opened up a large yellow umbrella, which made her easy to spot as she headed toward the south side of campus. Cat jogged to catch up to the other girl, and by the time Delaney reached the border of campus at College Street, Cat was right behind her.

The noise of her footsteps gave her away because Delaney spun around before crossing the street.

"What do you want?" she demanded.

Cat stopped. They were on the grass near the street, which was empty of traffic in the rain. Underneath the umbrella, Delaney was dry, her brown hair full and wavy. Her dark eyes were wary. Cat knew she must look a sight, with her clothes soaked and her hair pasted to her face. Cat was older than Delaney by three years, but the other girl was several inches taller, which made Cat feel small.

"My name's Cat—"

"I know who you are."

"Oh. Okay." Cat tried to make a joke out of it. "Usually, it's not a good thing when people know who I am."

"Don't be cute," Delaney snapped back. "Yes, I know all about you from the papers, and I know you're smart because you keep beating me on math tests, but most of all, I know you're connected to that detective. Serena. I don't want to talk to her, and I don't want to talk to you."

Cat held up her hands in surrender. "Look, I just wanted to say hi."

"Hi. Is that all? Are we done?"

"Sure, fine, sorry to bother you," Cat said with an edge in her voice. She began to walk away, but then she stopped and took a breath. The rain was harder than ever. "No, actually, I want to say something else."

"What is it?"

Cat took a step closer to the other girl. "Hey, if you want to act like a bitch, that's fine, go ahead. Believe me, I've been where you are, and I've got the act down cold. It's a lot easier than letting your guard down. We don't have to talk. That's okay. But you and me, we're not so different. We've both been through shit."

"You don't know anything about me."

"No? I think you'd be surprised how much I know. Like I said, I've been there. And I know something else, too. It's about Zach."

Delaney's wide mouth pressed into a flat, unhappy frown. "What about him?"

"He's still in love with you."

Cat watched the girl's lower lip tremble. Her eyes grew glassy with tears, but her face twisted in defiance.

"Don't talk to me about Zach. Get away from me. I don't need this."

"Okay. Whatever you want."

Cat turned her back on Delaney and started toward campus, but she hadn't gone far when she heard a low voice calling after her. The word was barely audible above the rain.

"Wait."

Cat reversed her steps. Delaney stood in the same place near the street, trying to hold the umbrella straight against the wind.

"Is that really true?" she asked. "About Zach?"

Cat nodded. "Yes, it is."

"I heard he likes *you*."

"He doesn't. He hasn't gotten over you. I could tell that after talking with him for five minutes."

"Well, he needs to move on," Delaney said.

"He can't. He wants to know why you dumped him."

Delaney opened her mouth, then shut it tight and said nothing. One tear slipped down her cheek.

Cat looked up and down College Street. A few cars were parked along the curbs. Directly across from them was a row of old houses, most of them now used for student apartments. The rain poured down over her face, making it hard to see.

"Hey, do you mind if we share that umbrella?" she asked.

Delaney shrugged and tilted it upward. Cat came under the protection of the rim, standing close to the other girl. Delaney had a long, slender nose and perfect creamy skin, which was in contrast to Cat's golden face. Her brown eyes stared at Cat with a mixture of loneliness and resentment. Cat remembered how much time she'd spent feeling the same way. Alone. Bitter. Suspicious of the world and everyone in it.

"I don't know if it was in the articles about me," Cat said, "but my mom died when I was six. My dad killed her."

Delaney nodded with something that looked like sympathy. "Yeah, I read that."

"It sucked then, and it still sucks."

"I know how you feel."

"I bet you do," Cat said.

They stood awkwardly under the umbrella, neither one moving.

"I should go," Delaney said. "If you talk to Zach—"

"Do you want me to tell him something?"

She shook her head. "No. That's okay."

"Zach's cute. Kind of a big bear."

"Yeah." A little nostalgia shined in the girl's eyes.

Cat made a snap decision. "Listen, I'm hungry, and I haven't eaten. You want to order a pizza or something?"

"I can't." After an awkward pause, she added, "Not tonight."

"Okay."

She offered up the tiniest smile. "Maybe another time, though?"

"Okay."

"You're right," Delaney went on. "I'm not really a bitch."

"Yeah, I can tell."

It was a strange moment, when it was obvious to both of them that they actually liked each other.

"Look, I appreciate you reaching out to me," the other girl said. "You didn't have to do that. Particularly when you know I'm going to kick your ass on the next test."

Cat grinned. "You think so, huh?"

Delaney's smile got wider, and she had a face that was born to smile. It was so dazzling that it made Cat a little jealous.

"Listen, for what it's worth, I've been in some bad places and done some bad things," Cat told her. "The only reason I'm on the other side of all that is because of two people, and one of them is Serena. You don't have to talk to her, but if you ever want to, you can trust her. She'll protect you. I promise."

"That's good to know," Delaney replied.

"She's been through shit, too. Like us."

"I know. She told me some of it."

"There's a lot more."

"Okay."

"Anyway," Cat said. "That's all I wanted to say."

"Thanks." Delaney gestured at one of the houses across the street. "That's me. My apartment is over there. Gotta crack the books."

"Sure. Me too."

"I feel bad leaving you without the umbrella."

"I'm fine," Cat said.

Delaney smiled again, that high-wattage smile. She turned away and walked out into the street, her umbrella the one splash of color on a dark night. Cat felt the cold rain again and grimaced. She kept her eyes on Delaney as the other girl reached the middle of College Street.

That was when, half a block away, headlights burned to life.

Cat heard the screech of tires on wet asphalt. A car that had been parked at the far curb accelerated like a rocket, shooting through the rain directly at Delaney. Cat screamed, but the other girl didn't hear her. Delaney seemed lost in thought, not noticing the car as it bore down on her, gathering speed. Cat sprinted into the street, shouting Delaney's name. The other girl had reached the opposite curb, but Cat saw the car bump off the street and tear through the green grass.

The headlights loomed like two monster's eyes. Their brightness finally jolted Delaney out of her trance. She realized what was happening, but the shock of it froze her in place, and she stood on the grass, not moving as the car roared toward her with a new burst of speed. It wasn't slowing down or turning away; it wasn't out of control. The driver knew exactly what he was doing. Cat raced onto the grass and threw herself at Delaney's back, hitting her so hard that the two of them flew into the air.

A fraction of a second later, the car cleared them by inches, covering both of them with spray and mud. It carved furrows into the lawn before lurching back onto the street and speeding away.

Delaney was facedown. Cat grabbed frantically at her shoulder.

"Are you okay? Delaney, are you hurt? Are you all right?"

With a choking cough, the younger girl pushed herself up in the wet grass. Her sneakers were in the ruts left by the car. That was how close it had come to killing them both. Delaney's brown eyes were wide. She shook her head in shock, and Cat quickly threw her arms around the girl.

"It's okay. We're okay."

Delaney gasped for breath. The impact of Cat landing on her back had knocked the wind out of her. When she could suck in a little bit of air, she managed to say, "How could he not see me?"

Cat hesitated. She wasn't sure whether to tell her the truth.

"He saw you, Delaney. He was aiming for you. He was trying to kill you."

30

Stride watched Gavin Webster's face, which changed color in the firelight. Reflections of the flames danced in the man's blue eyes. The lawyer was home, in the old house on Observation Hill overlooking the lake. The damaged front door had been repaired. He wore jeans and a rust-colored wool sweater with fraying cuffs and tears at the elbows. He was drinking, too. Hard stuff, straight gin.

"So you talked to Broadway?" the lawyer asked. His voice was part grief, part outrage.

"Yes."

"So did he tell you that he gave me one hundred thousand dollars in cash to pay the ransom? Not ten thousand?"

"He did," Stride said.

Gavin studied Stride's impassive expression. Like a good defense lawyer, he always anticipated the prosecution's case. "But that doesn't prove how much cash was in the backpack when I tossed it to the man in the boat. Right?"

"Right."

"I could have buried the rest of the money somewhere for all you know."

"True."

"And then there's the missing gun," Gavin added. "I suppose I probably tossed that in the river after I killed Hink."

"I don't know. Did you?"

"No, because I didn't do it." Gavin got up and used a poker to jostle the logs in the fireplace, causing a shower of sparks. "Let me ask you something, Stride. What's my motive in all of your fantastic theories? Why would I want to harm my wife? I could have divorced Chelsey if I really wanted to get rid of her, and there was no way she was going to get her hands on any of that cash."

"Divorce is still ugly," Stride said.

"So is murder. If I'm caught, I go to prison, rather than enjoying my wealth. That seems like a risky bet to make. Besides, it's a moot point anyway, because I loved her." He heard what he'd said, and he corrected the tense. "*Love* her."

Stride stared at Gavin as the man took a seat on the brick hearth near the fire. His skin was flushed red, and his blue eyes still had that weirdly charismatic glow. Maybe it was the alcohol, or maybe the lawyer was taunting him, but Stride knew that Gavin was right. Despite those three million dollars, he had no obvious motive to kill his wife.

If Gavin had really done it, there was something else he was trying to hide.

But what?

Stride still had one more card to play.

"We have a major search underway," he told the lawyer. "We've been covering an area north of the city for most of the day."

Concern spread across Gavin's face. Stride couldn't decide whether it was real or faked. "A search? You think you've found the location where Hink took Chelsey?"

"We don't know yet. It's a big area, and it will take us time to work our way through it. We have dogs following Chelsey's scent, but the rain makes the process more difficult."

Gavin frowned. "Where are you searching?"

"The woods near Fredenberg Lake," Stride said, watching the lawyer's face for any reaction.

"Fredenberg Lake? Well, I was just up in that area last—" Gavin stopped. He glanced away and shook his head with a hiss of disgust. "Of course. You know that already. That's why you're searching up there."

Stride waited for Gavin to go on.

"The tow-truck driver? He's your source?"

"That's right."

"What a time to get a flat tire, huh? While I'm out scouting the woods to figure out where to bury my wife's body?"

"If that's a joke, it's not funny," Stride said.

"You're right. This isn't funny. It's pathetic."

"You told us you went to visit your parents on Sunday evening," Stride went on. "That's the same day you were in the woods near Fredenberg Lake. You went up there on Sunday morning, and later that day, you headed off to visit your parents for a couple of days?"

"Yes. So what?"

"Then you got back to Duluth on Tuesday evening, and that's when you discovered that Chelsey was missing?"

"Exactly."

Stride frowned. "So far we haven't found anyone who can confirm that Chelsey was still alive on Sunday. We can't locate anyone who saw or talked to Chelsey on Sunday, Monday, or Tuesday."

"*I* talked to her," Gavin protested.

"Did anyone else? Did your parents?"

"No, but you can check her phone records. You'll see that I called. Twice. Each call lasted several minutes."

"That only means that someone answered the phone," Stride said, "but we don't have any way to prove it was actually your wife. It could have been Hink Miller, for example."

Gavin nearly spit with exasperation. "Oh, for fuck's sake, Stride."

"Your wife didn't make any calls after Saturday afternoon. She didn't receive any other calls. She didn't send any emails. She didn't use her credit cards. None of the neighbors saw her. What was she doing for those three days?"

"Chelsey enjoyed time alone in the house," Gavin insisted. "I don't know, maybe she enjoyed time away from *me*. She didn't like to go anywhere when I was gone, because she considered it a vacation. She never told anyone that she was alone, because otherwise, people would have stopped by, invited her to dinner, forced her to make other plans. When she was alone, she liked being able to stay home and watch all the movies that I hated."

Stride let his outburst run its course. Then he said, "She enjoyed time away from you?"

Gavin sighed. "Figure of speech. I told you, we weren't always in sync. It happens in marriages. I'm sure you know that. Couples have ups and downs, and I admit, much of ours was down in recent months. But you can't make the leap from there to murder."

"Except Chelsey is missing."

"Because someone took her!" Gavin shouted. He jumped to his feet. "Someone kidnapped her! I paid them a ransom! You can search the woods around Fredenberg Lake all you want, but you're wasting your time. I had *nothing* to do with her disappearance."

"It's a remote location," Stride pointed out. "So what were you doing up there?"

Gavin sat down in the chair near the fireplace and poured himself more gin. "You wouldn't believe me if I told you."

"Try me."

The lawyer sipped his drink. "Have you ever heard of geocaching?"

"It's some kind of GPS treasure hunt, isn't it?" Stride asked, his eyes narrowing.

"That's right. People hide things in various locations. Urban, rural, suburban, wherever. None of it is valuable. It's just poems, trinkets, plastic toys, whatever. They keep records of the GPS coordinates of the hiding places and post them online. Seekers try to locate the things that are hidden. There are caches everywhere. Millions of people go out looking for them."

"Including you?"

"Including me. We all have our hobbies."

"How long have you been doing this?" Stride asked.

"Years. A decade or more. Sunday mornings are my searching time. Some people go to church. Me, I dig around for geocaches."

"And that's what you were doing near Fredenberg Lake?"

"Yes."

"Why there?" Stride asked. "I assume there must be hundreds or thousands of these geocaches around the Northland. What brought you to that particular area on Sunday morning?"

"A puzzle."

"What do you mean? What kind of puzzle?"

"There are local clubs, Stride. Message boards. We set up games and contests with each other. It's all anonymous, all done under secret identities. I know that may sound odd, but it's part of the mystery. I've been playing a private game with one of the members for a few weeks."

"Who?"

"I told you, I don't know. It's anonymous. We use private email accounts. There's nothing sinister about it. Whoever it is doesn't know who I am, either. He—or she, I have no idea—approached me after seeing some of my posts on the local message board. He'd hidden a medallion somewhere in the Northland, like the way they do in Saint Paul during the Winter Carnival. He invited me to look for the clues and try to find it. That's why I was on that road near Fredenberg Lake. I was hunting for the medallion."

"Did you find it?" Stride asked.

"Yes, I did."

"Can I see it?"

Gavin got up and left the room. He returned a few seconds later and handed a gold plastic medallion to Stride. It was about four inches in diameter, and it was decorated with the signs of the Zodiac. There were no signs that it had been outside; it had been scrubbed clean.

"This is what you were looking for?"

"That's right. As you can see, it's not expensive. I mean, we always run the risk that some hiker will stumble across a cache by accident, so we never hide valuable things. These are just games."

"I'll need to see the emails you exchanged with this person," Stride said.

"Sure, if that's what you want. I doubt it'll help, though. It's just a generic Gmail account. The handle was *Razrsharp*, whatever that means."

"Did it occur to you that this person could be the kidnapper?" Stride asked.

Gavin looked genuinely startled. "No. It didn't. I have no reason to think that this person even knows who I am. Just like I don't know who he is."

"But he might know, right?"

"I suppose."

"Who else knows about this hobby of yours?" Stride asked.

"I don't hide it. I talk about it all the time."

"Including at Broadway's games?"

Gavin hesitated. "Yes."

Stride turned the medallion over in his hands, then handed it back to Gavin.

A generic Gmail account.

It would be difficult, maybe impossible, to trace the account to its owner. Stride was also well aware that the account could belong to Gavin himself. The puzzles. The medallion. That could all have been him, anticipating every twist in the game. If the police stumbled onto a body in the woods, if anyone spotted him or remembered him, he had an explanation for why he was in the area. A mysterious, anonymous suspect to lay in front of them.

Razrsharp.

Stride stared into Gavin's blue eyes. Those strange blue eyes stared back at him. He definitely could have done it. He was intelligent enough to develop a brilliant scheme to kidnap and kill his wife. But if he had, *why?*

They still didn't have a motive.

His phone started ringing. It was Maggie.

Stride answered the phone and listened without saying anything. The call was quick. Signal was bad. He hung up the phone, and he could see a wave of anxiety cross Gavin's face. In that moment, Stride tried to listen to his instincts, to figure out what secrets the man was keeping. Like a geocache hidden in the trees.

Innocent or guilty. They'd have an answer soon.

"We've found your wife, Gavin," Stride told him. "Chelsey's alive."

31

Chelsey Webster lay on her back in an indentation dug out of the gully. It resembled a shallow grave. There were mounds of dirt and dead leaves piled around the hole, as if whoever had brought her here had intended to bury her, but then left her uncovered instead for the wolves to find. One of the search dogs had zeroed in on her scent—or on the aroma of urine and feces soiling her clothes—and led a police officer with a flashlight directly to her.

She wore what she must have been wearing when she'd been taken from her house. A rose-colored turtleneck. A bulky sweater. Wool slacks and heavy socks, but no shoes. All her clothes were muddy and soaking wet now from the daylong rain, but before that, they would have given her a small bit of protection while she was outside. That was probably what had kept her alive. She was gagged with an old T-shirt in her mouth and gray tape, allowing her to make nothing more than desperate whimpers. Her wrists and ankles were tightly bound with tape, too. Wherever skin showed, it was black with dirt, and her face was bruised. Her body wasn't secured to anything, but the hole had been dug on a slope above a narrow creek. If she'd struggled enough to roll out, she could easily have drowned in the water.

Maggie knelt beside her. She squeezed Chelsey's hand, which was ice-cold. She could feel the woman trembling. Guppo and the other cops and the dogs pressed close in around her, and Maggie waved them back to give her more space and to begin to establish a perimeter for the crime scene. She looked for injuries beyond the bruising—cuts, abrasions, broken bones, knife or gun wounds—but she didn't see any signs of additional trauma. The woman's face was sunken, and she looked dehydrated. In the beams of a dozen flashlights, her eyes were wide open and scared.

But she was alive.

"Mrs. Webster, my name is Lieutenant Maggie Bei with the Duluth Police. We are very, very glad to see you. Don't worry, you're safe now. An ambulance will be here soon. They'll get you to a hospital so the doctors can check you out and clean you up. Rather than carry you out immediately, we'd like to wait and let the paramedics examine you to make sure you're safe to move. But we'll stay right here until they arrive. Do you understand?"

Slowly, with some confusion on her face, Chelsey nodded.

"My apologies for the bright lights," Maggie went on. "You might want to close your eyes if that's more comfortable."

Chelsey did, and Maggie used her camera phone to take a series of pictures and videos of the scene. When she had a rough photographic record of the area, she gestured at Guppo, who handed her two thick blankets he'd retrieved from the squad car.

"Let's see if we can keep you a little warmer while we wait, okay?" Maggie said, spreading the blankets over Chelsey's body. "I know the tape is uncomfortable, but I don't want to remove it myself, because your skin is probably pretty raw where you've been bound. Better to do that at the hospital. But I'm going to cut a slit across the tape on your mouth and see if I can get that shirt out, okay? That should help you breathe a lot easier."

Again Chelsey nodded. Her eyes were open again, despite the harshness of the light shining down on her.

Maggie extracted a Swiss army knife from her pocket and carefully cut an opening in the tape that was stretched across Chelsey's face. With her fingers, she gingerly nudged the flaps of the tape apart, until the gap was wide enough for her to slowly pull the sodden shirt from Chelsey's mouth. She did it inch by inch, gauging the woman's reaction, ready to stop if Chelsey showed any signs of pain or choking. She didn't. The shirt itself was wet and dirty and flecked with traces of blood. When it came free, she handed it to Guppo, who deposited it in a plastic evidence bag.

Chelsey took a gulp of fresh air and coughed raggedly. Maggie was afraid the woman would vomit, and she helped her up by her shoulders and held her until the coughing fit passed. Then, gently, she laid the woman down on her back again.

"Are you able to talk at all?" Maggie asked. "Don't strain yourself. Just give me a yes or no, and that's it."

The woman cleared her throat, wincing as she did. "Little bit."

"That's okay. Give it time."

She heard trampling in the brush and saw another officer arriving from a squad car at the road. The cop held up a hand with five fingers spread wide.

"The ambulance is five minutes out," Maggie told Chelsey quietly. "It won't be long now."

"Thank you."

"Like I said, you don't have to talk. Save your voice. If you're up for it, I'll ask you a few yes-or-no questions, and all you have to do is nod or shake your head. Is that okay? Don't worry if you'd rather wait. We don't have to do this now."

Chelsey hesitated, then nodded her approval.

"Good. I appreciate your help. Mrs. Webster, I know this has been a terrible ordeal, and we're incredibly relieved to find you. Can you tell me, do you know who did this to you?"

The woman shook her head. Her voice cracked as she tried to talk. "Hood."

"The kidnapper was wearing a hood?"

She nodded.

"Was it a man?"

Another nod.

"Did you hear his voice? Did he speak to you at all? Or did you hear him speaking to anyone else?"

She shook her head.

"Was there more than one man?"

Again she shook her head.

"One," she murmured. Then in a shaky voice she added, "Knocked me out."

"He hit you?"

She nodded.

"Do you have any idea how long you've been here in the woods?" Maggie asked.

Chelsey shook her head again.

"Your husband returned from Rice Lake late on Tuesday evening," Maggie went on. "He was with his parents, do you remember that? Was that the night you were taken?"

Chelsey closed her eyes and nodded.

"Did the kidnapper take you straight here?"

She shook her head and spoke again. "Later."

"Do you know where you were kept initially?"

"No."

"It's okay. Just nod or shake your head. Did the same man take you out here to the woods? Was it the man who abducted you from your home?"

"Not sure. Think so."

"Your husband says he talked to you on Thursday night before he delivered the ransom money to the kidnapper. Do you remember talking to him?"

"Yes."

"So you were taken out here after that? After that call?"

"Yes."

"Do you remember if it was the same night?"

"Not sure."

"If it was Thursday, that would mean you've been out here for four nights. Does that sound possible?"

"Don't know. Maybe."

"All right. Thank you, Chelsey. I won't ask you anything more for now. You just rest."

Maggie listened to the quiet of the forest. Distantly, she heard the overlapping wails of sirens getting closer. She stood up again. She studied the hole in which Chelsey had been placed, near the base of the sharp gully, several hundred yards from the nearest road. Chelsey wouldn't have lasted much longer outside. Either the wolves would have found her, or she would have succumbed to dehydration. It was a miracle they'd gotten to her in time.

In all the thousands of square miles of Northland woods, they'd found their way to the right place. Because Gavin had been in the same place days before the kidnapper had brought his wife here to die.

There were no coincidences.

She stared down at Chelsey Webster again. Why was she alive?

The kidnapper had driven her here, dragged or carried her through the woods, dug a hole for her body—and then failed to kill her. He hadn't strangled her, or shot her, or cut her throat, or buried her alive. Instead, he'd left her. As if, when it came to that horrible moment, he couldn't bring himself to do it. He couldn't murder this woman. He could leave her to suffer a slow, agonizing death, or a death at the hands of animals who would have torn her apart. But he couldn't deliver the blow himself.

Maggie thought to herself: *Like a husband.*

She heard the woman trying to talk again, and she knelt beside her. "What is it, Chelsey?"

Her mouth made nothing more than a low mumble. Maggie leaned close enough to make out what she was saying.

"Gavin," Chelsey whispered. "Where's Gavin?"

"You'll see him soon. We talked to your husband. He knows you're alive, and he'll see you at the hospital."

"Gavin," Chelsey said again.

Then she closed her eyes and didn't say anything more.

* * * * *

Serena sat in the darkness. She breathed in; she breathed out. Her last drink had been near one o'clock in the morning the previous night, and now it was almost ten o'clock. The time ticked toward midnight. She still wanted a drink, but that was nothing special. She *always* wanted one. She'd wanted one every night for 6,608 nights. But she was alone now, and alone was dangerous. She felt an impulse to get up and go outside, to drive back to that bar in West Duluth, to sit down in front of Jagger and order another Absolut Citron. The pull was like a magnet. Her brain came up with sweet, seductive lies for why she should give herself one last night.

This day was already a loss. The count was still at zero. Nothing would change that. So why resist? She could allow herself one more drink. Or a few drinks. A final farewell. She could quit at 11:59 p.m., and then tomorrow she would be free.

Lies.

Her purse was on the table next to the sofa. Her car keys were inside her purse. *You know you want it, darling.*

The voice inside her head, the voice telling the lies, belonged to Samantha. Her mother had always been the queen of excuses. In the shadows of the cottage, she imagined Samantha sitting in the opposite chair near the fireplace. Young again, the way she'd been when Serena was only fifteen. Perfect. Lush blond hair. Bright white smile. Dressed to kill in a red dress that bared her thighs. Only the eyes gave away a hint of recklessness, madness, lack of control.

"Come on, Serena. Let's go to the bar. You and me. It'll be like the old days."

Serena breathed in. Breathed out.

"That bartender. What's his name? Jagger? He's a juicy one. If you don't sleep with him, I will."

And then: *"One drink, baby. Do it for me. What the hell harm can one drink do?"*

And then with a hiss from her forked tongue: *"You owe me, sweet child of mine. You left me, you walked away. You let me die on a bench alone. And now you won't even have a drink with me?"*

The words shot into Serena's head like the bullets of a gun.

Her hands curled into fists. She got up from the sofa, but she left her purse where it was. The purse with the car keys. She walked across the great space to the empty chair and stared down at Samantha.

"I still love you," she murmured.

"If you love me, you'll buy me a drink."

"I've finally figured out that I'll never stop loving you."

"Daughters don't run away from their mothers."

Serena sank to the floor. She bent forward until her cheek lay on the cushion of the chair, and she could feel its warmth, as if she were doing what she'd done so many times as a child, laying her head on Samantha's knees.

Then came the hardest one of all: "I forgive you, Mother."

She hesitated. Did she really mean that? Was she telling herself the truth?

"I forgive what you did. It doesn't change anything, it doesn't make me forget a moment of it, it doesn't make you less evil, but I forgive you."

The words were like a breath of wind that could blow away the dust. With that, Samantha was silent and gone, and Serena was alone. The empty chair was an empty chair, and the voice in her head went away. She stood up in the darkness, feeling an urge to scream with joy. She wanted a drink, but she wasn't going to have one.

Not tonight.

The future was something else. The future was a lot of days strung together, and Serena was no fortune-teller.

But not tonight.

Then she spun as she heard a loud knocking on the cottage's front door. It was an urgent knocking, the kind that said something was wrong. She ran to the door and ripped it open.

Cat and Delaney stood side by side on the porch.

The first thing Serena saw was blood.

32

Their clothes were dirty and grass-stained. Mud streaked their faces. Dried blood made a ribbon down Cat's arm, and Delaney had a deep purplish bruise on one of her cheekbones and a gash on her forehead just below the line of her dark hair. Their eyes looked numb with fear.

"Oh my God, what happened?" Serena cried.

She took Cat by the hand and dragged her inside the cottage and then did the same with Delaney. She turned on the lights and ran to the bathroom and came back with damp towels, Bactine, and bandages. Cat nodded at her to help Delaney first, and Serena examined the girl carefully and began to clean and disinfect the wounds on her face. As she did, Delaney winced at the sting.

"What happened?" Serena asked again.

"Someone tried to run Delaney down," Cat said.

"*What?*"

Cat explained about the car on the street near UMD. Serena didn't ask any more questions immediately. Instead, she broke away from Delaney long enough to wrap Cat up in a fierce hug. Her embrace was long and tight enough that Cat complained that Serena was squeezing her to death. She finally let go.

"Thank God you're okay," Serena said, taking Cat's face with both hands and leaning her forehead against hers.

"I'm fine."

When Serena turned back to help Delaney, she saw the girl watching the two of them closely. Serena understood her emotions. She was lonely. And a little jealous. She was looking at a mother and daughter together, and she was missing things that were gone and things that had never been.

"Delaney, how are you?" Serena asked softly.

"I'm okay."

"Do you need to go to the hospital?"

"No. I just bumped my head a little when I landed on the ground. Cat saved me. I never even saw the car."

"You're a mess from all the mud, and you must be cold. Do you want to clean up? I've got clothes you can wear."

Delaney nodded. "Thanks. That would be great."

Serena went to her dresser in the other bedroom to gather up clothes. They might be a little big for Delaney, but she thought they would fit her fine. She made a folded pile that she took into the cottage's one bathroom, and then she returned to the living room.

"You're all set. Take your time. If you want to take a shower, too, go for it."

Delaney gave her a weak smile. "Thank you, Mrs. Stride."

"It's Serena. Please."

Delaney went into the bathroom and closed the door. When Serena was alone with Cat, she tended to the girl's scraped arm and did her best to clean up the dirt from her face and skin with the damp towel. Then she gave Cat another hug.

"You could have been killed."

"I was on autopilot. I didn't think about it."

"Give me more details. Tell me about the car."

The girl shook her head. "I wish I could, but it all happened too fast. It was dark; it was raining. All I saw were headlights. I don't have any idea what the car looked like. I mean, it wasn't an SUV or a truck. It was a car. But beyond that, I can't tell you color, make, anything like that."

"And the driver?"

"No clue."

"Are you absolutely sure that this person was targeting Delaney? Could it have been an accident? Maybe they didn't see her in the street."

"No way," Cat insisted. "The car was going after her. The driver must have been watching us and waiting until she crossed. It started up as soon as she was in the middle of the street, and it went over the curb and followed us onto the grass. The thing barely missed us."

"Did you see where it went afterward?"

"No. By that point, we were both too freaked."

"Did Delaney say anything?" Serena asked.

"No. She was in shock. She wanted to go inside her apartment and forget about it. No doctors, no police, no nothing. I persuaded her that we should at least come here and tell you about it."

"I'm glad you did."

"What the hell's going on?" Cat asked. "Why would someone would want to kill her?"

"I don't know, but I want to hear what she has to say."

When Delaney got out of the shower a few minutes later, dressed in Serena's clothes, Serena talked with her while Cat went into the bathroom to take her own shower. She knew not to push too hard with the girl. She didn't mention Nikki, or the man in the car, or Zach, or Zach's father. Instead, she asked about calculus and college and being a freshman and living on her own. Slowly, Delaney relaxed around her. She began to talk quickly, as if a lot of words had been bottled up inside her and she was letting them out all at once. Her smile came back. It was a pretty smile.

When Cat was out of the shower, they ordered pizza. Delaney told them she had never eaten at Sammy's before, a fact that brought stricken looks of horror to Serena's and Cat's faces. They called in an order for delivery, opened cans of Diet Coke, and continued to chat about school, books, movies, and clothes. Two hours later, when the pizza was gone, Serena shot Cat a look that the girl understood. Cat made an excuse and went inside her old bedroom and closed the door, leaving Serena and Delaney alone.

Serena could see the girl's anxiety rise, but Delaney didn't shut down this time or get angry or defensive. She sat on the sofa across from Serena and steeled herself, as if she knew she needed to open the closet door and go toe-to-toe with the monster inside.

"I need to ask you some questions," Serena said. "Do you have any idea who the person in the car could be?"

Delaney brushed her long hair back. Her voice was steady. "I don't. I can't imagine why anyone would want to hurt me."

"Has anything unusual happened recently?"

The girl's sharp eyes homed in on Serena. "Well, you. You happened."

"I started asking about your mom again."

"Yes."

"Well, that's fair. I may have opened Pandora's box, but that tells me there was something in the box to begin with."

Delaney was silent.

"You want another pop?" Serena asked.

The girl shook her head.

"Well, I need one." Serena went into the kitchen and opened a new can of Diet Coke and returned to the living room. This time, she sat on the sofa next to Delaney.

"I told you some things about my own life the other day," Serena went on. "My struggle with drinking. My mother. I don't share those things with a lot of people, but I thought you deserved to know why this case is important to me. And honestly, why I blew it the first time around. Because I did. I wrote off your mom's death, and now I think there was much more to it than I realized at the time. The thing is, the two of you—you and Nikki—pushed too many buttons for me. I wasn't ready to deal with the emotions you brought up for me. Does that make any sense?"

Delaney didn't say anything, but Serena saw her head bob slightly.

"See, I think you're holding on to secrets that would explain a lot of what's going on," Serena said. "I know how hard it is to open up about tough stuff. I really do. But I'd like you to trust me and tell me what you're hiding."

"I can't." Delaney swung her head this time and met Serena's eyes. "I'd like to. Believe me. I'd like to tell someone. And Cat—she said you've always protected her. But I can't say anything."

"Why not?"

The girl's voice dropped to barely more than a whisper. "I'd lose everything. I'd be kicked out of school. I'd go to prison."

"Prison?"

Delaney nodded fiercely.

"Have you talked to a lawyer about this?" Serena asked.

"No."

"Then whatever this secret is, you're probably in a lot less jeopardy than you think. Did this happen two years ago? You were what, fifteen years old back then? It takes a lot for someone that young to go to prison. I can't see you doing the kinds of things that would put you there."

Delaney hesitated. "Could we talk off the record or something? Could you promise not to tell anyone and not do anything about it?"

"I won't lie to you, Delaney. No. That's not possible. If you tell me something involving a crime, I have to pursue it. But I can promise to move heaven and earth to keep you safe."

She saw a dark misery overtake the girl's face. Whatever the secret was, it was destroying her. It had been festering inside her for two years, taking over her life like a cancer.

And still she didn't talk.

"Delaney, I met with Zach's parents today," Serena said.

Those words landed on the girl like a burning arrow. Her eyes flew open with terror. She inhaled sharply, and her hands squeezed into fists.

"I also talked to someone at the garage about Zach's father. It sounds like he and your mother had a serious argument shortly before her death. Do you know what that argument was about?"

The girl sat frozen in silence, but cracks had begun to form in the ice.

"Was it about you?" Serena asked.

She heard Delaney's quick, frightened breaths.

"Did Mr. Larsen do something to you?" Serena went on. "I know he took you home after the camping trip that Sunday. It was just you and him in the car. I know that the very next day, everything began to fall apart between you and Zach. Delaney, if he assaulted you in some way, he should be punished for it. It's not your fault. What's more, if your mother knew about it and confronted him, then it's possible that he was involved in your mother's death."

Delaney squeezed her eyes shut. She shook her head. "You're wrong."

"Am I?"

The girl was silent.

"*Did* something happen between you and Mr. Larsen?"

Delaney opened her eyes again and took Serena's wrist. "Please, can't you drop it? Can't you let it go?"

"No, I can't. If an adult assaulted an underage child, I'm not going to let that go. I'm going to follow it until I know what really happened. If he's guilty, I'm going to see that he's punished. And the fact that someone tried to kill you tonight tells me that whatever is going on is not over. Look, Delaney, I understand the shame you feel. I understand how you can blame yourself. I've been there. It happened to me. I carried the burden for years. I still carry it. But if I could tell my teenage self one thing, it would be to fight back, rather than run away."

The girl stared into space. Her breaths came quickly.

"It wasn't his fault," she murmured. "Mr. Larsen. It wasn't his fault. It was mine. It was me."

"You were fifteen years old. Nothing was your fault."

"No. It was my idea. I tricked him. I knew he had a thing for me, and so I gave him what he wanted. I needed his help, and I needed him not to tell anyone about it."

Serena shook her head in confusion. "I don't understand."

The floodgates opened. Delaney sobbed. Her whole body convulsed, and she threw her arms around Serena's neck. When she spoke, her voice was so clouded by tears that Serena struggled to understand her.

"There was an accident."

33

Stride and Maggie talked with the doctor in the darkened corridor outside Chelsey Webster's hospital room. Inside, they kept a close eye on Gavin as he sat in the chair beside his wife's bed and held her hand. Chelsey was sleeping, one arm hooked up to intravenous fluids. She'd been cleaned and treated, and her hair washed, and she again looked like the beautiful woman she was.

"What's her condition?" Stride asked. "How is she?"

The doctor was a slim woman in her fifties with short gray hair. She sipped a cup of coffee as she spoke to them. It was nearly midnight, and the hospital corridor was dark and quiet.

"Given what she's been through, she's very lucky," the doctor said. "The wounds she suffered during the abduction were superficial and have mostly healed already. There's no evidence of concussion. She was dehydrated, but we've had her on fluids and liquid nutrients since she got here, and her numbers are already much better. My biggest concern in cases of extended exposure would be hypothermia, but as I say, she was lucky. She was wearing bulky clothes, and the hole in which they buried her must have provided a certain amount of insulation. Her body temperature was in the safe zone when the ambulance brought her in. Had she been out there much longer—given the heavy rain today—it's likely her condition would have deteriorated quickly. The fact that you found her when you did saved her life."

"How long would you expect her to stay in the hospital?"

"Well, we'll keep her overnight for observation, but there's really nothing wrong with her. I'm going to suggest some additional tests in the morning, but if those come back with no red flags, there's no reason she couldn't be released in the afternoon."

"Would we be able to ask her some questions when she awakens?"

"That'll be up to her. Just keep it short if you do."

"Thank you, Doctor," Stride said.

"Of course."

She walked away down the hospital corridor, and Stride and Maggie stayed outside Chelsey's room. Gavin noticed them hovering there, and he frowned unhappily. He had a rumpled look, his hair a mess. His blue eyes were shot with red, and his face was streaked where he'd been crying. The lawyer gently detached his hand from his wife's and then got up and joined them in the corridor.

"Do you have to be here now?" he whispered impatiently.

"We want to make sure your wife is okay," Stride told him. "She's been through a traumatic experience."

"Then let her rest."

"We will, but we'll need to talk to her when she wakes up."

"I want to be there when you do," Gavin snapped.

Maggie, who still looked ice-cold even though she'd changed into dry clothes at the station after returning from Fredenberg Lake, shook her head firmly. "We need to talk to her alone."

"I'm her husband. And a lawyer."

"You're also a suspect in her abduction," Maggie snapped.

Gavin exhaled with disgust. "Are you still pursuing that nonsense? Chelsey confirmed everything I told you, didn't she? The home invasion on Tuesday? The phone calls?"

"We still have questions," Stride told him.

The lawyer inhaled as if to fire back another sharp reply, but then he closed his eyes, and his shoulders sagged. He looked over his shoulder at his wife in the hospital bed. His lower lip trembled with emotion, the way a husband's would who had given up on the love of his life being found alive. Now here she was, back in his arms, and the relief on his face was palpable.

Stride wondered again: was he acting?

If so, he was good at it, but lawyers always were.

"I'm going to the cafeteria," Gavin said. He added sarcastically, "Do I need a police escort to do that?"

The man disappeared toward the elevators. They waited until he was gone, and then they went inside the hospital room, where they stood over Chelsey's bed. She lay on her back, the unattractive hospital gown revealing most of her neck and bare shoulders. Her blond hair was clean but still damp. Without makeup, she looked older, and her face looked drawn in the shadows, but she had a willowy elegance regardless of her surroundings.

As they stood there, her eyes popped open, surprising them. She'd been feigning sleep. She focused on Stride with a degree of anxiety, but then she saw and recognized Maggie, and she relaxed.

Maggie took the chair where Gavin had been sitting. Stride stayed standing behind her.

"Hello, Mrs. Webster. We met a few hours ago in the woods. I'm with the police. Lieutenant Maggie Bei."

"I remember." Her voice was stronger than Stride expected.

"My name's Jonathan Stride," he added. "I'm with the police, also."

It sounded strange to say that again after so long.

"How are you feeling?" Maggie asked.

"Much better. Night and day. I really thought I was going to die out there. I was running out of hope." Her head swiveled, and she glanced around the room, searching for Gavin. But Stride suspected that she'd been awake during their conversation in the doorway. "Where is my husband?"

"He went to the cafeteria. He'll be back soon."

"Ah."

Her eyes traveled back and forth between them, reading their faces.

Like Gavin, she had a smart, calculating stare. It made Stride think the lawyer had chosen a wife who was every bit his equal. He could guess the question she wanted to ask, based on what she'd overheard.

My husband is a suspect?

But she didn't ask it.

"We'd like to talk to you a bit more," Maggie went on. "The longer we wait to interview a victim, the more likely that their memories of the events grow vague and uncertain. That's why we want to nail down as many details as quickly as we can. However, this is only if you feel up to it. If you don't, say so, and we'll do this in the morning."

Chelsey nodded her approval. "It's fine. Go ahead."

"Can you tell us as much as you can remember about Tuesday evening when you were abducted?"

She was quiet for a little while, gathering her thoughts. "Gavin was gone, as you know. I was home alone. It was a cool night, but I had the windows open leading out to the porch. I like the chill. Rather than close the door or turn on the heat, I put on a heavy sweater. Odd, isn't it? The doctor said that helped save me. Anyway, I was reading a book and had some soft music playing. I don't know, I may even have fallen asleep in the chair. Then I heard a crash. A window breaking. I ran down the hallway toward the front door. By the time I got there, the man was already inside."

"Do you know what he looked like?"

Chelsey shook her head. "He wore a hood. I guess I vaguely noticed he was large, heavyset, but beyond that, it all happened too fast. He grabbed me. I struggled and tried to get free. I was able to tear away and run, but then he hit me, and it knocked me out. That's all I remember from inside the house."

Stride leaned his hands on the chair behind Maggie. "Do you remember anything else about the man? Height? Smell? Did he say anything?"

"No. It all happened in a few seconds."

"Had you received any threats recently?" Maggie asked. "Or had you noticed any strangers in the neighborhood? People watching the house?"

"Nothing like that."

Maggie reached inside to the pocket of her jacket and removed a mug shot that had been taken of Hink Miller when he'd been arrested. "Is this man familiar to you? Do you know who he is?"

Chelsey's head lifted off the pillow to examine the picture. "I don't think so, no."

"What about the name Hink Miller?"

"It doesn't ring any bells. It's an odd name, so I'm sure it would."

"He was a client of your husband's," Stride added.

"Well, I don't hang out with many of my husband's clients."

"He was murdered on Friday," Maggie added. "That was the day after the ransom was paid."

Chelsey's eyes narrowed. "I gather you believe this man Hink was involved in my kidnapping?"

"We think so. The backpack your husband used—as well as ten thousand dollars of the ransom money—was found hidden in Hink's basement." Then Maggie continued, "What do you remember next? After you came to?"

Chelsey blinked several times and grimaced as she thought back. "They woke me up to talk to Gavin."

"They?"

She shook her head. "Figure of speech. There was only the one man the whole time. I think it was the same man each time, but I can't honestly be sure. Anyway, when I talked to Gavin, I was disoriented, in panic. I begged him to help me, but then the man took away the phone. I don't know much about where I was. It was damp and dark, like a basement or a warehouse. There was no light to see. I don't know whether there were no windows or whether they'd blacked them out. I was bound, and most of the time, I was gagged. Sometimes he'd come and take off the gag and give me something to eat or drink and let me use a bucket to go to the bathroom. One time when he took off the gag, I tried to scream, and he hit me. I didn't try again after that."

"Do you remember hearing anything while you were there?" Stride asked. "Noises outside? Traffic? Trains? Planes?"

"No. The neighborhood was very quiet."

"Do you know how long you were there?"

"I don't." A thought seemed to occur to her. "I don't even know what day it is now."

"It's almost midnight on Monday evening."

"It felt like I was out there forever. You could have told me it was a month, and I wouldn't have been surprised."

"What happened next?" Stride asked.

"Sometime later—I don't know how long—I talked to Gavin again. He said he was paying them a ransom, that they'd release me as soon as he did, that I shouldn't be afraid. Then the man took away the phone and left me alone."

"He didn't take you with him?"

"No. He gagged me again and left me there. I remember I heard rain outside. It sounded heavy."

Maggie glanced up at Stride. "Thursday evening."

Stride nodded.

"Then what?" he asked Chelsey.

"Eventually, he came back. I don't know how long it was after that. I had no sense of time at that point, but the rain had definitely stopped. He blindfolded me and carried me out of wherever I was. I was hoping he was taking me to Gavin, that he was going to free me. I assumed by then that Gavin had paid him whatever money he wanted. He put me in the trunk of a car, and we drove a long way. Or at least, it seemed that way to me. I kept jostling around in the back. Then the car stopped, and he opened the trunk. He left the blindfold on, so I couldn't see where I was. But we were definitely in the woods somewhere. He carried me over his shoulder, and I could feel the tree branches. We went a long way. The farther we went, the more scared I got. And finally, he put me down on the ground, on this slope above a little creek. He took off the blindfold, but he was still wearing a hood. I saw that he had a shovel. I was terrified. I was sure he was going to kill me. He used the shovel to dig a hole in the bank of the slope, and he put me in it. I was begging him through the gag not to hurt me, not to kill me. He had the shovel in his hands, and I was waiting for him to swing it at me. But he didn't. He just left me there in the hole. At first, I was relieved, but then I knew he wasn't coming back. He'd left me there to die. And I don't know, that was like a thousand times worse."

She stopped and squeezed her eyes shut.

The silence stretched out.

"I'm very sorry," Stride said. "That must have been a terrifying experience."

Chelsey didn't answer. She didn't even nod.

"This may seem like an odd question," he went on, "but your husband says that one of his hobbies is geocaching."

Chelsey opened her eyes again with surprise. "Yes, that's right."

"He told me he often does this on Sunday mornings."

"Yes."

"Last Sunday, Gavin was seen in the woods near Fredenberg Lake. He told me he was geocaching."

Chelsey looked puzzled. "So?"

"So that location was not far from where you were found," Stride said. "Within a few hundred yards, in fact."

Stride could see a shadow of horror form in Chelsey's eyes. Her mind worked furiously, searching for explanations. And she couldn't find any. Just like them.

"What are you saying . . . ?" she began, but her words trailed off.

"Well, it's a strange coincidence that we're trying to explain," Stride said. "Gavin mentioned a puzzle that an anonymous geocacher from one of his clubs had sent him. Did he talk to you about that? He claims this person directed him to Fredenberg Lake."

"No. He never mentioned it."

"He said the person's email handle was *Razrsharp*. Does that mean anything to you?"

She shook her head. "No."

In the quiet of the late-night hospital, Stride heard the ding of the elevator at the far end of the dark hallway. He suspected it meant Gavin was coming back from the cafeteria. Maggie heard it, too.

"Just one more question, Mrs. Webster," she said, with a hint of urgency in her voice.

"What?"

"Does your husband own a gun?"

"Yes. Given the people he represents? I made sure he bought one."

"Where does he keep it?"

"On the back of a shelf in our bedroom closet. Why?"

"When did you last see it?"

"I'm not sure. I think a couple of weeks ago when I was putting laundry away." The shadow on her face now crept like a stain into Chelsey's voice, and she repeated her previous demand. "Why is that important?"

"It may not be important at all," Maggie said.

"Don't lie to me," Chelsey snapped. "Tell me the truth."

They heard footsteps in the hallway, getting closer. Gavin was almost there.

"The man named Hink Miller," Maggie went on quickly. "The client of your husband's who may have been involved in the kidnapping. He was shot. And Gavin's gun is missing."

34

"Delaney, I will protect you in any way I can," Serena told her, hoping it was a promise she could actually keep. "Tell me about the accident. Tell me what happened. You've been holding onto this secret for too long, and you need to let go of it."

The teenager pulled her knees onto the sofa. She looked away from Serena and stared at the fireplace, twisting strands of her long dark hair around her fingers. Her eyes were far away, and her bright smile had gone missing again. She was young, but she looked even younger now.

"That Sunday, Mr. Larsen drove me home," Delaney said, her voice low.

"This was after the camping trip?"

"Yes. I was feeling so good. Zach and I were in a really great place. I love—loved him. It was May, and school was going to be over soon, and I was thinking about me and him spending the summer together. Mr. Larsen was flirting with me like he usually did, but I tuned it out. He dropped me off at home, and then he left, and I went inside."

Serena waited. Delaney bit her lip, not wanting to go on.

"You know how my mom could be, right?" the girl continued finally.

"She was drunk?" Serena murmured.

Delaney nodded. "Yeah, but this was worse than that. She was unconscious. It was late Sunday afternoon, and she was still in bed. I struggled to get her up at all. She was really, really out of it this time. When I finally got her up, I made her take a cold shower and have some coffee. That helped."

Serena thought about this fifteen-year-old coming home from a camping trip and suddenly becoming the mother of the house again.

"Go on," she said, as she watched Delaney hesitate.

"I asked her what had been going on while I was gone, and she didn't know. She didn't remember any of it. That happened a lot. She couldn't tell me if she'd gone out drinking or stayed home or whether she was alone or with someone. She felt bad about it. She always felt bad. I could tell when she looked at me that she was ashamed that it had happened again."

"And you told her it was fine," Serena guessed.

"Sure, I did. It *was* fine. As long as one of us could take care of things, it was okay."

Serena shook her head and spoke quietly. "No, it really wasn't."

Delaney looked ready to object, but she didn't. "Anyway, I let Mom sober up for a while. When it was evening, we were starting to get hungry. She suggested we go to Big Daddy's for a burger. I thought that sounded great, but I made her promise no bars, no drinking. She was good about not drinking when I was with her. She would never drive drunk if I was in the car."

She said it as if this was a great accomplishment. A huge sacrifice.

"Your grandfather told me there were times when you had to pick your mom up yourself. You didn't even have a driver's license."

Delaney shrugged. "Gramps taught me how to drive when I was thirteen. I knew what I was doing. And it was only a couple of times. Usually, if Mom had a problem, she could get somebody else to take her home."

"Men?"

"Yeah, but I didn't care about that."

Serena held back because she didn't want the teenager retreating into her shell again. "Tell me what happened next."

Delaney was silent for a while. The girl's face was pale, and she tugged at her long hair in quick, nervous gestures. They'd reached the crisis point. Serena reached out and took hold of her hand. "Tell me," she repeated gently. "It's okay."

"We went out to the garage," Delaney said, her voice stumbling on the words. "That's when I saw it."

"Saw what?"

"The damage."

Serena felt her stomach lurch. She opened her mouth to say something, but she shut it again, letting Delaney find her own words. The girl looked as if she might cry, but then she closed her eyes and steadied herself.

"Mom owned a Highlander," she finally went on. "It was red. She loved that truck."

A red Toyota Highlander.

Just like that, a warning bell went off in Serena's memory, but she didn't remember the significance of the vehicle right away.

"When I opened the garage door, I saw that something had happened," Delaney continued. "The front end was all damaged and dented. Broken headlight. The bumper practically falling off. Mom had been in an accident. I asked her what had happened, but she didn't know. She didn't remember anything. She couldn't remember where she'd been or what she'd done. I knew this was trouble, so I closed the door right away to make sure no one would see anything if they drove by. And then I started running some searches on my phone."

Serena remembered now. She remembered the case. The name. The accident near Proctor.

"Jonah Fallon. The jogger killed in a hit-and-run."

Delaney nodded, and she couldn't hold back the tears anymore. They dripped silently down her cheeks. "I didn't know for sure. I mean, I found the headlines about the accident. It was all over the news. But I didn't want to believe it, you know? The papers said the accident happened up in Bayview Heights, and there's nothing up there. No bars or anything. Mom had no reason to be driving in that area. I thought maybe she'd hit another deer."

"The deer whistles," Serena murmured under her breath, as one of the puzzle pieces fell into place. "That's why she ordered them. They got knocked off in the accident. She was replacing them."

The girl nodded again.

"Delaney, you knew the truth," Serena said softly. "Didn't you?"

"Yeah. I was pretty sure that Mom had killed that man. I kept the garage closed, and we didn't go anywhere. I stayed home from school. I didn't want anyone seeing the condition of the truck. I knew if somebody saw it, they'd call the police."

Serena waited.

"Mom couldn't deal with it. So it was up to me to fix this for us. At first, I thought if we waited long enough, people would forget. If they couldn't figure out what kind of car it was, we could hold on for a while, and we would be okay. Then the police had a press conference the next day. They said the vehicle in the accident was a red Toyota Highlander. And that was that. If anyone saw our truck, we'd be screwed. I needed to do something."

As Delaney told the story, Serena watched her take on a false maturity that she knew only too well. *I needed to do something.*

"I kept pushing Mom to remember, but she didn't. Nothing came back. It was a total blackout. I knew that wouldn't matter if anyone found out. You would have arrested her. She'd have gone to prison. Probably for years. I wasn't wrong about that, was I?"

"No, you weren't wrong," Serena acknowledged. "This was criminal vehicular homicide. Given her prior DUIs, she probably would have been looking at significant prison time."

"I would have lost her. I wasn't going to let that happen."

"Delaney, a man died."

"I know that. And I felt horrible about it. So did my mom. What made it even worse was that she knew Mr. Fallon."

"She knew him? How?"

"He and his wife used my mom to cater their wedding. It was one of her first jobs, and they picked her because she was local. She was really grateful for that. It helped get her business off the ground. Now he was dead because of her. We couldn't believe it."

"The angel figurine," Serena said. "The message on it. *I'm sorry.*"

Delaney nodded. "She wanted me to drop it off at their house anonymously for his wife. But I wasn't going to do that. I didn't think we could take any chances. I thought maybe the police would be watching their house, or they'd have cameras installed."

Serena felt a little chill, listening to Delaney map it all out. There was a strange ruthlessness in her voice. A cold calculation as she laid out the details of making sure Nikki never got caught for her crime.

You do what you have to do.

It was as if Delaney could hear what she was thinking, because she said the same thing.

"You do what you have to do," the girl went on. "I made a plan for us. I had my mom take a bus to town and rent a car for a few days. I went with her to make sure she didn't say anything stupid. At that point, we didn't have to use the Highlander for a while. But I needed to do something about it. We couldn't just leave it like that. I thought about trying to ditch it somewhere, but even driving it out of the area wasn't safe. The police would be looking for it. Plus, no matter how far I took it or where I tried to hide it, somebody would find it eventually, and the vehicle ID would send people right back to my mom. So I needed to get it fixed. Repair the damage and get it painted. But I was sure the police had gone to every garage in town—probably around the state and over in Wisconsin, too—and told them to be on the lookout for a red Highlander with front-end damage."

Serena felt a terrible sickness again. She knew what was coming next.

"Zach's father," she guessed.

Delaney's whole face hardened. *You do what you have to do.*

"Yeah. I decided that was our only chance. Zach's father had a garage, and he could fix the Highlander. But I knew he'd tell someone, unless I gave him a reason to keep quiet."

"Oh, Delaney."

"I went to the garage. It was late. He was the only one there. It wasn't hard to convince him. He'd always had a weird fetish about me. Zach didn't see it, but I knew. One time he even stole my underwear, the big pervert. So yeah, I knew he wouldn't say no. I mean, to me it was no big deal. It was just sex, right? And when it was done, I told him what he was going to do for me in return. Pick up the Highlander at night, fix it in his garage, make sure nobody found out. Because if they did, I'd tell everybody about him and me."

Serena closed her eyes. All the flashbacks came. Her and Blue Dog. The things Cat had gone through, too. Years went by, and the world never changed. She listened to the monotone of the girl's voice as she described giving herself to Zach's father as no big deal, when in fact it was a huge, ugly, life-changing big deal.

"That's an awful thing," Serena murmured. "I'm so sorry."

"Well, like I said, it was my idea. My plan. And it worked. He fixed the Highlander, and we got it back, and it was perfect. A cool shade of blue, too. Nobody ever noticed. We were free."

Free.

That was the last thing Nikki and Delaney were.

"Your mom found out what you did?" Serena asked.

She nodded. "Yeah. After Mr. Larsen delivered the truck back to us, I had to show it to her. She wanted to know how I got it done, how I was sure that nobody would find out. At first, I just said Mr. Larsen knew me and he'd agreed to keep it quiet. But she saw through that. She knew I'd broken it off with Zach, and she guessed why. I couldn't see him anymore. I just couldn't. I couldn't be with him after what had happened with his dad. And to be honest, at that point, I was just dead inside, you know? I didn't feel anything. It wasn't fair to Zach to stay with him when I was pretty sure I could never love anybody."

The calmness with which this seventeen-year-old described never loving another human being was like a knife to Serena's heart. She put a hand on the girl's shoulder, and Delaney closed her eyes briefly but didn't cry. The numbness returned to her face. That was the only way she could deal with what had happened. When Serena looked up, she saw that the bedroom door was open. Cat had been listening, too. Serena was about to wave her away, but Delaney shook her head.

"It's okay."

Cat came and curled up in front of the sofa and took the younger girl's hand and didn't let go.

"Anyway, Mom saw through it," Delaney went on. "I had to tell her what I did. She went berserk. I tried to stop her, but she confronted Mr. Larsen. She said she wanted to kill him. When she got back home, it was like her life was over. I'd done all of this to save her, and instead, she acted like I'd made it worse. She kept talking about turning herself in. I made her swear she wouldn't, but I didn't believe her. That next weekend, I went to see my grandparents in Mora. Mom wanted me to go. She said I needed time to be a girl again, whatever that meant. She hugged me so hard when I left. I told her again and again not to tell anybody, not to go to the police, that it was done and over, that it was all behind us. She said okay. She told me she was fine. But when I got back on Sunday, there she was."

Delaney shook her head.

"See? It was all my fault."

Serena and Cat said in unison, "It *wasn't*."

But the girl didn't listen to them. "Now you know why I didn't want to deal with any of this again. Nobody killed my mom. Nobody murdered her. You were wrong about that, Serena. She just couldn't handle the guilt anymore. She killed herself, and that's the end of the story. She killed herself because of me."

35

"Jonah Fallon," Stride said, as he lay in bed with Serena later that night. "After all this time. That case drove Abel Teitscher crazy. Most of the time, with hit-and-runs, you catch them eventually. Guilt wins out, or someone sees the car and calls it in. But Abel was never able to put that one to bed. I'll have to call him in New Mexico and tell him we finally know what happened."

He watched Serena, who lay next to him, her eyes wide open. He hadn't turned out the lights yet. It was almost two in the morning, and the cottage was quiet. Cat was asleep in her bedroom, and Delaney was there, too, using a sleeping bag on the floor. They hadn't wanted the girl to be alone.

Serena didn't say anything, not at first.

"Are you okay?" he asked.

"The things we do for our mothers," she said.

"Even those that don't deserve it."

"Yes, even them."

"Delaney's a very resourceful girl."

"She is. I just hope her life doesn't get ruined by this." Serena raised herself on one elbow with new concern on her face. "Jonny, seriously, do you think I should stay quiet? Not report this?"

He shook his head. "You know you can't do that."

"I know, but now I wonder if I was wrong. Did I make a mistake? Maybe this is one secret that should have stayed buried."

"We don't have the luxury to decide that," he reminded her. "You'll help her through it. She'll get a good lawyer who will walk her through the whole process. She was fifteen years old. She was protecting her mother, and she's already paid a hell of a price for the things she did. No way the county attorney will try to press charges against her. They'll work out a deal. In the meantime, we'll make sure Ben Larsen is punished for taking advantage of her. And we'll finally be able to give a little bit of peace to Jonah Fallon's family, too. It may not be perfect, but it's how the system is supposed to work."

Serena nodded. "I'll look up Jonah's wife in the morning and go see her. I'm worried that she may not feel as charitably toward Delaney as we do. She must have gone through a lot of pain not knowing what happened."

"Well, people can surprise you," Stride said. "Let's hope she focuses on the big picture. Nikki didn't get away with what she did. She killed a man in a terrible accident, but within two weeks, she was dead, too."

"Yeah."

He heard hesitation in Serena's voice. "What is it?"

Her mouth curled into a frown, but she said nothing.

"In the end, Delaney will come out of this stronger," Stride went on, wanting to believe that was true. "She's obviously strong to begin with, but you can't keep that kind of secret without it screwing up your head. Telling the truth is the first step in getting her life back."

"I hope you're right."

"Give yourself some credit, too," he said. "You solved a cold case. One that's been open for two years."

"Did I?"

Stride brushed a few loose dark strands from her troubled face. "What's going on? Talk to me."

Serena got out of bed and went to the light switch and turned it off. She opened the window a little farther to let in cold air—she knew he liked that—and got back under the blanket with him. She kissed him in a way that told him they'd found the rhythm they'd lost for a while.

Then her voice came out of the darkness. "Do you remember where Jonah Fallon was killed?"

"It was somewhere in Bayview Heights, wasn't it? I took a look at the file in Abel's office the other day. Getchell Road, I think."

"Yes, exactly."

"That's a remote area," Stride said. "A two-lane road and no overhead lights, and the accident happened at night. Even if Jonah was wearing reflective gear, Nikki probably never saw him. I remember the forensics team concluded that the vehicle didn't even slow down. She was too drunk to know she'd hit him."

"That's what it looks like."

"Except you don't sound convinced. Why not?"

"Well, it was something Delaney said. I may be making too much of it, but it's been bothering me. There's nothing up there. No bars, restaurants, nothing. What was Nikki even doing in that area?"

"Does she need a reason? She was drunk. At night, most rural roads look the same. She got lost."

"And then what? She was too drunk to know where she was or what she'd done, but she was sober enough to find her way home and park in the garage?"

Stride narrowed his eyes. "What are you saying?"

"I'm saying that the accident gives Nikki a reason to kill herself. Fair enough. I didn't know about that before, and if that was the end of it, I'd say okay. I'd say we can close the book on the case. And on Jonah Fallon's death, too. But someone tried to kill Delaney tonight. Someone tried to run her down. It has to be connected. And if it is, that means I'm still missing something."

He frowned. "What about Ben Larsen? He had to be worried when you showed up asking questions after all this time. Maybe he was afraid that Delaney would talk about what happened between them."

"I thought that, too. That's the only explanation that makes any sense."

"But?"

"But I checked. I called Ben's house. He has an alibi. I shook him up, no doubt about that. When he got home from work, he got into a big fight with his wife. He put a fist into a mirror and cut up his hand. He spent the whole evening in the emergency room. Ben didn't do it."

Stride listened to the cold breeze whistling through the window. "Who else would want to harm Delaney?"

"That's what I can't figure out," Serena said. "According to Delaney, only three people knew the truth about what happened to Jonah Fallon. Her, Nikki, and Ben. Except now we have someone else who's willing to commit murder to keep Delaney from revealing the secret. *Why?*"

36

Chelsey Webster awoke in her own bed. She glanced at the clock on her nightstand and saw that it was almost four o'clock in the afternoon. She'd checked out of the hospital in the late morning, after the next battery of tests showed no further signs of physical trauma. Gavin had driven her home, and she'd been able to force down a little soup, but her stomach wasn't up to much more. Then she'd felt a new wave of exhaustion and had gone to take a nap.

Now three more hours had passed.

Gavin sat on their bed, staring at her with his luminous eyes. While she'd been asleep, he'd showered, and he looked refreshed. His curly hair was damp. He wore a black sweater and tan slacks, but his feet were bare. Seeing that she was awake, he grabbed and hugged her, and she winced.

"Sorry," he said, easing her back onto the pillow. "I forgot. You must be sore."

Chelsey simply stared back at him. Her husband.

"I'm relieved that you're safe," he went on. "I'd nearly given up hope."

"Here I am," she replied.

"It must have been horrible."

"Yes, it was."

"But it's over now. How do you feel?"

"How do you think I feel?" Chelsey replied, her voice like the edge of a knife.

Gavin blinked nervously. He reached out for her hand, but she yanked it away. "I know it will take time for you to get past this. That's understandable. But you'll get counseling. Everything will be fine."

Chelsey kept staring at him. This fraud. This hypocrite. Did he really think she had any interest in his fake sincerity? His sugar-sweet lies?

"I did everything they asked," Gavin continued, his eyes oddly desperate for her to believe him. "I got the cash. I gave it to them. I followed all of their instructions. The only thing I wanted was to get you back safely. They said they'd tell me where you were."

"Instead, they left me to die," Chelsey said.

"I know."

"Gavin, who is Hink Miller?" she asked.

He hesitated. "You know about him?"

"The police told me."

He shook his head bitterly. "Hink was a client. I represented him on an assault charge last year. That was all. I haven't seen him since then."

"They found part of the ransom money in his house."

"I heard that, yes."

"He was murdered. Someone shot him the day after you paid the ransom."

"I don't know anything about that."

Chelsey threw back the blanket and got out of bed. She swayed a little as she stood, but then she steadied herself.

"Are you sure you should be getting up so soon?" Gavin asked.

"Don't worry about me."

She went to their walk-in closet and turned on the light. At the back wall, she reached to a shelf over the hangers and threw several sweaters to the floor. With both hands, she felt around the rear of the shelf. There was nothing there. She returned to the doorway and folded her arms across her chest.

"Where's your gun?"

Gavin took a long time to answer. Finally, he said, "I don't know. It's missing."

"Missing? It was there a couple of weeks ago. I saw it. The gun and a box of bullets."

"I went to look for it on Thursday, and it was gone. The kidnapper must have taken it."

"How would the kidnapper know where we keep the gun?"

His voice rose with a wave of outrage. "What, are you a prosecutor now? Is this some kind of cross-examination? I don't know how he found it! The house was bugged. He was listening to us for days. One of us must have said something about it."

"It wasn't me," she said.

"Well, maybe he searched the house."

"He was there to abduct me, Gavin. Why would he take the time to steal a gun?"

"I have no idea!"

She came and sat next to him on the bed. "Was it you? Did you do this?"

"*What?*"

"Did you arrange for me to be kidnapped? Did you kill this man Hink? Did you ask him to kill *me*?"

"Did I—? Are you out of your mind? No!"

"The police seem to think you did."

"The police are wrong. That's what they do. They choose an easy suspect, and then they cherry-pick and misconstrue the evidence so that it looks the way they want it to look. I see that with my clients all the time. For God's sake, Chelsey, I would never do this. You know me."

"Do I?"

"Of course, you do."

"The look in your eyes in the hospital," Chelsey murmured, shaking her head. "You couldn't believe I was alive. You were certain you would never see me again."

Gavin banged his fists against his forehead. "You'd been gone for days! I told you, I was terrified! I thought you were dead!"

"Or did you assume Hink had killed me and buried my body? Like you'd paid him to do?"

Her husband shot off the bed. "This is nuts. I'm not going to listen to this."

He crossed the bedroom, then stopped where he was and turned back to her, his face stricken. He approached the bed and slid to the floor in front of her and put his head in her lap. When he spoke, his voice was muffled.

"I know you're upset. I don't blame you. But you have to believe me, I didn't do this."

She listened to his labored breathing. After a while, she summoned a smile and reached down and cupped his cheeks with her hands. "All right, Gavin. If you say you're innocent, then I have to accept that."

"You believe me? Really?"

"We've had our differences over the years, but you're still my husband."

"That's right."

Chelsey stroked her fingers through his curly hair. She knew he liked it when she did that. "I'm not thinking straight. Plus, I'm starving. I think I'm finally ready to eat something."

"What can I make for us?" Gavin asked.

"Actually, I'd love pizza. What about Thirsty Pagan?"

"Sure. We can drive over there."

She shook her head. "No, I'm not up for that. I'm not ready to leave the house. Would you go get one for us and bring it back?"

"Are you sure you'll be okay alone?"

"I'll be fine."

"It won't take long. An hour or so at most."

"Good."

He stood up, then bent down and pressed his lips against hers. They were dry and cracked. "We can start over, can't we?"

"Whatever you say."

Gavin grabbed socks from his dresser and sat down on the bed to put them on. He slipped his feet into loafers, then disappeared down the hallway to the stairs that led to the lower level. She heard the outside door open and shut, and she went into the hallway and stood beside the front window. A few seconds later, she watched Gavin's car drive away.

When he was gone, she hurried into his office. His MacBook was on the desk. She knew the password to access his files—she knew all his passwords; he reused the same one over and over with slight variations—and she accessed his desktop screen and loaded the internet browser. She went to Gmail and logged into the private account he kept for his geocaching activities.

There were no secrets between husband and wife.

She stared at the lineup of messages in his in-box. Her eyes flicked down the list of unread emails and stopped when she got to one that had been sent overnight, around two in the morning.

The sender's email handle was Razrsharp. The subject of the message said:

A new treasure hunt

Chelsey clicked on the message to open it. The email consisted of nothing but two rows of numbers:

46.7104776
92.2194869

GPS coordinates.

She copied the numbers and plugged them into a mapping utility, and the location came back on the west side of the city. When she checked the street view, she found herself staring at a remote section of Skyline Drive in the woods near Spirit Mountain.

Chelsey turned off the computer. She headed for her car.

* * * * *

Serena pulled onto the shoulder of Getchell Road, near a point where a small white cross was dug into the ground. She got out and walked into the weeds and squatted near the cross. There were rosary beads and dirty plastic flowers hanging over the post. A name had been painted on the cross in black, but two years had gone by, and the paint was fading. She could barely make it out.

Jonah Fallon.

It had happened right here. She stood up and looked in both directions down the lonely highway, seeing nothing but endless lines of trees. She'd been in this location once before, when she'd been helping Abel Teitscher scour the forest during the early part of the investigation.

Irony of ironies, she'd been called away from the case to deal with the suicide of Nikki Candis.

The road was arrow-straight. No curves at all. The accident had happened at ten thirty on a Saturday night. Fallon was a fitness geek, a man who ran every night, the same route on the same roads. He'd been wearing orange reflective tape on the back of his jacket and flashers on the heels of his running shoes. But the night would have been black as coal, and Nikki Candis would have been drunk to the point of unconsciousness, and Serena had no idea how fast the woman had been driving. Jonah Fallon didn't stand a chance. The Highlander had taken him out at full speed and kept going. The coroner said he died instantly, his body broken.

Serena got back into her car. A mile north, she turned left on a road called Wildrose Trail. The forest had been chopped away here to make large, grassy lots for executive home sites. They were sprawling, expensive properties, some fetching close to a million dollars, which was still a lot of money in the Duluth market. She parked outside a house with multiple gables and a white-brick exterior. There was a neat garden in the front yard, and the lawn had been recently mowed. A car with Wisconsin plates was parked in the driveway.

She'd never met Susan Fallon. This was Abel's case, and he'd been the one to deal with Jonah's wife. There was no record in the file that Abel had contacted her in more than a year; he'd had nothing to report on the status of the cold case. Now Abel was retired in New Mexico, and it fell to Serena to tell this woman that they finally knew who had been behind the wheel when Jonah died.

It was much later in the day than she'd planned to be here. Most of the day had been taken up in finding a lawyer for Delaney and in taking her statement at police headquarters. They'd also discussed possible charges for Ben Larsen with the county attorney. Serena had finally been able to get away, but she deliberately hadn't called Susan Fallon before showing up. After two years, this was the kind of news that she wanted to break in person.

At the door, Serena rang the bell and waited. It was a long time before she heard footsteps inside. She had no photograph of Jonah's wife, so she didn't know what to expect, but when the door opened, she saw two people standing on the threshold. One was a tall older man; the other was a short older woman. She *knew* them. They were familiar to her. She'd talked with them very recently, but she struggled to place them because she had no idea why she was seeing them *here*.

Something was wrong.

Something made no sense.

"Oh, Detective, hello," the woman greeted her. She didn't sound surprised at all to see Serena on the doorstep. "We heard about Chelsey. That's such wonderful news."

Serena blinked, forcing her mind to catch up to her eyes. She studied their faces again and glanced at the car in the driveway with Wisconsin plates.

Then, in a rush, she knew. She remembered.

Mary and Tim Webster.

Gavin Webster's parents from Rice Lake.

"It's very kind of you to come out here to tell us in person," Mary Webster went on. "Of course, Gavin called us as soon as he got word. It sounds like Chelsey is healthy and fine. We're so relieved."

Serena tried to find the words to ask the questions that were in her head.

"What are the two of you doing here?" she asked.

"Well, we put it off as long as we could," Mary replied. "Someone had to start cleaning out Susan's house. Given everything, Gavin wasn't going to be much help. He asked if we could take the lead, and we said we would. But I can't tell you how painful it is. Her spirit is still here. This is where she died, you know. She didn't want to pass away in a hospital."

"Susan," Serena murmured.

"That's right."

"Susan *Fallon*. Your daughter—Gavin's sister—was Jonah Fallon's *wife*."

"Yes, as we told you, it's just been tragedy upon tragedy for us. First Gavin lost everything, and then Susan received the cancer diagnosis so soon after getting married. And then for her to lose Jonah in that horrible, horrible accident. Well, God can be cruel sometimes. But at least He isn't cruel today. Today Gavin got Chelsey back, so that's something. It simply would have been too much for him to lose his sister and his wife in the same year."

37

"I called Abel Teitscher in New Mexico," Stride announced to Serena, Maggie, and Guppo in the police conference room. "Gavin's name never came up during the investigation of Jonah Fallon's hit-and-run. With Susan having a different last name, Abel never made the connection. Not that he would have or should have under the circumstances. It wouldn't have seemed relevant."

Maggie stood up and went to the window, where she leaned against the ledge. After staring at the forest for a while, she turned back and blurted out what they were all thinking.

"Does anyone believe this is just a coincidence?" she asked. "Because if not, what exactly do we think happened here?"

Stride stood in front of the whiteboard and studied the four names that he'd written there:

Jonah Fallon
Nikki Candis
Susan Webster Fallon
Gavin Webster

Somehow, the lives of those four people had intersected violently. And for Gavin, lucratively. Three of them were dead, and Gavin was rich.

"Six years ago, Gavin's law firm partner was arrested for embezzling client funds," Stride began, laying out the timeline for them. "The firm dissolved, and Gavin lost everything. He went bankrupt. He lost his house, his reputation, and most of his savings. He had to start over doing defense work for low-income clients, usually on public defender rates."

He used a black marker to circle Susan's name on the board.

"Then three years ago, Gavin's sister, Susan, married Jonah Fallon. Jonah was a senior health-care executive with money in the bank and a high six-figure income. Susan and Jonah honeymooned in a luxury resort in Aruba. They bought a mansion in Bayview Heights. Suddenly, Gavin's sister had everything in her life that Gavin had lost in his. It's not hard to think there was some sibling jealousy over that. But there wasn't anything Gavin could do about it." Stride paused. "Until."

"Until Susan was diagnosed with an aggressive form of uterine cancer just a few months after she got married," Serena finished his thought.

"Exactly."

Guppo shook his head. "Holy crap. Holy effing crap."

Stride sat down again and took a minute to contemplate the horror of what they were describing. "Yeah. That's what we're thinking, right? Gavin is bankrupt and down on his luck, and over here is his sister, with a lot of money thanks to her new husband. But then he finds out that his sister is going to die. It's just a matter of time. If she dies with Jonah alive, nothing changes for Gavin. On the other hand, if Jonah dies *before* Susan, then Susan inherits her husband's money. Plus a sizable life insurance policy, I imagine."

"So when Susan ultimately dies of cancer—with no kids, no other family—all of that money goes to Gavin," Serena concluded.

Stride nodded. "I think we're looking at an unbelievably insidious murder conspiracy that's been playing out for the last two years. With three million dollars as the pot of gold at the end of the rainbow."

"Fucking lawyers," Maggie snorted from the window ledge.

Guppo crunched on his Fritos. "Do you think Chelsey Webster knows about any of this?"

"She was pretty quick to have doubts about her husband," Maggie pointed out.

"Right, and if Chelsey suspects, it gives us the one thing we've been missing," Stride went on. "A motive. If it was just about money, Gavin could have divorced her and walked away with the inheritance. On the other hand, if Chelsey had even a whiff of foul play in Jonah's death, that's totally different. That's a reason to get rid of her permanently. Gavin keeps the money, and his wife never raises any awkward questions about his dead brother-in-law."

Serena went to the whiteboard, too. "It makes perfect sense, and we all think that's what probably happened. Except we have a big problem."

"We have no proof," Stride said.

"Exactly."

Serena drew an asterisk beside the name of the woman in the middle of everything. *Nikki Candis.*

"According to what we know right now, Gavin *didn't* kill Jonah Fallon," she went on. "Nikki Candis did. It was her vehicle. The red Highlander was parked in her garage. And Nikki had a history of drunk driving. Everything points to her."

"So there must be a connection between Nikki and Gavin," Maggie said.

"I agree," Serena replied, "but right now, the only connection we have is thin. According to Delaney, Nikki catered Jonah and Susan's wedding. She would have been at the reception, and presumably, so would Gavin. So we can put them in the same room at the same time. But that was one event three years ago. As a lawyer, Gavin would say that doesn't prove a damn thing, and he'd be right. We don't have any evidence that Nikki and Gavin even met, let alone that they teamed up on a grotesque conspiracy to kill Jonah Fallon."

"Did Gavin ever represent Nikki?" Stride asked. "Maybe on one of her DUIs?"

Guppo shook his head and replied with his mouth full of chips, "I went back and checked the court records. There's no indication that she was ever one of Gavin's clients."

"What about an affair?" Maggie asked.

"It sounds like Nikki did her share of sleeping around," Serena replied. "Particularly when she was drinking. So it's possible. I'll talk to Delaney and see if she recognizes Gavin's picture. I'll also take another look at Nikki's credit card and phone records in case anything jumps out that would tie her to Gavin."

Stride eased back in the chair.

He realized how normal and comfortable it felt to be here. He'd done this in this same room with these same people hundreds of times over the years. When he glanced at the window, he saw Maggie watching him with a strange little smirk on her face. He was sure she was thinking the same thing. But there was more to it than that. He'd also fallen into the role of command without even thinking about it. He was running the meeting, but technically, he wasn't the one in charge. Maggie was.

If he was really back, if he was really going to stay, then they were going to have to decide which one of them was the leader. But for the time being, the look on her face told him to keep going.

"Let's focus on Jonah Fallon," Stride went on. "He's the newest piece in the puzzle. Jonah's death proved to be extraordinarily fortuitous for Gavin. But as Serena points out, it was *Nikki's* SUV that killed him. The question is, was this really something more than a drunken hit-and-run?"

Serena frowned. "Delaney says her mother didn't remember the accident. She blacked out all of Saturday night. So that doesn't help us."

"Could she have been lying about it?" Stride asked.

"Maybe, but her behavior afterward doesn't mesh with that. Delaney says her mother was horrified by the damage to the Highlander. Plus, she'd had multiple blackout episodes like that in the past. It's part of a pattern."

"Well, that means we only know two things for sure," Stride said. "Nikki drank *a lot*, enough to get blackout drunk. And sometime after ten o'clock, her Highlander was out on Getchell Road near Jonah's house. Do we know how she got there or where she was drinking? Was there any activity on her credit cards that Saturday night?"

Serena shook her head. "No. And there were no phone calls on her cell phone, either. Delaney was with the Larsens on their camping trip. She and her mother didn't talk while she was gone."

"So we don't know where Nikki was or what she was doing until we get to the time of the accident," Stride said.

"We don't even know that," Maggie interrupted.

Stride's brow furrowed. "What do you mean?"

"We don't actually *know* that Nikki was behind the wheel," Maggie said. "We know it was her SUV, but we can't be certain that she was the one driving."

"That's true," Serena agreed. "For all we know, it could have been Gavin. Nikki had no reason to be out on Getchell Road, but Gavin sure did."

Stride drummed his fingers on the desk. "The only way that works is if Gavin had a significant relationship with Nikki Candis. That's what we need to establish. He needed access to her and to her vehicle. He had to know she was subject to blackouts. We have to prove he knew her, knew who she was, what she drove, where she lived. If we can't find an intersection in their lives, we'll never make a case." He looked at Serena. "This is your discovery. What do you want to do?"

"I'll talk to Delaney."

Serena grabbed her coat from the back of the chair. She headed for the doorway, but then she stopped. Her face darkened with a look that Stride knew well. It was the look she got when she was getting closer to the truth.

"You know, we're not just talking about the murder of Jonah Fallon. We could be talking about Nikki's death, too."

Stride nodded. "Gavin may have killed her to make sure we never linked him to the accident."

"Or maybe it's more than that," Serena said. "Maybe Nikki started to remember what really happened."

* * * * *

The mapping app told Chelsey Webster when she was closing in on the location of the GPS coordinates. She pulled onto the shoulder of

Skyline Drive, which was terraced into the steep hillside, and stopped. With a shiver, she got out into the cool evening. Most of the trees had given up their leaves, and through the empty birches, she could see the islands dotting the Saint Louis River.

It was almost dark. She had to move quickly.

She opened the trunk of her Volvo and removed a dirty shovel. When she checked her phone, she saw that she was fifty yards or so away from the GPS position she'd found in the email. The route led her uphill. She climbed across a bed of wet leaves and maneuvered around the young trees that grew closely together.

Halfway up the hillside, she stopped. The map told her she'd reached the spot, like finding an *X* scrawled by a pirate. The numbers matched.

Around her was a web of gnarled branches. The ground was thick with yellow-and-gold leaves. Gavin had always told her that this was the challenge of geocaching. The coordinates would get you only so far, and once you were there, you had to figure out exactly where the treasure was hidden.

Chelsey looked for a clue because she knew there would be one. She glanced around at the trees, her gaze moving methodically from one to the next. At first she saw nothing, but then in the dim shadows, she spotted a flash of color. A thin strand of pink ribbon was tied around the end of a long branch. It fluttered in the breeze.

She made her way to the spot. When she kicked away the leaves at her feet, she could see that the ground had been recently disturbed. The dirt had been shoveled away and then roughly replaced. The area made a small square, around two feet on each side.

Chelsey glanced down the hillside toward Skyline Drive. No one was there. No one was watching. The road was empty. She felt sweat on the back of her neck, and a wave of tiredness and fear broke across her mind. But she didn't listen to it. She knew what she had to do.

With her foot on the top of the blade, she thrust the shovel into the soft earth and began to dig.

38

A stalled car in the westbound lanes of the Superior bridge slowed Gavin on his way back to Duluth. When he finally pulled into their driveway, he noticed that the upstairs lights were off. The house was dark. He wondered if Chelsey had gone back to bed. He parked the car outside the garage, grabbed the pizza box, and went inside. Rather than call out to his wife, he climbed the steps in the darkness.

On the main level, he smelled the acrid waft of cigarette smoke. There was a breath of cold air through what must have been an open window. He could see the lights of the city glowing beyond the far end of the house, and when he headed that way, he saw Chelsey sitting in an armchair near the open door to the deck. She was almost invisible in the shadows of the porch. As he watched, she exhaled a cloud of smoke. Chelsey didn't smoke often, but when she did, he knew that something was wrong.

"Sorry it took me a while," Gavin said. "There was traffic."

He reached for the light switch, but Chelsey stopped him. "No, don't. I like it dark."

"Okay."

Gavin put the pizza on the counter of the wet bar. "I should probably heat this up before we eat."

"It doesn't matter. I'm not hungry anymore."

"Oh. That's fine."

He went behind the bar and poured himself a generous quantity of gin. He inhaled the aroma of the drink, enjoyed a sip, then took it to the open patio door.

"Are you okay?" he asked.

"Actually, I'm perfect now."

"Really? Well, that's good news. I'm glad to hear it."

"Are you going to get me a drink, too?" Chelsey asked.

"I can, but are you up for it? Maybe you should wait a while before trying alcohol again."

"Vodka tonic," she snapped, ignoring his warning.

"Fine."

As he returned to the bar, she added, "Let me see you make it."

Gavin stopped. "What?"

"I'd rather make sure you don't put anything in it," Chelsey explained.

"Are you kidding?"

"You did it once before. Ecstasy, don't you remember?"

"Yes, I do. And I remember that it was *your* idea to try it, not mine. You asked me to get some. You said you wanted to see what it was like, see how it made you feel. Everything is drama with you, Chelsey."

"Well, I need drama, darling, because life with you is so goddamn *boring*."

He closed his eyes. A roaring filled his head. He breathed through his nose, his anger growing along with his humiliation. "Do we have to do this again? Now?"

"What? You were expecting me to come back as the devoted wife?"

"Hardly."

"Did you think I'd get rescued and suddenly fall back into your arms?" she sneered.

"No. I knew you'd never change."

"That's better. What a fake you are, Gavin. 'We'll get counseling.' 'I'm so relieved you're safe.' Who do you think you're talking to?"

He swore through clenched teeth. "God! You're such a bitch!"

"There you go," she retorted with a sparkling burst of laughter. "That's the most honest thing you've said to me in years. Get it all out. Tell me how you really feel, Gavin."

He was tired of lying. Tired of pretending. "I hate your fucking guts."

"Good for you. It's refreshing to see you show some balls for once in your life."

He did feel better. He liked saying it out loud after all this time. "I hate the sight of you. I loathe waking up to you in my bed. You make me feel utterly worthless. Like a total failure."

"That's because you *are* worthless, darling. You *are* a total failure."

"Stop it!"

"Oh, no, we can't stop now. This is too good. Go on. Tell me more. What did you think when you found out I was gone?"

"I was *hoping* you were dead."

"Of course, you were. I bet it was hard pretending to be upset when you talked to the police."

"It was."

"'Oh, my loving wife! She's gone!' Good thing you're such a fraud."

"I've had plenty of practice."

"But it must have been such a shock when they found me," Chelsey said, making an exaggerated frown.

"They told me you were alive, and I wanted to puke."

"Aw, you poor thing."

Gavin stalked away to the patio door. His nostrils flared as he inhaled the evening air on the hillside. He downed his gin and wiped his mouth. Then, with a roar, he took his empty lowball glass and hurled it over the railing toward the trees. He turned back to his wife, and his lip curled with revulsion.

"We're finally down to it, aren't we?" he said from the gloom.

"Yes, we are. No more lies. All our cards on the table. It's better this way, isn't it?"

"You're right."

"Admit it. You've wanted to be rid of me for years."

"Of course, I have. And I'm *going* to be rid of you, too. I'm going to take every fucking dollar in the divorce. All three million. There's nothing you can do about it. You can go whore yourself out on the street for all I care."

"Charming."

The night seemed to get deeper. He couldn't look away from his wife. He stared at Chelsey, and she stared back at him. His eyes had adjusted, and he could see now that she'd changed clothes. When he looked harder, he saw streaks of dirt on her hands and face.

"Did you go somewhere?" he asked, immediately suspicious.

"Yes, I did."

"Where? What were you doing?"

She gave him a cold smile. "Geocaching."

"What?"

Chelsey reached down to the brick hearth in front of the fireplace. For the first time, he noticed a padded plastic bag in the shadows there. It had been ripped open at the top. She lifted it and put it on her lap.

"Razrsharp sent you a message," she said.

"*Razrsharp?* What are you talking about?"

"The police said you told them that an anonymous email account had sent you to the woods where I was found. That sounded odd to me, Gavin. Very, very odd. So I looked in your account and found that Razrsharp had sent you more GPS coordinates. I decided to see what treasure he'd hidden for you this time."

He studied the bag. "What's in it? What did you find?"

"Are you saying you don't know?" She dug a hand deep into the bag and removed a semiautomatic pistol that she placed on the arm of the chair. It was a 9 mm Glock. "This is what was inside. Your gun, Gavin."

He stared wide-eyed at the Glock. And then at his wife.

A chill rippled up his spine.

"What do you think, darling?" she asked him. "Is this the gun that killed Hink Miller? Because I think it is. I'm going to give it to the police."

"I don't know anything about that gun. I don't know how it got there."

"Do you really expect anyone to believe you, Gavin? The police already think you're a liar. After they test this gun, they're going to arrest you for murder."

"Let them try. I'll embarrass them in court."

She counted off on her fingers. "Your gun. Your client. You scouting the woods in the middle of nowhere right where I was found."

"Razrsharp did this. It's *him*."

"Who is Razrsharp?"

"I have no idea."

She was quiet for a long time. "I'm betting the police will think it's you."

"That's crazy."

"Is it, Gavin? Without this Razrsharp, this mystery man, everything points to you. He's your alibi for being in the woods. He's your alibi for the murder weapon."

"*He's* the one. It's not me."

Chelsey pursed her lips in thought. The back of her hand grazed the butt of the gun on the armchair. "While I was waiting for you, I got a strange phone call."

"From who?"

"Maggie Bei of the Duluth Police."

"What did she want?"

"She wants to talk to me tomorrow. They're looking into the hit-and-run again. Jonah's death."

"*Jonah?*" Gavin asked. "What does he have to do with anything?"

"Ms. Bei didn't say, but I could read between the lines. They're wondering if you had something to do with the accident that killed him."

"Me? Why the hell would I—?"

"For the money."

"Kill Jonah?" Gavin felt the walls begin to close around him, the ceiling to come down on his head. "Murder my own sister's husband over money? And then wait for her to die? That's the sickest thing I ever heard. No one will believe that."

Chelsey shook her head slowly back and forth. He followed it like the swinging of a pendulum. "You're wrong, darling. *Everyone* will believe that. You know they will. Just like everyone will believe you wanted me dead."

His eyelids narrowed until they were practically closed. His teeth clamped together. His face flushed. He could feel the heat of his skin burning like the summer sun. He took a step toward Chelsey, but her fingers covered the gun.

Gavin stopped where he was.

They stared at each other. Husband and wife. The air crackled with violence. In his head, he measured the distance to the gun and the time it would take to get to it. She saw him making his calculations. Her body coiled like a taut spring, as if she knew exactly what he was planning. As if she were daring him to try.

"What now, Gavin?" Chelsey asked calmly. "What happens next?"

* * * * *

Serena drove through the open gate into the self-storage facility in Proctor. Delaney sat next to her in anxious silence. The facility wasn't large, just a long warehouse next to the trees, with a row of white metal doors marking individual storage units. The area around the warehouse was unpaved. Serena drove down the length of the building and stopped outside the unit number that Delaney had given her.

She looked at the teenager. "Are you up for this?"

Delaney shrugged. "I guess I had to come here sooner or later. I've had the key for a long time, but I never used it. Gramps arranged for Mom's stuff to be moved over here. If it had been up to me, I would have just given it all away. But he thought someday I might want to see it again."

"I can go in there by myself if you prefer."

"No, I'll come, too."

They got out of the Mustang. The location of the facility wasn't far from the interstate, and they could hear the roar of traffic on I-35 to the south. The night sky overhead was clear. Delaney took a small key ring from her pocket and fumbled with the keys in the darkness. Serena used her flashlight to make it easier. When the girl had isolated the correct key, she unlocked the unit, and Serena bent down and opened the door. Inside, she located a light switch, which illuminated a single LED bulb overhead.

The unit had a musty, shut-up smell. Cobwebs dangled from the corners of the ceiling. It was crowded with furniture, chairs balanced on top of sofas, mattresses and box springs propped against the walls, and boxes of clothes and kitchenware stacked high in precarious towers. There was almost no room to move among the remnants of a lost life.

Delaney hesitated in the doorway. She took one tentative step, then ran a hand across the dusty surface of an oak dresser. "I can still feel her here," she murmured. "Like time was standing still, you know?"

"Possessions have a life force," Serena said. "It's like the memories inside them are frozen, and suddenly they thaw out."

"Yeah." The girl sniffled and wiped her nose. "I really miss her."

"I know you do."

"Do you miss your mom, too? Despite what she did?"

Serena put an arm around Delaney. "Actually, I do. It feels strange to say that, but I do. She was abusive to me in horrible ways. But I wish she was still alive, even if it just meant I could scream at her again."

"I yelled at my mom once," Delaney said. "I put her in a cold shower when she was drunk. I told her she had to quit, she had to get help, she was killing herself, she was killing me. I told her I—I told her that I hated her. I felt awful saying that. But she got sober for a few months after that. Then it all came back. It always came back sooner or later."

"I know."

"This man you talked about," Delaney said. "Gavin Webster. Can you show me his picture again?"

Serena took her phone and found the best photograph she had of Gavin. She enlarged it to zoom in on his face. Delaney took the phone and stared at the man long and hard. Then she shook her head.

"I don't remember him. He's not one of the ones I found in her bed."

"And your mom never mentioned his name? She didn't talk about him?"

"I don't think so."

"Did you meet most of the men your mom dated?" Serena asked.

"No, there were a lot of nights when she didn't come home."

"She left you alone?"

"Yeah, but that was okay. I knew how to take care of myself."

"How old were you when that started?"

"I'm not sure. Nine, ten."

Serena shook her head. She wanted to say: *No, that was not okay.*

"I get what you're trying to do," Delaney went on, "but I think you're wrong. I don't see how the accident could have been anything other than what it was. It was our truck. Mom got drunk and hit somebody."

"I'm not so sure about that," Serena insisted.

"But why?"

"Because I think there was a connection between Gavin and your mom, even if you don't remember him. That's why I want to find the records that Nikki kept from the Fallon wedding. Maybe there's something in there to tie the two of them together."

"Well, we can look," Delaney agreed, but she didn't sound hopeful.

They squeezed their way through the storage unit. With her flashlight, Serena spotted dead bugs and mouse droppings on the concrete floor. Their footsteps disturbed the dust, and she had to cover her mouth as she coughed. They reached the back wall without finding any business records, and Serena was beginning to wonder if Delaney's grandfather had jettisoned his daughter's files when emptying the house. Then Delaney tugged on her sleeve and said, "There."

Several bankers boxes were stacked like children's blocks on a wooden kitchen table in a far corner of the unit. They were labeled in neat square letters with black marker. Serena illuminated each of the boxes until she found one labeled *Susan & Jonah Fallon*. She had to shift several other boxes to retrieve it.

"I remember that wedding," Delaney commented.

"You were there?"

"Yeah, I was at the reception helping my mom. I told you, that was one of her first big jobs. She was really stressed about getting everything right. Mrs. Fallon rented out this beautiful private estate in Cloquet for the event. I think it belonged to an old lumber baron years ago. It was super elegant and old-fashioned. Mom did different themes for the food in each room. The whole thing was great. I was so proud of her."

"Did you meet the bride and groom?"

"Sure. I liked Mrs. Fallon. Some of the women Mom did events for, they were pretty stuck-up. But Mrs. Fallon was sweet, easy to like. She said it was her wedding, but my mom was the food expert, and she wanted her to run the show. I thought that was cool."

"And Jonah Fallon?"

"I only met him on that day. I don't remember him very well. He was handsome, I think. A big man."

"But you don't remember Gavin? Susan's brother?"

Delaney shook her head. "No. I'm sorry."

Serena took the box in her arms. "Well, let's look at this in the car, okay?"

She brought the box to the Mustang and helped Delaney relock the storage unit. Inside the car, she removed the lid and began to methodically examine the papers in the box. Nikki Candis may have been an alcoholic in her personal life, but she kept neat, organized records related to her business. Everything about the event was in a separate folder: menu and recipes, food orders, equipment orders, wine and alcohol, serving staff. As she pulled out the folders, she also noticed a computer thumb drive in the bottom of the box.

"Do you know what this is?" she asked Delaney.

The girl nodded. "Mom took pictures of everything. I helped her with that. She wanted a complete record of every event, so we got photos of the food, serving trays, decorations, everything. During the reception, I took a lot of pics, so Mom could see which rooms were crowded and which weren't, what people liked and what they didn't, that kind of thing. She was really serious about research. I mean, that's what's so frustrating. She was good at what she did. The business could have been huge. But—"

"But she had a disease," Serena said.

"Yeah."

Serena reached around to the back seat and grabbed her laptop. She booted it up with Nikki's thumb drive in the USB port, then loaded the photographs and examined them one by one. The early pictures had been taken before the event began, showing elaborate presentations of gourmet food. Later, Delaney had taken photographs while the reception was in progress. The girl had gone from room to room in the Cloquet estate. The library. The formal dining room. The gallery. The screened porch. Then outside, in the nighttime garden, near an elaborate fountain. There was a large white tent on the lawn where a dance floor had been built and a small live orchestra played. Delaney had been thorough, capturing multiple shots in every location.

Serena saw several pictures of Susan and Jonah Fallon together, bride and groom. She wore an off-the-shoulder white dress and tiara; he was in a charcoal-gray tux. She had curly hair like her brother, and their faces had a family resemblance, although her eyes were brown, not luminous blue. Her smile radiated pure joy. Jonah Fallon looked as Delaney had described him, magnetic and handsome, with a fit build. Serena had seen him before, but only in pictures of his broken body by the side of the road.

"I always think it's weird to see pictures like this, when people don't know what the future holds," Delaney commented. "And how bad it's going to be."

"At least they had a beautiful wedding."

"Yeah, and a year later, he'd be dead, and she'd have cancer. Sucks."

Serena nodded. She kept going through the pictures.

She spotted Gavin a couple of times. He was in a black tux, dancing with his sister, then sitting at a table with his parents. Chelsey wasn't with him. And there was no sign of Nikki Candis in the pictures at all. There was absolutely nothing to suggest that Gavin and Nikki had met at the reception. If they'd had a relationship that started here, it had happened outside the camera's eye.

"Where was your mother?" she asked.

"Mostly in the kitchen," Delaney said. "Occasionally, she'd go from room to room and check on things, but not for long. That's the thing,

Serena. She was *busy* that whole evening. She didn't interact with any of the guests. She didn't have time for that. I don't think you're going to find what you want to find."

Serena nodded. "Unfortunately, I think you're right."

But she kept looking through the rest of the pictures anyway. One by one. Studying the faces. Then she stopped. She saw a photograph; it registered in her brain; she moved on to the next one. But almost immediately, she backed up to see it again. With a click of the mouse, she enlarged the picture to zoom in on the faces.

She recognized both of them with a wave of shock.

Two faces. A man and a woman.

Two faces in a corner of the garden, near the bubbling water of the fountain, lit only by twinkling fairy lights strung over their heads. But there was enough light in the picture to see them stealing a secret kiss. It was a passionate kiss, full of erotic energy and desire, the kiss of two hungry people enmeshed in a torrid affair.

"Oh my God," Serena murmured in horror.

She knew.

She knew what had happened and why. From then until now. From the beginning of the murder conspiracy until the very end. It was all there in that one picture.

And it wasn't over.

Delaney stared at her. "What is it?"

"I was wrong," Serena said. "All of us—me, Stride, Maggie. We were wrong about everything."

39

The burnt smell of the gunshot lingered on Gavin's porch. The breeze through the sliding door had done nothing to wash it away.

Stride stared down at the dead body at his feet. He noted the singed wound in Gavin's temple; the bone, blood, and brain on the carpeted floor; and the fingernail scratches on his hands. The lawyer's blue eyes were open, his enigmatic stare now permanently fixed on a far-off horizon.

Outside, on the deck, broken glass glittered under the exterior lights. A bullet had gone through the door, shattering it as Gavin and Chelsey struggled for the gun. Another had gone into the ceiling, causing a cloud of plaster dust to settle over the body.

The house was crowded with people. The coroner and her assistant had arrived. The police officers who'd responded to the 911 call were still here, along with half a dozen other uniformed cops, as well as Stride, Maggie, and Guppo. In the corner of the porch, Chelsey Webster sat on the floor, her arms wrapped around her knees, her body shivering. Blood had sprayed over her face and splattered her clothes. Her eyes were nearly as fixed as her dead husband's. She stared at Gavin's body on the floor and didn't even blink.

Maggie went and squatted in front of her. "Mrs. Webster? I'm sorry, but we're going to have to ask you to relocate. We need to process the scene. Can we help you get to another room? We need to ask some questions."

Chelsey didn't react. Her glazed eyes didn't move.

Maggie repeated her request, gently, and Stride positioned himself between Chelsey and her husband's body to interrupt her concentration. Chelsey finally came out of her trance and nodded. "Yes. Yes, of course."

They helped her to her feet and led her down the hallway to the living room, which was adjacent to the house's front door. Stride nodded at two police officers to vacate the space. Chelsey didn't sit down. She walked nervously back and forth between the front windows and the built-in bookshelves.

"We'll need to take pictures of you," Stride said. "And we'll need a swab of your hands for gunshot residue."

Chelsey shrugged. "Yes, fine, but I've already told you that I fired the gun."

"It's standard procedure. We'll also need to take the clothes you're wearing as evidence, so you'll have to change into something else. A policewoman will accompany you. After that, you can clean yourself up."

"I can't stay here tonight," she murmured.

"No."

"I guess I'll go to a hotel." Then she stopped as a thought occurred to her. "That is, if I'm free to go. Am I under arrest? You're not going to arrest me, are you?"

"Right now, we'd like you to tell us exactly what happened," Maggie said.

"It was self-defense."

"I understand."

"Should I talk to a lawyer?"

"That's entirely up to you," Stride said.

Chelsey paced more quickly. "Lawyer or no lawyer, I don't know what difference it makes. I didn't have a choice. Gavin was trying to kill me."

"Maybe you'd like to sit down," Maggie suggested.

Chelsey stopped in the middle of the floor. Her face was distracted.

Finally, she took a seat on the sofa near the windows, and she smoothed her long hair with quivering fingers. "We had an argument."

"About what?"

"Everything. It got out of control. And then he lunged at me." She shook her head. "You were right. It was him. The whole thing was him. He arranged for the kidnapping. He said he hated me. He wanted me dead."

"Did he actually confess to the kidnapping?" Maggie asked.

Her words spilled out quickly. "He didn't need to. I saw it in his eyes. Once I told him what I'd found, once I showed him the gun, the façade fell away."

"Tomorrow you'll have to show us exactly where you found it," Stride said.

She nodded. "Of course. I can do that."

"Did Gavin say anything else?" Maggie asked.

"He denied it. Well, what else would he say? But I told him about your call. About you suspecting him in Jonah's murder. I think that was the breaking point. That's when he knew everything was going to come out."

"Do you believe it's possible that Gavin was responsible for Jonah Fallon's death?" Stride asked.

She looked up at the ceiling. "I don't know. It's hard for me to imagine. It's so horrible. But Gavin was desperate about money. He'd lost everything. I suppose he could have convinced himself that the ends justified the means. Susan was going to die anyway."

"After the accident, did you ever suspect he was involved?"

Chelsey hesitated. "No. But—I don't know—sometimes thoughts go through your head and you pretend you're not thinking what you're thinking."

"Tell us exactly what happened on the porch," Stride said. "You confronted Gavin. You argued. What did he do?"

Chelsey took a deep breath in and out. "I was in the chair. He was standing over me. We didn't say anything, and I wasn't sure what he was going to do. Then he went for the gun and grabbed it. I knew he was going to kill me. I got hold of his wrist and forced his arm away, and he fired. The bullet went through the patio door. Then I swung his arm up, and he fired again, and the bullet went into the ceiling. I was able to get my finger on the trigger, but Gavin is stronger than me, and I'm still very weak from the abduction. I managed to get my foot around Gavin's ankle. That was what saved me. He lost his balance and fell backward, and I fell with him. As we fell, the gun went off again. This time it was—it was pointed at Gavin's head. I landed on top of him, and he was dead. I screamed, I just screamed. Then I called 911."

Stride had heard a recording of the emergency call, including the panicked voice on the phone.

This is—this is Chelsey Webster. My husband's dead! He was trying to kill me, and I shot him! He's dead! Send the police, please send them right now!

It was a very convincing performance.

"Is there anything else you can tell us?" he asked.

"No, that's everything. I really need to rest now."

"Yes, of course."

"I'll get a policewoman," Maggie interjected. "She can go to your bedroom with you. She'll take pictures and collect your clothes. After that, we can have someone take you to a hotel if you'd like."

"Thank you." Chelsey exhaled and closed her eyes, and her whole body seemed to relax. "You're both very kind."

Stride and Maggie left the living room together. He waited in the hallway while Maggie located a policewoman, and then they took the stairs to the lower level of the house. The medical and crime-scene teams were still gathering evidence on the porch. The two of them went outside into the cool night air and walked across the back lawn that overlooked the lake.

They stood next to each other.

"What do you think?" Maggie asked.

Her question hung there in the darkness. In Stride's mind, he kept seeing the image of Gavin dead on the floor.

The blood on his face.

His surprised blue eyes.

"The scene backs up what she's saying," Maggie went on. "There was a struggle for the gun."

"Definitely."

Maggie heard doubt in his voice. "But?"

"But was Gavin behind the kidnapping? I'm not so sure."

"Why go for the gun if he was innocent?" Maggie asked.

"Fair point. Then again, why send himself an email from a fake account that leads to *his gun*?"

Maggie frowned. "To point the finger away from himself? To prove that someone else was working with Hink? He could tell us about the email, and we could go dig up the gun. Gavin could say, 'See? You guys got it wrong.'"

"And the rest of the ransom money?"

"Buried somewhere else, I assume," Maggie said. "Gavin couldn't let us find that. A kidnapper wouldn't give back the money."

Stride stared out at the dark mass of the lake. Then he murmured, "A neat little package tied with a bow."

"Sometimes that's the way it works."

That was true, he knew. Sometimes, but not very often.

"Do you believe in coincidences?" Stride asked.

"You know I don't."

"Neither do I. Then again, they do happen. Do you remember that case in Anoka County a few years ago? A depressed old woman tried to kill her husband and herself. She wanted the two of them to die together. So she turned on the gas line, and she wrote to her friends to say goodbye. Except in the morning, they were both still alive, and the police arrested her for attempted murder. She went to jail, but nobody wanted her there for long. Not the judge, not the prosecutor, and not her husband. He just wanted his wife back, and she swore she wouldn't do it again. So they let her go. She came home, and a few hours later, her husband was dead."

"Jesus," Maggie said. "She killed him?"

Stride smiled. "No. The coroner concluded that he died of natural causes. But that's a hell of a coincidence."

"What are you saying, boss?"

He eyed her in the darkness. The way she said the word had a message for him. "Boss?"

"Yeah. Boss."

Stride let that sink in for a moment, and then he pushed it aside. "Either Jonah Fallon's death and Chelsey Webster's kidnapping are two unrelated events, or else they're part of an elaborate plot to steal three million dollars. Right? It's a conspiracy or a coincidence."

"Earlier, you were pretty sure it was a conspiracy," Maggie said.

"Earlier, Gavin wasn't dead."

"So?"

"So I don't think a lawyer smart enough to come up with a murder plot like this would be careless enough to let himself get killed at the end of it. If Gavin wanted Chelsey dead, she'd be dead."

"Does that mean you think the hit-and-run was an accident?"

He let that idea walk through his mind for a moment, but then he shook his head. "No. I don't. Strange coincidences may happen, but not when we're talking about that kind of money. This was a premeditated conspiracy. This was murder. But Gavin isn't our only suspect."

"He had a hell of a motive to kill Jonah," Maggie pointed out.

"So did his wife."

Maggie cocked her head. "*Chelsey?*"

"She was never a suspect because we thought she was dead. But now? Chelsey is about to walk away free and clear with three million dollars and no husband. That's a pretty elegant outcome, don't you think? If Gavin had died in any other way—murder, accident, whatever—Chelsey would have been our prime suspect. We would have turned over every rock to prove that she was involved. But with the evidence in the kidnapping pointing at Gavin, she can simply *admit* she killed him. An open-and-shut case of self-defense. And that also is a neat little package tied with a bow."

"Son of a bitch," Maggie swore. "You think it's possible she arranged all of this herself? She kidnapped *herself*?"

"I think Chelsey Webster is one very cool customer."

Maggie was quiet for a moment. Down the hillside, the Duluth skyline glittered. "She couldn't have done this alone."

"You're right," Stride agreed. "If it really was her behind all of this, then she had help. Not only in faking the kidnapping, but in killing Jonah Fallon, too. She's had a partner from the very beginning."

40

Serena walked into the bar on Grand Avenue.

Aerosmith rocked the jukebox, loud enough that she couldn't hear anything else. A few customers played pull tabs; someone shouted as they got a lucky card. The closed-up air smelled of beer and cheap perfume. Serena could imagine Nikki Candis here, night after night. Nikki playing darts, clapping for the country band, watching the Super Bowl. Nikki drinking until closing time, trying to drown her pain. Nikki hitching a ride with a man who would take her home and take her to bed.

The dead woman's presence lingered in the bar like an echo. Delaney had told Serena at the beginning: *If my mother was going to haunt anywhere, it would be there. That was her place.*

Yes, it was.

Nikki's credit card records showed dozens of visits to the bar. They all knew her here. They knew what she was like. A blackout drunk. If you were looking for someone to take the fall for an accident that was really a murder, Nikki Candis was the perfect patsy. She wouldn't remember a thing.

It was a busy night inside. Twenty- and thirtysomethings crowded shoulder to shoulder, talking, laughing, and dancing. Standing by the bar door, Serena felt hunger washing over her like a wave. The desire never went away. Pour me a drink, and keep pouring. Absolut Citron. Two ice cubes. God, it would taste good. Smell good. The glass would be chilled in her hand, and the vodka would be silky on her lips. She could imagine the bliss of that first swallow.

No.

No.

Never again.

Serena made her way to the bar. There was one empty stool, and she took it. When she glanced at the person next to her, she noticed a woman about her own age who had messy, highlighted brown hair. If this were another life, if the woman were wearing skinny red jeans, it could have been Nikki. But then the woman, sensing Serena's stare, glanced her way. She was a stranger. Nikki was long gone.

"Well, hello again," said a smooth voice from the other side of the bar.

There he was. Jagger.

Hot, literally hot, with a glow of sweat on his forehead. He made being sexy look so effortless. His eyes were laser beams that drilled inside her, as if she were the only other person in the bar. Serena noticed the woman on the adjacent stool taking jealous note of Jagger's interest in her. Some men just had instant erotic appeal, particularly for women of a certain age.

Even married women.

Women like Chelsey Webster.

"I thought you weren't coming back," Jagger said, slipping his hands into the pockets of his jeans.

Serena didn't smile. "That's what I said, but I came back for you."

"Lucky me. Do you want a drink?"

"Club soda."

His eyebrows arched in surprise. "Good choice. Good for you."

Serena saw him examining her face with wary concern. She could tell that he saw something that he didn't like. It was probably the new hardness on Serena's mouth and in her eyes. The flirtiness, the desire, the vulnerability of the woman who'd crashed off the wagon, was gone.

She was sure he'd already guessed why she was there.

You're scared, Jagger.

You're scared because I'm here to take you down.

But the bartender pretended that nothing had changed. Tonight was just like the other two nights. He flipped a pilsner glass in his hand, then went to the fountain and filled the glass with ice and unleashed a spray of club soda. He reached under the bar for a lime wedge and draped it over the edge of the glass with a flourish. Then he slid the club soda across the bar.

Another smile. So suave. So cool.

He was very attractive. She still felt it, but now she was disgusted with how she'd behaved. She'd almost let herself be seduced by a monster.

"We need to talk," Serena told him over the tumult of the crowd. The heat of the bar made her thirsty, and she drank the club soda in a couple of swallows.

"So talk."

"Outside."

"I'm working," Jagger said.

"Not anymore. You're done for the night."

His easy smile couldn't hide a ripple of fear. She reached into her jacket and pulled out her phone. She saw that she'd missed two calls from Stride, but she didn't call him back, not yet. She went to her photo stream and opened up the picture she'd taken from her laptop.

She put her phone on the bar for Jagger to see.

It was the photograph she'd found in Nikki's files. The photograph Delaney had taken in the dark fairyland of the reception, a picture of a man and a woman locked in a passionate embrace.

It was a photograph of Jagger and Chelsey, kissing like lovers at the wedding of Susan and Jonah Fallon.

Serena leaned close enough to whisper to him. "I know what you did. I know *everything*."

He stared at the picture. The smile bled from his face. So did the charm. Steel and ice took over his features, and just like that, he was a dangerous man. He was capable of violence. He was the kind of man who could climb into Nikki's Toyota Highlander and go hunting for a jogger on the back roads.

Serena used her finger to slide the screen to the next picture, where she'd scanned the staff list Nikki had assembled for the Fallon wedding. These were the people she'd hired to serve at the reception.

She used her long nail to point at the name she'd found on the list. *Mick "Jagger" Galloway.*

He'd bartended the reception.

Somewhere during the night, he'd also seduced Chelsey Webster, or Chelsey had seduced him. Either way, it was the beginning of an affair that would lead them both to murder.

"Outside," Serena said again.

Jagger waved at the other bartender and mouthed, "Break."

He grabbed his leather jacket, and the two of them left the bar together. The cool air outside was a relief, but the echo of the jukebox left an odd ringing in Serena's ears that refused to go away. In the darkness, she stood next to her Mustang, which was parked at the curb. Casually, Jagger took a few steps down the sidewalk, but he didn't look ready to run. He still looked unconcerned with everything that was happening. As she watched him, he reached into his back pocket, and Serena tensed, ready to draw her weapon. Instead, his hand emerged with a pack of cigarettes, and he lit one and allowed the smoke to form a cloud around his head.

"So what is it I can do for you?" Jagger asked.

"The best thing you can do is confess," she told him. "Tell us everything. As soon as we talk to Chelsey, she'll turn on you in a split second. When we get a little older, we women aren't so sentimental, even when the sex is great. She'll throw you under the bus, Jagger. She'll say it was all your idea. You forced her, or you blackmailed her, to go along with your scheme. The whole sick murder conspiracy, starting with Jonah Fallon. Trust me, she'll cut a deal and let you take the fall."

Jagger stood on the corner, smoking, watching her carefully like a predator eyeing prey. "I have no idea what you're talking about."

"It's too late for games. You're Razrsharp. It's your account, right? You sent Gavin the emails. You lured him to Fredenberg Lake on your little treasure hunt, and then—what? Did you slash his tire while he was in the woods? That way, you knew he'd have to call a tow truck. Someone would see him up there."

Jagger blew a smoke ring and listened to her with a smirk frozen on his face. Serena shook her head, as if shooing away a mosquito. The odd buzzing in her ears got louder.

"Once we knew Gavin had been up in those woods, you knew we'd start searching the area," she went on. "Is that when you took Chelsey up there? I bet she'd only been in that hole for a few hours when we found her. Did you stay close by? Just to make sure she was safe?"

"If you're trying to scare me, it's not working."

"I think I do scare you. And I should. I have enough for a warrant. Once we get a look at your apartment, your computer, and your phone, we're going to find everything we need to put both of you away."

"A warrant? Good luck with that. I tended bar at a wedding. I kissed a drunk wife. Big deal."

"You also *lied* about knowing Nikki Candis," Serena said. Despite the cold night air, she was feeling hot. Sweat gathered like dew on the back of her neck, and a flush rose on her cheeks.

"I worked for Nikki a couple of times. That's all."

"Really? I think you met her right here. You told me you only got the bartending job a few months ago, but you've lived a couple of blocks away from the bar for five years. This was your place, right? Just like it was Nikki's place. You were both regulars. How many times did you take her home? How many times did you wake up next to her, and she didn't even remember the previous night? That's what gave you the idea, isn't it? That's how you figured out you could get rid of Jonah Fallon without anyone suspecting he'd been murdered."

"That's quite the story. Do you think you can prove it?"

"Let's see."

Beside her, the passenger door of the Mustang swung open, and Delaney Candis got out of the car. She stood next to Serena on the sidewalk and stared at Jagger, her young face ice-cold with rage.

"Do you recognize him, Delaney?" Serena said.

"*Yes*," she hissed. "Yes, I know him. I'll never forget him. I found him in my mother's bed half a dozen times. He would get her drunk and take her home. He knew all about her blackouts."

A stiffness came over Jagger's body. He dropped his cigarette and crushed it under his shoe on the sidewalk. He stared at the teenager for a long moment, and then he exhaled with a quick, cynical laugh. "Chelsey said I should kill the girl. I said no. But she was right."

"You tried to run her down last night. Didn't you?"

Jagger shrugged. "You were in the bar talking about Nikki. That freaked me out. I knew we had trouble."

"Delaney, get back in the car," Serena told her. And then to Jagger: "Get on your knees. Put your hands on top of your head."

"No, I don't think so."

"On your knees. Do it."

He made no effort to move. "Did you really think I wouldn't have an exit strategy? A backup plan? I figured I might have to run. That's okay. I told you, I'm a rolling stone."

Serena reached around to the small of her back and removed her gun. Delaney was still standing next to her on the sidewalk. "Back in the car," she repeated to the girl. "Right now."

Wait.

Did she even say that?

She heard the words, but they floated away into the air, and she didn't know if they'd made it to her lips. She hesitated, feeling strange. Delaney was looking at her with a confused, horrified expression on her face. Meanwhile, Jagger was grinning. That damn sexy grin.

"You don't look so good, Serena," he said.

He was right. Her eyes blinked in and out of focus. She took a step toward him, and the ground undulated under her feet, as if carried by an ocean wave. Dizziness swept through her mind.

"*Serena!*" Delaney cried, but the girl's voice sounded far away.

She felt a surge of nausea, and she knew. The truth blinded her in one helpless instant. Jagger had seen her come into the bar; he'd seen her face; he'd known why she was there. He'd been ready for her.

What had he put in her drink? GHB? Rohypnol? Ketamine? Whatever it was, it was hitting her hard and fast.

Her fingers felt numb. She struggled to keep her gun steady, but her arms felt disconnected from the rest of her body, like a marionette with broken strings. She couldn't walk; she couldn't stand anymore. As her knees buckled, she was vaguely conscious of Delaney kneeling beside her and trying to hold her up, and then of Jagger closing the distance between them and peeling the gun away from her fingers.

He grabbed Delaney as the teenager tried to run. He choked off her scream.

That was all.

Then Serena's mind spiraled down like a crashing plane, and the world went black.

* * * * *

"Serena's still not answering her phone," Stride said. "It goes straight to voice mail. Cat hasn't heard from her, either. And the locater app doesn't show it at all. It's turned off."

Maggie frowned at him. "Could she be . . . ?"

"Drinking? No. I know her. She's in control of that again. She was with Delaney Candis, but Delaney's not answering her phone either. I don't like this. She shouldn't be off the grid tonight."

He stared over the trees at the lake, listening to his instincts, which told him that something was wrong. Then he grabbed his phone and dialed. A few seconds later, Curt Dickes answered.

"Stride! Hey, long time, man! What's shakin'?"

"Curt, I don't have time to talk. You sent Serena to a massage therapist who works with Chelsey Webster. She told Serena she thought Chelsey was having an affair. Did you ever hear *who* it was with?"

"No, I hear a lot of gossip, but nothing about that. Why, what's up?"

Stride ignored the question. "I need Broadway's phone number. Quickly."

The easy tone of Curt's voice changed immediately. "Are you kidding,

Stride? He finds out I'm doxing him, and that's not good for my business. Or my health."

"Give it to me, and I owe you one. A get-out-of-jail-free card."

Curt unleashed a loud sigh. "Shit, okay, fine, fine, I'll text you the number."

"Thank you, Curt."

Stride hung up. A few seconds later, his text tone sounded, and he checked his messages. Curt had sent him a contact file with a phone number and no name attached to it. He opened it up and quickly dialed the number.

The youthful voice of Broadway answered on the first ring. He didn't sound surprised to get the call. "Well, Lieutenant Stride, hello. How resourceful of you to find me. Let me guess, Curt?"

"No comment."

"Oh, I really have no issue with Curt giving you my number. I would have given it to you myself if you'd asked. I assumed it wasn't Gavin, because I hear that he won't be joining me for Friday games anymore. That's a shame."

Stride shook his head, wondering how Broadway had heard the news of Gavin's death so quickly. But he didn't bother asking about the man's sources.

"I need information," he said.

"Go on."

"Did Gavin ever mention—or did you hear anything—about Chelsey Webster having an affair? Do you know who she was seeing?"

Even in the silence, Stride could hear the man smiling. Whatever else Broadway was, he was shrewd. "Ah, Chelsey. The fact that you're asking about her makes me think your investigation has taken some interesting turns. I did tell you that I thought there were some deep waters with that woman."

"Is there anything you can tell me?"

"Alas, no. Gavin never mentioned any suspicions about an affair, and those kinds of rumors never reached my ears. Having met Chelsey, I also suspect she knows how to be discreet."

Stride was frustrated. "All right."

"However, I can pass along one bit of information," Broadway said. "I don't know whether it will be helpful."

"What is it?"

"I told you I was doing an audit of my personnel, looking for connections that might prove useful to you. I was particularly interested in whether Hink Miller had a friend who may have assisted him in the kidnapping plot."

"Did you find someone?" Stride asked.

"Well, yes and no. I found someone with a connection to Hink, but it's unlikely they'd be partners. If anything, this man would have loved to put a bullet in Hink's skull just for the hell of it. Apparently, the two of them both worked at the same bar a few years ago. Hink was a bouncer. He caught this man slipping something into a woman's drink, and he dragged him outside and delivered a beating that broke three of the man's ribs. Had I known this, of course, I wouldn't have hired either one of them. Apparently, Hink told someone about the incident when he saw the man at one of my parties. Not long after that, Hink developed legal problems of his own, and I fired him, so the story never made its way to me."

"Who was this other man?" Stride asked.

"A bartender," Broadway replied. "Quite a popular one with the ladies. His name is Mick Galloway, but he goes by the nickname Jagger."

Stride swore and hung up.

"Get an alert out on Serena's Mustang," he told Maggie. "We need to find her right now."

* * * * *

Delaney's eyes burned across the front seat of the car.

The man called Jagger had one hand on the wheel, and the other hand was pointing a gun at her chest. He sped down the southbound lanes of I-35, and already, Duluth was several miles behind them. In the back seat, she heard Serena groaning, starting to awaken.

"You *murdered* my mother," Delaney said, spitting the words at him.

Next to her, Jagger shot an eye at the rearview mirror. His gaze kept going back and forth between the teenager and the highway. Delaney wanted a moment of distraction—something, anything—when he wasn't looking her way, and then she could knock the gun from his hand.

"You made it look like she killed herself, but it was *you*," she went on.

"I really didn't want to kill Nikki," he replied, as if the decision were something casual, something that meant nothing to him either way. "That wasn't part of the plan. I figured the police would arrest her for the hit-and-run. Once the cops had the Toyota, they'd put her in prison."

Jagger's face was black with shadow. When he turned his head, all she saw were his eyes. "Nikki made it easy. I figured she would. When I went over there that Saturday night, I made sure she partied hard. It wasn't just the booze. I spiked her drinks, too, so when she crashed, she was *out*. At that point, all I had to do was take the Highlander and go looking for Jonah. When it was done, I came back and parked the truck in the garage. Nikki was still out cold. I didn't think there was a chance in hell she'd remember me being there."

Delaney glanced out the window. The nighttime forest whipped by beyond the guardrails. She knew what was going to happen next. When they were far enough away, when Jagger felt safe, he'd shoot them both and leave their bodies somewhere in the woods.

"But she did," Delaney murmured. "She finally remembered, didn't she? My mom remembered what you did. It was you, not her."

"Yeah, she was starting to put it together," Jagger went on. "She came into the bar, and it was the first time since the accident. She said you were staying with your grandparents, and she was alone, and did I want to buy her a drink? But I wasn't crazy about being seen with her. I said we should go back to her place. Maybe that was a mistake. Maybe that's what started triggering things. We got to the house, and the longer we were there, the more she kept *looking* at me. Like something wasn't adding up. She started going on about Saturday night, saying she couldn't remember what had happened, but she felt like we'd been together. That was when I knew. She had to go."

Delaney squeezed her eyes shut. She swallowed down her grief and fury. It had all been for nothing. It had all been a hideous mistake. Her mother hadn't done anything wrong. She hadn't been behind the wheel of the Highlander. And what Delaney herself had been forced to do—to make it all go away—

This man.

This man was the devil. He'd killed Jonah Fallon on the road. Killed her mother. And now he was going to kill her, too.

Jagger gave her a sideways look, sensing her rage on the other side of the car and guessing how much she wanted to put her hands around his throat. "Don't even think about it."

She breathed hard and turned her head away. She watched the woods come and go. There was nothing she could do. She'd failed her mother. She'd ruined both of their lives. *For nothing.*

Then Delaney heard Jagger mutter under his breath. "Shit."

She looked across the car in time to see a highway patrol car passing in the opposite lanes, heading north. Jagger tensed as his eyes locked on the side mirror, watching the squad car disappear, waiting to see what it did. Delaney looked back, too, praying, hoping. The squad car drove, and drove, and drove, getting farther away from them like a pinpoint of light. She wanted to cry with disappointment.

Then Jagger swore again.

Much louder this time.

Flashing lights erupted on the car behind them. So did its siren. The squad car wheeled into the median to reverse direction. The police were coming after them. Immediately, Jagger's foot shoved down on the accelerator, and the engine of the Mustang growled. The car took off.

He wasn't watching her anymore. He was focused on the mirror and the road.

This was her chance. Through the darkness, Delaney saw an overpass looming over the freeway. She counted off the seconds as they bore down on it, and then she leaped across the seat at Jagger.

With one hand, she forced away the gun.

With the other, she grabbed the steering wheel and spun it hard, sending the Mustang careening toward the concrete pillar of the overpass.

41

Serena didn't know how much time had passed. She remembered the harsh squeal of brakes, the twisted tearing of metal, and then the thud of impact and the sensation of flying. After that, nothing. She blinked, opening her eyes. Her muscles groaned with pain when she tried to move. Up was down, and down was up, and when she managed to orient herself, she realized that she was on her back on the roof of the car. It had flipped. When she moved her hands over her body, sharp fragments scraped her fingers. Glass. There was glass everywhere.

Light dazzled her eyes from outside. A flashlight. The rear car door was open, the frame twisted. She squinted, seeing the concerned face of a highway patrol officer leaning into the Mustang.

"Are you hurt, ma'am?"

Serena had no idea if she was hurt or not, but she said, "No. Get me out of here."

"The paramedics are on the way. We should wait for them."

"Officer, I'm Serena Stride with the Duluth Police. Is there anyone else in the car? Anyone in the front seat?"

"No. Just you."

"Then that means we've got a murderer and a hostage on the run. Get me out of here."

"Yes, ma'am."

Serena felt strong hands underneath her shoulder blades. The highway cop dragged her from the vehicle, and she felt a wild relief being freed from the claustrophobic compartment. He helped her up, but her head spun, and she sank back to her knees. Then she tried again, focusing on the solid ground underneath her feet. The aftereffects of the drug lingered in her head, but the combination of adrenaline and fear had begun to purge it from her system.

She studied her Mustang, which was a total loss. Its front end was crushed, the airbags deployed, all of its doors open, its windows shattered. It lay upside down, diagonally across the freeway lane, underneath an overpass.

"Where are we?" she asked.

"That's Jay Cooke Road over our heads," the cop replied.

"Did you see the other two get out of the car?"

"No, they were gone when I got here."

Serena glanced at the concrete slope of the highway bridge and saw dark stains that looked like a blood trail leading up to the road over their heads.

"Are more police on their way?"

"Oh, yeah, we've scrambled everybody. Police, fire, medical. Southbound lanes are already shut down a mile back, and we're doing the same on the northbound lanes."

"How long was I out?"

"Maybe ten minutes."

Serena winced as a stab of pain knifed through her back. "Get hold of Lieutenant Jonathan Stride with the Duluth Police. Tell him we've got a murder suspect on the run. Mick 'Jagger' Galloway. He's armed and dangerous, and he most likely has a seventeen-year-old girl named Delaney Candis as a hostage. Odds are, this guy will try to jack another car as soon as possible, so we need a perimeter around the area to keep him contained."

"Mick Jagger? Seriously?"

"Yeah, seriously. You got all that?"

"Got it."

Serena took a step toward the freeway shoulder, stopped to let the dizziness pass, then started walking again.

"You look like you should stay here," the cop told her. "You're in bad shape."

"I'm not letting Delaney get killed," Serena replied.

She crossed the highway lane to the guardrail, which had been flattened by the Mustang. She stepped over it, then climbed the slope of the overpass, following the blood trail. Everything hurt. Her arms, her legs, her chest, her head, even her teeth, as if she'd bitten down hard during the impact. She moved slowly. Near the top, she shifted into the weeds, which grew nearly waist-high, and she used her arms to scrape through the brambles. The effort left her gasping for breath.

Finally, she broke onto the hilltop. She winced at the headache that felt like a drill boring into her skull. With a groan, she swung her legs over another metal guardrail and stood on the asphalt surface of Jay Cooke Road. It was a two-lane country highway heading off into the night in both directions. Trees butted up to the road. There were no overhead lights, but the sky was clear, with a sliver of moon. She saw nothing down the road in both directions. Below her, the lanes of I-35 were devoid of traffic, too, except for the squad car with its flashing light bar. She looked at her feet and saw a few dark bloodstains leading away from the interstate toward Highway 61 half a mile away.

Serena tried to run, but she couldn't muster the effort. The most she could manage was a fast, stumbling walk, and even that speed left her head throbbing. She squinted into the darkness. Where were they? There was still blood at her feet. They were still ahead of her.

She stopped to catch her breath again, and somewhere in the distance, she heard a stifled scream.

Delaney.

The girl's voice wasn't far away. Serena willed her legs to carry her faster, straight down the middle of Jay Cooke Road, with the evergreens squeezing in on both sides. A random cloud covered the moon, making the night even darker. She couldn't let Jagger get away. She couldn't let him take that girl. And yet her strength was waning. Her mind was barely holding it together.

Down the road, headlights gleamed as a car turned off Highway 61 and headed toward her.

No!

If Jagger got to that car, he'd escape. She heard a shout, heard the screech of tires, heard two gunshots in quick succession. The headlights veered sideways but kept coming. The car accelerated wildly in a serpentine fashion, getting closer. Serena froze like a deer, hypnotized by the lights that pinned her on the highway, and then at the last moment, she threw herself onto the shoulder. The car rocketed past her, barely missing her.

With another shudder of pain, she stood up. She'd twisted an ankle as she fell, and when she tried to walk, putting any pressure on her foot felt like the clamp of a bear trap. She was close to fainting.

But she saw them. There they were.

The cloud slipped past the moon, and the dim light revealed two figures in the middle of the road.

"*Jagger!*" she screamed.

He didn't try to run. She limped toward the two of them, her right leg dragging. As she got closer, she saw him standing like a dark tower, one arm locked around Delaney's neck, her own gun pointed at the girl's temple. Delaney's eyes were wide with terror.

Jagger stayed where he was. Serena realized that he was badly hurt. His white face was ribboned with blood. His legs shuddered like trees in the wind, but he held fast to the girl and the gun.

"Delaney, are you okay?" Serena called.

Despite her fear, the girl nodded.

"Jagger, give it up," Serena told him. "It's over. The police are coming."

She took a step closer.

"*Don't*," he hissed at her, his voice raspy. "Don't move. I'll shoot the girl."

"You're not going to do that," Serena said. "You're going to let her go. You want a hostage? Take me. I'm unarmed, Jagger. Let Delaney go, and I'll go with you. That's how you stay alive."

She took another step toward him. She kept her arms out, her fingers spread wide, so he could see that she wasn't lying. No gun.

"Come on, Jagger. Be smart."

They were only about twenty feet apart now. With a snarl, he jabbed the gun harder against Delaney's head. "*Stop!*"

"Let her go," Serena said again. "You want to kill someone? Kill me. You don't need to hurt that girl."

Jagger stared back with his eyes glazed by pain. His jaw was clenched, his teeth bared. He yanked the pistol away from Delaney and pointed it across the short distance at Serena. They faced each other down the yellow line of the highway. His arm wobbled, the barrel unsteady.

If he fired, he might hit her, or he might not. She took one more step. The closer she got, the easier target she was, but Serena didn't care. Sometimes you have to stare down the devil to see how tough he really is.

"Let Delaney go," she said again, her voice as steady as a rock.

The barrel of the gun was so close.

If he fired . . .

Serena heard a cacophony of wails getting louder and closer. It was the noise of sirens, drawing in on them from both directions. Beyond Jagger and Delaney, at the intersection with Highway 61, she saw the flashing red lights of at least four squad cars. They were behind her, too, roaring closer from I-35. The cars screeched to a stop. She didn't have to look back to know they were blocking the road. The whirling lights made a kaleidoscope across the pavement and onto Jagger's face.

"It's over," Serena said again. "There's no way out."

Over their heads, she heard the throb of a police helicopter hovering like an insect above the road. A cannon of white light shot from the machine, like theatre lights highlighting the three of them center stage.

"Let the girl go."

He still had the gun aimed at Serena's chest.

"*Let. Her. Go.*"

Slowly, Jagger dropped his other arm, releasing his grip on Delaney.

The girl stayed where she was, frozen. Tears rolled down her face. Her eyes were wide, two white orbs staring back at Serena.

"Put your arms in the air, Delaney," Serena told her, "and walk away slowly. Head to the police cars behind you. Do it right now."

The teenager still froze, as if not willing to move, not willing to leave her.

"Delaney, *go*."

Finally, the girl did. She put her hands in the air, then backed away from Jagger. She kept walking backward, and when she was ten feet away, she turned and ran. Floodlights from the squad cars lit her up, and she bolted that way. Serena watched the girl until she saw a police officer scoop her into his arms.

She was free. She was safe.

"Put down the gun, Jagger."

Serena took another step toward him.

"Nobody else has to get hurt," she said.

Another step.

"Kneel down, put the gun on the ground. There's a sharpshooter in that helicopter, Jagger. I can tell you what's happening up there. He's asking for a green light to take you out. You have about ten seconds before he puts a bullet in your head. What's it going to be? Do you live or die?"

The devil stared at her. Dressed in black. Covered in red.

Jagger's arm sagged. The gun shifted, barrel pointing at the ground. He knelt to put it down, but he didn't even get that far. His grip loosened, and the gun fell away. He slumped sideways to the highway, unconscious, losing blood. Serena closed the last few painful steps, and then she kicked the gun away and stood over him. The helicopter throbbed over her head. The bright light made her squint. Running footsteps pounded from all sides, cops charging from the squad cars. Chaos. Shouts. And one voice above all the others.

"*Serena!*"

It was Jonny. Running for her.

She tried to focus. She tried to see what was real and what was in her head. There were so many people around her. Friends and ghosts. Maggie. Guppo. Delaney. And Nikki. And Samantha, too. Just for a moment, Samantha was there, standing by the trees, before she became mist.

"Serena," Stride murmured, rushing up to her, reaching for her.

She smiled a tired smile and collapsed into his arms.

42

Stride expected to find Maggie sitting behind her desk. Instead, she sat in front of the desk, her feet up. She had a Big Mac on a paper wrapper in her lap and a large Coke in one hand. He looked around the office and realized that it wasn't her office anymore. It was his office again, almost exactly the way it had been fourteen months ago. His photographs—Serena, Cat—were back in frames on the desk. His pictures hung on the walls.

"Hey, boss," she said casually, taking a large bite from her Big Mac with one hand and then wiping her mouth.

He looked around, feeling as if time had marched backward. This was the world before he was shot. It wasn't today's world. "What the hell, Mags?"

"I moved my stuff into Abel's office," she replied.

Stride shook his head. "No. We need to talk about this."

"Too late. It's already done."

"That's not what I want."

Maggie shrugged. "Are you back? I mean, for good?"

He didn't hesitate this time. There was no longer any doubt. "Yes, I'm back, but that's not the point. It's been over a year. The job's yours. I talked to K-2. I told him I wanted you to stay in charge."

"I know you did. Thank you for that. And also, I told him to stuff it. Well, not exactly like that." She grinned. "Okay, yeah, exactly like that."

"This isn't fair to you."

Maggie spread her arms wide, spilling a little Coke. "So what? Life's not fair. It wasn't fair you getting shot. I filled in, but this will always be your job. Besides, if you want the truth, I really hate being the boss. It ain't me. Add in the fact that most of the cops hate *me* when I'm in charge, and I'd rather be number two again. Then I can piss and moan about you like everybody else."

Stride went over to the window and leaned against the ledge. He studied the leather chair behind the desk. It was his chair. She'd moved it back here from Abel Teitscher's office.

All he had to do was sit down.

"I'm not happy about this, Mags," Stride said.

"You'll get over it."

"Are you sure?"

"I'm not being noble, boss. It's what I *want*."

"K-2 better make sure you keep your rank and benefits."

"Oh, yeah. Don't worry about that. I'm incredibly gracious, but I'm not stupid. I'm still Lieutenant Mags as far as my pension goes."

He didn't know what to say. He'd had plenty of second chances in life, more than he deserved. This was another. He glanced out the window and wondered what other surprises the future held, but then he realized that thinking about the future was a waste of time. It would come no matter what he did.

Yes, he was really back.

"So tell me about our songbirds," Stride said.

Maggie's smile widened. She drank more of her Coke. "Oh, those two can't turn on each other fast enough. Jagger says the whole thing was Chelsey's idea. Chelsey says Jagger came up with the scheme, and she just went along for the ride. The bottom line is, we'll put them both away for a long time."

"Did they meet at the Fallon wedding?"

"Yeah. It was sex at first sight. Sounds like it was a torrid affair worthy of a romance novel. You know, Jagger shirtless, Chelsey caressing his turgid manhood. Anyway, they were going at it hot and heavy for months, and then Chelsey found out about Susan's cancer. One of them—doesn't really matter who—began to speculate about the idea of Jonah's money going to Susan . . . and then to Gavin . . . and then to Chelsey. The question was how to do it without fingers being pointed at either one of them. The first half of the plot worked exactly as planned. Jagger used Nikki's Highlander to run down Jonah, and nobody knew he'd done it. Honestly, if Serena hadn't gone to the bar to ask about those hundred-dollar bills—and the bar hadn't triggered her memories of Nikki's case file—they probably would have gotten away with the whole thing. I'm not sure we'd ever have made a connection to the Fallon murder otherwise."

"How about the kidnapping?" Stride asked.

"They planned it months ago. Then they really began laying the groundwork after Susan died and Gavin got the money. Chelsey started talking to people about how Gavin was making her nervous, how she was afraid of what he might do to her. They wanted us to see him as a suspect from the beginning. Jagger planted the surveillance camera to make the abduction look legit, and then they staged the kidnapping while Gavin was gone. It was just the two of them, nobody else. Hink Miller had nothing to do with it. Jagger killed Hink to point the finger at Gavin. The scheme was actually pretty smart—just enough conspiracy to make us suspicious, without making it too obvious. Use one of Gavin's clients as his 'partner,' leave behind part of the ransom and some of Chelsey's hair and perfume in the trunk of Hink's car, and use Gavin's gun for the murder. Then they'd make sure we found the gun later. The point was to make us think that Gavin hired Hink to kidnap and kill Chelsey, and then he killed Hink to cover it up, assuming Chelsey was already dead in the woods somewhere according to his plan. They didn't really care whether we had enough evidence to actually arrest Gavin. The plan was always for Chelsey to kill him and claim self-defense."

"And was Chelsey in Jagger's apartment the whole time?"

"Right. That's also where the rest of the ransom money was, by the way. After they steered us to Fredenberg Lake, Jagger hid Chelsey in the woods and waited for us to find her. Once we did, Chelsey could claim that the kidnapper—we'd assume it was Hink—didn't have the balls to kill her and simply left her to die in the woods. Hence her miraculous escape."

"Nice," Stride said. "Chelsey's alive, Hink's dead, and a few hours later, so is Gavin."

"Yeah. And the two of them are three million dollars richer. You have to admire their dedication, by the way. Chelsey kept her own urine and feces for several days so she could soil her clothes. She starved and dehydrated herself too, just to make it look legit. Yuck."

Stride shook his head. "We've dealt with some evil people over the years, but these two may take the prize."

"Delaney called Jagger the devil," she replied. "I'm not so sure she's wrong."

Maggie finished her Big Mac, slurped up the rest of the Coke, and stuffed the wrappers into the bag. "I'm curious about one thing, though," she went on.

"What's that?"

"At the end of the day, do you think Gavin figured it out? Is that why he went for the gun?"

"Oh, I have to think it finally dawned on him," Stride replied. "He was being framed, and there was only one other person beside himself who knew where he hid that gun in the house—and knew all his passwords, too. That was Chelsey. So yeah, I think that last fight was a fight to the death."

Maggie stood up from the chair, and Stride stayed by the window. They stared at each other. It was just like the old days.

"I'm heading out," she said. Then she added, "I left you the Teeling."

"Thanks."

"Pour a shot. Celebrate. No matter what the doctor says, you need to live sometimes, too."

"You're right."

Maggie gave him a wink, and she left him in the office. His office.

His past, his present, his future. He inhaled deeply, feeling the tug in his chest, the little pain that was always there, always reminding him that life was short.

Then Stride sat down in his chair and got to work.

* * * * *

Serena was alone in the cottage that night. Jonny was late coming home, but she didn't mind. She knew, when he came through the door, that he'd be smiling. He'd have his life back. And his wife back, too. She felt as if they'd finally closed the door on fourteen months of recovery. They'd walked through hell together and come out clean on the other side.

For him, it was his job.

For her, it was the number she would whisper to herself after midnight. *One.*

She found herself walking around the house, looking at ordinary objects in a new way. The candlesticks on the table. The old map of Duluth on the wall. The fading wooden sign above the fireplace with a single word: *Believe.* They were things she'd seen a million times, but they gave her a strange new comfort now. A sense of belonging.

When she went into the spare bedroom, she began unpacking her clothes from the dresser and moving them back into the closet in the master bedroom with Jonny's. She wanted no distance between them anymore. The closet space was cramped, but she didn't care. If they were getting up in the middle of the night now, they'd get up together.

At last, when her restlessness became calm, she sat down in the armchair by the fireplace. She listened to the silence of the cottage and felt its ghosts. In her hands, she turned over the small padded envelope that had been delivered in the mail that day. The return address was from the sheriff's office in Maricopa County, Arizona. She'd been putting off the moment of opening it. Whatever was inside was a part of Samantha's life. Her legacy. Serena didn't really know if there was anything she wanted from her mother.

But she undid the flap and reached inside. The first thing she removed was a handwritten note.

Ms. Stride,

Your mother did not have much in the way of possessions when she died. I'm afraid the few clothes and personal items she did have were in a state of contamination that would make it impossible to ship to you. However, I thought you would like to have this one piece of jewelry. She wasn't wearing it around her neck when we found her. She had it clasped in her hand.

With condolences,
Deputy Lawrence Moray

Serena closed her eyes, then reached inside the envelope again. She came away with a small gold locket and chain. It wasn't expensive, and the etched design—a scripted letter *S*—had mostly faded, as if it had been rubbed away over time. *S* for Samantha. *S* for Serena. She lifted the locket up in the dim light and let it dangle at the end of the chain like a talisman. When she could hold back no longer, she undid the clasp and separated the locket to see the old photograph inside.

It had faded, too, like the letter *S* on the outside. Its colors had worn away. But she recognized the little girl in the picture, the girl with the jet-black hair and the emerald eyes. The girl smiling at the camera, smiling at her mother. Serena had no recollection of when the picture had been taken. It was just one photograph. One lost memory. How old was she then? Eight? Nine?

She had it clasped in her hand.

Serena closed the locket gently. Then she slung the chain around her neck and felt the cool metal close to her warm skin.

"What's that?"

She looked up in surprise. Jonny was standing over her. She hadn't even heard him come in through the back door.

"It's my past," she told him. "I was thinking it's okay for me to keep it a little closer."

Stride knelt beside the chair. There was something different, something warm and happy, in his eyes. He kissed her, and she expected him to tell her about his day, about being back, about life starting over again after an extended pause. Instead, he whispered, "I have a surprise for you."

"What is it?"

He gave a shout toward the cottage's front door, and with a shudder, the door burst inward. Serena saw Cat there, biting her lip and unable to suppress a huge grin. Behind her was Delaney, face flushed with excitement. The two girls looked like conspirators in a secret plot. Like sisters.

Cat looked at Stride and said, "Ready?"

He nodded. "Ready."

Cat held the door open. Delaney disappeared onto the porch and was gone for a moment. And then there was a bark.

A dog's bark.

Serena's hands flew to her face. In an instant, she began to cry. With a blur of black-and-white fur, Elton galloped from the porch into the house. The Border collie froze on the carpet, looking left, looking right, looking everywhere, until he spotted Serena in the chair by the fireplace. Unleashing another loud bark of excitement, the dog bolted toward her at full speed. Serena slid off the chair onto her knees to welcome him, and Elton landed against her so hard that she toppled backward. Then the dog was on top of her, licking away the flood of tears.

When she was finally able to sit up, she hugged Elton against her chest and said in a broken voice to Jonny, "How? How did you do it?"

He shook his head. "It wasn't me. Elton did it."

"What?"

"Dale Sacks called me. He said ever since they brought the dog back, he's been peeing in every room. And particularly in Dale's bed. They finally decided that Elton was making it very clear that he wanted alternate arrangements. So here he is."

Serena shook her head, still crying. "He's mine?"

"He's yours. Well, actually, he's ours."

Serena looked at Jonny and thought about how incredibly lucky she was to love a man like him. She looked up at the two girls grinning at her from the front door and felt love for them, too. She looked around at the cottage, and she also loved this place and all of its memories. And it occurred to her that none of this love would be in her heart if her life had gone differently, if she hadn't suffered, if she hadn't run away. She wouldn't be here at all to savor this moment without Samantha. For better and for worse, every twist and turn, every pain and regret, had led her here.

Serena fingered the locket under her shirt.

"Well, come on," she said to the girls.

With squeals of excitement, Cat and Delaney ran across the room, and then everyone was laughing and hugging Elton, and the dog was wagging his tail like a tornado. He let loose a loud woof that Serena had no trouble translating, because she was thinking exactly the same thing.

I'm home.

FROM THE AUTHOR

Thanks for reading the latest Jonathan Stride novel!

If you like this novel, be sure to check out all of my other books, too. Visit my website at BFreemanBooks.com to join my mailing list, get book-club discussion questions, and find out more about me and my books.

Finally, if you enjoy my books, please post your reviews online at Audible, Goodreads, Amazon, and other sites for booklovers—and spread the word to your reader friends. Thanks!

You can write to me with your feedback at Brian@BFreemanBooks.com. I love to get emails from listeners and readers around the world, and yes, I reply personally. You can also "like" my official fan page on Facebook at facebook.com/BFreemanFans or follow me on Twitter or Instagram using the handle BFreemanBooks.

BOOKS BY BRIAN FREEMAN

THE JONATHAN STRIDE SERIES

The Zero Night
Funeral for a Friend
*Alter Ego**
Marathon
Goodbye to the Dead
The Cold Nowhere
Turn to Stone (e-novella)
Spitting Devil (e-short story)
The Burying Place
In the Dark
Stalked
Stripped
Immoral

THE FROST EASTON SERIES

The Crooked Street
The Voice Inside
The Night Bird

THE CAB BOLTON SERIES

Season of Fear
The Bone House
*Cab Bolton also appears in *Alter Ego*

ROBERT LUDLUM'S JASON BOURNE SERIES

The Bourne Sacrifice
The Bourne Treachery
The Bourne Evolution

STANDALONE NOVELS

I Remember You
The Ursulina
Infinite
Thief River Falls
The Deep, Deep Snow
Spilled Blood